The Calling

The Calling

Authored, Edited and Published by
Teresa McCoy

ISBN
978-1-7345828-0-2

Library of Congress
2020901972

Cover, Layout and Artwork by
Stephanie McCoy

First Edition

Dedication

This book is dedicated to all those seekers of family origin and history,
who understand that knowing where we came from has much to do with where we want to go.

A note from the author on her choice to use dialect
in
The Calling:

Language is like music. The same tunes can be
played in a variety of styles, octaves, keys and
tempos. Music enhances our emotions, and I believe
the use of dialect augments a character's authenticity
and likeability. My hope is that Merrick's dialect,
though of a different rhythm and cadence,
harmonizes with Kerry's in the mind of the reader.

To quote author James Kelman, "Language is
culture—if you lose your language you've lost your
culture."

What a loss that would be for us all!

The Calling
by Teresa McCoy

It has always seemed to me
I had to answer questions which fate had posed to my
forefathers
which had not yet been answered,
or as if I had to complete, or perhaps continue,
things which previous ages had left unfinished.
Carl Jung (1875 - 1961)

Prologue:

The Time Between Times

It is easy to be wise after the event.
—English 17th Century

1792

"*What have I done?*" the young woman whispered in disbelief as she assessed her situation. While unwilling to acknowledge the error of her most recent impulsive decision, she could not ignore the forceful gusts of wind that had already ripped away her control of the boat—her brother Rowse's boat that she had taken without his knowledge or consent. The lack of visibility caused by the slashing rain was worrisome enough, but as she battled with the oars of the faithful *Sea Bird*, she remembered with acute regret the many times she had shrugged and laughed away Rowse's warning that her brash and willful daring might someday invite her demise.

She just may have extended that very invitation this night. She surely was not laughing now, and her arms were so weary from rowing against the wind and riotous waters that she could not have shrugged for a pardon.

It was supposed to have been an easy run. Rowse had said so himself before he began retching two days ago, unable to keep anything in his stomach. The illness left his body sapped of its usual vitality and he admitted that in his weakened state he could not even imagine the rise and fall of waves beneath him without feeling sick. That was a pity, for he had been most eager to share in the profits this venture promised.

Therefore, his bold sister had made the furtive decision to make the run in his place. After all, the coastline had been her playground since she had been old enough to tag along with Rowse and his friends. After the early death of their parents, she and her brother had been on their

i

own. Over the years, the two of them had sailed together many times from Porth Harbor to a French ship anchored near Fowey or Mevagissey and back again, carrying barrels of French brandy under the fake bottom Rowse had built into their boat.

By the time she was seventeen, that little girl had grown into a striking young woman who caused her brother worry, especially after he had taken on the added concerns of a wife. However, his sister remained enamored only by the sea and the excitement of their work. For the next five years, she continued to feed on adventure and danger mixed with the spray of salt water and the frigid sea breezes she adored.

Then there was Myghal.

Myghal, the handsome artist from Sennen, admitted it was as much her recklessness that had drawn him to her as it was her emerald-eyed beauty. She found peace in his tranquility and assurance in the protection he offered even as he gave her rein. However, now that they were betrothed, Myghal suggested that she settle down and let him fill her need for adventure.

She looked forward to her future as Myghal's wife, but there was an edge to her contentment. She had grown up wild, and the sea beckoned. Rowse's ailment provided the justification she needed to feel the thrill of a run just one more time before she married and more than likely became permanently beached in a delicate condition. *Was not a sister to help her brother in his time of need?*

When she left the bay at dusk, dark and angry clouds were moving westward along the horizon. Nights like these were best because boats shrouded in fog were invisible from the shore. Timing was the trick, and by her calculation, she would have the *Sea Bird* anchored in the harbor before the outlying disturbance could morph into a respectable coastal storm.

The transfer from the French vessel had gone well. Dressed in her brother's clothes with her bright hair stuffed in an oversized cap, her gender remained undetected as she worked alongside men in the inky darkness. There was no conversation to give her away. Successful transfers were always done in silence in case authorities were lurking in the mists.

There were only two other boats from neighboring villages that had chanced to participate, so the cut in the profits would be appreciatively reduced. Rowse would be pleased and Myghal would surely be forgiving.

The *Sea Bird* was full and the bold lass rode waves of self-satisfaction on her way back home when the scene she saw developing on the horizon stunned her. The innocuous dark clouds that had been scooting across the sky had at some point assembled in a threatening mass. She had not noticed when the storm shifted direction, but it was now brutally clear that it would lay siege to the tiny fishing village of Porth.

It should have been easy coming into the harbor with the tide, but the squall's competing winds had forced her to take down the sails. She rowed frantically, but the boat only spun and made no headway. Her arms and shoulders screamed with fatigue, and through her rain-soaked clothing, her body began to chill.

It was the fear that took her by surprise. She had always been oblivious to fear and failure. Her uncanny surefootedness and understanding of the rigs and sails belonged more to a boy than a young maiden. All her peers had married and born children while she worked in the open sea beside her brother and his mates—matching her intelligence and daring to their greater strengths. She needed some of that brute strength to battle this storm, and it was becoming more apparent by the second that she did not possess it.

It was cold, too. She had not prepared for the sudden change in temperature. Soaked by the rain her body had become lethargic, but she was not sure if it was the cold or the fear that was fast becoming her nemesis.

When she saw the flicker of a lantern on the shore, she knew it was surely Myghal. He would be quick to ascertain that his missing fiancé and Rowse's missing boat were not coincidental. While the lamp's beam oscillated like a tiny beacon, she recognized his bellows over the howl of the wind and the beat of the rain. In keeping with the rhythm of her beloved sea, his shouts started out strong with fury, intensified with a crescendo of fear and then abated in heartbreak.

With heroic effort, she pushed aside the threatening panic to search for the outcrop of jagged rocks that marked her way, but it was near impossible to see past the bullets of stinging rain that came at her from all directions. Then, in a flash of lightening, she located the landmark when waves crashed into those rocks and sent up a soaring spray of seawater. She picked up the oars once more. All she had to do was make it around the rocks and turn into the harbor. Maybe luck would be with her and the storm would push her on and into Myghal's arms.

So focused she was on maneuvering the boat that she neither heard nor saw the gigantic wave until it was almost upon her. It was a massive wall of water; the kind that ancient mariners spoke of in reverent tones.

The young woman, who had never before known fear, cringed as she braced for impact. *This cannot be happening*, she thought just seconds before the wave slammed into the boat and drove it starboard into the rocks with the crack of splintering wood. The force of the collision pitched the lithe young woman overboard into the churning water, barely missing the rocks.

The wave continued past her toward shore, and she prayed that Myghal would flee to higher ground. That was the final crushing blow, that she might be responsible for ending his life as well.

When understanding of her futile situation finally drained the fight from her body, a calm acceptance filled her soul. The strength of the powerful undertow had defeated the hope she had clung to—that the tide would push her toward shore. In fact, each wave pulled her further and further out to sea. She could hear her brother's boat crash into the rocks again and again. A pile of firewood it would soon become, while the precious contraband spilled into the sea. *All for naught this was*—she had to admit with shame and much regret. *There was now no brandy, no boat…no life with Myghal.*

As it became clear what she had done, she could only pray for some way to atone. Even after the traitorous sea pulled her under it seemed she could still hear the gruff helplessness of Myghal's voice calling, calling.

Thus began their time between the times.

- 1 -

It is in your moments of decision that your destiny is shaped.
—Tony Robbins

"Is there any way I can talk you out of this, Kerry?" Tania called from the kitchen where she was making hot chocolate. "You get lost here in Wilmington where you grew up. How in the world will you find your way around in the UK?"

Kerry let the cursor hover over the "confirm" button for a full thirty seconds as she mentally scanned one last time the pros and cons of this decision. Several wise quotations from her collection flashed through her mind before silenced by the persuasive summons that had been haunting her for weeks.

Though Kerry had grown cautious in recent years and had developed a habit of second-guessing every decision she made, her instincts told her this was right. She squeezed her eyes shut and with a resolute nod, clicked the mouse to confirm her one-way plane ticket to London.

She closed her laptop with calm decisiveness, pushed her riot of curly flame-colored hair away from her face and joined her roommate in the cozy living area of their tiny apartment. "It's done, Tania," she informed her friend. "My leave of absence was approved today, and I just purchased my plane ticket."

"It was that easy…getting a year's leave?"

Kerry nodded setting her springy curls in motion, "I'm entitled to it now that I've completed three years. Besides that, my reason is sound. I stated on the application that I wanted *to take an educational journey in my teaching field, as well as embark on a venture of self-improvement in order to grow from a good teacher into an inspiring educator and leader.* Evidently the powers-that-be thought it was a good idea."

She smiled her thanks at Tania as she took the steaming mug of hot cocoa and moved to settle down among the assortment of homemade pillows on their second-hand sofa. Just when she was getting comfortable, she turned and caught sight of Tania's skeptical expression.

"*What?*" She barked at Tania and almost upset the mug she held in her lap. She thought better of making sharp movements and asked Tania again, calmly this time, although a tad caustically, "What was that look about?"

Tania gave her a slightly apologetic smile. "I was just trying to picture you as a leader. You know I love you Kerry, but in three years I've never known you to lead the way off an elevator."

Kerry was neither angered nor hurt by this because, sadly, it was true. She had always been more of a follower. But she was now determined to make a change, so with narrowed eyes she challenged her friend, "Maybe that's because I've always been the first one on."

Tania laughed, delighted with Kerry's usual quick wit. "So...back to your leave application, are you looking to win the teacher of the year award? I thought you were too modest for all that."

"Well, besides the fact that it would look good on a resume, I really do want to improve my knowledge and myself. It would benefit my students as well." Kerry glanced at Tania and braced herself for the persuasive speech she knew was coming.

Tania did not disappoint. "Then why don't you just take the year off and go out to your Dad's place in the country? You could spend your days at the local library studying the British Empire and reading Eckhart Tolle and Richard Carlson."

Kerry rolled her eyes at Tania's suggestion. "Because total immersion in a culture is so much better than simple research—everyone knows that. At least there won't be a language barrier. And not having anyone close to fix things for me will force me into self-reliance."

Tania sat in the cushioned rocking chair opposite Kerry, leaned forward and tried again. "But Kerry—*girl*—you've never done anything daring in the three years I've known you, and now all of a sudden you want to quit your job and take off to England where you've never been and where you don't know a soul? What happens if you get lost? You *know* how you panic."

"I'm not quitting my job—I'm taking a year's leave. And anyway, don't you think it's time I gained some confidence and sophistication?" Kerry changed tactics to put Tania on the defensive. "Maybe I have something to prove to those of you who think I'm just a clumsy oaf. Maybe I have something to prove to myself." She turned away from Tania and watched the swirl made by melting marshmallows as she stirred her hot cocoa.

After waiting for a response Kerry added, "Besides that, I have another reason for going."

Tania almost leaped from her chair to join Kerry on the couch, her dark eyes wide with regret and solace. "I knew it! I could kick myself for setting you up with that Ian. I never thought he'd be such a jerk, and I am so sorry, Kerry, and I'd do anything to rewind all that, but..." She cocked her head just like Kerry's school principal did when urging one toward self-reflection, "... maybe Myrtle Beach would be a better getaway?"

Kerry turned incredulous green eyes on her friend. "What are you talking about? You really thought Ian and I were hitting it off—*that way*?"

"But you went out every weekend for two months. I thought things were developing between you two and then I saw him at Pepino's kissing that blonde. I wasn't sure if you knew, but I guess you did. Why didn't you talk to me about it?"

"Oh my gosh, Tania, did I ever give you any indication that Ian and I had become romantically involved? We both knew after one date that we would be great friends, but nothing more. I don't even need to leave the neighborhood because of him, much less the country."

Tania's face was a mask of confusion. "But you went out together as much as Robert and I..."

"Tania," Kerry interrupted with an indulgent smile. "You introduced me to a good friend, and I thank you for that. We were each other's security date—you know—someone to do things with so we didn't have to be alone. A date for company parties and fundraisers and all those other functions where you need a comfortable date that will let you relax and focus on business instead of wooing."

Tania's eyebrows arched as she grinned at Kerry. "Did you say *wooing*?"

Kerry frowned at her. "What? Don't people *woo* each other these days?"

"You know?" Tania's shoulders slumped and her face fell into thoughtfulness. "Not much really. That's kinda sad, isn't it?"

"Well, if you ask me I think our society is in trouble if wooing is a thing of the past." She heaved a heavy sigh as she set her mug on a nearby coaster. "I was just born in the wrong century. I hate the loss of all those pretty manners."

Tania was quick with a comeback. "Yeah, well in a former century you could have been married off to someone you didn't even know. And as his *property*, what need would there be to *woo*?"

Kerry picked up her mug again to salute Tania. "You've got me there. I just need to get with the program, I guess."

Tania giggled and her eyes softened. "Oh, Kerry, that would ruin the 'Old World' romanticisms that make you who you are. So you and Ian didn't click?"

"We still keep in touch, and if I ever needed him, Ian would be there for me as I would for him. But he has a real girlfriend now, and I'm happy for him. I would never want to take his time away from her. He just wasn't the one for me, Tania. There was no spark between us." She laid her head back on the couch's soft cushion, thought about the two other prospects Tania had lined up for her in the last six months and sighed. "Maybe I just don't spark."

Tania studied the young woman beside her. Kerry always seemed so lost and alone. She shouldered her burdens with resignation and without complaint. The fixer in Tania wanted to find someone for her friend—someone who could connect with the old soul that lived within her. Kerry had so much to offer, but it would take someone special to discover what a treasure she was. "You just wait," she fussed. "Find the right one and you'll go off like a Roman candle. Maybe you should try one of those dating websites…"

Kerry's eyes rolled. "Why do you think all my troubles would go away if I had a man in my life? It seems to me it would be better to get myself in order first before bringing someone else into the fray. I brought you in, and here you are getting into a frenzy over this trip. You're not my mother, my dear, and you have your own life to live."

Tania heard the determination in her friend's voice, but she quickly pushed on. "Kerry, please. Spend some time thinking hard about what you're doing. I love you girl, but you know you're a trouble magnet. I don't think you're a doofus, how could I? You are just somewhat naïve and… you have no filter." Tania shook her head at Kerry's crestfallen expression. "What I mean to say is you have no experience with the world, Kerry. Your view of the modern world is…well…antiquated. Life isn't simple anymore Kerry, and you just…well…you just need a good dose of cynicism before you go out there on your own. And let me just mention that teachers in this twenty-first century are allowed a life outside the classroom besides summer camps, you know. You should go out…meet people…*experience life…*"

"Which is exactly what I'm trying to do and you're fighting me."

Tania recognized the grit in Kerry's expression. She sighed heavily, knowing she was losing the battle. "I can't bear the thought of you overseas by yourself. What does your brother think about this? You have told him, haven't you?"

"Oh, you know Owen. As long as he doesn't have to let go of any time or cash, he doesn't care. Although he did say, I'd be better off giving him the money I'll spend for this trip and let him invest it for me. What else would you expect from a stockbroker?"

She did expect more, however, and it stung. He was her brother and her *only* living relative. *Was it too much to ask that he care a little for his kid sister?* "Look Tania, I know you mean well, and I do love you for caring, but I need this and I'm going to do it. I'm twenty-five years old. I don't have to ask my brother or anyone else for permission. I can make my own decisions. Owen has certainly made his." Out of the corner of her eye, she watched Tania chew on that statement briefly, but her friend surprisingly let it pass.

Instead, she continued to throw buckets of cold water on Kerry's plans. "But aren't you concerned about traveling overseas these days? London is a hotspot for terrorism, you know."

Kerry took in a deep breath, gathered her riotous hair into a ponytail, twisted it around several times and then pushed it into a knot at the back of her head. She stared into Tania's worried face, her eyes challenging with unwavering logic. "Tania, is there any place in this world where safety is guaranteed?"

Tania glanced briefly toward a shelf that displayed a picture of Kerry with her mom and dad taken shortly after Kerry's high school graduation. It was the last there would ever be of such photos. Tania decided it was best to remain silent and listen as Kerry went on.

"I'm going, Tania, and it's going to be fine. Look, I know you're right—I'm not worldly and I'll admit I have no sense of direction and tend to get lost and be afraid. I also know my tongue is apt to trip over itself as my body has a tendency to trip over things. But please understand that I need to prove, if only to myself, that I'm not a hopeless incompetent. I need to build confidence and a reasonable trust of the world around me. I need to do this for me, Tania, and this might be my one chance."

Tania sighed in defeat. "Well, what is this other reason for going then?"

Kerry's expression softened. "I want to continue Dad's genealogy research on site. It was important to him. As an orphan, he had no living family to share with us, but he wanted to leave his grandchildren some roots. I owe him that."

"You owe it to him to live to have grandchildren," Tania weakly tried this one last argument, but she knew by that look in her friend's eyes that this trip was happening. "So who's going to take care of your Dad's place while you stumble around England?" she asked with an attempt at humor.

Kerry relaxed with a smile. "Me? Stumble?" She rolled her denim capris past her knees and stretched her legs out to expose two nearly identical purple splotches, one on each knee, "Well, you know I can't function without a good bruise or two—keeps me honest."

Tania's sigh included a slight whimper as she inspected Kerry's wounded knees. "What on earth happened this time?"

"My heels caught on the steps leading down to the teacher's lounge. Mark Phillips, our gym teacher, gallantly tried to stop me from falling, but…stop, Tania—he's happily married with two kids," she hastened to squash the hope that suddenly flashed in Tania's eyes.

Darn! "He didn't reach you in time?"

"Oh, yeah, he did. But my forward momentum took him with me. He's in a boot. Just a bad sprain, though. Not broken."

"Oh, God, Kerry, do you think you can keep from getting arrested in London?"

"As far as I know, clumsiness is not a crime," Kerry huffed. "It may be a crime of decorum—especially in imperial England, but nothing worthy of the Tower I'm sure. You know, you'd better save your worries for yourself. I don't know what you'll do the next time you need someone to sit up all night to help you sew those meticulous costumes you create. And who's going to throw the victory parties when you win more awards for those amazing conceptions?"

Tania's eyes traveled to the bookcase behind Kerry where those trophies now sat on the highest shelf. "You have a point, but your most valuable service has been your glue gun talent. That day they all crashed onto the floor and broke into so many small pieces, I thought they were destined for the trash. However, you and your glue gun brought them back to life." She casually tipped her head toward Kerry, catching her eyes. "You remember that day, don't you? It was during that dramatic off-key sing-along you had with Christina Agularia."

Kerry flinched as she glanced at the three silver awards with their barely discernible cracks. "You did say those repairs were works of art. That was another all-nighter I pulled for your benefit, by the way." Her head snapped back to Tania, her eyes narrowing. "And what do you mean *off-key*?"

Tania could not help laughing. "Let me see…that night you sat up repairing my poor broken trophies—wasn't that also the night the glue gun caught fire and burned that section of carpet under the rug there?"

Kerry glanced down at the spot Tania referred to, recalling that night. "Well, I first had to save my students' midterm exams from their proximity to the flames. Otherwise, the burn would have covered a much smaller area. But see? That proves I can prioritize even in a crisis."

Tania studied her friend fondly. They were the same age, but Kerry seemed more like a younger sister. There were reasons, of course. The responsibilities that had weighed on Kerry since before adulthood had stunted her social growth and probably added to her insecurities as well. She was so inexperienced for her age in some regards, yet in other ways life had forced her to grow up too fast. Maybe this trip would be good for her. Tania heaved another sigh. "I'll miss you, Kerry."

"And I'll miss you." Kerry's eyes dropped to the pretty patchwork rug Tania had made to cover the burned carpet. She would never cease to be amazed at what Tania could make out of scrap materials she scavenged from the theatre where she worked. Her mother would have liked Tania, would have respected her talent.

As she leaned toward the floor and ran the palm of her hand over the textured rug, Kerry began quietly, "In answer to your question about my parent's place, my brother—in his much older wisdom—has decided to sell it." At Tania's stunned expression, she hurried to explain. "In all fairness I've agreed. I'll admit I was angry at first, but then I realized the property taxes and maintenance on the place would be huge strains for my teacher's salary. Owen could really use the money—he has his family and that fancy lifestyle to support. My half of the estate will give me a comfortable cushion and makes this trip possible. It's just so sad, though. Dad kept everything just as it was when Mom was alive, and I don't think I could stand seeing their whole life taken apart and sold to the highest bidders. I want to be out of here before the estate sale." She paused for a second and drew a breath. Catching Tania's eyes, she continued, "And there is one more thing. You're going to think I'm a little weird."

Tania focused all her attention on her friend. "I already know you're a little weird, so spill it, sister."

Kerry leaned in toward Tania and spoke in a quiet, conspiratorial voice. "Every time I open Dad's genealogy files, I feel this strange pull, like a…a calling sort of thing, reaching out to me from across the Atlantic. I can't help but feel there is something over there I'm suppose to find or…

7

do. And those occasional nightmares I have? They're coming much more frequently. I've had trouble sleeping for weeks now. I feel think these things are connected in some way. Does that seem utterly fanciful to you?"

Tania's eyes opened wide. She let out the breath she had held, leaned over and covered Kerry's hand with her own. "*Kerry*, you didn't tell me you'd felt a *calling*. That's a different matter altogether. A calling isn't something to ignore."

Kerry sighed heavily. "Oh, I most certainly can't ignore it. You know, I've never been a superstitious person, but I can't disregard this…this summons, for lack of a better word. It's like I've been served a subpoena and I have to show up at court."

"Then I guess you got to go," Tania said in resignation. "And I knew that about the nightmares." Kerry's eyebrows went up in question and Tania hurried on, "Oh, you never woke me up, but if I happened to be awake I could hear you thrashing about, gasping for air. You'd wake up just about the time I reached your door. They're pretty intense, huh? You know they have storms in England, too. Worse, more likely—it's an island you know."

Kerry nodded, slightly embarrassed that Tania had heard her, but relieved she had gained her friend's support. Her eyes dropped to the rug again and she changed the subject. "I promise I'll pay for that carpet repair before I go."

"Oh, our deposit will take care of that. Lord knows we've fixed a jillion other things in this little place out of our own pockets. So…how long do I have to find another roommate?"

Kerry warmed to the new topic of conversation. "I want to leave as soon as I finish the school year, so about eight weeks. Hopefully you'll find someone as nice as I am."

Tania's forlorn face lifted with a sly smile. "Or maybe I'll purposefully choose someone I just can't stand so we won't feel bad about somehow driving her out when you return."

Kerry's green eyes glittered. "You could try breaking her hard-earned treasures."

"Or a little accidental arson?"

Kerry laughed and let her eyes sweep the small apartment they had shared for three years. Tania's African decor mixed well with her eclectic style, their individual tastes weaving a comfortable and homey atmosphere. Heaving a sad sigh, she fixed Tania's eyes with her own.

"Realistically, Tania, you and I both know I won't be back, not here anyway." Tania's eyebrows drew together to argue, but Kerry continued. "This was going to happen eventually. You and Robert are getting closer and closer, and you know the two of you will either move in together or maybe even get married. You'll need this klutzy white girl out of the way. This was bound to happen, one way or another."

Tania reluctantly nodded. She also recognized this as a turning point in both their lives. Three years ago when Kerry had answered Tania's ad for a roommate, she literally tripped over the apartment's threshold onto the floor and into Tania's life. Within the space of the half hour interview Kerry had inadvertently stepped on Tania's musical, religious and political preferences in addition to breaking a teacup, but Tania recognized the honesty and kindness in the girl's eyes. So she gave Kerry a chance, and as it turned out, not only did they make ideal roommates, they also became best friends. "Promise me you'll call me if you need anything—even just to hear a familiar voice?"

"I will, but I'll be fine, Tania. Don't worry. I'll text and email you often with pictures and all the dirt I find out about the old homeland folks." She wiggled her eyebrows wickedly. "There might be some really juicy stuff hidden over there." She looked into Tania's sad, worried eyes and sought to assure her, "I'll be fine, Tania. I promise."

- 2 -

An important key to self-confidence is preparation.
—Arthur Ashe

What in blazes was I thinking? Kerry thought to herself several times during the weeks leading up to her trip. After all, she had never ventured to even Texas or California on her own. To fly across thousands of miles of ocean to a different continent where she knew not a single soul was downright scary. Nonetheless, the pull was inescapable. There was simply no other course to take.

As a teacher of middle school Social Studies, Kerry was a genius at research and planning. *Planning is what saves teachers from the mutiny of the masses; it is also the key to getting subject content embedded in the age-afflicted mind of the middle school creature.* The yearly evaluations in her employee file proved that Kerry did this well. She also had an inherent gift in making her lesson plans fun, kinetic, and relevant, so she had become a favorite among the students. In the classroom, she was buoyant and self-assured.

Outside the classroom Kerry's confidence dwindled. She lacked her brother's polish and the easy-going social understanding that allowed him sail through to the lucrative position he now held. Owen was smart as well as physically impressive. He was tall and bulky with a handsomely chiseled green-eyed face and straight dark brown hair—all clearly inherited from their parents. Kerry, however, was small with soft but slightly irregular features, and those physical traits combined with her red uncontrollable mane made her for years the brunt of teasing about milkmen and cabbage patches.

Owen was the popular athlete while Kerry tended to fly under the radar, hiding behind books and studies. She was a classic introvert, but at the same time aware of latent and inhibited passions that caused her confusion and uncertainty. Like a bird that wanted desperately to fly but was not quite developed. Kerry was grateful that their parents had always

11

been supportive, but what was so easy for Owen seemed out of reach for Kerry. She felt she had definitely missed something in the gene pool.

Before she really began to worry about her social ineptitude, her mom's accident put all social expectations in the irrelevant category. After her mother's death, Kerry spent her college breaks with her lonely father. She had friends on campus, but no time or inclination for socializing. And for the last three years, unlike Owen—with his six-figure income, fancy cars, his beautiful wife and daughter in the opulent home in the affluent neighborhood in Beaufort where they entertain almost weekly—Kerry survived on her teacher's salary by splitting the rent on a 'vintage' apartment in Wilmington and spending weekends in the country with her dad. That ended six months ago.

Among her positive dominate traits, however, was steadfast determination. Once an idea took root in Kerry's head, that determination brought it to fruition. Kerry did not hesitate to put to work her professional strong points, research and planning, to ensure the success of this journey. She had drawn up a timeline weeks ago, and the checkmarks on her lists did much to ease her worries and boost her confidence. She applied for her passport, her airline ticket was secure and she had bought a book about backpacking through Britain which she has since read from cover to cover, dog-eared pages and highlighted important points. She made the announcement to a few of her closest friends, and the next thing was to liquidate some "stuff" and purchase a good backpack.

"What do you mean, *backpack*?" asked Tania with wide eyes. "Don't you need one of those steamer trunk things? How are you going to pack enough clothes in a backpack? What about accessories?"

"Tania, look at this," Kerry opened wide her *Guide to Backpacking in Britain* that offered a full checklist of what and how to pack. "I'm not staying at hotels and eating in fancy restaurants. I'm riding buses and staying in hostels. I only need easy-to-pack clothes like shorts, jeans and t-shirts, a good pair of hiking shoes, flip-flops and a rain poncho. If I decide to stay through the winter, I'll buy long-johns, a couple of sweaters, and a heavy coat. But minimizing is the name of the game for now."

"But you never know what might come up. I hope you have room for a fairy-godmother in this backpack thing."

Kerry grinned at her friend. "Are you worried about me going into the Queen's country without formal wear? I thought I would, you know, just slip in incognito. The Queen won't feel the need to invite me to the palace if she doesn't even know I'm there."

Tania made a face. "What if you meet some English lord and he asks you out? Oh! What will you carry for protection? Have you thought of that?"

Kerry snapped the book shut. "I'll borrow Robert's wallet. I know he carries little else in that thing."

Tania's eyes narrowed. "That's an unfortunate truth, but I didn't mean that kind of protection. Seriously, you…"

"Tania," Kerry interrupted. "Look at me."

"I am. That's why I'm worried.

Kerry let out a frustrated sigh. "Listen to me, then. I'm going to be in populated areas—mostly. I won't get into cars with strange guys, won't accept candy from strangers, and by all accounts the hostels are safe. I'll keep my passport and credit cards in a money belt next to my skin at all times. I'm really excited about this trip, so stop with the negativity, okay? Go shopping with me." She opened the book to one of those dog-eared pages and held it out to Tania. "Help me find the items on this list."

Tania reluctantly took the book and scanned the items. "Well, at least it includes some toiletries. But how about makeup? A little enhancement never hurts, you know."

An intense premonition of loneliness smothered Kerry's laugh. *Who would she banter with like this in England?* "I wish you could come with me," she blurted.

"No way!" Tania gave the book back to Kerry. "When I visit a rainy country with this humidity-challenged hair, I'll need something bigger than this backpack of yours just for my hair products alone. Ponytails don't work for me. And by the way—you seriously plan to tote this thing containing all your worldly possessions around on your back? Uh, uh. No way, baby. I'm a costume designer, not a turtle!"

⚓

Three weeks later, Tania came in from work to find Kerry in her room where stacks of clothing and piles of articles covered her bed. Kerry's face was aglow as she greeted Tania with a quick hug. "My passport came in the mail this morning. The stars are lining up, Tania."

"Yeah? Well, this is exciting. Let me see your passport."

Kerry turned around and fished a brand new money belt out of her brand new backpack that leaned against the bed. Excitement turned to astonishment and then to exasperation when she found no passport. "I thought I put it right in here. Maybe I laid it out to show you as soon as you got home." Frantically she searched through the piles on her bed.

Tania watched for a few seconds as neat stacks morphed into a mess, then said simply, "Um, hmm" as she turned and left the room.

"Don't you use that tone with me," called Kerry from the bedroom. "Maybe I put it…"

Her panic subsided when she heard Tania call from the kitchen, "… right here on the bar with my mail?" Tania was opening the passport just as Kerry joined her in the front room, a sheepish expression on her face. "Nice mug shot," Tania continued. "Anyone who looks at this picture might be fooled into thinking this is someone who has it all together."

"Thanks," said Kerry with a scowl, reaching for the passport. "I should have left it in my backpack until you got home. This was my first lesson in safeguarding my passport."

"*Your first lesson?* How many lessons do you think it will take…*Kerenza* Carter?" Tania smiled at the legal name on Kerry's passport. "I forget sometimes that Kerry is your nickname." Giggling softly she added, "Remember when Robert first found out that your name is Kerenza? He thought he was so clever making up those silly rhymes—*Who knows what's in Kerenza's credenza?* And *has poor Kerenza got influenza?*"

Kerry gave her a wry smile. "Yeah, good ole' Ro-bert the per-vert, the eternal adolescent."

Tania stuck out her tongue and followed up with a smile and a wink. "But he's *my* adolescent."

Kerry held out her hand for the passport. "Yes, he's all yours, but that's mine, and I'll put it in its home right now where it will stay until duty calls." After sheathing the passport in the money belt, she raised her tee shirt, strapped on the belt, and then let her shirt drop back into place. "See? It's hardly noticeable." She did not let Tania's doubtful expression dampen her spirits. "Speaking of Slobbert, is he coming over tonight? Do you think he would help me move some of this stuff into storage?"

Tania let the familiar jibe go. Instead of a clever comeback, she twirled around and led the way back into Kerry's bedroom. "Already?" She took in the neat stack of boxes sitting on top of a small dresser and a desk pushed into a corner. "You're down to just a bed and a chair, and you have three weeks left."

"It's time to get used to my new minimized lifestyle. Besides, I can't wait until the last minute. You've lived with me long enough to know how hectic the last two weeks of school are. Grades, permanent records, awards, post-planning—all are so time consuming—and this year I have to move everything out of my classroom and take it to storage. Then I have to go to the closing on Dad's place, have a garage sale, pack, and attend the bon voyage party my grade level staff is giving me. That's a lot in three weeks. I'm starting to panic that I won't get it all done. Plus I keep getting distracted by the all this genealogy stuff of Dad's. I'm getting obsessed to find out what kind of genes I have running through my veins. Do you ever wonder about why you are the way you are?"

At Tania's blank expression, Kerry tried to explain. "As the only child of an adopted orphan, Dad didn't have any blood relatives that we could look to and say 'I look somewhat like *her* or I got that trait from *him*.' I mean look at this mop!" She gathered up her hair in both hands, "I'd like to know where this came from. And besides that, Ralph Waldo Emerson himself said, 'Every man is a quotation from all his ancestors', I want to know what mine have said down through the ages and why. I want to know the story leading up to me. Does that make sense?"

Tania nodded, wide-eyed.

"And who knows?" Kerry added as she gathered her hair into a ponytail, securing it with the band she always wore on her wrist. "I may even find a living family member or two—some distant cousin by marriage or the like. That's the main reason this trip is important to me."

Tania let her eyes travel over Kerry. They took in her friend's ponytailed hair and make-up free face framed by uncontainable wispy curls, standing barefoot in her stripped-down room, her money belt visible underneath her thin tee shirt. In her mind, she cursed Kerry's brother, Owen, for his self-centered attitude. Kerry needed family. She let out a shaky sigh. "Robert will be happy to help move your things. And if you'd like, I'll help you with the garage sale." Tania glanced at the stacks of Kerry's clothes, mostly jeans, t-shirts and professional clothes. "Are you selling all of this stuff? I'm not interested for myself, I couldn't squeeze into a size two if my life depended on it, but I might buy some things for my little sister and help your cause." She shuffled through a couple of stacks, and then shook her head. "I don't know though, this stuff is a little old-fashioned."

Kerry's gaze spanned the piles of clothes. "*Old-fashioned?*"

"Yeah, I mean…very conservative and basic. Girl, this is the wardrobe of a fortyish woman. I'll bet you don't own one thing cut low enough or high enough to show off the nice physical attributes you have or the tattoos you don't. Your skin is as unmarked as a baby's behind. I'm not sayin' that's bad—just unusual these days. Old-fashioned."

Kerry considered this. "I guess after all the necessary stitches I've had over the years I can't imagine offering myself up as a volunteer pin cushion. Of course, a tattoo would be a sure way for someone to identify a body if…"

Tania interrupted Kerry with a gasp, her beautiful chocolate eyes horrified. "What an unspeakable thing to joke about! Look, girl, don't get upset, but I have to say this. You look terribly young and small and unsure, Kerry. You'll be a prime target for the wrong people—you know what I'm saying? You need to be very careful."

"I know, Tania. Just keep telling me I'm going to be fine. I know I say it all the time but hearing it from you would lend it…credibility."

Tania gripped Kerry's shoulders and looked into her eyes. In her most convincing voice, she assured her friend. "Kerry, you've got good instincts. Listen to them. Be alert, remain cautious, and you'll be just fine."

Tania sounded almost convincing.

- 3 -

With every goodbye, you learn.
—Veronica A. Shoffstall

Kerry should be better at goodbyes by now. She has certainly had
enough practice in the last seven years.

Near the end of Kerry's junior year of high school, an intoxicated
driver ran a red light and slammed into her mother's car on her way
home from work. The young man suffered minor injuries, but the accident
rendered Kerry's once robust mother, Jean, a quadriplegic. Jean worked
hard to rehabilitate and had even begun to adapt to the continuation of
her job as an editor for a small publishing house. However, the frequent
bouts with pneumonia weakened her, and after one life-threatening
episode Kerry made the decision to turn down her UNC acceptance to
become Jean's full-time caretaker.

The sacrifices made by her husband and daughter began to weigh
heavily on Jean. She fought against a hovering depression, and her body
continued to weaken. Shortly after Kerry's graduation, Jean's mind and
body gave up its fight. It was as if she had seen her daughter to adulthood
and could now get out of her way. Kerry and her father had been with
Jean to say their goodbyes as she passed.

Six months ago, Kerry's dad had a fatal heart attack in his sleep just
hours after she had returned to the city. They had spent the weekend
together fishing at the creek and playing checkers on the wrap-around
porch of her childhood home. Her last image of him alive was waving
goodbye as she drove down the tree-lined drive.

Last week Kerry had signed the 'goodbye' papers to that home, and
last night she had been the guest of honor at a bon voyage party given by
teachers at her school. Over the last three years, she had said goodbyes
to hundreds of students as they moved from her care and supervision
toward high school. Tonight she was to meet her closest friends at Matt's
Bar for a "till we meet again" sort of farewell. If there was a lesson in

goodbyes, she was still as oblivious to it as some of her students had been to the implications of the Clayton-Bulwar Treaty of 1850.

..

Kerry was twenty minutes late and frantic when she walked into the cheerful atmosphere of Matt's Bar. Robert was the first to see her and waved her over to their table. Tania looked as striking as ever, and was happily snuggled up to Robert. When she saw Kerry approaching, she poured Kerry's favorite wine in a glass and passed it to her as she joined the group. "Here's the lady of the hour," she beamed, "or what's left of it anyway. Where did you find your keys this time?"

Kerry grinned at their next-door neighbor Lucy. "I was just about to go across the hall and knock on your door when I realized you were probably already here. I found them hiding under a towel in the bathroom."

Lucy, the mother figure who lived across the hall from Kerry and Tania, had for the last two years kept duplicate sets of keys for those repeated occasions when Kerry misplaced her own. The woman's smile did not quite hide her exasperation. "It's a long way from London to Wilmington, Sweet pea. You need to somehow keep up with your keys or find a British Lucy."

Kerry laughed and gave the woman a quick hug. "Lucy, you know there's not another like you in the whole world. Besides, I'll only need to keep up with one hostel key at a time."

"And you think that's going to be easier?" Lucy's eyebrows shot up her forehead. "You'd better wear it around your neck." She looked across the table. "You boys have any words of advice for this world traveler?"

Brandon and Blake, the couple who owned the local coffee shop she and Tania had frequented for two years, were among Kerry's close circle of friends. Blake spoke first. "Yeah, always order a small coffee in a large cup. Then maybe you won't slosh all over yourself...and the floor...other customers..."

Brandon gave him a disapproving look. "That hasn't happened in...a while now."

Blake let out a snort and countered, "Because I deliver her coffees to her table. It'll take her a while to get those British baristas trained."

Brandon gave Kerry an apologetic glance and then turned a frown on Tai Luong, the young foreign exchange student who had wandered into the coffee shop a year ago. She was now their collective charge. "Can you believe he's being so mean to her? Tonight of all nights?"

Tai Luong smiled in her usual sweet way. "Blake just trying not to cry. He know he going to miss carrying coffee for her."

Blake huffed again, "Yeah, right. It's what I live for." Then his obstinate countenance fell when he focused on Kerry's face. "This whole business of you going off alone is killing me."

Kerry gave him a warm smile and patted his hand where it lay on the table. "But you won't always be around, Blake, and sooner or later I have to learn to carry my own coffee. Understand? Charlotte Bronte said, 'The more unsustained I am, the more I will respect myself'."

Blake squeezed her hand. "Well, kudos for Charlotte, but Kerry, baby, it'll break our hearts if anything happens to you."

For a moment, everyone was silent, all in agreement with Blake's statement. Brandon was the first to recognize the need to lighten the moment. "Well, Kerry, are you all packed?"

Kerry brightened immediately. "I am. All my gels and liquids are in three ounce containers, my phone and iPad are charged for the plane ride, and…" her eyes cutting to Tania, "my passport is in its proper place."

"What time do you leave tomorrow?" asked Blake. "Is there anything we can do? Need a ride to the airport?"

"Thank you, but my brother is taking me." She could not keep the delight out of her voice. "He's in from Beaufort on business and can see me off before he leaves."

"That's great," said Brandon. "What time do you leave?"

"My flight leaves at 1:30, putting me in London at 3:30 a.m. their time."

"Oh, honey, please be careful," this from Lucy. "The wee hours of the morning can't be a good time for a lone woman to be on the streets of London."

Kerry smiled to assure the woman. "The Piccadilly Line of the London Underground train system leaves Heathrow at 5:15 that morning. I checked. I figured by the time I get through customs and have a leisurely breakfast somewhere in the airport, I shouldn't have to wait long to board. The train will take me to a station within blocks of my first hostel. It's a good forty-five minute trip, so it should be light outside when I arrive." Everyone nodded and Kerry went on, "The sale of Dad's home went through Wednesday without a hitch. I have two major credit cards so I won't need much cash, and, yes, Tania, they are tucked away with my passport. I've studied British currency so I won't have to depend on strangers to help me pay for things, and I have the U.S. Embassy's number memorized."

"You're probably going to be homesick at first," said Lucy. "But just immerse yourself—become a Londoner. It will pass. And please don't forget to keep in touch."

Tai Luong spoke quietly. "It take about three week to get over worst of it. Then you meet friends..." her smile took in everyone at the table, "... and you be much better."

"I will keep in touch," Kerry promised. "I'm really going to miss all of you—you've been like family to me."

"Promise me you'll wear flip-flops in those hostel showers. Ew! You never know what you can pick up in those public places," warned Blake with a shiver of repulsion. "And OMG! What about the beds?"

Kerry rolled her eyes and chuckled. "I have a sleeping bag, Blake, one that rolls up tight and fits into the straps on my backpack. Don't worry guys, I've researched every book and website I could find on this subject. Tania can vouch for me."

"Kerry is going to be just fine," assured Tania. "It's us I'm worried about. What are we going to do for entertainment now? Who's going to enlighten us with her collection of pertinent quotes?"

"I guess I'm probably the only person here not entirely broken up about you leaving," this from Robert, which gained him a punch in the ribs from Tania's elbow but caused a bright smile to spread across Kerry's face.

"Now why would that be, Robert? Could it be that Tania found no one good enough to replace me as roommate and had to settle for *your* sorry ass?"

"Hey, I'm the pick of the litter. I'll pay your portion of the rent but I won't take up that other bedroom." He looked at Tania and smiled sweetly. "Now Tania can have a real sewing room all to herself—a room where she can design to her heart's content and then close the door on it at night."

Kerry looked at Tania and winked. "So you have him believing that's not an all consuming career you've got there? Oh, Robert—you've a lot to learn. I hope you're not a stranger to needle and thread!"

Robert's smug smile stiffened as he looked down at Tania, who ignored him and pushed an elegantly wrapped package across the table to Kerry. "From all of us."

"Oh, guys...you didn't have to do anything, but what a nice surprise!" Kerry made eye contact with each friend as she tore the teal blue ribbon and paper from the box. Inside was a small frame that displayed a picture of her six smiling friends holding a banner that read, *Always remember—you're braver than you believe. A.A. Milne*

Kerry felt her eyes water and her throat tighten, but she pushed through it. "Thanks so much, y'all. I'll pull it out every night and put it beside my bed where I'll see it first thing every morning. It will start my day out right. This quote of Milne's is especially meaningful to me, as you know. Actually, Milne has a plethora of significant quotes."

"He must talk a lot, then. Who is he—a preacher or a politician?" asked Robert, chuckling at his own joke.

Kerry smiled and shrugged. "He'd probably do well as a preacher but he's too decent to be a politi…" she caught herself, remembering too late that Brandon's father was mayor of his hometown, "…to be like *some* politicians," she finished as she stole a glance at Brandon's smiling face while hers grew rosy with embarrassment.

"Don't worry about it," he said. "No offense taken. Everyone knows it's an unscrupulous business. So tell Robert who Milne is."

Kerry turned a relieved face back to Robert, "Winnie the Pooh. Milne is the genius behind the infinite wisdom of Winnie the Pooh and his friend Christopher Robin."

"Pooh Bear?" Robert was skeptical. "I thought he was just some yellow dude with a red sweater who was always getting into trouble—usually with honey."

Brandon winked at Kerry. "But he had a special friend with amazing insight, Pooh did, and he appreciated learning about the important things in life. Like friends."

Tania raised her glass in toast and everyone at the table followed suit. "Here's to friends. May Kerry find new friends in the UK so she won't be alone, but remember she can always count on her old friends here at home."

⚓

That night before she climbed into bed, Kerry placed the framed picture of her friends on the chair beside her bed where she would see it when she woke up. She ran her fingers over the smiling faces of her friends, thought about her mom and dad and wondered once more about the lesson in goodbyes.

On a whim, she jumped out of bed and went to her iPad to search for more quotes from A. A. Milne. Scrolling down the list, she caught her breath when the answer revealed itself in crystal clarity. She grabbed her notebook of collected quotes and copied what Winnie the Pooh had known all along—*How lucky I am to have something that makes saying goodbye so hard.*

- 4 -

We are all formed of frailty and error;
Let us pardon reciprocally each other's folly—
that is the first law of nature.
—Voltaire

Kerry was not new to flying. Before her grandfather died, she and her mother, father and brother would fly twice a year to upstate New York to visit him. Even so, she had not lost the thrill of that huge mechanical bird taking off into the sky, nor appreciation for that feeling of peace up in clouds that sometimes looked so much like big fluffy pillows she imagined jumping out of the plane and burrowing into their billowy softness.

It was pleasant anticipation that enabled Kerry to put aside the embarrassment she suffered at the flight desk and board the 757 airliner. She settled into her window seat located just in front of the wing, her backpack stowed in the overhead storage, her earphones plugged in and her iPad ready for use. At a bookstore near the gate, she had picked up a book of Sudoku and other puzzles that she tucked into the seat pocket along with her new writing journal from Tania and her cherished collection of favorite quotes. She had plenty to keep her busy on the long flight to London. While other passengers boarded, she looked out the window at the tarmac hubbub and thought back on her morning…

She awakened after a peaceful sleep—which she took as a good omen—to the early morning sun shining through the lace curtains of Tania's new sewing room. She showered and dressed and was standing in front of the open refrigerator trying to decide between yogurt and cereal when Tania surprised her with an invitation to breakfast at the cute little pancake house nearby—just the two of them. There Tania presented her friend with another going away gift, a journal with a paisley cover in Kerry's favorite combination of colors–fuchsia, teal, and black.

"Now this is not to be used as a trip diary or another volume of collected quotes. This is for story writing. You have a flair for writing, Kerry. I've seen it in the writing samples you've written for your students. You should exercise it, and you'll have lots of down time during travel to do just that."

Kerry was touched that someone thought her little hobby of making up stories had any positive merit. "I will, Tania. How thoughtful of you. Who knows, maybe I'll get something published one day and we'll both become famous."

There were a few moments of panic when Owen did not show up to take her to the airport. Worried that something terrible might have happened to him, she had frantically called his cell phone. After the third try, a groggy Owen answered and admitted that after schmoozing clients the night before he was too hung-over to make it.

"You can call a taxi, right Sis? I couldn't walk you to the gate anyway—it would just be a drop off and run situation. Not really worth the trouble…well, you know what I mean."

Kerry was not surprised, and she tried not to let it hurt, but it did. "Don't worry, Owen, I'll be fine. I'll keep in touch."

Same old, same old.

When she climbed into the taxi a few minutes later, Kerry had to remind herself to breathe. This was it. *Her plans had come together!* In less than ten hours, she would be in London, and most important to Kerry this morning—the weather forecast was clear all the way.

No storms!

She passed through security with ease, although the money belt around her waist under her shirt had been a temporary item of concern. She felt a little tremor of panic when she had to take it off and go through the screening device while it went through the scanner on its own, but as soon as the two were reunited, Kerry had felt in control again.

Once through security, Kerry bought a sandwich and chips to take on the plane with her. With her hands full, she waited at her gate, eyeing her fellow passengers that were also waiting. She picked out a couple in the crowd that would make good characters for potential short stories.

The next snag in her trip happened just before boarding the plane. Juggling her pack, her sandwich and chips and bookstore purchases, Kerry's ticket had unknowingly fluttered to the floor. When it was time for Kerry to scan her ticket and board the plane, her ticket was no longer on her person. Kerry was near tears, the flight desk was about to have a conniption, and a short-lived panic ensued until a Good Samaritan brought to the desk the wayward ticket he had found on the floor. As a red-faced Kerry finally boarded the plane, she was acutely aware of the scowls and rolling eyes that expressed irritation in the boarding delay.

Now safely in her seat, she was glad to be able to enjoy a few minutes of thoughtful solitude. Then the occupant of the seat next to hers arrived. It seemed things were to get worse before they got better.

She could not resist texting Tania. "John Goodman's twin just squeezed into the seat next to mine."

In less than thirty seconds, Tania's response rang in. "You lucky girl! What's he doing?"

Kerry's thumbs flew over the keyboard. "Looking very nervous and sweating profusely. Taking up part of my space. *Why me?*"

"He could be thinking the same thing. If you weren't there, he'd have more room," Tania pointed out.

"As always, you are the voice of reason. I'll make the best of it. Leaving gate now. Signing off. Love you much."

Kerry turned off her phone and put it in the seat pocket. She glanced at the man beside her. His hands were gripping the chair arms, his eyes squeezed tight. "Sir, are you okay?" she asked with concern.

The man opened his eyes to find interest and concern on Kerry's young face. "I'll be okay in a minute. I don't do well with take-offs. Or landings. Don't much care for anything in-between either." He motioned to a prescription bottle he had tucked into the seat pocket. "But I'll be fine… just took a valium. It helps me relax."

"I usually enjoy flying myself, but this is my first international flight. Have you done this before?"

"Many times. It doesn't get any easier. But it's my job—my responsibility." The man turned his head fully to look straight at her. "Are you doing this for a lark?" He looked incredulous.

Kerry thought a moment about her calling before she answered, "No, I have to do this, too."

His expression relaxed into empathy. "Oh, well. It's the pits, isn't it?"

Kerry thought conversation would keep his mind off the movement of the plane as it backed out of the gate. "So the valium really helps?"

"Like a charm. I take one for takeoff, and then another a little more than halfway so I'm good during landing. It's just anxiety about being out of control, you know?" He talked on nervously, "I make sure I bring extras just in case I lose one or something. Don't want to take any chances," then a wry chuckle. "I'd hate to have a panic attack about losing the medicine I take for panic attacks."

Kerry wondered what his panic attacks might look like and decided it would be better not to find out. Her own were hard enough to face. "I understand completely. I have a phobia of my own."

"Oh, yeah?" he looked at her curiously.

"I'm ashamed to admit it, because it is so childish, but I'm deathly afraid of storms. They paralyze me."

"Really? Have you had a bad experience in the past?"

"You mean like a trigger experience? Not that anyone remembers. My parents think I was born with it. I would wake up at the first lightning strike or roll of thunder and scream for the duration. I don't scream anymore, but I find it hard to breathe until it's over. Sometimes I have nightmares about storms."

"Huh. I feel for you. I guess we all have our crosses to bear. Fortunately, the weather is supposed to be perfect during this flight. Nice and smooth they said. Better for us both, right?"

"Right. Well, I hope you have a pleasant, uneventful trip, sir."

"Thanks. I appreciate that. You, too."

Kerry plugged in her earphones, turned on her music and watched out the window. Once the airplane had taxied to the runway, and was second in line for takeoff, she stole a glance at the man again. His grip on the chair arms had relaxed, his eyelids were fluttering down, and by the time the engines revved up for takeoff, he was snoring steadily.

The first three hours passed in flying bliss—the steady noise of the engines and the sound of circulating air encased her in the cocoon she looked forward to when flying. Except for the occasional forced shifting of the man next to her by the flight attendants in an attempt to reduce the noise level of his snores, Kerry was undisturbed, surrounded by her music and the white noise of the airplane. It was an uninterrupted time during which nothing was required of her and she could, without guilt, do nothing but read, work puzzles, and get lost in thought. She just tried to keep those thoughts away from the ocean water undulating 30,000 feet below. The sea, she was ashamed to admit, was her other adversary.

Even though Kerry knew one was supposed to keep hydrated during flight, she began to doubt the wisdom of those two bottles of water she had consumed in the last three hours. She really needed to go to the bathroom, but just like Rip Van Winkle, her neighbor was down for the count.

Finally, she could wait no longer. She attempted to excuse herself, but got no response from Mr. Goodman. Her several attempts to climb over him were thwarted by his large frame. It was going to take some strategic planning, and after a bit of forethought, Kerry stood up in her seat hunched over beneath the overhead bins. She placed her right hand on the corner of his headrest and her left on the headrest of the seat in front of his. Very carefully, she lifted her right leg up and over his mid-section. She used her arms to lift her body up and over far enough to place her right foot in the aisle. Once her footing felt firm, she twisted around, switched her arms on the headrests and then very carefully pulled her left leg over into the aisle.

She blushed to hear a quiet applause from a few of her fellow travelers and beamed inwardly that she had completed such a task with perfect balance. Unfortunately her first step toward the restroom met resistance. When she looked back, she saw that her wristwatch had apparently grazed Goodman's shoulder just enough to be caught in the threads of his tweed vest.

She heard a chuckle and looked behind her. A man who looked to be about forty raised his eyebrows at her. He was definitely a sleazy sort, and Kerry currently didn't have the time or inclination to interact with him at all. She simply unfastened the watch clasp and left it dangling from the vest.

On her way up the aisle, she stepped on an errant squeak toy and startled several passengers that had just nodded off, including the owner of the toy who immediately began to thrash and wail in his mother's arms. Several pairs of eyes speared her, and in some, she saw recognition. *Yes, it's me again. The same as held up the boarding line.*

By the time she made it to the restroom, Kerry's face was burning and her shoulders felt heavy. It crossed her mind to stay in the restroom until they reached London. Silly thought, *however…*

A few minutes later, Kerry returned and was dismayed that her watch was no longer clinging to her travel mate's vest. She cast a dreading glance at Sleezeball and, sure enough, he held up her watch and gave her what he probably thought was a sensuous wink. She turned on her teacher look—the one that usually caused any nonsense in her classroom to disintegrate, and held out her hand. "Thank you," she said, sincerely but not overfriendly.

Instead of returning the watch, he pulled it back toward his chest and smiled. "This good sport here," his tilt of the head indicated a young boy of about twelve years, "has agreed to switch places with you. You'll be much more comfortable here I think, and we can talk about how in the world you will make it through Heathrow without my help."

The boy started to rise, but Kerry put a hand on his shoulder and smiled. "That's not necessary. I'm fine where I am. I think they're about to show a movie so ask your grandpa to please give me my watch and I'll get out of your way."

The boy snickered slightly. "Yeah, *Grandpa*, I think you just struck out."

"May I help here?" asked an approaching flight attendant.

Sleezeball scowled, handed Kerry her watch, and retreated behind his newspaper. Kerry winked at the boy and turned to the flight attendant. "I don't think I can get back in there," she explained as she gestured toward her seat.

"I see what you mean," said the woman with understanding. "There is one empty seat near the back that you are welcome to use."

"That would be great!" Kerry thanked the flight attendant and followed her to an aisle seat next to an elderly woman who was reading the book that lay in her lap. She never acknowledged Kerry's presence, but just kept reading as if a quiz awaited her on landing.

Certain there was not going to be any conversation on this leg of the trip, Kerry settled in her seat and realized she had not one thing to do. All that forethought about music, puzzle books, cloud watching—all that was at her seat next to the Goodman twin. She groaned slightly and closed her eyes. There was nothing to do now but let her mind wander ahead of her to London.

She started out with pleasant thoughts about touring Buckingham Palace, London Bridge, Big Ben, Oxford College, and especially the Library of the Society of Genealogists. After a few minutes, however, she became apprehensive about the separation from her stuff. Thank God, her money belt was still strapped securely around her waist. She was suddenly aware of how quickly vulnerability could take over.

Kerry realized she had dozed off when she heard the woman beside her ask the flight attendant for a blanket. She glanced at the window and saw it was very dark outside—the only hint of light was that flashing from the wings of the aircraft. Kerry stretched her neck to see what was going on up at her assigned seat. The man was gone—apparently answering the call of nature. Kerry felt a rush of relief as she recognized this chance to retrieve her belongings.

She quickly made her way up the aisle and slid in to her seat to gather her possessions. The Sudoku book and pencil were not there. She took another second to scan the area and found them stuffed in the man's seat pocket, probably retrieved from the floor and hurriedly stashed there.

The "Available" light flashed on over the bathroom, and the door was opening. Ready to make a quick getaway to her new seat, Kerry grabbed the book of puzzles and jerked, causing the prescription bottle of valium to come flying out with it. Apparently the lid had not been secured, because when it hit the floor, the cap dislodged and little pills smaller than M&M Minis scattered all over the floor. Kerry jerked her head up to assess the man's progress back to his seat and figured she had less than ten seconds to rectify her actions and clear out.

She quickly threw all her stuff in his seat and dropped to the floor. Oblivious to the fact that her bottom was blocking the aisle, she hurriedly picked up the pills and put them back into the bottle where they belonged and secured the lid. She returned the bottle to the seat pocket and sat down a fraction of a second before the man returned looking a bit flushed and disgruntled at the sight of her stuff in his seat.

"Sorry," apologized Kerry as she pulled her belongings out of his seat and into her lap. He fell into the seat and reached for the valium.

"Did you lose something back here?" he asked as he popped a pill in his mouth and swallowed.

"What? Umm…no. I think it's all here."

"Good." The man leaned back in his seat and closed his eyes.

"You're feeling alright? Not airsick?"

"No, I'm fine, thank you." Kerry thought he must have read the alarm in her eyes and may have even been able to hear her heart as it beat wildly in her chest. She could feel the heat in her face and knew it probably looked fevered as well.

"Well, let me know if you need to get by."

The hilarity in that statement brought on a fit of laughter that she battled to swallow. When she recovered, she asked him if he would like to change seats with her so she would not disturb him if she needed to get out.

"Hell, no. I'm sorry, what I mean is I get claustrophobic in that seat. Feel all trapped in. I'm fine here, but thanks."

She looked at him for a few seconds in amazement, then leaned back in her seat, hugged her belongings to her chest and let out a sigh of exasperation. He was already snoring again.

A glance at her watch told Kerry that in four hours the plane would began its initial approach to Heathrow Airport. Depending on when they would actually land and how long it took to get through customs, she determined she would be ready to leave the airport around 4:30 am. She would have a half hour to grab breakfast before locating the train that would take her to Kensington.

After a snack and cup of hot tea, Kerry leaned further back in her seat, anticipating a good nap before arriving in London. She was looking forward to emailing Tania about her in-flight adventures.

Before she was fully relaxed, however, an uneasy thought began to wiggle into her brain. Had she recovered all those little pills from the floor? Were there any missing from that prescription bottle? What if he had other flights around Europe before coming back to the states and ran out of his precious pills. What if he could not get them refilled overseas? Would that cause him to freak out beside some innocent unsuspecting passenger? Get sick? Have a heart attack? Moreover, what if a stray pill was hiding somewhere on the floor and was later found by a child?

She could already feel the guilt upon reading the headlines: *International Jet Liner Forced to Make Emergency Landing*...where? In the ocean?

Groaning inwardly, Kerry sat up and tore out a blank page of her new journal. After scribbling a quick note, she pressed the button to call the flight attendant.

- 5 -

Our actions are like ships we may watch put out to sea,
and not know when or with what cargo they will return to port.
—Iris Murdock, The Bell

He stared at her without fully comprehending for a moment, then took the prescription bottle out of his coat pocket, spilled the pills into his hand and silently counted them. He looked up at her and stared again. "You could've not said anything," he told her. "You could have just gone about your merry way and not said a thing."

"No, I couldn't. Just thinking of all the inconvenience I may have caused you, not to mention the fact that you might frea…become concerned about your itinerary…"

"It's okay—that you were going to say I might freak out? It's a fair assumption."

"Well, I just couldn't do that. And I felt it would more prudent to tell you after we landed and got off the plane."

They were sitting at a small table in a food court at Heathrow amid the throngs of people waiting in lines for something besides the meager airline food. Outside the one wall of windows, they could see the busy activity of taxis and shuttles.

"Well, you are a very perceptive and nice young lady to be concerned about a complete stranger," he said. "One who no doubt drove you crazy. I'm fully aware that I am not the ideal travel companion."

"You are very nice to not blow up at me, and I've had a lot of practice owning up to things. Are you set, then? Everything's okay?"

"Everything is fine. I have to call for a car. Is someone meeting you outside? Do you need a lift?"

Kerry suddenly thought of her promise to Tania. She had only just stepped on British soil and already she was talking to a stranger and contemplating getting into a car with him. "No, thank you. That's nice of you, but I'm fine. I'm going to take the train into London. It should be

31

light by then, so I'll tour around a bit, take some pictures."

He seemed to notice her back pack for the first time. He appeared deep in thought for a minute, then reached into his suit pocket and pulled out a business card. "My name is Ralph Wilesky," he informed her, "I work for a chain of international hotels." He shuffled through another set of cards and laid one on the table in front of her. "If you need anything while you're in London, call this number and ask for Olivia Tesmer. She's the manager of the Traveler's Haven near Heathrow here and a very decent person." He hesitated a moment and then held up a hand while he pulled out his mobile, dialed and then spoke into the phone, "Olivia please, thank you." He frowned and drummed his fingers on the table for a few seconds, then his face broke into an affectionate smile, "Olivia, Ralph Wilesky. Oh, as good as it ever is. Listen, I met a young American lady on the plane who did me, and possibly other airline passengers, a great favor and I want to return it. She needs a room while she gets her bearings and recovers from the trip. She sat by me—I'm sure she didn't get much rest. Will you set her up there, take care of her? Her name is…" He raised his eyebrows at Kerry in question.

Stunned by this unexpected turn of events, and not quite sure she trusted it, Kerry sat gaping until his impatient hand gesture commanded her to speak, "Kerry. Carter."

"Kerry Carter. That's right. Thanks Olivia. No, I'm supposed to meet with the new manager in Kensington, so I'll call for a car here in a minute and go…oh, you will? You're a sweetheart. Maybe I'll see you next trip. Thanks again, Olivia."

Looking back at Kerry, Ralph smiled, "There you go, Miss Carter. The hotel has a shuttle van that will pick you up in about ten minutes. Just look for Heathrow Traveler's Haven on the side."

Kerry was speechless for a moment, unable to find the words to express her gratitude. She did need a good bed this first night, and she almost melted at the thought of a long hot shower. "I don't know what to say, Mr. Wilesky. Thank you so much!"

"You just have a good time. How long are you staying?"

"That's undetermined at the moment. I have a year's leave, so we'll see."

"Leave? Leave from what?"

"I teach middle school Social Studies in Wilmington. Our curriculum includes a study of England. I'm here to soak up the culture to share with my students."

After a few seconds of contemplation, he asked, "How old are you, if I may be so bold to ask?"

"Twenty-five."

"Huh. I took you for not a day over eighteen. You're still pretty young for traveling internationally on your own. Bet your parents are wringing their hands as we speak."

"They're both deceased," she said matter-of-factly, but when his eyebrows drew together she quickly added, "I have an older brother. I'm staying in contact with him."

His eyes squinted at her for a moment, and then he reached over to tap the business card lying in front of her. "Talk to her. She's the British Statue of Liberty—send me your lost, your lonely, your scared. She'll help you." He glanced out the window. "There's my car. The shuttle van will be here shortly. Take care and enjoy yourself, Miss Carter. I'm going to get some decent breakfast and then go see a man about how to run a hotel."

She watched him squeeze into the back seat of the town car and waved goodbye. She smiled to herself. Mr. Ralph Wilesky wasn't such a bad travel mate after all.

Kerry texted Tania to let her know she had arrived safely, promising to send her an email later. Then she texted Owen in case he might worry. She looked up just in time to see the hotel shuttle pull to the curb. She grabbed her backpack and exited the double doors.

"Kerry?" asked the driver when she approached. When she smiled and nodded, he opened the passenger door for her.

This is just too cool, thought Kerry as she climbed aboard. *With a start like this, what did the rest of her trip hold in store?*

Kerry opened the door to her room at Traveler's Haven and looked around. She went back into the hall, checked the number on the door and compared it to her key card. *300. Right.* She walked back in for another look. *This can't be right*, she said to herself.

She went back to the lobby and asked the young man at the desk if there had been a mistake. He checked his computer and affirmed. "Room 300? That's right. Is anything amiss, Miss?" he smiled crookedly at his own humor.

"Oh, no. Nothing's wrong. It's just so *big*."

A middle-aged man with a rolling bag and brief case had just walked up to the desk. "I bet you don't hear that much, huh, Sport?" He snickered at his coarse joke while Kerry and the young man both blinked awkwardly.

At that same moment a tiny woman, her hair coiled into a bun at the back of her head and eyeglasses sitting down near the end of her pinched little nose, came out of an adjacent office to join them at the desk. "Sir, we are booked solid tonight. I'm sorry, but there are no more rooms available."

"But I have a reservation," he almost whined. "For Elliot. George Elliot. I asked for an early check-in?" Up onto the counter came the briefcase whose contents would undoubtedly prove this.

But to no avail. "There are no rooms here, sir." The tiny woman seemed to double in stature, somehow becoming a force you would want to walk away from rather than confront. "You might try the Marriott down the street."

The man slowly lowered his briefcase, looked at each of them briefly, and then left the lobby in a huff. His rolling bag wheel caught in the door behind him, jerked him backwards and robbed him of storming out in a dignified manner.

"Edward," said the woman. "You may take your break now. Ten minutes."

"Thank you, Ms. Tesmer." With a quick smile at Kerry, he left the front desk.

"Kerry?"

Kerry nodded and took the offered hand. "Ms. Tesmer." The woman transformed back into a warm and welcoming personality. Kerry guessed her to be in her late seventies, but her voice was strong and decisive. "Ralph Wilesky is one of the most honorable men I know. When he asks me to take care of someone he is concerned about, I know it is the right thing to do. Therefore, I personally took care of the reservation. Have you been to your room? 300?"

"Yes, thank you. It's just so grand. I wasn't expecting anything like that. I was planning on staying in a hostel tonight."

"And you will. But right now, you need some rest, and 300 is located in a quiet corner. It must be past midnight back in the states. You're probably exhausted. I'll send up a tray shortly after noon our time. Does that sound about right? We'll give you a late checkout time of 2:30. Welcome to the Traveler's Haven Heathrow."

"Thank you so much. Umm…I didn't take that man's reservation?" Her head indicated the exit door.

The little woman's nose wrinkled as if she had smelled something a bit rancid. "Of course not. And we've several rooms available. Just not for him. If he can't treat my staff and guests with respect, he can sleep on the street for all I care."

"Oh," Kerry tried to keep the dismay off her face. "Well, thanks again. I don't know how to tell you how much I appreciate this."

"You're fine. Rest well and let us know if there is anything we can do to make your stay more enjoyable."

The thought flashed through Kerry's mind that Olivia Tesmer was certainly someone you wanted on your side, as she could be brutal. She was smiling at the little warrior woman as she took two steps backward, turned…and collided with a luggage cart.

There was a flurry of activity as the bellhop pushing the cart almost fell apart with embarrassment, spewing apologies to the lobby at large. The concierge hurried over to reload the small luggage that had fallen off the cart during the collision, and Mrs. Tesmer was there to assess Kerry's damage. "Are you alright, child?"

Kerry was holding a hand to her face, trying to absolve blame from the bellhop and reassure him at the same time. "It's just a bloody nose. I should have looked before I moved…so clumsy of me."

"Come over here and get some tissue…Liam, get her an ice pack please."

Less than five minutes later, Mrs. Tesmer had the lobby operating serenely again and Kerry was almost unaffected. Mrs. Tesmer doled out first aid without gushing, which Kerry appreciated. The less fuss the better had always been her preference.

"Thank you, Mrs. Tesmer. I'm so sorry for the commotion."

"It's fine, dear. I'm glad your injury wasn't more severe, although you will probably have a bruise tomorrow. Take that ice pack with you to your room and continue to use it for a while. And Kerry…while you are in Britain, *your nose is bleeding*—try to refrain from using the term bloody. It's a very vulgar term here."

Kerry could feel her face heating up. "I knew that…it just slipped out. *Sorry*."

"I know, dear. Just didn't want you to cause yourself more…notoriety."

"Thanks. Which way is the elevator again?"

"The lift is around that corner."

"Lift. Right. Thanks."

Kerry turned slowly, made sure the way was clear, and walked to the *lift*, chastising herself. *Notoriety*—that was a nice of saying 'making a

35

spectacle of yourself'.

Back in her lavish room decorated in soothing colors of green and blue, Kerry ran a tub of hot water in the Jacuzzi. After a twenty-minute soak in pure luxury with the ice pack balanced on her nose, she toweled off, slipped on a fresh sleep shirt, and checked out the snacks in the courtesy basket that came with the room. After selecting a banana, some shortbread and a packet of Nutella, she made herself a cup of hot cocoa and climbed into the huge bed among a throng of pillows with her iPad, intending to send a long email to her friends back home. She was exhausted, however, and the drowsiness brought on by the warm drink and Jacuzzi shortened her correspondence to a brief note of assurance. It ended with *I've become a huge John Goodman fan.*

Kerry closed the curtains against the rising sun, and then snuggled into the voluptuous bed. Just before nodding off, she remembered her new bedtime ritual. She threw off the covers and padded to her backpack, took out the framed picture of her friends and set it on the nightstand beside the alarm clock. *If y'all could see me now*, she thought as she settled back into luxurious sheets. *The truth doesn't only set you free—it can also set you up.*

- 6 -

When the traveler goes alone he gets acquainted with himself.
—Liberty Hyde Bailey

Kerry slept fitfully throughout the morning hours. She tossed through intermittent dreams that left her feeling vulnerable and unbalanced—and alone. Finally, she got up to find tranquility in her collection of quotes.

In that collection, she could usually find an antidote for a negative mood or a review for life's most valuable lessons. Kerry's mother had started the collection as a gift to Kerry on her sixteenth birthday. While she was alive, Jean helped Kerry with the collection, praising her daughter's choices. Since her mother's death, the ever-growing collection had become, in essence, motherly advice by proxy.

Flipping through the book, Kerry found one that soothed her. Albert Einstein had once said, "…intuition is nothing but the outcome of earlier intellectual experience." Kerry turned that over in her mind. *Okay then,* she thought, *I can trust my intuitions about people and circumstances because all my earlier experiences have taught me intellectually what to look for in trustworthiness.* For a twenty-five-year-old, Kerry had a lot of experience with all kinds of people. As a result of her mother's condition–doctors, hospital workers, insurance reps, rehab personnel; home health care workers and hospice; funeral directors and lawyers. At school she dealt with parents, children, co-workers, and DEFACS. She had learned to read people pretty well by now. She knew intuitively those to trust and those to avoid. Considering both Ralph Wilesky and Mrs. Tesmer, Kerry felt fate was smiling on her.

From her child psychology classes and since working with children and counselors at school, Kerry had developed a strong understanding of the phenomena of 'self-fulfilled prophecy'. She could not help feeling that most people saw her as a clumsy air-head, but maybe that was because it was how she saw herself. It dawned on her that she had grown into that image—it was what she portrayed. After reflecting on this, Kerry realized it was time to make a change. What a blessed opportunity she had here where no one knew her. It was an exhilarating freedom.

Kerry recalled a famous quote: *That which we manifest is before us…* For the first time since she had read those words, their lesson became clear: *Whatever you dwell on becomes you.*

Determined to dwell only on positive thoughts and virtues, Kerry was finally able to go back to sleep and slept soundly until the cleaning crews making their morning rounds woke her. Fully rested, she took a shower, dressed, and sent a long email to her friends and a shorter one to Owen (he liked short and to the point). Room service brought her a bountiful breakfast of poached eggs, pancakes, sausage and fruit. *The day was off to a wonderful start.*

Before Kerry left her room, she wrote thank you notes to Mrs. Tesmer and Mr. Wilesky on the hotel stationery she found in the desk, took one long last look at luxury and comfort, and after adjusting her backpack, made her way to the elevator—*lift.*

Kerry entered the hotel lobby to drop off her key and notes and was surprised to have a card from Mrs. Tesmer as well. In it, the kind little woman asked Kerry to call periodically and let her know how she was doing. That was a comforting thoughtfulness, even though it did irk her just a bit that Ms. Tesmer probably thought Kerry was going to require extra care during her stay.

But, no!! Ignoring any negative vibes that might cloud her London debut, Kerry put aside her chagrin and donned an optimistic smile as she pushed her way through the revolving door and out into the reality of London.

The smile vanished immediately.

She had planned to take the train from the airport into downtown London, but she was not certain what to do now that she was at the hotel, several miles away from the airport. Maybe the hotel shuttle would take her back? Any unfamiliar place is quite intimidating, and Kerry's first reaction was to go back inside the hotel and arrange for a flight home to Wilmington. It took several breaths before Kerry forced herself to focus on her newly adopted mantra: *You are braver than you believe!*

She did go back into the hotel to the concierge's desk, but for help with transportation. The kind man at the desk told her that luckily this hotel was on the route of the National Express bus system between Heathrow and Central London, and only marginally more expensive than the train. Kerry exited the hotel with renewed confidence and waited where the concierge had instructed to wait for the bus.

As it turned out, traveling by bus was much better than taking the underground train because Kerry, having snagged a window seat, was able to appreciate the scenery along the way. Holding tightly in one hand the name and address of the hostel in Kensington where she had made reservations, and frequently checking her money belt with the other, she took in the sights of the city with wide eyes until excitement and appreciation replaced her fear and anxiety.

If there ever was a place to realize self-reliance and gain confidence, thought Kerry, it was here in London. The city itself is proof of a people whose shared stubborn resilience has seen them through countless battles and bombardments over hundreds of years. Kerry remembered hearing Winston Churchill's speech that contained his famous quote, "Nevah, nevah, nevah give up!"

As she observed the people of London, Kerry could feel her dad's presence somehow. She could see him in the resolute facial expressions of the middle-aged Englishmen that got on and off the bus, and in the language of their body movements she recognized that same dogged willfulness. Somewhere along the way, she relaxed and began to feel more at home.

After getting off at her stop, Kerry quickly found the hostel, and confirmed her reservation. She was in a room with six bunks. That was a little daunting, but Kerry resolved to look at it as an opportunity to converse with five different people, ask questions, and to learn. Rooming with five others was quite economical as well.

After securing the room and locking her pack in a locker, Kerry spent the rest of the afternoon touring on foot the area around her hostel. She took pictures of the red double-decker buses, old churches, new architecture, and the beautiful plants that adorned the lampposts and window boxes along the streets.

She found Londoners to be not *unfriendly*, but busy and hurried like those of any other big city. As she caught bits of conversations from the people she passed on the street, it was a bit unnerving that she could not understand much of what she overheard. Although most of the spoken language was English, she was surprised that it all sounded so foreign.

At Boots—a popular pharmacy and store affiliated with Walgreens in the States—she bought a bath towel, washcloth and bath soap for the remainder of her stays in hostels. Her research had informed her that most hostels do not supply bath linen as hotels do, and she wanted to be prepared. She was surprised to learn that if she wanted to carry the items out of the store in a plastic bag, she had to pay for the bag. That is the UK way—part of their plans to tackle pollution. Kerry decided to buy the bag and make it reusable by taking it with her everywhere, just in case. She also bought some picture postcards to send to her friends back home.

Her choice of hostel had been a lucky one, as it was only three blocks to the subway station. While she was there she bought a map, a schedule and an "Oyster Pass" to fund her future touring. For dinner, she found a pizzeria one block from the hostel. Day One down, things were looking up.

As she sat on her bed scheduling tours for the next day, her five roommates returned—all at the same time. It did not take Kerry long to understand they were a party of five, Slavic she thought, traveling together and with little to no English. They didn't seem overjoyed to find Kerry in the room. She knew they were talking about her and eyeing her belongings. She held out a package of gum as a friendship offering, but they folded in among themselves and laughed, making sidelong glances at her from time to time.

On her iPad, Kerry went to the top of the list she was working on and wrote—*Priority One: Find another hostel.* This hostel did provide lockers at least, and thanks to her backpacking guide, she had purchased a combination lock. That night before going to bed, she even took off her money belt in the bathroom and discreetly placed it in her locker with her other things. She didn't trust this group should she actually fall asleep, which was looking highly unlikely now. It was a loud, rude party group that she was stuck with, and party they did. Kerry had gone from one end of the spectrum to the other—from the Traveler's Haven to Traveler's *Hell.*

After a night of broken sleep, Kerry arose early, quietly dressed and slipped out of the room leaving behind a hovel of chip bags, beer bottles, and snoring girls. She patted her concealed money belt as she left the hostel, hoping and praying she would find more comfortable accommodations elsewhere.

Her friend Tai Luong, said it took about three weeks to really acclimate. As Kerry looked around at the people hustling and bustling, she made a promise to herself. She would give herself three weeks before allowing thoughts of going home. This was, after all, as much her home as North Carolina. Her roots were here. No second thoughts—she was where she was supposed to be for now.

London is an old lady who mutters and has the second sight.
She is slightly deaf, and doesn't suffer fools gladly.
—A.A. Gill

Hi, Tania! I'm sitting on a park bench in Soho across from the impressive Palace Theater built in the late 1800's. Interesting fact: Les Miserables ran for nineteen years straight here in the 70's and 80's. Classic entertainment never dies! Aladdin is currently playing. I'd like to go IF I could get a ticket, but there is so much to see and do. I'll put that on hold for a while.

Soho is an interesting place. For one thing, it was the setting for the home of Robert Louis Steveson's Mr. Hyde—the bad dude. Historically, it has a rather sordid past but has become in modern times the artsy part of London, kinda like Greenich Village in New York. Brandon and Blake would feel right at home here, too. Very trendy and progressive.

I love London! I know I'm still in the honeymoon stage, having only been here for a month, but I'm totally infatuated. The history here is incredible. Actually seeing the places I've only read about makes it all come alive. Next year I won't blindly teach this stuff.

The weather kinda sucks, though. I'd love to see some sun. I'm glad I brought more jeans than shorts because sunless days mean cooler temps.

The diversity in the population of London surprised me. I read about it before coming, but just figured the reporter hadn't taught in a North Carolina school. Talk about diversity, right? But it truly is, like this quote I found (imagine that!) "A roost for every bird." There are a lot of middle easterners here, as well as Poles and French, and Africans—you name it, it's here. Even a North Carolinian schoolteacher—though I still can't believe it!

The city is as sprawling as New York is tall. It's so easy to get lost, and I have to admit I have been lost on several occasions. But don't worry. While Londoners are brash and no-nonsense types, when they do decide to help you, they do go out of their way. I have even ventured into the countryside to find the headstones for two generations of ancestors that preceded my great grandfather, thanks to Dad's research. Sadly, the only information I've found on the man that sent my grandfather to safety in Canada is that he went missing during the war. Anyway, the people are not much friendlier out in the country—very clannish. If you can somehow find a way through their figurative motes and armor, they are also quite endearing and helpful, and I seem to be one of the lucky ones.

It just occurred to me right this minute that if I were to give London a human personification, it would be Mrs. Tesmer of the hotel! Both are small in stature, yet are intimidating forces that refuse to give up certain traditions and decorum. I do think the world of Mrs. Tesmer. She must be approaching eighty, but she's so cool.

I've seen her once a week since I've been here. She asked me to keep in touch, so I have tea with her on Tuesday afternoons and tell her what I've done and she helps me plan what to do next. It's like having my own personal tour guide.

It's easy to get around now that I've learned the bus schedules (I love the red double-decker busses) and I've also have mastered the The Tube (subway system). I've seen so much, and I've taken a bjillion pictures. My bulletin boards and power point lessons will be the envy of the entire seventh and eighth grade faculty.

The hostels have not been bad. I've stayed in three so far. The first one was too much on the outskirts of everything. It was also the only one where I rented a room with six bunks—never, ever again. Evidently, I can only handle one roommate at a time. I moved a little further into the city, and now I'm just off the Square Mile or City of London where everything happens, and always has since the days of the Romans. The only trouble I've had at my current hostel was that I infuriated my Austrian roommate by throwing out her stale beer. I thought I was being helpful, tidying up our room and all. Evidently, she was going to use it on her hair the next day. However, we've got that straightened out now—I don't touch her stuff, although it has been hard looking at that unwrapped, half-eaten Snickers bar lying on her bedside table for two days. I keep expecting the infamous London rodents to get wind of it and we'll wake up and find our room taken over by the Rats of Nimh.

You asked what I do at night at the hostel. There is a lounge area in front where I go sometimes for a cup of hot cocoa or tea and chitchat with English speaking travelers. I do my laundry—almost an everyday thing since I have very few clothes with me. I organize my notes and ideas for next year's Social Studies classes. I research landmarks and tourist sites. In addition—this is so cool—I've starting writing these little short stories about people I observe. Thank you so much for the journal! Even when I leave my backpack locked up at the hostel, I always carry that journal and a pen. One day while waiting out the rain in a coffee shop, I wrote a story about a homeless man I saw in the city and now I'm hooked. I love it! I've written stories about people on The Tube, people in museums—there are characters everywhere, and I give them new stories. It's a blast!

Anyway, I think I have given the primary reason for this trip enough time and effort to take a break from it this afternoon. I've been anxious to go to the Family Records Centre, which is just down the street from the Library of the Society of Genealogists and close to my current hostel. I hope that I can find information to fill in the blanks of my family tree further back in time. It would be so cool to get back to at least the 1700's. I'll let you know.

I'm doing fine, Tania. I have been lost, but have found my way... eventually. I'm sure I've pissed a few people off, as I am slow to decipher what they are saying—some of them talk so fast—but I'm getting better. I've had a few little injuries, mostly to my pride. I hope you never know the humiliation of falling flat on your face in front of Buckingham Palace. And you know what? Those guards really are like statues—they appeared not to even notice all the stuff that flew out of my bag when I hit the ground, even though my chap stick rolled under the iron fence to within two inches of one booted foot. I was scared to death they might suspect that chap stick to be some sort of mini bomb and that I'd be locked up in The Tower! The guards didn't flinch, and they didn't laugh at me, so I figured all was well. But as I limped away, I swear one of them winked at me. We'll just keep that between us, right?

Say hi to Robert. I want a picture of him modeling that Spanish calypso costume you're working on. Hilarious! He can't say I didn't warn him.

Love you and miss you,
Kerry

⚓

Kerry locked her iPad and put it back into the smaller bag she had purchased for daytrips. Her big backpack was in the locker back at the hostel, sharing the room with that half-eaten Snickers bar. Thinking of Snickers made her aware of her hunger, so she looked around for a place to eat before leaving Soho.

She headed in the direction of Moor Street and turned left. The street was crowded, but it was a lucky move because just ahead she saw a sign marking *The Spice of Life Pub*. She was only a few yards from the entrance of the apparently popular establishment when her attention was drawn to a group of young men filing inside, one wearing—*of all things!*—a University of North Carolina sweatshirt. She suddenly felt like crying. She had been successful at keeping her homesickness at bay, but she could not let the opportunity to talk with someone from home slip by. If only for a few moments, she needed to relate with someone.

She threw her bag up over her shoulder and yelled the rivalry charge, "Go to Hell, Duke!" It had the desired effect. The young man stopped and turned, obviously confused amid an equally confused crowd.

"Which Duke?" someone in the crowd asked.

"Duke Who?" mumbled another.

"Another Duke caught in some kind o' mischief, no doubt," assumed an older man.

Who other than Kerry Carter would yell such a thing in the middle of a British street?

But she had no time for misgivings. She charged on until coming to an abrupt stop a few feet from her target. "What I mean is…Go Tar Heels?" she said.

A slow smile spread across the sweatshirt wearer's face. "Go Tar Heels, indeed," his eyes warmed at the sight of her. "Where'd you come from, Darlin'? I thought you were about to start a riot or somethin'."

Oh, how she had missed that southern drawl! "Can I buy you a drink and just listen to you talk for a while?"

"You can do anything you want with me for a while, Sugar." He waved his friends on in, took her arm and led her to a seat at the bar. The four other young men shot her dazzling smiles and slapped her new friend on the back as they walked to a booth further into the dimly lit café.

"I don't mean to take you from your friends," Kerry apologized. " I just didn't realize I was so homesick…until I saw your shirt. It will be so nice to talk to someone who gets me. Where are you from? What are you doing here?"

He was a senior member of a high school band from Ashville invited to play at the Heritage Festival of Music in London and who was currently the envy of his buddies for having been "picked up" by a pretty girl. He did not consider her an intrusion at all, but admitted that they were to meet the school chaperones back at their hotel in two hours.

Kerry spent an hour with him. Over sandwiches and soft drinks, they talked about football, England, music and travel, but in the end, even though she loved listening to how he said his words, those words did not amount to much more than one could expect of a high school boy. Before she left, Kerry gave him one more feather for his cap by kissing his cheek, which brought on whoops and hollers from his classmates.

After a three-block walk during which she vowed never to yell out anything in a group of foreigners ever again, she climbed on a bus that would take her to the area called the Charterhouse Buildings.

⚓

The Library of the Society of Genealogists is an amazing comprehensive collection of information, but with very strict rules, Kerry learned. She had to leave her bag and everything in it, except coins for the copiers, secured in a locker on the main floor. A guard directed her to the lower library and showed her how to use the computers and copiers.

It was a bit overwhelming at first, and it took Kerry half an hour to figure out the process, but because of her talent and perseverance for research, she was soon following the pre-war threads of her family. After two hours of crosschecking census records, birth and death records, and marriage registrations, she identified the father of Stephen Carter, not in the London area as she had surmised, but in Cornwall. Rowen, her father's great, great, grandfather, died in St. Austell, Cornwall, in 1857. She even found the name of the parish to which he had belonged.

Kerry barely smothered a squeal of delight at the discovery that her dad's family had come from Cornwall, the setting of her favorite dark and mysterious novels. Near the town of Fowey sat the estate that had inspired the fictional Manderly in Daphne du Murier's haunting novel, *Rebecca*. She was disappointed to learn that the estate was not open to the public, but Kerry was in awe of just getting near the place that had dominated her book choices and imagination since she was a teen.

She made three photocopies, picked up her belongings from the locker room, and sailed out of the library. As she rode the bus back to the stop near her hostel, she felt that strange pull again. It had been somewhat reticent since she had arrived in London, but now it was back whirlwind-strong. She was convinced that whatever it was that called to her she would find it in Cornwall.

⚓

Back in her hostel room, Kerry sat on her bed and devoured a turkey sandwich from the corner deli as she researched St. Austell on her iPad. She studied the city's location and history for an hour. Since Annya, her roommate of ten days, had not yet returned Kerry continued her research to include available St. Austell hostels and compared travel rates by bus and by train. She decided to travel by train, and chose a hostel from the website.

She sent a quick email to Mrs. Tesmer confirming their teatime ritual for the next day. She hoped her wise friend would give her some tips on traveling to and around Cornwall. She glanced at the time on her iPad and realized how late it was. Her roommate was not in yet. She must have found a party somewhere. Annya was very much into parties.

Kerry put away her iPad, brushed her teeth and said goodnight to her framed friends as she climbed into her sleeping bag. Before she turned out her light, her eyes fell on the half-eaten Snickers bar. A half-eaten pastry from the café downstairs sat beside it. Groaning, Kerry turned to face the wall, thinking to herself that maybe she would make it to Cornwall before Annya's new little roommates moved in. As she drifted off to sleep, her thoughts were of Cornwall and the story *Rebecca*. The first sentence of that novel played repeatedly in her mind, "Last night I dreamt I went to Manderly again..."

⚓

Kerry jumped out of the sound sleep. She took in great gulps of air as if she had been under water for a time. When her eyes adjusted to the dark, her eyes fell upon the Snickers and pastry and her sleeping roommate. So great was her relief, she could do no more than fall back into the safety of her sleeping bag and let her heart rate slow back to normal.

Kerry frequently had these dreams—her entire life. She was sure they perpetuated her fear of storms, but she did not understand why. Her parents and Owen took storms as a matter of life. They respected storms, but had never promoted a fear of them. When Kerry was a child, a night storm would send her screaming to her parents' bed where they would cuddle her tightly and assure her that everything would be fine. As she got older, they insisted she face her fears alone and overcome them. Nothing worked. She still felt first the knots in her stomach, and then the disorientation of a full-blown panic attack. She was obsessed with weather forecasts, and laughed ruefully at herself when supervising her students through storm drills. She had always hoped her protective instincts would kick in if there ever was a real storm and that she could maintain her wits and not freeze into a pillar of worthlessness.

Every nightmare she ever had included a storm, and in this one she had been in danger of drowning. She was glad she was already safely in England, for if there had been a storm in the forecast for her trip over the

Atlantic, she would have postponed, paid the penalty gladly.

She listened carefully, but outside all seemed calm. It had all just been a dream.

⚓

Kerry spent the morning repacking laundry and inventorying her belongings, making sure everything was ready for another trip. By the time she sat down at the sidewalk café where she was to meet Mrs. Tesmer for tea, she was sure her nightmare resulted from thinking about the story *Rebecca* before going to sleep. In her dream, she must have been playing the part of the ill-fated title character, Rebecca, who had drowned in the inlet behind the De Winter mansion. That had happened during a storm.

Kerry heard Mrs. Tesmer coming before she actually saw her. The tiny woman was little more than waist high to most people when she stood up straight, but Kerry could hear her gravelly voice shooing away pigeons and fussing at people who blocked the foot traffic when they stopped to leisurely look in the shop windows. Kerry smiled at the approaching older woman, wondering why she liked the stiff little woman so much. There had been some sort of connection between them from the first meeting. Kerry stood and pulled out a chair.

"Ah, thank you dear," said Mrs. Tesmer as she lowered herself into the chair. "I'm sorry I'm late. I esteem punctuality, and am embarrassed when I do not achieve it. It seems I have to leave earlier every day. I don't know if London is getting more crowded or I'm getting slower. How was your week?"

Kerry began by recounting her week day by day, including all the sights, museums and people she met. "I took the Beatles London Walking Tour on Saturday. It was so crowded. It's amazing what a fan base there still is after all this time."

Mrs. Tesmer smiled and her eyes sparkled, giving Kerry a glimpse of the young Olivia. "I was such a fan—still am for that matter, even though my favorite Beatle, George, no longer sings…God rest his soul."

"*You* were a Beatles fan?" Kerry tried to imagine the proper, no-nonsense woman sitting across from her as a young Beatlemanian. "Did you ever go to a concert?"

"Many."

"Really? Did you scream and swoon?" Kerry smiled accusingly.

Mrs. Tesmer made a face. "I've never been much of a screamer or swooner, even back then." A devilish glint in her eyes, she continued, "There are other ways to show one's appreciation." That said she turned to ask the waiter for more tea.

Kerry sat stunned for a few seconds, wondering at the meaning of that statement. When the waiter was out of earshot, she asked, "Mrs. Tesmer, were you a groupee?"

Mrs. Tesmer smiled a wicked little grin. "Well, not in the truest sense, but let's just say my aim was good, and I went through a lot of knickers in those days."

"Ha! *That's so cool!*" Kerry felt conspiratorial, knowing she had just received privileged information. "I bet you were something back in the day." Catching the tiniest flash glitter in Mrs. Tesmer's eyes, Kerry hurried to remedy her statement. "I mean…not that you aren't something now. I think you're wonderful. I just meant…"

The older woman dismissed Kerry's words with a wave of her hand. "I was a little fool back then. And George brought out the devil in me. I wasn't too far the other side of twenty, but should have known better. Ah, well, I was unmarried and free as a bird, as was George at the time, and it didn't seem to have done me any harm—except the depletion of my knickers cabinet."

Kerry suddenly realized the wealth of information sitting across from her. Quickly doing the math in her head, Kerry calculated that Mrs. Tesmer was not old enough to remember much about being a child during the London blackouts of World War II, but she surely had heard first-hand accounts about what it had been like to huddle with her family and listen to the prime minister's rallying speeches on the radio. Here was great knowledge of London's darker days as well as those of her glory.

"Mrs. Tesmer, do you mind if I interview you?" At the woman's startled expression, she hurried to explain. "Touring buildings and reading snippets of history on placards and monuments is one thing, but a firsthand account? That is truly educational."

"What? Right now?"

"Do you have a few more minutes today? I'd like to do it now if possible as I'm leaving tomorrow to spend a few days in Cornwall."

"Cornwall? Why by all that's holy do you want to go to Cornwall? We consider Cornwall our poor step-child county."

Kerry explained the evidence she had found at the genealogy center. "I really need to go there to continue the research. Graveyards, churches, local museums—I'm starting to understand how to get the most from genealogical research. Why do you view Cornwall that way?"

Mrs. Tesmer cocked her head and considered. "It's old British snobbery. The Celts settled Cornwall, not the Anglos. Might as well be Scots," she said with a visible shudder.

Kerry raised an eyebrow at that. *People are the same everywhere*, she thought.

"Haven't you tried ancestry.com?" asked the older woman. "It seems to be all the rage."

"It's like I just said of touring. Reading the history and seeing pictures can give you information, but to get the feeling of living where my ancestors lived, I need to go there—walk where they walked, immerse in their culture."

Mrs. Tesmer was quiet a minute and then said, "You're the brave one, aren't you? Venturing out into strange territories, determined to complete your mission—all alone?"

Kerry sat back in her chair. "You're the first person to ever consider me brave. And no. I've seen bravery. This is not nearly the same."

Mrs. Tesmer regarded the younger woman closely, and understanding dawned on her face. "Your mother or your father?" she asked. She knew Kerry's parents were both deceased, but had never pried.

Kerry recognized the discernment in her older friend's eyes. "My mom," she explained. "Dad died suddenly of a heart attack—his first clue that he even had a heart condition. But mom…she had to face a new existence after an accident left her paralyzed. She had to face the fact that her marriage, family, career—nothing would ever be the same again. Add to that the recurring pneumonia that chipped away her strength and all while she tried to keep up a good front to protect us from her suffering. That was the bravest thing I've ever witnessed."

Mrs. Tesmer patted Kerry's hand where it lay on the table. "I'm so sorry. It was the same with my daughter, although she didn't suffer as long. She was just so unprepared."

Kerry quickly responded to the sadness in the little woman. "What happened?"

"Rose was actually in the states when she had the sudden onset. She was in her third year at Yale, her late father's alma mater. She collapsed while on Spring Break in a hotel lobby in St. Petersburg, Florida. It took me fifteen hours to get to her."

"Oh how awful for you both. She must have been so scared."

"Thank God she had an angel looking over her. A real one. The manager of the hotel rode with her in the ambulance and stayed with her in the hospital until I got there so she wouldn't be alone. I'll never forget that kindness."

Kerry was clumsy, but quick-minded. "The manager of that hotel—Mr. Wilesky?"

The older woman looked at her and smiled. "The same. Rose died of a brain tumor, resisted the powerful pain medication as long as she could. She didn't want to miss out on what time we had left."

Kerry remembered her nightmare, remembered how that desperate longing to live had rallied her weakening body to struggle against the engulfing water. It must have been the same for Rose.

"We had four days together before she gave in," continued Mrs. Tesmer. "She passed away two days later. Ralph procured a room for me at the hotel and helped me arrange Rose's transport back home. He made sure I ate. He told me to call him if there was ever anything he could do. And then ten years later, when his chain of hotels went international, he got me my job at Heathrow. He takes me to dinner whenever he's in town. A wonderful man, it's a shame he never had a family of his own." Kerry nodded thoughtfully. "He must be very influential with corporate headquarters to be able to put people up and take care of them like he does."

Mrs. Tesmer smiled. "Ralph Wilesky *is* corporate headquarters. He owns the hotels." At Kerry's unbelieving expression, her smile widened and she added, "You'd never know it, would you? He's so unassuming and…well, for lack of a better word…ordinary. He's worth a fortune *and* extremely generous."

They were quiet for a while, each lost in their own thoughts. Kerry marveled at the connection between them all. *Coincidence? Fate?*

Mrs. Tesmer broke the silence. "So it's a small world. Now, about traveling to Cornwall. I can't help but worry. I don't know anyone even near the area to look after you or to call upon."

Kerry groaned inwardly. *Why did everyone assume she needed someone to look after her? Did she really send out incompetent I'm-a-fool-so-look-after-me vibes? Of course, Mrs. Tesmer had witnessed her encounter with the luggage cart that first night, and she had listened to Kerry's accounts of similar mishaps around London.* Again she had to argue her case. "Mrs. Tesmer, I appreciate the concern, but surely Cornwall is civilized with all the amenities one might need. I like to think I'm not so foolish as to invite trouble, and if it finds me surely there's law enforcement, church refuges—what could happen?" When she looked up into Mrs. Tesmer's eyes, she saw the memory of her daughter's tragedy was still fresh in her mind. "I'm… so sorry, Mrs. Tesmer. I just need someone to look after my mouth. That was a terribly insensitive thing to say."

"Oh, dear, you are just young," Mrs. Tesmer words rode out on a sigh. "The young never see themselves as mortal. Optimism is what fuels them to reach for the stars, conquer the world. Where would we be without them? So, you are going to Cornwall. Knowing you, I know you've done research. Let's see what you've got."

Kerry gave her a brilliant smile. "An interview for a peek at my files?"

Mrs. Tesmer flung her arms in the air. "Oh, why not? I have nothing else to do on my day off other than clean the apartment and talk to my cats. The cats can do without me today. Probably would be grateful for the reprieve. Have you dinner plans? We'll just make a day of it."

That night after dinner and a very illuminating discussion with Mrs. Tesmer, Kerry emailed Tania. She told her about the exciting eighteenth-century family information she had found, about her plans to travel to Cornwall, and about the amazing connections she'd made in London. She also wrote—*I've always resented people treating me as if I have no brains to look after myself. I even started to doubt my own capabilities. I think I'm finally realizing that sometimes people don't want to take care of you because they think you need it, but because they need to fill an abyss in their own hearts, or to pay forward a kindness that they at one time received. So I've decided to change my attitude. People can look after me all they want. Quote of the day, "No one can make you feel inferior without your consent," Eleanor Roosevelt.*

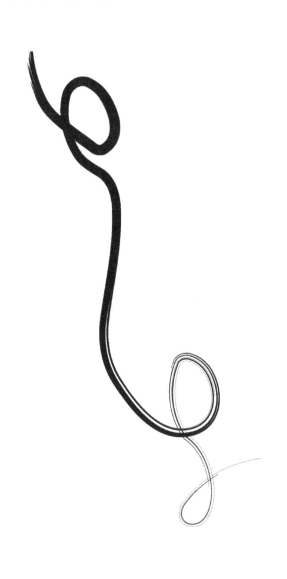

- 8 -

Those who desire to understand the Cornish, and their country,
must use their imagination and travel back in time.
—Daphne du Murier, Vanishing Cornwall

Kerry's excitement escalated during the entire four-hour trip to
Cornwall. She could not shake the feeling that something significant was
just around the corner. She had no idea what to expect, but when she
stepped off the train in St. Austell and breathed in the smell of the ocean
air, she felt amazingly like she had come home. She knew instinctively it
was not the fact that the scent reminded her of Wilmington, which it did
somewhat, but it was the sense of belonging that warmed her in spite of
the chilly air.

She made her way to Fore Street, a main road through town, and took
in the sights and sounds as she traversed the brick-laid street. Cornwall
was such a contrast to London, not only due to its rural nature and
proximity to the coast, but in the tranquil feel of the place.

She noticed right away that the dialect was different here than in
London. As she listened to the conversations around her, she realized the
vernacular was similar to that of students who had transferred into the
Wilmington school district from the Appalachian part of the Carolinas.
It was not difficult for Kerry to decipher. *I be wi'e drekly* was *I'll be with
you directly.* The speed with which the Cornish spoke their words taxed
her Southern ear somewhat, but if she concentrated, she could follow
their meanings.

Towering above the storefronts of Fore Street, she found the Holy
Trinity Church. According to her research, this church was originally
dedicated to a sixth century priest, St. Austol, but then in 1150 became
known as the Priory of Tywardeath. *Such ancient history!* The impressive
tower with its elaborate carvings became Holy Trinity during the
fifteenth century and had remained so to present day. Its last restoration
was in 1872.

After taking pictures of the exterior from every possible angle, Kerry finally heeded her hunger pangs. Just across the street, her eyes landed on an eating establishment that boasted tables behind large plate glass windows where one could people watch, one of her favorite pastimes. Unsure of what to order on the unfamiliar menu, she decided to play it safe and ordered a small vegetable salad with the delicious looking bread she had spied on display near the counter.

After a very satisfying and entertaining lunch, Kerry decided it was time to stop lugging her backpack around and check in at the hostel where she had made reservations. As she paid her bill, she asked the proprietor for directions. It was further away than she had expected according to her map, but after the four-hour train ride today, she thought the exercise would do her good.

St. Austell was much larger and busier than Kerry had expected. There was much construction and renovation going on, so it was not a particularly attractive city yet, but if one looked past the scaffolding and the busy workers, there was definite potential, a nice melding of ancient and modern.

When Kerry finally sighted her destination, she had grown weary. She thought of Tania's comment about being a turtle and winced. *Poor creatures. No wonder they move so slowly.* Now just two blocks ahead and on the other side of the street was a bed with her name on it.

She had just stepped from the curb when a carefree young teen on a bicycle whooshed into the street and would have knocked her down if not for a pair of strong arms that came out of nowhere. Those arms encircled her slight frame, including the backpack, turned her slightly to shield her with his body and protect her from the scrape of the handlebar and pedal as the dervish whizzed past.

"Young punk! Didna even look back now did 'e? Some heller e'is! You okay, luv?"

The strong arms loosened, and Kerry turned within them to meet her rescuer. "I'm fine, really," she began as her eyes traveled up a broad chest and past wide shoulders. "If there's an accident waiting to happen you can bet your bottom dollar I'll be..." Her words trailed off when her eyes met his face—a full head above her own. He was ruggedly handsome, and...*familiar* somehow. Kerry's mind flashed with possible scenarios and finally settled on the only one that made sense—he looked like the romantic image of the Cornish pirates that lived in historical fiction. His eyes were almost black and lit with all manner of mischievousness—

straight black hair that reminded her of a raven's wings, but too clean cut for a real pirate—a sun darkened face partially covered with a thick five o'clock shadow but not so copious as to hide the cleft in his chin. Yeah, his likeness could have been on the cover of any number of paperback novels.

He was looking at her intently. "'E'll…what? Assumin' I'd wager me last *pound*?" His lips curved up in a friendly smile, exposing well cared for white teeth that stood out against his bronzed face.

Embarrassed, Kerry rushed to finish, "That I'll…that I'll somehow manage to step in the middle of it. Trouble that is." She shook her head slightly, glanced around quickly. "Where did you come from, anyway?"

"Penzance, up the road aways," he had dropped his arms to his sides, but the dark eyes continued to hold hers.

Seriously? Kerry mocked herself. *A pirate from Penzance?* She gave him a dubious look. "That's quite a speedy trip. What are you, the Cornish Superman?"

His friendly smile morphed quickly into a somewhat rakish grin. "Aye, well…there's been some talk…"

A soft chuckled escaped Kerry as she recited the quote that immediately popped into her head. "*All things are subject to interpretation…*"

His eyes widened, sparkled with interest and appreciation. "*And facts do not cease to exist because they are ignored…*"

Kerry laughed outright, unable to mask her pleasure. "Huxley," she said through her smile.

"Aye, good. I'm sorry I cannot spit out the originator of your quote, but…it's something German?"

"Yes! Neitzsche," she agreed with a smile of delight.

His eyes travel over her face, apparent interest lighting up his dark eyes. "We've met before, aye?"

Kerry's eyes went round as he spoke her very thoughts, but then she narrowed them and she made herself huff out a flat little laugh. "I thought that line originated in the States."

He chuckled. "Probably in the Garden of Eden, truth be told. A testament to what the sight of a pretty girl can do to a man's brain. But seriously, 'e seemed familiar for a spell there. Are 'e on holiday from school?"

"Yes, but not from studying—from teaching."

"Yer not a schoolgirl, then? 'E look young."

Kerry's brows drew together, slightly annoyed. "I get that all the time, carded everywhere I go. I am of the legal age to both drink and vote, and enough years beyond to know better than to do both at the same time."

"Ah. A senior citizen, then. From the States, are 'ee? The southern parts?"

"What was your first clue?" She giggled slightly. "Well, I must thank you. If not for your swift action both that biker and I would probably be in a tangled and blood…uh, I mean…terrible mess right now." Kerry colored slightly at her near miss regarding the English vulgarity. "Do you always move that fast?"

He hadn't missed the slight color that spread over her face. "Not always," he stated flatly, but his smile spread wider.

Kerry knew he was testing her thoughts but she could not prevent her face catching fire as she shifted a bit and threw a quick glance around at her surroundings. His stance changed immediately. "And I should probably take it down to a turtle's pace 'ere. I'm forgettin' me manners." He stepped back and bowed like an English lord. "Me name is Merrek Walles. I'm a citizen o' the crown, I reside in Penzance, and I'm in St. Austell on business. And I'm wonderin' if you might be takin' a chance and joinin' me for denner tonight, Miss…?

"What?" Kerry looked around again, seeking some kind of assurance. *What if this guy really was a pirate?*

"Somewheres very public where you'll feel safe," he read her mind, "I can be a fitty gent on the side."

Kerry studied his good-humored expression and could not stop her smile. It felt good to banter with someone. She had missed that. "On the side of what?" she asked.

"Well, on the side of findin' an excuse to wrap me arms about a pretty lady in the middle of the street, savin' her arse to boot."

"I was not in the middle of the street! That hooligan cut that corner like…like…" Kerry's eyes flashed.

Merrek's danced. That she was quick to temper up seemed to please him. "A hoolie—what did 'e say?" his smile teasing. "I don't understand… explain it ta me over denner?"

Kerry took a minute to study this man. He seemed to be about the age of her brother. He obviously liked to tease, and was apparently having a good time goading her, but he was also perceptive and considerate, and his eyes were kind behind the mischievousness that glimmered there. He seemed…*trustworthy.*

She contemplated her evening. It would be nice not to eat alone…again. Maybe he felt the same way, being away from home and all. "Well, would it be alright with Mrs. Walles, or your special someone?"

She didn't think his smile could get any more brilliant, but it did just seconds before he turned serious and held up his unadorned left hand. "Unattached—completely," he assured her.

"It will have to be somewhere very casual. I only brought clothes for backpacking," she slapped her pack. "No cocktail dresses or heels in here."

"Perfect. There's a friendly little kiddlywink just across from that chemist's shop there, y'see?" He pointed up the road, back toward the center of town, "Fish and chips…"

"Excuse me? A friendly what?"

"Kiddly…Sorry. A tavern, a pub. A bar is it 'e Yankees say? A kiddlywink is an old Cornish name for beer shops that sell 'behind me back brews', if you know what I mean."

"Oh. Unlicensed stuff…like southern moonshine. Great. It'll probably be raided if I go in there. That's the kind of thing that happens with me…Kerry Carter, by the way," she held out her hand, found it swallowed by his with just the right pressure. "You seem to know your way around town." His grip loosened and she immediately withdrew her hand.

"Like I said, I do business here."

"Oh, yeah. What kind of business are you in?"

"Imports and exports."

Uh-huh, thought Kerry. *Piracy.* "Well, then…sure. Is six okay? I'll just meet you there?"

He grimaced slightly. "A little modern and ungentlemanly in my opinion, but I can live with it under the circumstances. Till then, luv. And be careful, will 'ee? That pavement there? Amazin' concept. Designed ta keep pedestrians like yourself contained, out th'way…" he was chuckling at her exasperated expression as he walked away.

In a rather nice imitation of his Cornish dialect, Kerry said to his back as he retreated, "I'm takin' me denner with a smart arse is it then?"

Merrek laughed, turned around and, walking backwards, gave her a dashing smile and a jaunty little salute. "'E've got me pegged proper, Miss Carter. Must be that teacher thing." Then he turned and disappeared between the buildings.

Tania's concerned face came into Kerry's mind, as did her friend's words of warning about being a prime target for the wrong people. Merrek Walles was dangerously appealing, but her instincts did not feel threatened—although she still could not shake the feeling that they had met before. Well, they say that everyone has a twin. It was just strange that they were both seeing double.

Fifteen minutes later Kerry had checked into the hostel. The only space left was in a room of six beds. *Just my luck*, Kerry thought as she let herself into the room with three sets of bunk beds. There was no one in the room, but stacked in one corner she saw a collection of water sport paraphernalia—flippers, goggles and snorkels, and the like. Taped on one wall there was a collage of photos, young people hiking, swimming, one taken at a bar, and one on a boat. Kerry quickly summed it up—a group on vacation, traveling together and sharing experiences. She would be the one out of the loop again, the one that did not fit in. That was okay, she just abhorred the feeling of being an unwelcomed intruder. Maybe they were leaving tomorrow. Maybe a smaller room would open up.

She could make it through one night surely.

She organized her things in her locker and then sat down to type out a quick email to tell Tania and her friends that she had made it to Cornwall. Kerry did not mention her dinner date—she would write about that later when she could answer all of the questions she knew they would ask.

After a much needed and undisturbed nap, Kerry showered and changed into fresh jeans and a light green t-shirt. She started to put her hair up in the usual ponytail, but decided to leave it down. This maybe wasn't a date really—just two unattached people in town on business, but it had been a while since Kerry had taken any time with her appearance and it felt good to fix up for a change. She ran her fingers through her hair, trying to give it some order, but let it curl freely around her face and down her back. She opened the mascara and lipstick that Tania had insisted she pack—just in case—and carefully applied the enhancements. *Bless your heart, Tania.*

Kerry arrived at the crowded pub a little later than six o'clock. She had asked a kind looking pedestrian she met on the street corner about the chemist's shop and learned that it was a pharmacy. Once she found that landmark, she saw the little pub across the street sandwiched between a florist and a company that arranged bus tours.

When Kerry entered the noisy pub, she paused for a moment while her eyes adjusted to the dim lights and smoky haze. She let her gaze roam the crowded establishment searching for a familiar face. It seemed to be a happy and popular place. There was a lot of dark wood, and she could smell the beeswax used to keep it looking rich. In the back, there was a well-used pool table still in demand, and all ages of clientele sat at crowded tables engaged in both serious and raucous conversations.

At the bar, she caught sight of Merrek waving to her. He turned to say something to the bartender and then vacated his seat to walk toward her. Kerry was glad she had taken the extra time with her appearance. As he approached, she took in his favorable perusal and complimentary smile. She noticed that his eyes also shimmered with straightforward friendliness—no leer, no hint of hidden agendas. Feeling safe, she answered his smile with her own.

Merrek Walles stood and met his new acquaintance halfway. *She's a bonny lass,* he thought as he gazed at her, but he still could not believe he had asked her to dinner that impulsively. He had at least day's worth of paperwork waiting for him in Penzance, but the attraction had been immediate. It had caught him totally off guard, and he was a very guarded person. But those eyes…he was sure he had admired them before. *When? Where?* As she approached, they were as green as summer foliage, reflecting the color of her shirt.

"An to think I almost went on me merry way home this mornin'and woulda missed this lovely vision," he said as he took her hand and led her to a table for two. He motioned to the waiter to bring over two mugs of beer, and then turned to grace her with his smile. "I thought 'ee were a 'andsome cheel in the early day, luv, but tonight …if 'e don't mind me sayin' it…yer some fetchin'."

Kerry blushed, never at ease with compliments. "Tonight I have on makeup," she admitted honestly.

His eyes excited her as they scanned her face. " 'Beauty—be not caused, luv, it just is.' That's the gist of it anyway."

"Oh‚ I know this one…Emily Bronte?"

"Ah, yer slippin', darlin'. Dickinson."

"You're wonderful, you know that?" She did not miss the flash in those dark eyes and she felt the heat rising in her cheeks. "I mean, I've never known anyone to love quotes like I do—especially not a guy."

"There's a lot ta be had from quotes," he said almost defensively. "A whole book o' thoughts can sometimes be summed up in just a few well chosen words. Philanthropies and philosophies snared in a single line o' wisdom from even the most unlikely individuals. Some of me favorites come from Jim Morrison."

"Oh, I know. I found a kinship with Morrison long ago."

Merrek leaned forward. His eyebrows drew together and his dark gaze narrowed. He tested her. "And which quote in particular did that for 'e, young Kerry?"

Kerry smiled bashfully but was ready with her answer, "The one that states, 'I see myself as an intelligent sensitive human with the soul of a clown, which forces me to blow it at the most important moments'."

Merrek's eyebrows arched slowly and his intense eyes softened, "Yer wonderful, 'e know that?" he repeated back to Kerry. *Was that a blush creeping into her face again?*

"Did you say you were on your way back to Penzance earlier?" Kerry changed the subject.

"Aye, I was. Then somethin' tole me ta linger a bit and stroll down the street here. Put me in just the right place ta meet me denner date. I am one lucky bloke, aye?"

Kerry leaned forward, a serious expression stealing over her face. "Something told you? You mean like a calling sort of thing?"

Merrek's smile faded as wariness crept into his gaze, "I, uh…where are we goin' with this, luv?"

"What I mean is—I've felt a pull to come here, like…I don't know, like I had to come here…to England, to Cornwall." The bewilderment on his face made her realize what meaning her words might have conveyed. "No! No, I'm sorry. It's just that I've been trying to extend the research my dad started a few years ago, tracing his family's genealogy. I know it sounds farfetched, but I believe I was called here to find out some…truth or something."

Merrek's smile held a hint of relief. "Are ye sure the piskies 'aven't been playin' around in yer brain, Luv?"

"Piskies? Oh, no. No pixies. I don't know…fate? Do you believe in fate?"

"I…hmm…would you like to order some fish and chips? They go really well with the beer. Tis *their* fate, mayhap," he smiled crookedly.

Kerry's heart skipped a beat at that charming grin. "I'm sorry. I know I sound a little crazy." Kerry could see her embarrassment amused him, making her blush deepen. "It's just that I've had this strange feeling for months now. I've been trying to understand it. Yes, some fish and chips sound wonderful. I'm sorry," she concluded with a wry chuckle. "this is a terrible way to start an acquaintance."

Merrek studied her for a long moment, a deeper interest in her taking root. She had a refreshing honesty about her that he was convinced had grown extinct among modern women. Her expressive green eyes were easy to read, and in them, he saw contradictions that fed his curiosity. There was insecurity there, but countered by innocent hope and a courageous resolve. Earlier in the day, he had seen those same eyes literally sparkle with impish wit and intelligence. He found himself extremely interested in drawing her out while preserving her becoming attributes. She reminded him of someone, but he could not search out the source of that impression.

He turned and shouted out their order to the man behind the bar. Turning back to Kerry, he gave her a friendly smile, "Then why don't we just try again from the start? Your name is Kerry Carter and you're from the States. Tell me more."

Kerry stared for a moment into his compelling eyes, took a deep breath and started slowly at first. She told him she was from North Carolina, that she was taking a year's leave from teaching to travel around England to gather material for her classroom and at the same time, work on extending her dad's genealogy research.

At this point, she began talking faster, her face and hand gestures more animated, her manner much more relaxed. Her cheeks flushed from the beer and the intensiveness with which she told her story. As Merrek watched her artless facial expressions and the honest emotions in her stunning eyes, his interest became fascination. He made himself concentrate on what she was saying.

"Dad's father was part of a government operation called Pied Piper. Do you know about it? It involved a group of evacuees including children sent from London to Canada in 1939 to protect them from German bombings. His papers show the names of his mother, who was deceased, and father, but his father went missing during the war. A couple in New York did adopt him eventually, but he was old enough to insist on keeping his own surname. My grandfather married a Canadian woman, my grandmother, who died when my dad was ten. When Dad grew up, he met my mom at a meeting for descendents of Operation Pied Piper looking to reconnect with lost families in Britain. Neither one of them had a tangible family. They always wanted extended family for my brother and me–for big reunions, Thanksgiving dinners and such. But Mom died six years ago, and Dad was trying to find what family he might have back here in England when he died last year. He had gone back two generations looking for descendants. I got interested as I looked through his research, and I spent quite a bit of time on the various websites that offer genealogy help. Through ancestry.com I got back another two generations—to the mid 1800's, and that's when I began to feel…and this is what I'm talking about…something that seemed to tell me research wasn't good enough. I felt compelled to come here to continue the search. That nagging feeling is the underlying reason I'm here."

Kerry knew Merrek had carefully followed every word. She appreciated that he did not seem to feign interest, and he waited without interrupting until she was finished. Then he leaned toward her and said in a soft and gentle tone, "'E're young to have already lost both parents. I'm sorry, Kerry."

The sincerity in his voice washed over her, stirring emotions she had pressed down over the years. Strange, that she would have to travel so far to hear the empathy she longed for, and from a stranger—although looking into his eyes, she still felt that odd familiarity.

She let her eyes drop to her lap, but not before Merrek saw the sorrow and loneliness that shimmered there. "Siblins'?" he coaxed.

"I have one older brother, who is about your age if my guess is right. He has a wife and baby, lives two hours from me. We aren't very close. What about you? Do you have family in Penzance?"

Merrek decided not to pry into her relationship with her brother, and leaned back, unable to keep a smile from spreading across his face. "I have a huge, loud, mostly annoying family who grabs every opportunity to gather—sometimes to celebrate, sometimes to fight—but we are always together. I can't imagine not having that…connection. I know of that wartime evacuation you mentioned. We learned of it in school. How lonely for your da. What of your mum?"

"She grew up in upstate New York in foster homes. She has no family connections either. I understand Dad's need to feel a part of a family tree of some sort. So here I am, playing detective."

Merrek smiled warmly, " 'History remembers only the celebrated, genealogy remembers them all,' aye? 'Tis a noble mission 'e've undertaken. I wish 'e success."

He watched, mesmerized, as Kerry's face lit up with pleasure at his words. It made him feel like the Cornish Superman indeed to have affected that sudden radiance. She happily drained her mug and took another bite of chips dipped in the pub's special sauce. "This is great food by the way," she announced.

Merrek smiled at her enthusiasm. He also smiled at her apparent oblivion that she was now wearing some of the special sauce on her shirt. "Aye, I like it. Another beer?"

"Sure, thank you. Now, what about you? Tell me about your big family."

"Me? I come from generations of fishermen. We've lived on the Cornish coast for centuries. Loud, crude brawlers—the lot of them." He smiled broadly. "They're fantastic. Pretty women, too—me sisters, female cousins. Could be we have some of that Carter blood in there somewhere."

The subtle compliment was lost on Kerry. Merrek's version of family contrasted significantly with her own. His frank but proud account of his numerous relatives intrigued her, and a gaping void grew deep within her. She was…lonely. "How many sisters?" she wanted to know.

"Four. I have one brother. He's the piggy widden." At Kerry's raised eyebrows, Merrek smiled. "The runt. The baby. There's the four girls between us, and what a pair of bookends we make. Ne're see eye-to-eye on anythin'. I fear Trev's only desire in life is to get by with as little effort as possible. A fitty playboy 'e is. A veritable flirt. Since Da's heart attack last year, I'm back ta workin' the boats again part time with Trev and two hirelings. Maybe I should say we work and Trev listens ta his music. I don't think he even notices the fish, an' I'm fair certain 'e never notices the flirty looks my youngest sisters cast at our ship mates as the boat comes to dock. They're a handful, they are. Keep me busy lookin' out for 'em. I could use Trev's help."

"Sounds like you're busy doing lots of things. Imports, exports, fishing…chaperoning."

"Aye, well, we do what we have ta do, right? And glad we're able. It's not been all that cumbersome. I do Da's accountin' when I do mine—his billin' with mine…it's workin' out fitty well. Mum has never 'andled the finances—she would 'ave been lost."

"My dad was okay in that department, but cooking nutritiously? He would have existed entirely on peanut butter. And the laundry! He was shocked and disturbed by his pink underwear. He'd never learned to sort laundry and needed help with all that. And like you said, I was glad I was close enough to help him. But I didn't have to take on raising siblings."

"Aye, well, I didna take on the raisin' of 'em, just the lookin' out. 'E know, keepin' the blokes away from me sisters until they're fully grown and makin' sure Trev didna get too far behind in 'is studies."

Kerry loved the way Merrek slipped back and forth between London and Cornish dialect. She asked questions mainly to listen to his speech patterns, but she learned his older sisters were married, the two youngest were in their late teens. His dad had semi-retired two years ago due to a heart condition, and completely retired since his heart attack. His mom was a devout Catholic who took care of everyone—in and outside the family, lighting candles every evening at the church for those that had passed. There were so many aunts and uncles and cousins that one could not walk to town without running into a few relatives along the way. All this fascinated Kerry. She had known people from large families in the States, but most of them had relatives scattered across the country, gathering in one place only on special occasions. According to Merrek, even though his family's closeness was somewhat irksome when it came to his privacy, it was reassuring to know someone was always close by in times of need. *Security*. Kerry could only imagine what a comfort that could be.

Merrek touched her hand. "I'm sorry—I'm boring you."

Kerry's eyes widened in alarm and she gave her head a demonstrative shake. "No...no! I was taking it all in and thinking how wonderful it sounds. I'm jealous to tell you the truth. Your family is very interesting, but now tell me about you...as an individual."

He did, and Kerry learned that Merrek was six years her senior, had worked his way through the University of London's Queen Mary campus with the help of an academic scholarship. He and a friend had painstakingly built a thriving business. Merrek worked in seafood exports and his friend in imports. They had an office in Kingston, but he did a lot of his research and built contacts from his laptop at his parents' home where he had moved in to take over the head of household duties for his dad—freeing his mother to care for her husband.

"Business has been good so far. Fish consumption has been on the rise since the 1970's. Touted as the *healthier diet choice*, 'e know."

"So, you export seafood and then turn around and import it, too?"

"Aye, our fishing industry brings in a lot of mackerel, prawns, scallops, and shellfish. But we Brits love whitefish, and those landings 'ere 'ave been droppin' off since the 1950's. So the import o' those types is big business. We sell our resources to clients in France, Spain, Italy, the Irish Republic—we buy salmon, haddock, tilapia, and the like from places like Denmark, Iceland, and Norway. Although a lot of our Salmon and Pollock come from your Pacific coast."

Kerry soon realized that here was another rich source of information on British commerce, from the trade worker to the corporate level, so she concentrated on accessing and mentally storing as much as she could. She hoped she would have an opportunity to interview Merrick formally while they were both in the area. He was easy to talk to, she enjoyed listening to him, and watching his unguarded, and...handsome...face.

After finishing the second beer, Kerry could not suppress her yawns, apologizing in the midst of them. "I promise you it's not present company, just an early and exciting morning topped off by a very satisfying dinner. I've really enjoyed this, thank you."

"Ah, pleasure's been mine. 'E's dark out—I'll walk 'e home." When she started to protest, he gave her a look with those dark eyes that clearly meant he was going to walk her home, so she did not even try to argue.

"How long are 'e here for, Kerry? I 'ave ta go inta London tomorrow, but I'll be back the day after. I'd like ta see 'e again. Maybe I can help 'e some with yer genealogy research or with yer cultural experiences."

Kerry was delighted. "I'd like that if you have the time. It would be nice to share what I find out with someone, especially someone who knows the area and the people. Could you leave me a message—say...at this bar?"

"I'll give you me phone number since it's clear you'll not be givin' me yours," he teased with a smile.

"A girl can't be too careful," Kerry said apologetically.

"Aye, no—'e's good. Wish me sisters would follow that creed. They'd drop their phone numbers over the city from a fly over if Da gave them phones. I said they were 'ansome, not canny."

The walk back to the hostel was delightfully informative. Merrek could not keep the pride out of his voice as he talked about Cornwall's history and demography. Kerry could not believe how short the trip had seemed, and the light shining through the window of her room signaled the occupancy of her new roommates. Merrick did not miss the slight slump of Kerry's shoulders as they neared the door. "They don't sound tired," he surmised. "Sounds like they're just gettin' started. You're not gettin' much sleep here tonight, luv."

"Not getting much sleep doesn't bother me so much. I just hate being the party crasher. They'll undoubtedly give me that look that says *if you stay don't expect to be included. In fact, please go find another party to crash.*" The sound of Merrek's chuckle made her realize the facial animations she employed as she impersonated her roommates. She blushed, much to his delight. She made herself smile. "Hopefully it will only be for one night. Thank you so much for seeing me safely home."

Merrek shot a dubious glance toward her room from which music suddenly pelted through the walls. "Hold a minute for me." He walked a few paces away and spoke to someone on his phone. Kerry knew he was up to something on her behalf, and could not help suspicion from taking root.

He was wearing a triumphant smile when he returned. "I 'appen to have a cousin twice removed who owns a bed and breakfast six blocks from here. She's empty tonight, so it would be doing'her a favor to 'ave a guest."

"But I've already paid for my night here. I appreciate it, but I'll be fine."

Merrek looked toward the hostel room door and his brows drew together. "Kerry, I cannot leave 'e here in good conscience, luv. I'd have the man's hide who would leave one o' me sisters 'ere alone." He leaned down until his face was close to hers, his eyes commanding in their intensity. "It'd be wise ta reconsider." He watched her expression and knew she took exception to his authoritativeness, but he also saw the struggle going on behind her eyes as she came to recognize the soundness of his suggestion. He added with a knowing smile, "I promise I'll not have a key and I'll be in Penzance before midnight. My cousin is licensed and...what do you call it?"

"Like...bonded?" Kerry supplied.

"The very same. She'll also make you a fitty breakfast in the mornin'. Bacon, eggs, scones and jam...Min's some good cook."

Kerry calculated that she could afford to splurge every now and then, and a night or two in a room alone with a breakfast waiting for her when she woke up sounded heavenly. The sound of a shattered glass came from inside her room and was the decisive factor, "Sold! Just wait here while I get my things?"

Kerry used her key, but there was no need as the door swung freely open. There was indeed a party in progress. From the looks of it, her five roommates had found a few Cornish friends of their own. Kerry zigzagged through the dancing on her way to take her things out of her locker. A young man with menacing eyes suddenly turned and blocked her way. Kerry mistook his insolent expression for one of accusation and immediately turned apologetic. "Oh, dear, and I just got here. What did I do?"

66

A slow grin spread over the stranger's face. "Nothing yet, babe, but be assured you'll be doin' it with me." His grin broadened as Kerry's eyes went wide. He reached for her arm but never made contact. Merrek materialized between them without a word and placed Kerry at his back. The other man glanced at Merrek's scowl and his smile faded. He shrugged slightly, winked at Kerry over Merrek's shoulder and staggered back into the crowd.

Kerry unlocked her locker and removed her things. Merrek kept his eyes trained on the offender until they were outside.

"You do that very effectively I've noticed—that look," Kerry said to Merrek as he took her backpack, hooked it over his shoulder and began to lead the way up the street. "You'd have made a great classroom disciplinarian with that look."

"Me evil eye? Practice, that. Me sisters 'ave seen to it that I've 'ad lots of practice. Every man knows the key to a successful evil eye is to smack of the ability to back it up while expressin' sincere hope for an opportunity. It's taken me years, and lots of bobber lips to boot. But now, a good old-fashioned stare down will usually do the trick, especially if the opponent is as deep in the cups as that bloke back there. Brawling weren't on 'is agenda tonight." He gave her a sideways glance. "He 'ad other activities in mind. See why I didn't want ta leave 'e 'ere?"

"But *I* didn't have any activities in mind," Kerry looked offended.

Merrek dipped his head forward to study her face. "I don't think that mattered to 'im, luv." He blew out through his mouth. "'E must have kept your own brother quite busy."

"Owen? No. I was such an awkward and clumsy girl everyone usually just tried to stay out of my way."

"I can't imagine that. 'E move quite gracefully now, and I'm sure 'e've attracted a host of admirers…as well as some busters like that back there."

Kerry sighed inwardly. It seemed like that was mostly what she had ever attracted. *Losers gravitate toward losers, right?* "Well, I would hope I was left with something after all those years of ballet and gymnastics. My mom and dad enrolled me in any activity in which building coordination was part of the training. I think Owen was always jealous of the attention I got, but he was perfect. He didn't need outside help."

"What's he like—your brother? 'E was alright with you comin' all this way alone?"

Kerry stared at the steeple of the Holy Trinity church peeking over the treetops. "Owen dresses immaculately, speaks eloquently, and moves through a room like he owns it. I have always been in awe of him. No, he had no problem with it. I doubt he's given me a second thought." Then, realizing the bitterness of her statement, she rushed to correct herself. "That's unfair of me. I'm sure he's been checking with my old roommate to make sure I'm okay. He's not much for phone conversations. He's a very busy man."

Merrek tried to refrain from making a quick judgment, but he could not help feeling animosity toward this Owen. Kerry was still very young to be without the support of parents; she needed her older brother. He could hear it in her voice. "What kind of work does Owen do?"

"He's a broker, and an extremely successful one. He's married to an exquisite ballet instructor, and they had a beautiful baby, a little girl, eighteen months ago. We never saw much of them, though. Owen and Millicent were always busy with their own affairs. He does have that one flaw—that disregard for family. Even after Mom died, he didn't take time for Dad. As mundane as I am I'm confident he's going to regret that someday, and I feel for him."

"Well, it's not me place to comment on any of that, but one thing I can say—you are not ordinary, Kerry Carter. I knew that from the moment we met."

This time Kerry swung her head to search his face. *Was that another line? He was so breathtakingly handsome, and he had perfected a look that allowed no resistance—did he also have a repertoire of lines in store to melt women?*

He stopped walking suddenly, halting her by laying a hand gently on her arm. "Well, now. Ye've quite a look there yerself, Miss Carter, and 'e use no veil ta conceal it. 'E are what 'e are, and right now 'e're blatantly questionin' my sincerity. That *'e can't put one over on me* look must've been quite 'andy in a classroom."

"Well…?" Kerry had no idea how to respond. He was standing fairly close to her, so she had to look up to try to read his eyes. They were so dark and presently glittering with amusement. "I… don't know what to say. An awkward moment—this."

"Nah. Usually a cheel would slap a bloke with some snippy, flirtatious comeback. Instead, 'e honestly challenged me. 'E just metaphorically held up a mirror to me face. Now if I were a slimy bloke tryin' ta make a move, seein' meself clearly in reflection might behoove me ta just slither back to the hole I came outta. But, as I'm not a slimy bloke, I can stand here without guile and say I think yours is a better way of handlin' things, and definitely not... *mundane.*"

They stood there in the middle of the walkway, staring into to one another's eyes. Finally, Merrek spoke with a slight smile. "Now *this* is an awkward moment."

Kerry burst into a delighted chuckle. She really liked this guy. He was funny and certainly articulate. He had so impressed the teacher in her by using words like *metaphorically* and *guile*, and who really ever uses the word *behoove* nowadays? He also shared her appreciation and respect for quotes. She found that to be an uncommon but pleasing trait. "Well," she began, her green eyes sparkling. "I'm glad you've assured me you're not a slimy bloke trying to make a move."

"Well, now...I didna go so far as to say I wasna makin' a move," that glint in his eyes again, "jus' not a slimy one."

Another chuckle bubbled up in Kerry's throat. Yeah, she would look forward to another evening of his company. She tucked her hand into the crook of the arm he offered her and they resumed their stroll along a sidewalk bordered with rosemary, its pleasant scent filling the cool night air. Merrek gave her a sideways glance. "'E didn't answer the second part o' me question, 'e know," he ventured.

Kerry looked at him, her dark auburn brows drawing together as she tried to remember. "What was that?"

"Well, probably none of me business, but I'm askin'. What about admirers back in the states...one in particular?"

"Oh, that..." Merrek was surprised that she looked embarrassed, "no...I mean, I've dated here and there, but...no. No one special. But the bright spot in not having had a serious relationship is that I've never had my heart broken."

She glanced up at him briefly. Maybe no one had broken her heart, but he did not miss the self-recrimination shimmering in her beautiful eyes before she looked away. Did she see herself as undesirable? *Wrongfully misinformed, then.*

"It's probably none of my business," she continued, her eyes focused on the dark sky, "but I'm asking anyway—what about you? No special woman in your life?"

Before he could answer, she rolled her eyes. "What am I thinking... you're probably the heart *breaker.*"

He cocked an eyebrow. "Ah, now...'e wound me with such an accusation. I'll admit t' 'avin' me own pride bruised...sorely... but me heart got out of it intact. I've been too busy of late to get muddled in relationships. Me sisters say I've become *aloof*. If that's what 'e are when trying to juggle several things at once, then I guess I'm *aloof*."

Kerry smiled up at him. "I don't think you're aloof. If you were, I'd probably still be tangled up with a bicycle right about now."

Merrek laughed and patted her hand where it rested on his arm, "'E know…I need t' find that young billyo and thank 'im for pushin' 'e inta me life today. It's been a fine time, Kerry. And 'ere we are."

The sign at the front gate to their destination read *Min's B&B*. Merrek opened the scrolled wrought iron gate and let her pass in front of him. "Min's a talker and a bit hard a' hearin'. When you've 'ad enough, just say you hear your phone ringin'—she'll never know if it did or didn't."

"That's mean," Kerry accused him.

"Just 'e wait," he promised. They entered a charming portico before reaching the front door. Prior to ringing the bell outside the door, Merrek leaned his head down slightly toward hers to look directly into her eyes. Kerry found herself very interested in the adventurous spark that lit them. "I'm serious about wantin' ta see 'e again, Kerry. Will 'e 'ave denner with me still? Day after the morrow?"

Kerry did not have to consider. "I'd love to. I had a great time tonight. Thank you."

His eyes left hers and dropped to her mouth. It crossed her mind that he meant to lean down further for a kiss, and she was considering how she felt about that when a short, round woman with a friendly face opened the door and ushered them inside with a string of Cornish dialect that required Kerry's full attention to decipher. "Dynnargh! Cummas-zon! Jus heave 'er bag in the catchpit there, we'll light 'er above-stairs dreckly. I 'ave tea on an' some oggies I made minutes agone, zam-zoodled tho' they be," without pausing to breathe she went on, "Merrek, 'ee's good ta see ya. Who's the cheel, uh?"

"It's good ta see 'e, too, Min," although he wished it had been a couple of minutes later. "This is Kerry Carter. And she's from the states, so ya might want ta speak more o'the Queen's English if ya want to be understood."

"Carter?" She stopped abruptly and turned to look curiously at Kerry. "'E's a Cornish name. Goes backalong years ago. Merrek, joinin' us for tea?"

"I've really got to go, so I'm leaving Kerry in your hands. Kerry, I'll see you for denner on Friday? I'll pick you up here at six."

Kerry caught the spark of interest that flashed in Min's eyes as she glanced back and forth between the two them. "I'll be here," she promised.

⚓

While Min fussed with the tea service, Kerry looked around her kitchen. It was very small and cluttered with pots, pans and herbs that hung from a rack above a table that held a dough bowl and an assortment of canisters. It smelled heavenly from whatever she had just baked, and the soft breeze drawn between two open windows cooled the air. There was a very small refrigerator opposite the huge stove, suggesting that Min shopped daily for fresh food. Kerry immediately felt at home in Min's kitchen. On the wall next to the refrigerator was a calendar with reminders and notations that revealed today's date as June 25. It struck Kerry that she had not been in a real home with a kitchen for almost five weeks.

Min set a steaming cup of tea in front of Kerry and sat down with her at the table. She pushed back a strand of gray hair that had escaped her braided bun, scooted a tray of pastries to within Kerry's reach, and then got right to the point. "So, when did you and Merrek meet?" she asked with sparkling eyes.

"We met today on Fore Street. He saved me from certain injury by a careless cyclist. Then we had dinner together."

The woman's face lit up. "Only today, and 'e asks 'e ta denner? 'E must've been taken with 'ee—Merrek's not much for spontaneity, that' un."

Kerry was surprised and secretly reveled in that tidbit of information. "Oh, I don't know about that. He was just being kind to a rattled foreigner."

The older woman guffawed at that. "There's bein' kind and there's pleasin' oneself ta boot. Driven as 'e is with 'is duties, 'e rarely takes time to please 'imself. And yer not forgettin' are 'ee, that 'e's ask you ta denner a second time?"

Kerry had not forgotten. *Far from it.* "Well, I'm so glad he's giving me some of his time. I'm researching the area for the purpose of genealogy. I think I have some relatives buried at St. Luke's cemetery—I'm going to check that out in the morning. Merrek has been helpful in giving me a brief overview of the history of the city—about the kaolin and tin mines, the competition among the fishermen. It helps to have a feel for where your relatives lived."

Min was quiet a moment, obviously turning things over in her mind. "They quit berrin people in some of the church cemeteries backalong the late 1800's ya know. Could be they's at the public cemetery—Watering 'e's called."

"I read that, but according to the Genealogy Society Library in London, Rowen Carter and his wife were buried at St. Luke's in the 1850's. I'd like to try to find those gravestones and see if there's anyone I can talk to that has access to church records. About how long would it take on foot to get there?"

"Better fit, I've a bike out back. It's years agone since it were new, but the tires still hold air and the chain's not latched up. Yer welcome to it. Everything's a stone's throw from 'ere. Jus' head out west on the carriageway, turn north on Bodmin Road. You'll not miss it."

"That would be wonderful—thank you. And if you still have a room available tomorrow night I would like to stay."

"Well, as Merrek is meetin' you here fer 'e denner date, I think that would be the thing to do. If ye don't mind m'asking how is Rowen Carter related to ya?"

"He would be my grandfather six generations back".

"Aye…I see. I've known people what's done genealogy work. Sometimes, ye 'ave to be prepared to take some bad with the good."

"I'm prepared for that. All families have black sheep. But I had no sheep at all to begin with, so I really don't care. Have you known some Carters from around here?"

"Not personally, nah. So, what do ya think of our Merrek?" The woman changed subjects so fast she caught Kerry off guard.

"He's…very nice."

"And a looker, too, huh? Stuggy—uh, sturdy like. Maids all over the county 'ave 'opes for that un, they do."

"Why hasn't he settled on any of them? He does like women, doesn't he?" Kerry realized too late how gauche that sounded, especially when she could almost see strands of hair wiggle out of Min's bun to stand on end. She hurriedly continued, "I mean two of my best friends back home are in a same sex relationship. I guess it's become second nature for me not to make assumptions."

"Oh, don't ya be worrin' about Merrek. 'E does like him some women, that I can tell ya," when Kerry raised her eyebrows at that statement it was Min's turn to stumble back over her words. "I mean, well…none of the male Walles are rabble rousers, least not while they's sober anyway. But that Merrek, 'e's as solid as they come, though a bit o'buster 'e is. Jus' been particular, that un, since…, well, I'll promise ya this—'e was taken with ya or you'd not be 'avin' denner with 'im a second time. Not one for dalliances, that un. Now, the two younger sisters? A different story they are. Cakey 'un's, the pair…underbaked. Trev, the young brother—oh and 'e's a lovely boy, too—'e calls 'em a *hot mess*. You 'ave siblings?"

"Just one, about the same age as Merrek. Owen is anything but a hot mess. He is a classic Wall Street type, you know what I mean?"

"The girls'll know it. They pour over American magazines like they should the Holy Book truth be told. You're looking all worn out, cheel. Ready for bed? Get your stuff an' let me show ya yer room."

"Oh, thank you so much. I am very sleepy all of a sudden. Was that chamomile tea?"

"And lavender," Min said with a wink. "Ye'll sleep like a bairn."

Min led Kerry upstairs to a small, cozy room to the left of a hallway bathroom. The room was everything she had ever thought a B&B should be. Min had seen to every comfort—a chocolate square on her pillow, dry sherry on the sideboard, current magazines, and sweet-smelling soaps. After a quick hot shower in the hall bathroom, Kerry opened the window in her room to let in the soft breeze, turned off the lamp beside the bed and burrowed down under a fresh, soft comforter. She was asleep almost instantly.

Kerry woke up just in time to swallow the scream that threatened to rend the night and wake every sleeping individual along the street. Another nightmare. Another storm of emotions. *Was she never to get a full night's sleep again?*

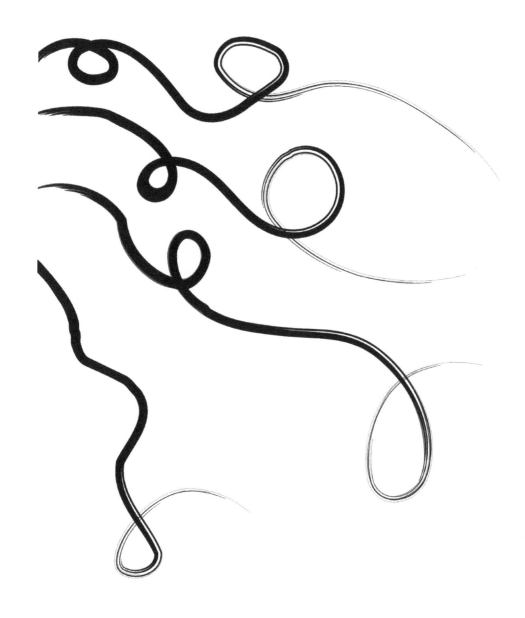

- 9 -

Fertility of imagination and an abundance of guesses at the truth are
among the first requisites of discovery.
—William Jevons

Min was 'some good cook' as Merrek had said. The berryfilled
pasties with clotted cream were so much better than Kerry anticipated.
They were actually a delicious follow-up to the fresh farm eggs with
bacon and oven roasted cherry tomatoes that Min served her that
morning. *I could get used to this,* Kerry said to herself as she thought
of the taste-challenged protein bar she usually had after waking up
rest challenged in a hostel room. Here in Min's cottage, except for the
interruption by the dream, she really had slept like a baby.

Kerry retrieved her backpack from the *catchpit* downstairs. She thought
the Cornish term most appropriate for the place in a home where the
occupants drop their stuff. "What ar'm in the States?," Min had asked
her. Frankly, Kerry could not answer her succinctly. *Coat closet? Mud
room?* She could think of nothing quite as efficient as catchpit.

Helping herself to Min's offer of the bike, Kerry had pedaled far down
the lane toward the main road when the sun came out from behind the
ever-present clouds, brightening the landscape and warming her skin.
Since she had come to Britain, she had only had glimpses of sun here
and there. It was the one thing about North Carolina that she missed
the most. That and warm temperatures. Summers back home meant
temperatures in the 90's and oftentimes above 100. So far, England had
not warmed to more than 66. But, she reminded herself, since she was
traveling mostly under her own steam, North Carolina heat was a good
thing to miss.

Excitement fluttered within her as she coasted the bicycle onto
the church grounds. The actual church building dated back to1828
according to the plaque beside the door. Rowen Carter would have been
twenty–two years old. As Kerry leaned the bike against the rock wall

that surrounded the cemetery, she wondered if her ancient relative had worshipped there. Her mother and father had been believers, but had never been members of a church. Owen had joined the Catholic Church before he married Millicent, but Kerry herself was still unattached to a religious institution.

"Ay? Zackly what can I do fer 'ee?" A small coverall clad man appeared at a gate in the wall. He had on thick garden gloves and carried a hammer in one hand and garden stakes in the other.

"Are you the grounds keeper?" Kerry asked. At the man's curt nod, she smiled amiably. Three years of working in a school had taught her the most influential and powerful people in a school building, the ones you wanted on your side, were the maintenance staff. They could make your life pleasant or not so much so. Kerry had learned to treat them with utmost respect. "My name is Kerry Carter. Mr...?"

"Trelawney," he answered.

"I'm sorry to interrupt you, Mr. Trelawney. I'm looking for the headstones of my relatives. My research has led me here. Is it alright if I look around?"

He looked her up and down for a moment, then opened the gate wide and held it for her. "I know where'n a lot of folks are restin'. What's the name?"

"Carter. Specifically, Rowen Carter. It would be great if you could point me in the right direction."

"Aye, they's Carters upaways around those trees," he pointed with the hammer, and then took off a glove, revealing a smashed thumb. "Ya need 'elp I'll be there dreckly. Got a gwidgee-gwee 'ere ta fix up."

Kerry winced in empathy. "Oh, by all means, yes, take care of that. I'm sure I can find what I'm looking for. I hope that heals fast for you."

The caretaker gave another little satisfied nod and left Kerry to her search. She walked up the hill in the direction the groundskeeper had indicated. This was not like the open and orderly public cemetery where her parents now rested. There, the neatly manicured lawns held sleek, modern headstones that were evenly spaced and in orderly rows. Here, some heavily engraved markers stood three to five feet tall, and some were simple markers lying on the ground. Some bore weathered Celtic crosses, and some were so time worn it was impossible to see what the engravings had been. All the tombstones were crowded in at odd angles enclosed by the rock wall. The caretaker had done a good job of keeping the ivy and other vines and weeds at bay, but it still took Kerry a good ten minutes of searching eroded etchings before she finally found a granite headstone that read simply: *Rowen Carter, 1793 – 1857.*

Kerry had read somewhere that it was a chilling experience to stand at the foot of another's grave. One had to wonder about the people who had stood in the same spot generations before in grief and mourning. She found that to be true. She looked at the headstone beside him and found Gwynn Carter who had died one month later.

It was interesting to put timelines into perspective, something that as a teacher of Social Studies had become second nature to Kerry. She thought it notable that in the same year her friends' American ancestors were reacting to the economic panic of 1857, hers were dying on the other side of the Atlantic during another kind of panic—diphtheria. Kerry wondered what they were doing during their last days together and felt a sudden rush of grief for her own parents.

Behind her, a man cleared his throat. She turned and faced a kind-looking fortyish man who apologized for intruding as he held out his hand. "I'm Patrick Pollak, the pastor here at St. Luke's." He nodded toward the Carter graves. "I see you have found someone?"

Kerry studied his kind face as she shook his hand. Here was someone who would help her, she thought to herself. "It's nice to meet you. I'm Kerry. Kerry *Carter*." She also indicated the headstones. "These were my grandparents, several generations back."

"And you are obviously from the States. Which one?"

"North Carolina. My father grew up in New York where he married my mom, and then they moved on down to the Carolinas. Dad used ancestry.com to get back two generations to England. I've come to finish his search, which has led me here."

"Welcome to the UK then, Miss Carter. I hope you're having a good go at it here in your mother country?"

Kerry's smile was genuine. "I've been having the best time. I've met so many nice people. You must enjoy your work here."

"It's rewarding, yes."

Glancing back at the grave marker Kerry's expression turned hopeful. "I know Rowen lived long ago, but do you know anything about him? Would there be anything in the church records?"

Reverend Pollak considered this. "We may be able to help you. I've been here ten years, and I don't know any Carters in the present congregation, but the previous pastors kept meticulous records. We take guardianship of those that rest here in our care as seriously as we do our concern for the living membership. I've a wedding to conduct this afternoon, but can you come back tomorrow just after noon? I'll try to have some information for you."

"Oh, thank you, sir. That would be so kind."

"It's my job. Stay as long as you'd like. It's rather peaceful here, aye?" As he walked away, he said over his shoulder, "You might want to be prepared to learn some unsavory information. Cornwall has a rich but rather seamy history."

⚓

Kerry had to pedal fast on the way back to Min's. Rain was coming in from the east, and she hoped it did not include thunder and lightning, at least not until she was in the privacy of her rented room.

As her legs pumped to the rhythms found in her favorite Don Henley tune, Kerry considered Pastor Pollak's warning. Min had said the same thing. *Were the Carters infamous in some way? What if they were?* Her dad had been a good, sweet man. She did not remember much about her grandfather, but her parents had spoken of him with affection. Every family had a black sheep or two. She had not expected to find a family of angels, just a family of her own.

She arrived at Min's just as the first fat raindrops turned into a stinging, driving downpour. She put the bike away and sprinted up the stairs to the covered back porch where Min was gathering fresh herbs from among her many colorful pots.

"Cuttin' it close there, cheel. I was expectin' a half drowned kitten to come through the door but it looks like 'e scared in just in the nick o' time."

"It came up fast, didn't it?"

"'E's the only way they come up 'round 'ere, but this one's just a water producer. No high winds or such. How 'bout an oggie? I did 'em up good this time."

Kerry took off her wet shoes and left them by the door before she followed Min into the aromatic kitchen. "I don't know how you could have improved those from last night. They were delicious."

"Just 'e wait. Did 'e find what 'e were lookin' for over ta St. Luke's?"

"I found the graves, and the pastor there is going to look in the church records to see what information he can give me tomorrow afternoon." She looked through the window at the weather and grimaced. "He has a wedding today."

"Oh, now—speakin' a weddins, Merrek called taday askin' after 'e. I think 'e's wantin' to invite 'e to the Golowan Festival in Penzance on Saturday. Said it would be good research for yer teachin', like I'm believin' that's all it were."

Kerry could not suppress a smile at the woman's lack of subtlety. "Seriously, Min. 'Speaking of weddings'? And what is the Golowan Festival?"

Min began to talk while Kerry sampled the pastries, which to her pleasant surprise really were tastier than her previous batch. Merrek had not exaggerated about how his cousin could cook...or talk. The chat lasted over two hours, but Kerry did not mind as she found Min an absolute treasure trove of information. Plus, the woman's gregariousness took Kerry's mind off the weather. Since it did not seem that Min needed verbal responses to fuel her soliloquies, Kerry was free to focus on listening.

As the rain peppered down on the roof of the B&B, Kerry learned about the local history and political activity through Min's eyes. Whether she wanted to or not, she also learned about the neighbors and the dynamics of the Walles family through Min's viewpoint and judgments. Kerry did not mind at all since she gained five new short story ideas from Min's narratives.

"'Bàrth an Jówl!" Min exclaimed when she took a breath to look at the clock. Jumping up out of her chair, she explained, "I've got me two new guests comin' in at five—a couple. I better scoot an' get the big room ready."

"Can I do anything to help?"

"Aye, if 'e don't mind. I'll never turn down a helpin' 'and. I don't get around as quick as I use'ta."

They worked together putting fresh sheets on the bed in 'the big room' and setting out all the niceties–the sherry, the flowers, the tea set. All the while, Kerry mentally outlined a short story about a woman who ran a Bed & Breakfast on the coast of North Carolina who had two rowdy daughters that gave her all kinds of humorous grief.

Kerry was in her room when she heard the couple come in— Americans. She heard them lumber up the staircase dragging what sounded like a trunk. She cringed as she anticipated the beating the staircase walls were taking. She heard Min giving them suggestions on places for dinner, and they left shortly afterward.

Assuming she had a couple of hours alone above stairs, Kerry went ahead and took her shower in the tiny hallway bathroom she would share with the new guests, washed some underwear, cleaned up after herself and went back to her room to hang up her things and let her wet curls begin to dry. Donning a pair of shorts and a light sweatshirt, she went downstairs to find Min fussing as she mopped up streaks of mud across the floor. "Bleddy dobecks the lot'o'em. Come in'ere like the didikoys they are."

"Oh, Min, I'm so sorry. Some people just don't think. You'd think they were raised in a barn."

That brought a chuckle to the older woman. "Can't all'o us be perfect now, aye? I've 'ad many guests from America before. Nice an' considerate people. Jus' goes to prove they's dobecks everwhere, an' once in a while yer goin' ta get'un."

Min invited Kerry to have dinner with her and Kerry accepted with the stipulation that she help with the meal. While they ate, Kerry asked if she might have time to go see the Bodmin moors, only a few miles beyond the church, before her meeting with Pastor Pollak.

"'E don' want ta be goin' onto the moors alone, cheel," Min warned. 'E's jus' not smart."

"You believe the myths and legends, then?" asked Kerry carefully.

"If 'e want to go take the guided tour. They's evidence o'cats roamin' the moors."

"Like feral cats?"

"Nah. Like big cats. Wild cats. Cats what rip things up."

Kerry did not get a chance to ask for details, because just then the new guests returned.

Min hopped up to greet them in the entry hall. Kerry followed for the chance to speak with fellow Americans. "I 'ope yer denner was some enjoyable?" Min asked so politely Kerry wondered if she had forgotten about the mud they had tracked in earlier.

"It was…not," answered the man, tall and slender, graying temples. "Might have been better if we'd actually received what we ordered but I was too hungry to wait for them to get their act together. Terrible service. Mediocre food."

Kerry glanced at the woman. Skinny and bottle-tanned, lots of big jewelry. The woman asked Min, "Do you happen to have an antacid? I'm afraid that food gave me heartburn. Strange—I *never* get heartburn."

Min offered to get something for her and left the room deflated, as if she had let her guests down with her restaurant suggestion. Kerry doubted these people would have been satisfied with a dinner at the Ritz, and she wished Min would come back with a laxative instead of an antacid.

Pasting on a pleasant smile, Kerry extended her hand. "Hi, I'm Kerry Carter from Wilmington, North Carolina. You are fellow Americans but I can't place the area from your accent."

They looked at her as if from a height of at least twenty feet. "That's because proper education eradicates accents," said the man as he took her hand. "We are Paul and Brandi Miller, from Tampa, Florida. What brings your family to this miserable part of the world?"

Kerry could not remember ever meeting such sour people, and part of her felt sorry for whatever had made them that way. "Oh, it's just me, solo. And you'll like it better when the rain stops—it's really quite beautiful. I'm here doing genealogy research for my family. You?"

Brandi appeared deep in thought. Kerry was sure it could not be too deep. Paul answered, "We are on our third tour of Europe. This is the first time we've tried Cornwall. Should have passed on it again, and the west side isn't any more impressive. What are you doing

1. traveling by yourself?"

Before Kerry could answer Brandi came out of her stupor. "*Carter?* Did you say your name was Carter? Do you think you might be related to that smuggling bunch we just read about over near Mount's Bay?"

You can read? was unfortunately the first thing that entered Kerry's mind. She always tried to see the best in people, but the Millers made the search seem a waste of time. She answered smoothly, "Might be. I haven't found anything like that yet, but who knows? That would be kind of exciting."

Paul spoke again. "Well, if you've traced your family back to this hellhole, you're bound to be related to some kind of miscreants. My condolences."

Min came in with a little bottle of Tums for Brandi, who without even a thank you took them and started up the stairs. Part way up, she turned and said, "We'll have breakfast at ten. Coffee, not tea. Fruit and plain toasted bagel only. And please don't over-toast the bagel." Paul fell in behind her and they disappeared upstairs.

As soon as they heard the bedroom door shut, Min and Kerry simultaneously made gagging gestures. Giggling at how much their minds were in accord, Min strutted to the kitchen with her chest puffed out and Kerry minced along behind her in imitation of the new houseguests. There they opened a bottle of Scotch, and when they had surely burned the Miller's ears quite enough, Kerry asked Min about the smuggling Carters.

"They was some brothers that ran up quite a successful smugglin' operation between Lizard Point and Mousehole backalong the late 1700's. Legend has it they was decent fellows, wouldn't allow no cussin' or brawlin' on the boats. Fishers by trade, they fell into the smuggling business in a big way. Once on a lark, one called hisself the King of Prussia, an' it stuck. The whole area were known as Prussia Point. The Mount Bay area is full o' caves and tunnels where they'd hide their loot till they could sell it. Tea, cloth, brandy—anythin' they could make a profit on. The townsfolk helped 'em, and even the authorities could be bought ta look th'other way. Story is, long about the early 1800's they got religion and gave up smugglin' altogether, although a few factions kept it up. They had a rather big family, all along the coast. Could be 'e are related. In fact, years agone smugglin' was just a way of life here in part o' Cornwall. Most families were into it somehow. Bother ya some, does it, that yer family could 'ave been pirates, criminals?"

Kerry shook her head, "Not at all. I think it would be exciting to have such a unique history. I've always played it so safe since I'm an accident waiting to happen—it would be ironic to have come from such daring people. What about your family? Were they in the smuggling business as well?"

"'Tis a possibility. They was jobs for lookouts, an' flackers, an' those what sold. Smugglin' were a big business. A boat maker could build boats with hidden compartments, women wi' bundles tied 'round their waists and hips underneath wide skirts could walk right under the noses o' authorities. Sometimes the runners'd sink barrels offshore and later, when it was safe, ordinary fishermen'd look for their markers an' haul the contraband in wi' the daily catch. Aye. Big business. A little B&B proprietor like meself could hide contraband, runners as well." She winked at Kerry. "Could be they's some leftover brandy down in my cellar right now. But as far as I know for sure, the Walles' have been fishermen forever wi' a few tin and kaolin miners here and there. Aye, and there was also an artist some generations agone—maybe six or seven. Some o' 'is paintin's are on display at the museum over ta Bude. 'E's our only claim to fame."

Kerry's mind was already spinning with characters and stories. She was also mentally working on creating a social studies project about events brought on by heavy taxation, such as smuggling. Min interrupted her thoughts. "Yer brother interested in this genealogy stuff like yerself?"

Kerry looked away. "No. He has no interest in it." Looking back at Min's kind and understanding face she continued, "While I'm busy trying to find a family I can call my own, Owen would rather be free of any ties. I love my brother, but he is entirely too self centered, and has never been content with his background. Owen wants to be more...Upper End. He treats me decently when we are alone, but I've always had the impression he doesn't want me around his friends or business associates since he's never invited me to any of the functions he hosts. No, he would never embrace the idea of coming from a family of smugglers. While I think it would be kind of romantic, Owen would think it...I don't know...vulgar."

"Can't be so—yer brother bein' ashamed o' ye. Better fit, maybe 'e's ashamed of 'is friends. Didde ever think o'that?"

"Well...no. I hadn't." Kerry turned that over in her mind. What did she know of the people with whom Owen associated? They would be like him, more than likely—a beautiful wife, an elegant home, fancy cars, one or two children in private schools. Drank too much, partied too hard and who knew what other vices they fell into? And always blamed the whole of it on the pressures of the job. Maybe all this time he had been protecting her from them. She began to warm to that idea.

Min broke into her thoughts. "Now, that Merrek? 'E's 'ad 'is share o' weighty burdens placed on 'is shoulders. And those younger girls are a brazen pair. But 'e adores 'em. All families have both good and bad, but most times, 'e's just a matter a' difference. 'E's bad for yer innards to turn away from yer family."

"I know, but I guess you never know what's really in each other's thoughts, especially if you don't truly talk to one another." Kerry sighed heavily. "Anyway, there's only the two of us now, and from what I've been able to gather, this branch of the Carter family wasn't very prolific either. I've yet to find any living relatives."

"Well, cheel, families—what do ya do wi'em? I've sure enjoyed jawin'wi' ya, but it's gettin'late and these old bones've got to get up in the mornin' and not over-toast the bagels, don't 'ee know."

⚓

Kerry got up early the next morning. As quietly as she could, she freshened up in the bathroom between her room and the Millers, and then tiptoed toward the stairs. As she passed in front of 'the big room', she heard snores through the walls. No early birds in that room, it seemed.

Min was already in the kitchen. She smiled a quiet good morning and motioned to the bowl of hot oats and the ever-present pastry she had prepared for her new young friend. "Oh, Min. You're spoiling me and making me fat," Kerry admonished.

"Don't think it would hurt you none—either of 'em. So…what's up for today besides St. Luke's and yer date tonight?"

Kerry did not miss the way Min's eyebrows wiggled at the mention of her date with Merrek. The woman was relentless. "Well, as soon as the Millers get up and go do whatever it is they are going to *endure* today, I need to wash a few clothes. Is there anything I can help you with?"

"I was jus' thinkin', as it's goin' ta be a sunny day, 'e might want ta go shoppin' down ta White River Place. Maybe get something special fer yer date tonight, or maybe somethin' for the Golowan Festival on Saturday."

Kerry laughed. "I told Merrek when he invited me to dinner the first time that I only had backpacking clothes. I'm sure he isn't planning to take me anywhere my jeans and t-shirts won't fit in. You know, I'm amazed he's is still a bachelor considering you're such a persistent match-maker." Kerry winced, "Do the Cornish have match-makers? You aren't really one, are you?"

"Nah," Min turned back toward the stove to check on the status of her boiling water, "I'm jus' sayin'…"

The closing of the bathroom door upstairs signaled the real beginning of the day. Min and Kerry shared an apprehensive look, and then Min poured the boiling water into the French press over pre-measured coffee. Kerry volunteered to cut the fruit. "You're on your own with the bagels," she told Min, "At my house, a meal was never ready until the bread was burned."

The Millers were thirty minutes late for their breakfast, blaming their tardiness on everything from not sleeping well on the too-soft mattress to the poor water pressure in the shower. As they picked at their food, they discussed their plans to tour the Lost Gardens of Heligan and the Eden Project and debated a place to eat lunch where they might find clean fare and decent service. Before she could stop herself, Kerry asked them if they might consider a picnic on the beautiful Bodmin Moors. Min had a coughing spell and had to excuse herself. Kerry offered the puzzled Millers an innocent smile.

⚓

While her laundry dried on hangers in her room in front of a small fan, Kerry readied herself for the ride to first St. Luke's, and then to the library for research. After dressing and securing her hair in a ponytail, she put on her passport/money belt and grabbed her iPod and earphones. She assured Min she would pick up some lunch somewhere and once again borrowed the bike.

On the way to St. Luke's Kerry realized she wasn't sure which she was looking forward to the most, receiving information from Pastor Pollak or seeing Merrek again. Min would have been disappointed to know there was even a contest.

Kerry suddenly thought of Mrs. Tesmer. She should call her soon to check in. What would the proper and stiff Mrs. Tesmer think of the homey and loquacious Min? Kerry decided she would not be surprised if they liked one another immensely. Better yet, what would Mrs. Tesmer think of the handsome Merrek Walles? That he was Kerry's George Harrison? Kerry decided she should keep that piece of her trip to Cornwall quiet for now, as there was a strong possibility that he could very well be. The same small-statured caretaker was painting the handrails to the church's front porch when Kerry rode into the parking area where she left the bike. "How's the thumb?" she asked, being careful not to brush against the rails on her way up to the door.

He smiled in recognition. "'E's good, thanks. The pastor's awaitenin' 'e inside."

Kerry entered through one of the double doors at the church's entrance. It took a moment for her eyes to adjust to the dimly lit chapel. The only light filtered in through small antique stained glass windows set high at four-foot intervals around the plastered walls. Oak beams adorned the ceiling, and the altar, made of matching oak and polished to a gleam, sat in the back upon a raised dais. Behind it there were chairs for a small choir and to the right sat an organ. Seven rows of oak pews marched along each side of the rich blue-carpeted aisle that led to the steps of the altar. Someone had scattered vases of fresh flowers around the chapel, adding to the quaint beauty and welcoming feel that contrasted with the stone exterior.

Through a plate glass window to her right, she spied Pastor Pollak in a small side office, obviously added in recent years. He looked up at her

85

approach. "Miss Carter," he smiled in greeting. "Did you survive that downpour yesterday?"

"I got home just in the nick of time. I so hope the wedding went well."

Pastor Pollak grimaced slightly. "I got them married. It's my hope a talented laundress can get the mud out of the bride's train. Now let me show you what I've found on your Carters."

He placed a very large bound book in front of Kerry. Its cloth cover, once maybe a rich burgundy, was faded and frayed. Before he opened it, he donned a pair of white gloves. "These old volumes are fragile," the pastor explained. "It would be a great loss if the pages were damaged." He opened the book to a pre-marked location. The pages did appear delicate, yellowed with age and smelled of centuries gone by. Kerry could hardly contain her excitement, but when her eyes scanned the Old English words that flourished across the page, she turned a bewildered face to Pastor Pollak.

"Oh, ye of little faith," he smiled patiently. He set another book, a newer one, beside the ancient one. "Some forward thinking church historian took the time to transcribe the older church records into easier reading for us today." He opened this book to a page he had marked with a ribbon. He pointed to a notation on the page. "This proves the correspondence to the page in this older book, and according to this it seems Rowen had a son who moved to London in 1859. His name was Stephan Carter."

"Stephan!" Kerry's enthusiasm renewed. "Yes! That matches with what I found in London."

"Yes, right here. Stephan. Born in 1834?"

"That's right," exclaimed Kerry, checking her notes. "I already have some information on him. Is there anything else about Rowen? Occupation maybe? Was he from this area?"

"Let's look further down. Yes, you'll see right here…" he sounded as excited as Kerry felt. "Rowen was a miner—moved here in 1840 to work in the local kaolin mines, and here is his baptism record in 1842. Both he and his wife died during the diphtheria epidemic, but of course, we have no way of knowing if that's what took them. It could just as well have been consumption—a common result of mining dust. Ah, and you're going to love this. Rowen was born in Porth, Cornwall to Rowse and Mary Carter."

Kerry felt a rush of exhilaration. "That's another generation back! Back to the 1700's. This is so wonderful!" Her hand actually shook as she wrote down this new information. "Where is Porth?" Even her voice quaked with thrill.

Pastor Pollak smiled as he carefully closed the books and took off the white gloves. "That's down on the coast, I think. Near Falmouth. Could be his parents are buried there. The churches in Porth might yield some information if you…" Pastor Pollak looked up in time to see the fireworks in Kerry's eyes.

"Falmouth? Oh, my goodness! Oh, sorry, not my goodness—I have very little, but—I am so excited about this! I've read so much about that area…historical fiction as well…du Maurier?" Pastor Pollak smiled and nodded in recognition. "Yes!! *Jamaica Inn* took place in that area. And that may be where my roots are? How cool is that?! Thank you so much."

"I'm glad we were able to help," the pastor smiled at her youthful enthusiasm as he stacked the books on a nearby shelf. "You know if you're going to be in town still on Sunday, come visit us during worship. We have a 10:00 and a 7:00 service."

"Thank you, but I think I'll be heading down to Porth on Sunday."

"Ah, Kerry, if you travel there, please be careful. The place still carries a rough reputation."

"Oh, I will. And thanks so much for all your help." A sudden thought occurred to Kerry. "Could I…leave a donation? An offering? It would make me happy."

"If it would make you happy, how can I turn you down?" He turned and indicated a small pedestal table in the corner to the left of the altar. "There are envelopes and offering plates on that table. It's been a pleasure to meet you. And Miss Carter? Take care, and God be with you."

After leaving her offering, and with her money belt safely replaced, Kerry all but skipped through the church doors onto the porch, her hand lightly skimming the handrail as she scampered down the steps. However, not lightly enough, as she belatedly remembered Trelawney's paint job. She looked at the white paint smeared on her hand and then back at the handrail. She had left definite skid marks in her wake.

Kerry climbed the steps once more and pulled open one of the double doors just as Pastor Pollak was exiting the other. "Forget something, Miss Carter?" he asked in surprise.

"Yes, I did, and I'd like to increase my offering," explained Kerry as she held out her hand revealing the white paint. The pastor looked confused until the caretaker appeared, his eyes zeroing in on the botched paint job. Mr. Trelawney did not even try to hide the scowl that spread over his face before his accusing eyes drifted up to Kerry.

"Ah," understanding dawned on the pastor's face. "Mr. Trelawney and I have been at loggerheads over whether those rails should get one or two coats. I said one, he said two. Looks like you'll get your two, my good man." Trelawney's scowl changed to a look of satisfaction. He tipped his hat to Kerry, and left to retrieve his painting materials.

Pastor Pollak smiled at Kerry. "I was trying to cut corners, much to Mr. Trelawney's aggravation and opposition. Thanks to you, dear child, we will no longer have to cut that corner. The Lord does indeed work in mysterious ways."

Kerry left the church in high spirits. Unlike the day before, the sun was out and everything looked fresh from the rain. Kerry could not imagine that the Millers found no beauty in Cornwall. All they had to do was look around.

As Kerry took in the sights and storefronts on her way to the local library, the display in the window of a boutique caught her eye. She slowed to a near stop as one mannequin in the display was wearing an especially pretty outfit—breezy, casual and feminine, a nice change from the jeans and t-shirts she had worn for weeks. She could not quite get that outfit out of her mind, even while at the library as she delved into the subject of the Carter brothers of Mount Bay.

The historical account was much as Min had told it. The three brothers—John, Henry, and Charles—had used three small inlets in the Mount Bay area for their rather successful operation. Pisky's Cove, Bessie's Cove, and King's Cove were in an area that was so secluded that the only way to see the boats in the inlets was from the sharp cliffs overhead. Natural caves and tunnels carved out by the ocean waters over the millenniums riddled the coastline and made convenient hiding places for contraband waiting distribution. The topography was also such that there was some protection from the Atlantic storms, although there had been a few to hit the area.

Kerry found Porth on a map of Cornwall. It was a small coastal village around Lizard Point to the west, approximately two miles from Mount Bay. What were the chances that her relatives and the King of Prussia Carters shared relatives? She had to know—had to have some proof.

Before leaving the library, Kerry also did a quick research of the Golowan Festival in Penzance. Golowan, Cornish for Midsummer, was the festival of St. John that the early inhabitants celebrated with huge bonfires and much merriment. In the late 1800's it was discontinued because the bonfires were oft times uncontrolled and dangerous, but in the early 1990's it was revived as an arts festival and celebration of local heritage. The possibility of attending sparked Kerry's imagination. Maybe her students could host a mock Golowan festival for the school and sell handmade arts and crafts, a very integrated learning experience.

On her way back to Min's, Kerry had to pass by the boutique again. She had not quite cleared the shop's parking lot when she slowed to a stop. If Merrek did invite her to the festival, that outfit would be so much fun to wear. She had been in the same jeans and shirts for weeks. The material looked to be something that would pack well and she would be able to wear it on other occasions. It would not hurt to just look at the price and see if her size was available.

⚓

Half an hour later Kerry stashed the bike and miraculously managed not to fall as she tripped up Min's porch steps at a break- neck speed. Her shopping spree had made her run a little late. She dashed up the stairs and into her room. Min was there, putting fresh flowers into the vase on the small dresser.

"Ow, and what ya been up ta now, Milady Carter?" Min asked as Kerry tore into her package to lay out the skirt and blouse, a wide rimstraw hat, and a new pair of sandals to complete the outfit. "I see ya took me advice ta doll up for Merrek tonight."

"Not tonight. I got it for the Golowan festival, and I didn't get it for Merrek—I got it for *me*. Won't this be fun to wear? I wasn't going to get the hat because I won't be able to pack it, but maybe I can strap it on the outside of my pack somehow. There's got to be a few more sunny days while I'm here." Noticing the flowers, she smiled at the older woman. "Thank you for the flowers, Min. They're such an uplifting touch."

"Well, now," smiled Min as her eyes twinkled. "Yer lookin' like yer a touch uplifted yerself."

Kerry chuckled. "This has been such a great day. My trip to St. Luke's proved fruitful and my research is taking me to Porth. It seems I had family in Porth on the coastline, likely related to smugglers for real. I'm so excited...and *late*," she exclaimed as she glanced at the clock. "I'm going to jump in the shower and..."

Min stopped her before she was completely out of the room. "Eh, Mr. Miller himself is indisposed at the moment," she indicated the bathroom with the tilt of her head.

"Oh. You think he'll be out soon?"

Min's voice was a whisper. "Can't say. Been in there for some time. It's beginnin' to get a bit worrisome, I'll tell ya."

"Have you knocked?"

"Would 'ee chance that? Don't hear nary a sound coming outta there to boot. Want ta use my water closet downstairs?"

"Oh, that's kind of you, Min, but I'll give him a few minutes. He can't stay in there forever, right? Where's Mrs. Miller?"

"Nappin'. Seems the gardens irritated her sensitivities and they 'ad to forego the rest of the day's plans so's they can rest up for the trip to Penzance in the mornin'."

"Are they going to the festival then?"

"Seems so. Takes the festiveness right out of it, aye?"

The door across the hall opened and revealed Mrs. Miller clad in a silky robe, her hand flung dramatically over her forehead. "Min, I need something for this headache, and you need to get these flowers out of here. They are adding insult to injury—my poor sinuses. And while you're at it, some coffee would be good."

"I'll take care of it, mum," Min said as she stepped around Mrs. Miller to retrieve the vase of flowers she had arranged for them that morning. On her way out of the room, she said cautiously, "Eh, Mr. Miller's been in the water closet for might a spell. Think 'e's okay?"

"He's fine. He likes to read in the bathroom. He'll be out when he gets to a good stopping place or he can no longer feel his legs. Please…I need to lie back down on my heating pad. Just bring up something with the coffee tray and leave it on the nightstand," Min was barely out of the room before the door shut behind her.

Reading? thought Kerry. *I have to get ready for my date—my rather hot date—and he's using our only bathroom as a reading room? Moreover, Min's being treated as a servant! This is too much.* When Min came back upstairs with the tray of coffee and aspirin, Kerry quietly asked where the circuit breaker box was located. Min glanced toward the bathroom and a slow smile spread across her face. "'E's in the pantry, far left corner. 'E's marked well."

Kerry sped down the stairs, found the box in the pantry, and switched off the electricity to the upstairs rooms. When she met Min coming back downstairs, the bathroom was available and Mr. Miller was in a state. Through the wall of the Miller's bedroom, they heard him bemoan the fact that his wife's heating pad could so easily overload the primitive

Cornish utility capabilities and Mrs. Miller was pleading with him to mind her headache. Kerry and Min shared a high five, and then Kerry went in for her shower. Several seconds later, the lights came back on thanks to Min.

By the time Kerry was dressed in fresh jeans and an apricot colored t-shirt, Merrek had been downstairs with Min for fifteen minutes. As she approached the kitchen, Kerry could hear them talking in low tones. During her last few steps, she clearly heard Min fuming at Merrek about having already mentioned the festival and was about to let it out that Kerry had bought something new to wear. *Was he not going to ask her?* She suddenly realized how much she had been looking forward to it. As soon as she came into their sight, they awkwardly stopped talking and turned toward Kerry.

Merrek rose from his chair to greet her. She noticed he was dressed in jeans and a chambray shirt. *He had remembered to keep it casual.* "I'm so sorry I'm late," Kerry apologized.

Merrek gave her one of those smiles that made everything all right. "Yer well worth the wait, luv, don't worry about it. Min told me ya 'ad ta rid the water closet o' varmints." Chuckling he added, "I do like yer style."

"My dad used to tell me even though I was physically clumsy my mind worked like a circus acrobat, a devious one at that."

Merrek beamed at her, and she blushed slightly. Min was obviously enjoying the whole thing. "Well, you two have fun. You've yer key, do ya cheel? I won't be waitin' up. I've already got me orders for breakfast of a mornin'. Merrek," she sent him a rather stern look, "remember what I said." She all but shooed them out the door.

⚓

"I thought we might have some traditional Cornish fare tonight if yer interested. Somethin' ta write in yer notes." Merrek put his hand at the small of her back as he guided her through the foot traffic. She liked his touch—gentlemanly, nothing more.

"Sure," said Kerry enthusiastically, although she quietly hoped it didn't involve squid or eel.

Merrek walked her to a quaint restaurant not far from Min's called The Gilliflower, named for an apple native to Cornwall. There he introduced her to squab pie, which contained no squab at all for which Kerry was abundantly thankful, but mutton and apples instead. She also enjoyed a variety of locally grown vegetables, flaky biscuits called Cornish splits,

Mead—a honey wine, and saffron cake with a raspberry sauce.

The restaurant owner, a big gregarious man with a shock of red hair and heavy beard to match, was Merrek's first cousin, Gorron. Kerry liked him instantly, and he was delighted in the American girl's interest in his food. He joined them for a few minutes at their table, and Kerry learned a bit about Cornish agriculture and methods of food preparations from him. She stared wide-eyed as a server passed their table carrying what she learned was Stargazy pie. The two men laughed at her bewilderment over the dish of fish heads protruding through the pastry, as if they were indeed gazing at the stars. She was so thankful Merrek had not ordered *that* dish.

As Kerry spooned the last of her saffron cake into her mouth, Merrek asked if she felt up to doing a bit of "pubbin" before going home. "I know one place in particular that ye'd like. Live music—traditional Cornish ditties—another cultural experience for 'ee."

"Sounds perfect," Kerry eagerly agreed. "Maybe they'll have CDs for sale that I could play for my students."

Merrek smiled at her enthusiasm. His eyes dropped to her chest and a sympathetic grimace crossed his face. Following his gaze, Kerry found a noticeably large dollop of raspberry sauce on her shirt. Her face colored with embarrassment while she let out an exasperated sigh.

"Maybe it won't stain," he attempted to sooth her. "Especially if 'e wash the spot now. The water closet's down that hall."

"Thanks. Sorry. I'll be back soon."

Merrek stood with her to hold back her chair. She was turning toward the restroom when he gently stopped her with his hand on her cheek, lifted her chin up so he could see her face, "Don't look so defeated, luv. 'Tis only a wee bit o' raspberry sauce."

She gave him a sad little smile. "It was the only unstained shirt I had left," and with a derisive little laugh added, "my wardrobe is like a scrapbook of dining experiences."

Merrek's smile was warm, his eyes warmer, "Then don't try overmuch to wash this away," he said quietly as his thumb brushed over the spot. He hadn't intended to feel the soft curve of her upper breast beneath that stain, but once done, he barely resisted the urge to do it again. "I'd like to think this dining experience has been somewhat memorable." Reluctantly he turned her, chuckling at the blush that stained her skin almost as vividly as the one on her shirt. "Off with 'e, then," he said and gave her a little push toward the restroom.

Kerry spent ten minutes with soap and water and finally accepted that she could wash away neither the red stain nor the shock of Merrek's touch. It had not been an unwelcome shock, but more of a…*spark*. A smile began to play at the corners of her mouth.

When she returned to the table sporting a huge water mark right in the center of her left breast and a crimson colored face, Merrek presented her with a Gilliflower souvenir t-shirt. "One arrow, two vultures." He shrugged and looked quite proud of himself.

Kerry's delight lit her face. "Oh, that's so thoughtful of you," she smiled as she stood on tiptoes to kiss his cheek. "This is perfect. How much do I owe you?"

"Well, since I took it upon meself to buy it for 'e, 'e owe me naught but more o'that smile. I want 'e to enjoy yerself tonight—no worries about stains. Besides, I like to support Gorran, and 'e'll be doin' some free marketin' for the Gilliflower."

Kerry gave him an even brighter smile. "I'll do so with pleasure. Thank you, Merrek."

She took the shirt back to the restroom to change. Merrek watched her go, admiring her gently curved body. He was attracted to her, but more than that, he *liked* her. She was an open book. As an eldest brother, he knew well the role of protector, and now he felt compelled to extend that duty to this little American. No one should ruin what she had, and there were those that would try if only for sport.

"It's a perfect fit," Kerry smiled at him when she returned. "Aye, well, having four sisters is quite an education. Are 'e ready for some fun?"

"I've been having fun all along," Kerry smiled up at him as they walked to the door, and felt the warmth of his gaze pass over her.

Merrek waved to his cousin as they were leaving, and Gorron hurried over to bid them goodbye. "Nice ta meet ya, Kerry. Enjoy yer stay. Nice shirt yer wearin' there. Merrek, 'e still staying over with us tonight? Hedren already made the guest room ready for 'e. She'll be mazed at havin' gone ta the trouble if 'e don't."

"Aye, and I appreciate the offer. I'll be back in time to 'elp 'e close."

"There'll be plenty ta be done. Always is." Gorron caught Merrek's arm as he went out the door. "Beware of that'un," he warned his cousin.

"Don't I know it?" Merrek replied with a wink at Kerry.

The name of the pub he took her to was Yeghes Da!—Cornish for 'cheers'. Kerry asked if the American TV sitcom had a role in the moniker, but no one knew. It was more open and lighted than the pub he had taken her to the first night, and there was a trio playing very lively music on guitar, base, and fiddle. Some of the words were old Celtic, some were English or a mix of the two. They added humor to their act, playing off each other and the crowd.

As the beer flowed freely, the crowd sometimes sang along, some even occasionally got up and danced. Kerry could not remember when she had had so much fun. She was even having a good time in spite of Merrek's frequent sidelong gazes at her. He still had not even mentioned the Penzance festival, and she really did not care that much as she was very excited about going down to Porth and digging up family roots. Tonight she was not going to let anything interfere with her enjoyment.

Merrek, however, knew the exact moment that the enjoyment was about to tilt the other way and quickly paid the tab. "Those two over there're arguin' over the attentions of the barmaid. The chucker out's gettin' nervous. Looks ta be a brawl shortwit'." Sure enough, Merrek and Kerry were barely out the door before someone threw the first punch and the real party began.

"The chucker out?" Kerry laughed, a little tipsy from the mead and ale.

"Aye, that rather large bloke standin' at the back? 'E's probably showin' those two the way out right about now."

Kerry could not stop giggling as she pondered his meaning. "You mean the bouncer?"

Merrek did not seem to mind her mirth. He laughed along with her—or maybe at her, but Kerry did not care. "Bouncer? I'm referrin' to the one what chucks out the undesirable behaviors."

"The chucker out," Kerry experimented with the feel of the term. "That's hilarious. The chucker out!"

"Aye, and what's a bouncer aboot? Bounces 'em out? " Kerry's giggles were infectious, and Merrek found himself chuckling along.

"Come to think of it I guess I'd rather be simply chucked out into the street than bounced out like a basketball. You English are much more civilized."

Suddenly audible were the sounds of fists flying, splintering wood, and shattering glass, "Does that sound civilized to 'e?" He smiled as her laughter almost covered the sounds of the melee. "We're in Cornwall, darlin'. London is another world away."

With a delighted sigh, Kerry tilted her head to the sky, spread her arms and loudly announced, "I love Cornwall!" Then she took Merrek's arm and smiled into his eyes, "Know a good quote about wonderful evenings,

Professor Walles?"

"Hmm, let me think," he caught Kerry about the waist and guided her around a pothole in the street. "How about, 'This has been the most wonderful evening I've had in some long time'."

"Nice..." Kerry smiled dreamily. "Who said that?"

Merrek laughed, and just then, in typical Kerry-style, she stumbled anyway—apparently over her own feet. But Merrek was quick. His arms went around her and held her securely. Laughing at her own clumsiness, Kerry twisted and tilted her head back to look up at him.

Merrek, mesmerized by how her curly red hair perfectly framed her face and made the green of her eyes pop, found he could not let go of her.

"Just so you know...," she stated as she looked up at him with slightly unfocused eyes, "...that bit of clumsiness wasn't my fault. The earth just quaked. It almost knocked me off my feet. Didn't you feel it?"

Merrek stared into dreamy green eyes. "Aye, I'm feelin' it still, Lass." His eyes dipped and he could not help but consider the promise of sweetness her smiling mouth beckoned him to taste. "And 'ere's that quote for 'e. From Scotsman Thomas Carlyle, 'If ever in doubt as to whether to kiss a pretty girl, always give 'er the benefit of the doubt'." He slowly lowered his head and brushed his lips gently across hers, and then took in a long breath. "Ah, lassie, I'll be havin' me some more o' that, if 'e don't mind—earthquake an' all." His arms tightened around her and his mouth covered hers. He watched as her eyes went limpid and then closed, let himself linger there, savoring her taste and the feel of her against his body.

Kerry went still at the onslaught of Merrek's kisses. In her experience, first kisses were somewhat experimental in approach, even awkward, and only slightly improved with frequency. But Merrek's were assertive and confident. The sensation felt proven, time-honored, familiar somehow. Foreign and exotic responses sparked within her, and yet at the same time she felt utterly secure, a sensation she had been without for far too long. She was disappointed when Merrek withdrew.

Her eyes flickered open when she heard a Cornish expletive ride out on his slowly expelled breath and saw her bewilderment mirrored in his expression. He loosened his arms, stepped back slightly. "Barth de Jowl, luv. What was that?"

"I don't know," she sighed, still clinging to his arms, "but thank God for the Scots." A burst of laughter escaped him, and he framed her face with his hands. "Ah, Kerry, 'e are a delightful lass. At first 'e seemed

familiar somehow, but I was wrong. I would've remembered you, darlin'."
He could not deny himself another prolonged kiss, recognizing his desire
for her to be on an unfamiliar plane, and unforgettable indeed.

Battling with himself to stop, he took her hand and Kerry almost
floated along with him as he continued their walk. After only a few
steps, he stopped. "Look, luv. Me plan was to invite you to the Golowan
Festival tomorrow—I guess Min told you already—the woman talks too
much..."

"Merrek, please. If something has come up or you've changed your
mind, no need to go into a lot of explanations. I've got plans to go to
Porth anyway, so..."

"...You're going to Porth?" he sounded worried. "By yourself?" Now
there was anger.

"Well, yeah. I came to London by myself, then here by myself. I think I
can do Porth, too."

"Damn," he said under his breath. "Okay, here's m' problem. Or maybe
I should say I'm afraid it would be your problem. Me oldest sister's family
has rented a place on the beach for the holiday and she has planned a
Golowan family get together there Saturday night, the only night I'm
free ta go. I want more than anythin' right now to take you to Golowan.
But I don't think I'd 'ave time to take 'e back to Min's before this family
thing. If I did our time would be eatin' up in travel, and..."

"Merrek. You need to go to your family gathering. I need to go on with
my research anyway. It's fine."

"Let me finish," he sounded frustrated. "I would really like to come
get you tomorrow mornin' and spend the whole day with 'ee, includin'
takin' ya to Elowen's for the bonfire an' all, but me family... I'm afraid...
no...I'm *certain* they'd embarrass ya'. They're a loud bunch and love ta
tease an' you'd take a load'a abuse on account o'... bein' me date."Kerry
searched his face. He was telling the truth. Her green eyes narrowed with
disapproval. "You're sounding a bit like my brother—embarrassed by your
family. And you don't think I could handle myself, do you?"

Merrek realized his mistake when he saw her eyes flash. He quickly
tried to make amends. "'E've said yerself 'e've not had extended family
experience. There will be several generations there, luv, all very familiar
an'well meanin'—mostly—but not very well mannered, especially after
the ale that's certain ta be consumed."

Her chin went up with a stubbornness he had not seen in her before.
"Merrek, I taught in a middle school for three years, not a convent. I'm

sure I've heard every foul word there is, or at least their derivations. I mean, pardon my French, but pussies cannot survive teaching middle school Americana."

Merrek laughed in surprise and then watched the blush creep up her face. "Ah, m'sweet. 'E may try to keep that spunk under raps but it does peek out from time ta time." *And what an aphrodisiac it was.* "Come w'me then? Walles family bonfire 'n all?"

"Aye," she smiled. "Porth can wait."

He took her hand in his and they resumed the walk back to Min's. "I feel complimented," he smiled as he walked beside her. "Puttin' your genealogy research at the back of the stove for me. I can feel me chest inflatin' even now."

⚓

Min was still up when Kerry slipped quietly into the kitchen for a drink of water. "Wot ya doin' home s'early?" she sounded genuinely disappointed.

"Well a girl's got to get some rest if she's going to spend the day and most the night in Penzance tomorrow."

Min's face lit up. "I tol' that boy not ta worry 'bout ya. Any lady wot 'as the gumption ta turn off the electric on a proper stranger 'as more than a bit o' fightin' spirit in 'er blood.""Speaking of toilet hogs, what's up with the Millers?" Kerry whispered.

"Gone to the Bugle Inn over near the Eden Project. And good riddance. Ordered dinner from me, they did. I 'ad ta explain to 'em the concept of a bed and breakfast and they huffed up and out, 'ad the gumption ta demand their money back fer the lost night o' stay."

"You didn't, did you, Min?"

"Wot ya take me for, cheel? Not some dobeck, no. Once in a while, that's just the way she goes. But 'ee, me girl, 'ave the water closet all to yerself in the mornin', so couldn'ta worked out better."

Knowing she would not go to sleep right away, Kerry emailed Mrs. Tesmer to update her on the recent discoveries, which were leading her to Porth. *Can you believe it could be that I am related to real "Jamaica Inn" type smugglers?* She wrote. *That possibility never entered my mind!* She also mentioned to Mrs. Tesmer that she was going to Penzance to experience the festival there, but kept the details to herself.

It was different with Tania's email. Kerry let Tania know how much she was looking forward to spending the day with Merrek. She also admitted her attraction to him. *I'll try to send you a picture*, she promised Tania. *Wait until you see him. Robert better not be around!*

⚓

Merrek put the last clean glass back in its place above the bar and glanced at his cousin's expectant face. "Aye, what is it, then?"

Gorron grinned. "So…what is it with you and this pretty little Yankee? I haven't seen 'e starry-eyed over a girl since…too long ago."

"I've never been starry-eyed," he threw the towel at his cousin's face, "but I do like 'er. And she's…intriguin'. Lot's o'layers ta that 'un."

"'E don't need complicated, m'boy."

"I didna mean complicated. Just some…multifaceted. Like…one minute she seems totally green, but then this intelligence and wit shows through. Another minute she seems so sweet, but if 'e push the right button, those green eyes snap with temper."

"Ah, and what other buttons 'ave 'e managed to push?"

Merrek grinned. "One minute she seems terribly innocent but then when I kissed 'er? I could taste some powerful passion simmerin' there, just below the surface. Aye, she's intriguin'."

"'E do look some good together, I'll tell 'e that. Seein' 'er again I guess?"

"Aye, takin' 'er to the Golowan Festival tomorrow and then over ta Elowen's rental for the cookout."

"Ah, bloody 'ell. Takin' 'er ta meet the folks, then?"

"Aye, it's a thing o'convenience. Don't go makin' more outta it than there is."

"Well, let's see. You like 'er, she's got all these intriguin' layers yer lookin' ta peel back, 'e like kissin' 'er. Not only are 'e seein' 'er again, but yer even willin' ta take the risk o' scarin' 'er off by subjectin' 'er to our bawdy family. What could I be makin' of that?"

Merrek ignored Gorron as a thought passed through the back of his mind. "Gorron, does she remind 'e of anyone?"

"No, and I'm sure I would've remembered someone that fetchin'. I'd 'ave thought to introduce 'er to 'e straightaway. Why? She remind 'e o'someone?"

"I've thought so since I first met 'er but I can't think where or when or who."

"Maybe she's the one, then. The counterpart ta that old soul o' yers."

"'E don't believe in all that bloody soul mate shite, do 'e?"

"Not in the sense that there's only one woman in the entire world for

98

each bloke, but I do believe we recognize ourselves in those we find…
intriguin'. She does look good beside 'e, me boy."

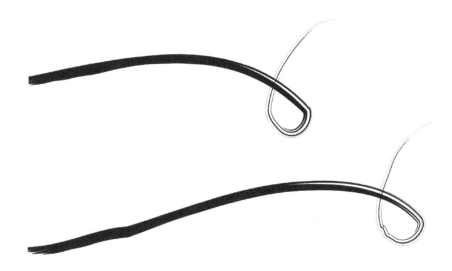

- 10 -

We all become great explorers
during our first few days in a new city,
or a new love affair.
—Mignon McLaughlin

Kerry was up before the sun the next morning. As she made up her bed she pondered a moment on the fact that she had become to feel quite at home at Min's, but she knew it would be over soon. She had perused Min's calendar down in the kitchen and knew both rooms were booked for the next several weeks. Kerry realized she really needed to think about leaving soon.

There was a bond between Kerry and Min, much like the one with Mrs. Tesmer. Kerry reflected that there was no older woman in the states that could fill in the emptiness left by her mother. Back in North Carolina, their neighbor, Lucy, was someone she felt she could ask for small favors, but Lucy had grown children of her own and grandchildren she looked after. She shared a different bond with these two British women. There was an almost familial feel to their relationship.

After her peaceful, unhurried shower and with ample time for her crop of springy curls to dry—somewhat—Kerry leisurely dressed and applied makeup. Min interrupted her once when she stopped by her room with a bottle of nail polish she had *just layin' 'round*. Kerry, touched by the woman's thoughtfulness, commented on how well the color went with her new outfit.

"Coincidence, I reckon," Min smiled with that twinkle in her eyes.

At nine o'clock, Kerry hardly recognized the girl in the reflection of the room's floor-length mirror. The soft, mid-calf-length skirt accentuated her femininity—the green, apricot and soft teal pastels in the shirt set off her green eyes.

When she heard Merrek's voice downstairs Kerry checked her money belt—now adapted to wear on her thigh and completely hidden by the free flowing skirt. She grabbed her hat and had to concentrate to walk serenely down the stairs and not trip into the kitchen where Merrek waited with Min. She could do without making that kind of an entrance today.

Merrek's reaction thrilled her. His dark eyes gleamed as he gave her a full-body perusal, from her freshly washed and curling hair to her recently painted toenails left exposed by her sandals. She was so encouraged by the admiration that shone in those eyes that she twirled once, causing the skirt to float around her, and then dropped into a brief curtsey.

"Damnation, luv. Yer all stripped up."

Kerry blinked twice. "By your tone I take it that means something good?"

He smiled broadly. "Oh, aye, Kerry. 'E look…beautiful."

Min was smiling as if she had a part in the whole thing.

"Is it appropriate?" Kerry turned this time in a slow circle. "I saw it in a little shop by the library. It looks festive, doesn't it?"

"Aye, yer a vision an' 'e know it." Merrek stepped close and reached around to the back of her neck. "Hold jus' one lil' bit here, luv," he explained. "'E should probably lose the price tag." With a little tug and snap, it was gone.

"Oh, thanks! I often forget about that. Dad used to say I'm like Minnie Pearl from the Grand Ole Opry." She laughed at the lost looks on their faces. "An American country singer from back in the day whose trademark was a price tag hanging from her hat. Oh! I wonder if I forgot the one on the hat, too. Check this out," she put on the wide-brimmed straw hat and struck a pose.

"Oh," Merrek frowned slightly. "Hell."

Kerry didn't know what to make of the expression on his face. "Is something wrong with it?" She took the hat off to examine it.

But Min understood immediately. She looked at Merrek accusingly, "*The BMW?* You brought the BMW!?"

Merrek began his defense. "I didna know she was going to dress up. She told me she only 'ad jeans and things…."

"Wait," Kerry was confused. "What could possibly be wrong with a BMW?"

Merrek looked apologetic. "Tis of the two wheeler sort."

Kerry's smile froze. "*A motorcycle?*"

Min looked at Merrek as if he had just broke wind at a cotillion. "An' look how lovely she looks…oh…" she raised her arms and then let them drop to her sides, dejected.

"I…we can take the train," Merrek tried. "I was plannin' on takin' the train back tonight anyway."

Kerry considered for only a second and then made what she considered a daring decision. "What's wrong with the motorcycle? I can hitch this skirt up, tuck it in, and we're good to go."

Min looked at her as if she had two heads. "But yer beautiful hair. Arg! The tangles! And your hat…oh…"

"That's why they invented braids. And I'll just take the hat back—more cash in my pocket. I've actually never been on a motorcycle before. I think it'll be a blast. Wait just a minute while I run up and fix my hair."

⚓

Outside, Merrek handed her a helmet. Kerry began having second thoughts as she climbed aboard the bike. She put the helmet on her head, but Merrek had to help her with the strap. "You've never been on one before, aye—a motorbike?" he asked as he watched Kerry's wary eyes travel over the machinery.

"No. I've only had one other opportunity, but I passed. It was much bigger than this one, and it was so loud."

"A Harley, maybe. Well, this one's fast but not so loud. Worried?"

Kerry disregarded the question before she had time to think about it. After all, *she was braver than she believed.* "It looks like fun," she stated emphatically and smiled at him.

"It does have its advantages—one bein' it makes parkin' some easier. Conversation is difficult because of the wind and the helmets, but the upside is you'll see more of the country and enjoy this sun. Not much good for the hair and skirt, though. I'm sorry about that. I didna think. There…how does that feel?" and gave her helmet a pat on top.

"It's fine," she answered, moving her head from side to side to get accustom to the weight. "Before we take off, I guess I should mention again that I'm terribly accident prone. You should be the worried one."

He pretended to consider that seriously for a moment, but then smiled that boyish grin. "Well, I'm not accident prone and I'm drivin', so 'e just hold on and trust me to keep 'e safe." With a wink he added, "I've been told I'm a trustworthy bloke."

Kerry returned his grin. "According to Ernest Hemingway, 'The best way to know if a man is trustworthy is to trust him'."

Merrek chuckled ruefully as he straddled the bike, "And the great Sophocles warns, 'Trust dies but mistrust blossoms.' So the pressure's on, then, aye? Don't worry, luv. I don't take chances on the road." He started the engine, waited for a few seconds, and then said over his shoulder, "If 'e don't 'old on, luv, ye'll be dumped on yer bum." Kerry put her hands lightly on either side of his waist. He heaved a sigh. "'Tis plain 'e've never ridden one o' these." He took her hands in his and guided her arms all the way around his waist. "Tight," he instructed. "Tighter." When he was satisfied, they were off with a powerful jerk that prompted Kerry to squeeze even tighter.

The trip was one hour from Min's door to the center of Penzance where the booth vendors and performers were located. As Merrek had warned, words blew away with the wind, but Kerry was too absorbed with their closeness to have carried on an intelligent conversation. Under the cotton t-shirt her arms surrounded was a body as hard as oak, and she was self-consciously aware that he could feel her softness pressed against his back. It took her a while to grow accustomed to the intimacy of bike riding, but when she finally relaxed, she was able to appreciate the Cornish countryside as it whipped by.

Kerry had not expected the almost tropical scenery she saw as they sped along the coastal highway, *carriageway* rather, toward Penzance. She was surprised to see palm trees and brilliant flora until she reminded herself that the warm gulf streams caressed the beaches of Southern Cornwall. She found it as breathtaking as anything she had seen in the states.

Coming up over a rise in the road, Kerry had her first glimpse of Penzance, lazily sprawled along that southern coast. She was instantly infatuated.

⚓

Merrek parked the bike between a booth on the far end of a long line of tents and an unloaded vendor's trailer. Kerry absentmindedly thought that a rather rude invasion of another's space, but she was the foreigner here. They obviously had a different way of doing things. At any rate, it was none of her business.

They arrived just as the festival was waking up, so they did not have to fight the crowds to see or sample until closer to the noon hour when it became extremely crowded and their progress slowed significantly. There were colorful booths displaying every kind of artwork and craft imaginable, and the food was extraordinary—pasties and sweets, seafood delicacies and local produce. There were pavilions where musicians played, there was folk dancing and, of course, there was no want for beer or ale.

By mid afternoon, Kerry had oohed and aahed over quilts and jewelry, pottery and metal sculpture, paintings and photography. One booth they explored sold matted and frame-ready name prints—attractive calligraphy-written names with the name meanings underneath.

"I've seen these at festivals back home," Kerry told Merrek. "But I bet there are different names here." They were in alphabetical order so it took her no time to find Merrek. "Your name means *the moors*. Well, that's appropriate."

"How so?"

"Ruggedly appealing; beguiling," she laughed when he rolled his eyes.

"Let's see if they 'ave yours," as he flipped through the C's.

"It's K-e-r-r-y," she corrected him.

"Not Carrie, like in *The Exorcist*?" he moved to the K's. "I'm relieved. I like Kerry with a K. It suits you better."

She had to stand on tiptoe to look over his shoulder. She let out a soft gasp when his fingers came upon the name Kerenza. "Shazam," she breathed softly, and stayed his hand.

"Sh—what?"

She pulled out the plastic envelope that contained her name. "Kerry is my nickname, the shortened form of my real name," she held up the envelope for him to see.

After a quick glance at the card, his eyes searched hers. "Your name is Kerenza? You're not jostlin' me up a bit, are ya now? That's an old-time Cornish name." He pointed to the meaning. "Means love."

"That's what you called me when we first met on the street," Kerry recalled, even though she knew it was just a casual greeting in the UK. "Guess you had it right from the start."

"Kerenza Carter, then?"

"Cover me a minute." Merrek's eyebrows rose slightly as Kerry reached up under her skirt to retrieve her passport and handed it to him. "See?" She watched his face. "My dad found the name in a list of names for little girls before I was born. He loved it. Mom thought it a little much, so they compromised by calling me Kerry. But Kerenza is on my birth certificate."

"You're jus' one surprise after another, aren't ya now, Kerenza… luv?"

He smiled as he put her passport back in her hand.

"I'm going to buy this, because I may never see another one." She laid her passport on the table and once again discreetly reached under her skirt to take some cash out of her belt while Merrek grinned.

"I rather like this security system o'yers. Need any help?"

Kerry glanced up at his devilish eyes. "Careful, me boy or I'll sic the piskies on 'e."

He laughed. "Yer a quick study, aren't 'e now?"

They walked the scope of the vendor area, took in a couple of parades, and sampled both food and drink before circling back to the booth where Merrek had parked the bike. The vendor now had photography on display, and what a display it was.

Kerry forgot all about Merrek's bike rudely invading the vendor's space when her eyes fell on the most amazing photos she had seen that day. Of the other photographers, half exhibited photos of ocean and beach scenes, pictures of sail boats, sea birds, and ocean life. The other half concentrated on the Bodmin Moors, beautiful landscapes, haunting photos of primitive rock formations. Both were gorgeous, but the pictures that now captured her admiration were in a different class. In these, the photographer had encapsulated commonplace moments in the lives of Cornwall's natives. In the faces of ordinary fishermen, miners, shopkeepers and homemakers, he disclosed the worries and dreams, the fears and pride of Cornwall, all with one click of the camera shutters. The photos told the story of a land—its history and its people. Kerry knew she had to have one of the smaller prints at least, but it was a painstaking decision.

"Like'em do ya?" asked the vendor.

"They're magnificent," replied Kerry. "I'm having a hard time making up my mind, but I think I'll take this one." It was of an old man and a young child working together on a weathered wooden boat. The photographer had caught them with their hands fisted into a fishnet side by side, the tautness of their arm muscles attesting to the weight of the load, and their matching expressions alluded to determination and a fierce pride. "There are so many story possibilities in this one." She glanced at Merrek. "It will make a great creative writing prompt, as would that one and that one, too," pointing to two others. "…But I like this one the best."

"May be that'un wot took the photo will givit to ya for a kiss," smiled the vendor.

Kerry speared him with an indignant look. Was this guy hitting on her? But when she turned to follow his eyes and the tilt of his head, there was Merrek, quietly watching her.

Understanding slowly dawned. "You took these?" she asked him, and recognized the hesitant and almost vulnerable expression in his eyes. "These wonderful photos—they're your work? I thought you were a pira…err…importer and exporter."

The corners of Merrek's mouth twitched, almost as if he wanted to smile, but was afraid that might be premature. "Aye. That pays me bills. This I do on the side, with hopes o' turnin' it into a proper career soon."

Kerry's eyes swept over the exhibit. "Well you are very good. I'm serious, this is more than taking photos—this is *art*. I want to buy this one." She held the plastic wrapped photo up for the vendor, but he deferred to Merrek.

"My gift to you," Merrek smiled. "In return for your appreciation of me work and a fine time at the festival today. Most people only like the ocean photos."

"You can't get…sentiment…passion… like this from ocean photos. Will you sign it for me?"

Merrek nodded slowly, and took the photo from her. "Funny that you'd pick that'un. 'E's one of me favorites. The ol' man 'e's me granfer, who you'll meet tonight. The cheel, me oldest sister's bairn. Four generations of fishermen we are. Many more before us." After writing on the back of the photo with a nearby pen, he turned to the seller. "Thanks, Danzel. I'll check with you later on the sales and your cut. Time ta take Kerry to meet the family."

"Ouch! Good luck ta ya, darlin'," he winked at Kerry before turning to a potential buyer.

Kerry shot a quick smile his way, but her attention was on Merrek's signature. *Thanks for a brilliant time at Golowan, Kerenza…love. Yours, Merrek Walles.*

⚓

Merrek placed the wrapped photo inside his bike's saddlebag while Kerry strapped on her helmet. Satisfied with its fit, she reached between her legs and grabbed the back of her long skirt, pulled it up and tucked it into the front waistband. Once she was on the bike, she gave him a quick nod to indicate she was ready. When he did not make a move to get on, she glanced up, anticipating a problem, and caught him gazing at her exposed legs. "Why don't you just take a picture?" she teased. "You're very good at it."

That slightly devilish look she found so exciting settled on his handsome face. Wrapping his long fingers around her chinstrap, he brought her face up to meet his as he bent toward her. "Aye, well, and 'e's not the only thing I'm good at," he promised, and then laughed as the color on her face deepened several shades. He let go of her chinstrap and straightened. "I'm also a fitty biker, aye? Trustworthy. 'E ready?"

Kerry tried to follow his flippant attitude in an effort to hide the release of the breath she had been holding. "Well, you betcha, then. Giddy-up, Mister Trustworthy."

Merrek's eyebrows shot up his forehead in amusement. "Ah, now. I love it when 'e talk hillbilly to me." Chuckling softly he seated himself and just before he started the engine she wrapped her arms tightly around him. He looked over his shoulder and shot her a lecherous smile.

"Well?" she asked defensively. "I don't want to fall on my fanny."

Merrek noticeably winced, and leaning back, he spoke quietly into her ear, "Luv, the word here is bum. In Britain—fanny is another word entirely. Same general area, just…more feminine in nature."

Kerry's arms broke away from him as if a furnace had burned her. Chuckling, he caught her hands and guided her arms back around his torso, "Ye'll be alright, luv? Just tryin' ta save 'e from future boners."

Kerry blinked several times. "What did you say?" She took her arms away from him again.

"What?" His confusion was real.

"Future what? Did you say…b—boners?" she finished in a whisper.

"Boners…aye. Mistakes. Misspeaks. Gaffes, if 'e will."

She saw no contradiction in his expression. She let out a long and shaky sigh. "And I thought I wouldn't encounter language barriers here."

"Ah, shite. That's right," he couldn't keep the laughter out of his voice. "Sorry, luv. George Shaw was right when he said England and America are the two countries separated by the same language. Guess we're educatin' each other, aye?"

"Well, I would like to get off the subject of anatomy if it's all the same to you."

He laughed outright then, completely enamored with her maidenly reaction. "I thought we were talkin' vocabulary, sweetheart."

She looked away from him, exasperated. "You...*bum,*" she whispered with venom.

He laughed again, harder, realizing he had done so more in one afternoon than he had in a month. Unable to resist the urge, twisted around, curled his hand around the back of her neck, and lifted her windshield to plant a fast and firm kiss on her pouting mouth. He was still chuckling when he turned and placed his hands on the handlebars. "Ah, Kerry girl, I never knew I'd find an American girl so..."

"What," she interrupted with a huff while she tried to shake off the effect of his kiss, "unsophisticated?"

"Unspoiled," his soft answer took all the huff right out of her. "Hold on, m'sweet. We're off."

⚓

They drove along the coast to the outskirts of the city. Kerry was so glad she had insisted they take the bike. She could hide behind Merrek's back and the noise of the motor while she tried to sort things out. *How was it she had become the center of attention to this handsome, accomplished man? Was he playing a game with her?* She had never been good at games, and she never attracted self-assured men. In the end, she reminded herself that he seemed trustworthy and that she was braver than she thought, so she may as well enjoy this time with him and for once not obsess about what may or may not be.

They pulled up into the drive of the holiday home and Merrek followed it all the way to the back lawn where they met a rock sea wall. The first thing Kerry noticed was the explosion of color along the wall.

"How pretty," she exclaimed. "Just look at those flowers! When I get my own place, I'm going to plant flowers everywhere."

"In the ground or in containers?" Merrek already knew the answer.

"Everywhere!" Kerry affirmed with a smile.

The second thing she noticed was the crowd. Kerry tried to guess the number of people that sat around a readied bonfire while children of all ages ran up stone steps from the beach. They ran to the feast laid out on three folding tables and snatched handfuls of snacks to take with them back to the beach. She could see five playpens set up under two large trees that kept infants and toddlers out of harm, and there were people playing and swimming in the water. She could not believe this was all one family. They were everywhere. This was what her dad had wanted, and she felt the longing in herself as well.

Kerry dismounted the bike, fixed her skirt and took off the helmet. Already children had spotted them and came running, leaping and climbing on Merrek like puppies. He acknowledged them all with a smile and by name, kissing the cheeks of the little girls, mussing the hair of the boys.

"Merrek, over here," shouted a very comely woman standing at the door of the two-story beachside cottage.

"That's me sister Elowen," Merrek guided her toward the door. "Four a' these hellers are hers and Penn's, me brother-in-law. Elowen 'as a good heart, an' she loves me dearly. She'll be yer champion. The rest a'the bunch—tis anyone's guess wot the mood o' the day might be."

Elowen came forward carrying a large tray of pasties with both hands. She gave Kerry a welcoming smile and Merreck a quick peck on the cheek. "I'm so glad you could join us, Kerry. I just can't believe this one brought you all the way from St. Austell on that bike of his." Kerry was vaguely aware of Merrek's grimace, as she could not quite take her eyes off Elowen. She was a beautiful woman in her late twenties, black hair with red highlights, and soft, smoky eyes. Her voice was kind. "If you'd like to freshen a bit before you meet all these people, the water closet is up those stairs third door on the left. Merrek, carry this tray out an' replenish what's on the tables, luv. Also, grab Trev if ya can find the buster and have him gather the empties. 'E knows where to put'em."

Merrek looked at Kerry. "'E see why I get invited to these soirees. I'm 'ere ta do 'er biddin'."

⚓

Kerry walked down a hall toward the bathroom. The sounds of the party outside faded slightly and she was relieved to have a moment to collect her thoughts and boost her confidence. She had never been at such a function—even at school. All of these people were relatives, and she was the outsider. Searching her memory for a quote on courage, she remembered one by John A. Shedd, 'A ship is safe in harbor, but that's not what ships are for.' Determined to sail into the unfamiliar waters, she first knocked on the third door on the left.

The door was slightly ajar, so she pushed it open. A beautiful dark haired toddler just pulling up her panties startled her. "I went peepee," said the little girl proudly, pointing down into a pot.

"Why, yes you did. That's a big girl!" From down the hall, she heard a woman's voice calling Merryn. "Is your name Merryn?" Kerry asked.

The little girl nodded. "That's my mommy."

Kerry called around the bathroom door, "She's in here."

Another lovely woman who was obviously Merrek's sister came forward, hand outstretched. "You must be Kerry, Merrek's date. So nice to meet ya. I'm Genna, the second sister. Did Merryn walk in on you? She waits until the last possible minute and then just expects everyone ta move outta 'er way."

"Oh, no. Quite the opposite. I walked in on her." Kerry winked at Merryn.

Merryn smiled and pointed a chubby finger at Kerry. "Her need go peepee, Mommy?"

"Merryn, really. I'm sorry, Kerry, she…" turning to face Kerry she paused, taking in Kerry's features, "'ave we met before? 'E look familiar."

"I don't think that's possible. I've only been in Cornwall for four days, and this is my first time to Penzance. Were you at the Golowan festival today?"

"No, we went yesterday." Genna made quick work of cleaning the potty. "I guess it's unlikely then that I've seen you before," she said hesitantly, as if she wasn't buying it. "Oh, well, Merryn, let's get out of Kerry's way. So happy you could join us tonight. Elowen always throws a good gathering. 'E should have a good time."

Alone in the bathroom, Kerry unbraided her wind-tattered ponytail and shook out her wild mane. Her hair was her most magnificent feature, but it could get a little uncontrollable at times. The braid had corralled it a bit. She pinched her cheeks and pressed her lips together, turned off the bathroom light, opened the door, and came eye to eye with a young teen of about fifteen years—a younger version of Merrek.

"You must be Trev? I'm Kerry."

He surveyed her up and down—rather too thoroughly Kerry thought—and with more than a bit of insolence. "Trevelyan, actually. *By Tre, Pol, and Pen ye'll know true Cornish men*, as the sayin' goes. Well, looks like maybe me brother's not gay after all. He hasn't brought a girl around in so long I was beginnin' ta think otherwise." Before Kerry knew what he was about, he reached around and put his hand on the small of her back, leaned his head down near her ear. "If he disappoints, though, darlin', I'll be around."

Kerry was used to dealing with boys this age, and was quick to parry.

"To do what?" she shot back. "Shoot marbles? Watch Barney, the big purple dinosaur?"

She saw the familiar quirk of a smile begin in the corner of his mouth, so much like his brother. His chin went up as if accepting the terms of a gauntlet and his hand returned to his side. "Touche, luv. Lookin' forward ta seein' 'e later." He sauntered slowly down the hall and out the back door.

Elowen came out of the kitchen with a tray of fruit and cheese, chuckling at the overheard exchange. "Well, good for you, Kerry. Trev actually likes it when people give it back to 'im. 'E's such a playboy. Would you be a dear and take this out to the table for me? You'll see where the desserts are. And Trev's right, by the way. Merrek hasn't brought a girl around in years. Ma and Da are going to flip out."

"It was very thoughtful of your brother to invite me to your Golowan celebration. He's helping me out with my research of English culture."

"No, dear," the woman smiled as she shook her head. "Bringin' ya here ta meet the family isn't bein' thoughtful, it's givin' ya fair warnin'. He's offerin' ya the chance to run before he starts his pursuit o' ya. He handles personal rejection a lot better than rejection o' 'is family."

Kerry doubted Elowen's assumption, but could not help fish for information. "I doubt he's had many personal rejections. He's very charming."

"Actually," piped in Genna, taking yet another toddler to the bathroom, "the only woman he ever brought to meet the family was, like, almost three, four years ago? Mum and Da disliked 'er right off. Merrek and Leif were working hard to establish their business at that time. Money was tight. She was a bitch, always complainin' about what Merrek couldn't afford and…"

"Genna," cut in Elowen. "This is old history, and Merrek's history ta boot. You shouldn't be tellin' it."

"Ee's never told me not to talk about it with anyone else…just not with 'im," Genna argued gently. Turning back to Kerry, "Merrek and this… woman…were involved only a short time, but long enough for him to find out that while she enjoyed 'is sublime looks and gorgeous body, charming wit, and everything else that Merrek has to offer, she was also taking the fast track to success in her own job…via her boss."

Kerry's eyes widened as Genna's meaning registered. "You mean…?"

"Aye, I mean," Genna sighed. "The doxy got 'er 'ard earned position—I say 'ard earned 'cos I got a gander at the ol' bugger at a charity function once. But Merrek was done with 'er. Threw 'er and everythin' associated with 'er outta 'is London apartment, outta 'is life, closed 'is heart like a steel trap against 'er and, as far as we know, any other woman that's crossed 'is path…until you, right El?"

"Well, I don't mean ta get in Merrek's business, but 'e did look at 'e sweet like. I 'aven't seen that expression in 'is eyes—ever I'd wager. E'en with that tart."

Kerry felt as if lead had entered her veins. This was complicated—real grown-up stuff. Out of her league. "I'm…just a…friend he's helping with research. I shouldn't know all this…"

Elowen slapped Genna's arm with a tea towel. "I told 'e ta shut yer mouth, didn't I? Are 'e tryin' ta help yer brother get on with 'is life or squelch all 'is chances?" Turning to Kerry, she offered her own explanation. "It's jus' that, since that time, Merrek's been so busy pickin' up the slack around 'ere since Da's been sick and then still workin' ta grow 'is own business. If 'e's 'ad time for women it's been with a certain amount of hesitancy I'm sure. Can 'e blame 'im? But 'e are the first one he's brought for us to meet since, so yeah, I agree that pursuit is a strong possibility. Are 'e stayin' in Cornwall long?"

"I…maybe a couple more days."

Elowen and Genna exchanged a look. "More than enough time…" Genna said to her sister.

Kerry looked down at the tray in her hands, thinking that if she were true to form it would never make it to the table in one piece, especially after this conversation. It did not seem that Merrek brought casual dates to meet his family, so for what purpose was this visit? Most likely just a convenience of timing. What would Merrek see in her that would be worth pursuing anyway? She was no match for the beauty in this family, and she was a klutz—an American klutz at that, a fact she was sure was not in her favor. She was confident before the night was over they would put aside this crazy idea.

But sometimes the way he looked at her? Not to mention those two kisses the night before…she looked back up at the two women who were already blatantly evaluating her and promised herself this tray was going to be delivered in pristine condition if only to keep her own pride intact. She remembered Maltz's words, 'Man maintains his balance, poise and sense of security only as he is moving forward.'

Kerry slowly began to make her way down the back stairs balancing the tray in both hands. If she caught a sandal on the steps, it was all over. Once she had successfully negotiated the steps, she still had several feet to traverse among crowds of adults and children before she reached her goal. When she finally set the tray down without mishap, she could not prevent the triumphant smile from spreading over her face while she turned in search of Merrek. She spotted him waving her over to where some elderly people were sitting around the beginnings of the fire, sipping mugs filled with amber ale. She hesitated while her gleeful expression turned to one of panic, but when Merrek smiled encouragingly at her, she hurried over before she lost her nerve.

"Ma, Da," he took her hand when she came within reach. "This is Kerry Carter. She's a schoolteacher from the States, and a genealogist. Seems her roots are here in Cornwall. In fact, Kerry is actually short for Kerenza—can't get much more Cornish than that. Kerry, these are me parents, grandparents and an assortment of aunts, uncles, and cousins. I'd introduce them but it seems unlikely you'd remember all the names. We'll let it just happen naturally as the evenin' goes."

Kerry smiled and nodded at all the faces.

"Kerry, is it?" Mrs. Walles leaned up from her chair to take Kerry's hand. "I didn't know Merrek was seeing anyone," she turned to her husband. "Did Merrek say anything to you?"

"Not a peep, and I don't know why 'e would be tightlipped 'bout 'er. Most young men would be braggin' ta snag such a pretty little thing…"

His wife nearly shouted his name in horror, then her eyes rolled back in her head and an exasperated sigh escaped her.

Mr. Walles defended himself. "I said *snag*, I did, old woman. Ya need to get some bloody 'earing aids, damn it, or get yer mind outta the gutter."

Laughter erupted among the crowd, and Mrs. Walles looked at Kerry apologetically. "Welcome, Kerry. Please forgive us. We tend to overwhelm."

Kerry quickly attempted to alleviate the woman's concern. "Oh, don't worry. Anyway, we only met a couple of days ago, so I doubt he would have…" and a new wave of laughter began, "…would have mentioned…" her stammered response revealed her confusion.

Merrek put his arm around Kerry's shoulder and turned her away from the group. "Thanks, dear family," he slung only half teasingly over his shoulder. "'E can't say I didna warn ya," he confided to Kerry.

"What was so funny to them?"

"Who knows?"

Kerry looked at him, and he read in her eyes the accusation that he was not clueless. "Well…" he admitted, "are 'e familiar with the British term *shag*"?

Kerry thought back over the conversation and Merrek chuckled as her cheeks pinkened. "Oh. No wonder your mother looked mortified. I mean…we only just met after all."

Merrek searched her face, and finding no pretense there, he smiled broadly. "Kerry, m'luv, 'e are a breath o' fresh air." He took her hand as they approached the food-laden tables.

"I met Genna and Trev. Where are your other sisters?"

"You met Trev? How was that?"

"Oh, he's a handsome boy. And knows it. But does he realize he's about fifteen years younger than you?"

Merrek looked up from the buffet with a stern scowl. "Did 'e make a pass? Where is that bleddy…"

"It's okay. I think we have an understanding."

"Aye, well, Trev has a distorted understandin' when it comes to manners and decorum. 'E'll let me know if I need to bobber 'is mouth."

"Oh, I don't think it would come to that. Surely he shares some of your charm."

Merrek gave her a skeptical look, and then glanced around for two available chairs. "Well, you might as well meet the rest of 'em."

Kerry followed him to two empty lawn chairs in a group of young people. There he introduced her to the two infamous younger sisters, Rosen and Lowenna. They were even more beautiful than the older two. They had dark hair like Merrek's, but with striking blue eyes. She could imagine the wolves they attracted.

"You're from the States?" Rosen, the younger one, asked with enthusiasm, her blue eyes sparkling. "North Carolina? I love Chris Daughtry. Do you know him?" Merrek rolled his eyes.

"No," Kerry acted as if it were a sensible question. "I'm sorry. I know who he is from American Idol and I like his music, too, but no, we've never crossed paths."

"Oh," Rosen looked deflated and lost interest in Kerry immediately, turning to an enamored eyed young man, probably a cousin—distant Kerry hoped—prompted by the depth of adoration on the boy's face.

The other beauty sat quietly, eyeing her suspiciously, "Where do I know you from?" she asked accusingly. "Where did you meet my brother?"

Merrek slammed his fork in his plate. "Could 'e please show some hospitality? 'E sound like yer already on the attack and 'e've just met."

"I've seen 'er before, I tell 'e. She's may been stalkin' 'e, ya know? But, of course, it's okay for 'e ta be chased by a skirt, but 'e'd better not ever catch me on a chase?" She turned back to Kerry. "Are 'e one of those bad girls, Kerry? One what me brother keeps telllin' me are loose? Easy? 'E doesn't want me ta be perceived that way, but is that why he likes you?"

"Enough," Merrek said tightly, softly, stabbing her with a threatening stare.

Nevertheless, on she marched. "Seems me brother 'as two sets of standards. 'E stays on me arse about being careful with boys, but then I guess 'e should know what's on their minds. I think 'e'd better be careful, too, Kerry, unless of course, yer the wicked one."

Merrek stood, dragging his sister up with him, his hand around her upper arm. "'E will not embarrass the family by making our guests uncomfortable," he said quietly near her ear. "And 'e'll not talk to Kerry as if she were yer equal. She's a teacher, for Christ's sake. Understood?"

Kerry watched the anger in Lowenna's eyes turn to quieted respect "Understood," she said compliantly. Merrek released her and sat back down to his dinner. Lowenna's eyes slowly traveled back to Kerry. "But I *know* I've seen 'e before."

Merrek had just bitten into a meat pastie, and before he could choke it down to reprimand his sister again, Kerry cut in, "Actually, your sister Genna said the same thing. I must have one of those faces. They say everyone has a double somewhere."

"Maybe, but..." Lowenna's eyes narrowed.

Trev broke the conversation by stepping in with a camera, which he handed to Merrek. "'Ere ye go. Ma says to take some pictures for the scrapbook." Then he bent down and put his arm around Kerry's shoulders, his hand hanging precariously close to Kerry's chest. "Take one 'a me and Kerry 'ere?" At Merrek's hot, warning glance, Trev laughed and stood. "Want me ta refill your ale there, Kerry?"

"Yes, thank you, Trev."

"What are brothers for?" he said with a wink at Merrek.

"Let's go for a swim before it gets too dark," said Rosen, pulling her t-shirt over her head, revealing a hot pink halter top. "Kerry, 'e want to swim? I'm sure between all of us we have a swimsuit 'e could wear."

Kerry looked toward the sea and off into the distance. Was that lightening she saw on the horizon? She felt the familiar knots beginning to form in her stomach. "No, no. Thanks, but I haven't finished eating yet."

Merrek tapped her foot with his. "When 'e're finished, go ahead if 'e'd like. I've got to walk around and take pictures."

"No, really. I'm fine."

"The water feels good this time o' year," offered Rosen. "'E can swim, can't 'e?"

"Not...well."

"Oh," this from Lowenna. "Well, then..."

The girls looked at her and then at Merrek. Kerry did not miss their eye-rolls as they turned and headed for the beach. "I really don't like to get in the ocean," she said more to herself than to him as she lowered her half-eaten plate to the ground.

Trev had just come back with Kerry's beer and overheard her comment. "Well 'e and Merrek are a match made in 'eaven, then."

Kerry eyes snapped back to Merrek's. "You're afraid of the ocean, too?"

Merrek threw a wadded up napkin at Trev's face. "Not afraid. Damn, I've fished out there most o' me life. I'm just not an enormous fan. The sea is fickle, can change in a heartbeat. I don't do well with fickle."

"So, Kerry, luv," teased Trev. "'E and I will jus' have to be careful. We've been warned." They could hear his laughter as he sauntered away.

Merrek moved so that he could peer closely at Kerry's face. "So which is it, luv? Dislike or fear?"

Kerry sighed with embarrassment. "I've...tried. But I tend to panic. It's just not worth it."

He took her hand in his, circled his thumb in her palm. "'Tis fine, luv. Swimmin's not a part o' the Golowan celebration." She smiled at him in thanks. He smiled back, filing this information in his mind to discuss later.

As sunset approached and the temperature dropped, the swimmers came out of the water and disappeared into the house for a quick shower and change of clothes. The young ones settled down with popcorn, hot cocoa and a movie inside with young teens watching over them. Outside, the men threw more wood on the fire as the evening grew darker and cooler. The ale and whiskey began to mellow the crowd and Kerry began to relax and socialize easier as Merrek walked around taking pictures. She could imagine how great those photos were going to look in the family album. Remembering those few of her own family—staged pictures of only four people—Kerry wondered if this group knew how lucky they were.

Someone turned on some lively music, which flowed through booming speakers. A cheer went up and dancing quickly followed suit. With his eyes on hers, Merrek set the camera down and Kerry read his intent.

As he approached her, she put up her hand in resistance. "I can't really. I'm not much of a dancer. No, really. I'm embarrassed of my lack of coordination."

Rosen saw Kerry's refusal and came forward, hands outstretched. "Dance with me, brother. Kerry?"

Merrek looked to her questioningly, and Kerry answered, "Please, yes, go ahead—dance with your sister."

Kerry was not expecting the show they put on, but apparently everyone else was because the group backed away to form a circle. Trev and Lowenna joined Merrek and Rosen. They were amazing to watch. Kerry had never seen such rhythm and precision. The two girls swapped partners several times without a break in the fluidity, their movements sharp, sexy, and full of attitude as the colorful dresses they had donned swirled and snapped. Trev was also wonderful, but Merrek held her attention. His moves were like liquid strength and sensuality. His timing and agility mesmerized her as he sometimes lifted, sometimes lowered his partner in his arms. Kerry watched with longing, but her dancing history was not a pretty one. Merrek glanced at her more than once, and must have read her thoughts. She colored profusely at the intent she saw in his eyes.

Following the enthusiastic applause at the end of the dance, the next song in the set was slow and romantic. Merrek left his sisters among a throng of dance partners and walked toward Kerry, crooking his finger for to her to join him. Kerry argued, "No, really, I'll step all over you. I have no grace—no sense of rhythm."

"Maybe 'e just never had a fitty partner," he smiled as he pulled her with him into the outskirts of the dancing area. He put one hand on the small of her back and the other cradled her hand. They moved a bit awkwardly at first until Merrek pulled her close. "'E can't see yer feet now," he explained. "Look at me."

Craning her head back so she could see his face she asked, "Where did you learn to dance like that? It was breathtaking."

He smiled down at her, flattered. "As the older brother of four sisters, I've had quite a bit o' practice, jus' playin' around, experimentin'. Trev's the one ta watch, though. Didn't 'e ever dance wi' yer brother?"

"No, never. He left for college when I was eleven. I never thought about dancing with boys then. They still had cooties...especially my brother." She stepped on his foot, gasped in embarrassment, and apologized as she pushed away from him.

Merrek pulled her back against his chest and brought their linked hands closer in. "Relax, Kerry," he coaxed as he dipped his head close to hers. "I'm fair certain I 'ave none of these…cooties?" She could hear the smile in his voice. After another four beats, he added, "Problem is, luv, 'e're tryin' ta lead."

"I know," Kerry sighed with exasperation. "I can't seem to help myself."

"'Tis a simple matter o' trust. Give yerself over ta me. Don't resist." He smiled at the wariness he saw in her expression. "I'm still trustworthy, aye?"

"Did you do much dancing in London?" Kerry could not believe she asked that. She saw the guarded look steal across his face and his features hardened. She wanted to take it back but it was blatantly out there.

"Me sisters been talkin' to 'e, aye?" She did not need to answer. The girl should never play poker with those adorably readable eyes. "They do a different dance in London," his eyes softened. "I didna like it."

His arm snaked further around her and she could feel his hand splay at her lower back, pressing her closer. He began to hum the song's melody next to her ear, his voice deep and resonating. His warm breath caused tendrils of her hair to stir and tickle her neck. The cool dampness of the evening had her unconsciously seeking his heat until she lost all focus except how amazing it felt to be in his arms and how their slow, easy movements gave her sensations of gracefulness. She never once thought about what her feet were supposed to do, or about losing the rhythm of the music. Her body simply glided with his, step for step, turn for turn. He was so completely in control of the dance that she thought her body might flow along with his even if he wasn't touching her at all.

Merrek knew the moment she began to enjoy the dance. He felt her tension slowly ebb, leaving her soft and pliant and moveable. He could not help but notice how nicely her body fit with his, how good she felt in his arms, and how sweetly she followed his lead. He gave up some resistance of his own and ran his lips across her temple, down the side of her face and across her jaw. To his delight, he felt her knees buckle ever so slightly, and so to compensate, he pulled her closer still.

She looked up at him just in time for his lips to capture hers. He groaned softly and she was sure she felt his knees wobble a bit.

As the end of the song drew near, Merrek slowly dipped her, arching her back over his arm. Her head fell back, and he thrilled the suddenly interested crowd by barely skimming his parted lips down her exposed throat before raising her up to face him, and then twirled her once as the song ended. Amid the unexpected burst of applause, Kerry looked up into his dark, glimmering eyes, and felt the blood rush to her face. He made her feel…pretty.

Merrek bowed and kissed her hands that he held in both of his. "Thank 'e for the dance, Kerenza girl. 'E dance some fine."

"That was so…much fun," her smile was brilliant, her eyes full of pure joy, her voice breathless.

He could not take his eyes off her, and it made him deliriously happy to know he had been the one to give her that experience, the one who was responsible for that look on her face.

The long whine of an electric guitar followed by a rumble of drumbeats broke the mood, and Merrek quietly cursed the acting DJ while he slowly and reluctantly slid his hands from hers. "I've got to go get the camera before someone sits on it," he said. "Bring me a beer?"

"Sure," she nodded. When she reached the keg, Elowen and Genna were there, both smiling knowingly.

"Well, what did we tell ya?" Genna turned to Elowen. "I'd say the pursuit has begun. And from the look o' yer radiant face, I'd say it was goin' well."

Elowen scowled gently at Genna. "Don't go embarrassin' the cheel, Gen. 'E can save that for our dear brother. Tell us, Kerry, what 'ave 'e found out about your ancestry 'ere in Cornwall?"

⚓

Merrek picked up the camera and snapped several pictures of his sisters and Kerry together at the keg, then examined them, zooming in on Kerry. He shook his head in amazement. Four days ago he had been focused, business driven, and did not even realize he was lonely. Since meeting Kerry he had difficulty concentrating during meetings, had to read contracts over three and sometimes four times, and stayed awake way into the night thinking of her smiles, the sincerity in those green, green eyes. Moreover, when he thought of her going back to America and not seeing her again, the loneliness broadsided him. He shook his head again to clear it. One just never knew how a chance meeting could change one's life.

⚓

Standing in line at the keg, Kerry enjoyed a brief conversation about her genealogy research. Elowen shared Kerry's enthusiasm about Porth. "I've seen pictures—it's a very pretty quaint village built into the walls—

like Porthoe. You'll like it very much."

Noticing Kerry's slight shiver she asked kindly, "Would you like to borrow a sweater? It is getting cooler all of a sudden. Surely, Merrek's not taking you home on that bike. He's hasn't been hitting the ale as heavily as usual, I've noticed, but still…"

"Oh, no. I'm fine. It's just the cold beer. And we're taking the train. I gathered he's staying overnight with Gorron and then returning tomorrow morning. It seems silly for him to have to make the round trip though—I could just go back myself."

"Oh, that's not going to happen, I can assure you. I know Merrek. He's got those protective eyes on you as we speak."

Kerry turned her head to see Merrek lowering himself into his vacated lawn chair, the camera strap draped around his neck, his eyes indeed watching her. She filled their mugs, thanked Elowen for her hospitality, and made her way through the crowd. Almost there, she stumbled on… something. She caught herself, but spilled half of the beer. Trev was there to witness her clumsiness. "Got a case of the headlighters, I see."

"What?" Kerry did not catch herself before dipping her head to inspect the front of her shirt. Trev had already walked past her and missed it, but she heard Merrek's sudden burst of laughter. Put out, she jerked her head up to face him.

Merrek saw the embarrassment in her face and shook his head, held up his hands in defense. "Trev meant you must be light-headed from the ale, that's all. That phrase evidently means something entirely different back in Wilmington, North Carolina," he chuckled.

Disgruntled, Kerry handed Merrek what was left of his beer, helped herself to a knitted shawl someone had left nearby, and stepped up onto the rock wall that faced the sea. She wrapped the throw around her shoulders and over her chest and watched the moonlight riding the incoming tide while searching for the signs of the lightening she had seen earlier. There was nothing there. Perhaps it had been the lights from a boat.

"Kerry?" Merrek called from his chair. She ignored him. "Come on, don't be mazed at me, luv. *Kerenza*."

She forgot whatever retort was on the tip of her tongue because when she turned into the wind to face him, he was ready with the camera. The flash caught her by surprise, but not before Merrek captured the glint of challenge in eyes that glittered like gemstones. "Ah, that's a good one," he said with satisfaction. "Aye, this is a definite keeper. Come see," he motioned to Kerry.

She grudgingly stepped down from the wall and stood to look over his shoulder. She almost did not recognize herself. The girl standing on the wall was *striking*—not beautiful like Merrek's dark haired sisters, but stunning just the same. The wind had blown against her skirt, plastering it against her legs and thighs, and her wild flamecolored hair was flying untamed around her head. Nevertheless, the eyes were the definite focal point. They were spitfire green.

"Let's see," Rosen and Lowenna, breathing heavily from dancing, crowded Kerry out to peer over their brother's shoulder. Rosen agreed it was a great picture, but Lowenna gasped and covered her mouth with her hands. "Jesus, Merrek, I knew I'd seen her before."

Before Merrek or Kerry could respond, Lowenna called to her sister across the lawn, "Genna! Come look at this."

Genna hurried over and took the camera from Merrek. She stared at the photo for a few seconds and then recognition dawned on her face. Looking up at Lowenna all she could say was, "Oh, my God." She even crossed herself as if to ward off bad spirits. Kerry began to feel she had somehow made the worse social faux pas of her life.

Merrek was getting angry at their reaction and Genna was quick to act. "Don't move..." she insisted, "...until I show you something. Lowenna, start explaining."

Merrek reached around and grabbed Kerry's hand, guiding her around his chair and into his lap. Kerry was too intrigued with the sisters' reaction to question the intimacy. Both of them looked at Lowenna expectantly.

"Last fall, Genna and I were helping clean out Granfer's attic, sorting out the things he wanted to give this one and that one when he dies. A morbid chore, that, aye? But we came across an old, old paintin'—of a woman on a sea wall. Kerry, I think...well obviously Genna and I both think you are the spittin' image of the woman in that paintin'. I couldn't place it before, where I knew you from, but with you in that wind, with your long skirt and the shawl wrapped around you, your hair...just wait. You'll see. Granfer said the painting had been in the family for over two hundred years. He told Genna to get it out of the attic and to an art conservator. So she has it right here, right now, to take to a studio in Penzance this week. How incredible is that?"

Genna called them to come to the house. "It's rather heavy, I don't want to bring it out, but you've got to see this."

As they approached, she turned the painting around for them.

There was no mistake.

Kerry and the girl in the painting could have been sisters. They shared the same clear green eyes laced with defiance, the same wildly curling red hair, and the facial features were too similar for coincidence.

Merrek looked several times between Kerry and the painting. "There's a resemblance even now, but this shot I got, those eyes—that's what makes it so indisputable. That fire comin' out of 'em." Staring at Kerry he asked only half jokingly, "Who are you?"

"Exactly what I asked before," chimed in Lowenna. "Why do we 'ave a paintin' that looks exactly like 'er? A two-hundred-year-old paintin', no less?" She turned to Kerry. "Have ya come back from the grave ta seduce me brother, Kerry?"

Trev had joined the group just outside the house in time to hear what was going on. "Let me see that picture you took," he said to Merrek. Looking back and forth between the painting and the photograph, he asked, "Am I the only one seein' the obvious 'ere? The marvel isn't only that the girls look alike, but also that Merrek photographed Kerry exactly the way the painter captured this woman. Similar clothing style, same pose caught in the wind with the sea as the backdrop. Maybe it's also Merrek what's come back from the grave. Recreatin' a masterpiece in modern media. Didde think of that? All that's missin' is that pendant this woman is wearin'. Looks like a peridot."

"My birthstone..." breathed Kerry.

For several seconds no one spoke, everyone's eyes riveted on the painting. Then Lowenna took action. "I'm going to go out and ask grandfer where in the world this painting came from—if anyone knows who she is. This is some spookiness, this is."

Kerry was speechless. It was spooky, and she needed to have some solitude to make sense of the whole thing. She began to long for the soft, billowy bedcovers at Min's B&B where she could get warm and not think about anything until she recovered not only from all the beer and excitement of the day, but also from this added shock.

Merrek pulled her to him and brushed her hair away from her face with a gentle hand. "A lot to take in one day, luv?"

"Yeah," she said, unable to control the shiver that had taken control of her. "It's been fun, but it has been a long day. Would it be rude to leave?"

"Not at all. I'll take 'e back ta Min's now." He turned to Genna. "Tell Elowen we had a good time and thanks. Tell Ma I'll be home in the mornin'. I'm takin' Kerry back to St. Austell."

"Oh, but don't ya want to wait and hear what Da and Granfer have to say?" Genna looked back and forth between her brother and Kerry.

Merrek sighed loudly. "Genna, Kerry's tired and chilled. Got a sweater or jacket I can take for her? She's shiverin' like a leaf." Genna grabbed a heavy sweater from the hooks by the door. "Thanks, Gen," Merrek said softly as he wrapped the sweater around Kerry's shoulders. "I'll talk to 'e later."

Before anyone besides Genna knew they were leaving, Merrek and Kerry were speeding along the road to the train station. Kerry was quiet, and Merrek's mind was running in opposing directions. He had felt familiarity from the moment he had met Kerry, but he had never seen that painting. How could he know her? There was simply no way. They had lived an ocean apart until the day they met. It was all very odd and somewhat...spooky, as Lowenna had said.

When they arrived at the station, Merrek chained his bike to a stand and then walked Kerry inside and bought the tickets back to St. Austell.

There were only a few people on the late train. Kerry and Merrek had almost the whole car to themselves. Merrek offered Kerry to snuggle against him for warmth and she could not resist. They were each lost in their own thoughts, and after a while, his heat and the rocking motion of the train soon lulled Kerry to sleep.

She wasn't asleep very long before a soft grumbling noise woke her. Checking out her surroundings, she saw that the train car had emptied and they had it to themselves. Merrek had moved his legs to stretch out across the double seat, Kerry's tucked beside them. He held her securely against him, her back against his chest and her head beneath his chin. He was also asleep, snoring softly. She did not move, completely contented to be wrapped in his warmth and strength. She drifted back to sleep as the rumble of the rails filled her ears and the lights along the way flashed by outside the window.

⚓

She heard the thunder roll and the lightning flashed through her closed eyelids. She felt the familiar panic began to rise from her core and spread to her extremities. She held her breath, realizing she did not know where she was and the fear moved in to control her. Her body jerked, and it was then that she realized she was not alone. His strong arms tightened around her reassuringly and he kissed her temple. She immediately calmed, listened to him breathe and knew it would be all right. He would keep her safe.

She turned in his arms, still half asleep, and reached up to caress the stubble on his cheek and around to the back of his neck. He shifted her as he lowered his head and found her mouth with his. She felt his hand move over her hip and down her leg as he deepened the kiss. Dipping under her skirt, his hand followed the bare skin up her calf and slid past the back of her knee, sending shivers of pleasure all over her. Just before his hand reached her thigh, she woke completely with a start...

"Oh! Oh, no!" Kerry leaped out of Merrek's arms and bolted into the opposite seat.

"Damnation." Merrek swore in frustration, swung his long legs to the floor and sat up. Sleep and confusion gathered in his clouded eyes. "I'm sorry, Kerry, but 'e can't start something like that and think I can just ignore it." His breath hitched when Kerry snatched her skirt up to her thighs. "Bloody hell, Kerry," he raked a hand through his hair and took a quick look around the train car. "As much as I'd love t' accommodate ya, darlin, this is a public system and even in Cornwall we have laws..."

"Oh, hush, Merrek. Just hush!" Her hands were on her money belt. "My passport! I left my passport at the Golowan Festival—at that name booth. I know you gave it back to me but I laid it down on the table to pay and I didn't put it back. Oh, God...I'm such a dimwit." She jerked her skirt back down and demurely tucked it around her legs and faced him with panicked green eyes. "I have to go to the American Embassy. You think there's a train to London that leaves tonight?"

Merrek's eyes narrowed on his otherwise placid face while his hand dipped inside his shirt pocket. "You mean this passport, luv, the one I picked up where 'e so carelessly left it?" He dangled it in front of her, laughed as her expression changed from panic to relief and then murderous. She lunged at him and tried to grab the passport but he moved it over his head just beyond her reach. "Forgot about it meself until jus' now. 'E's been in my pocket all this time." Smiling wickedly, he wrapped his free arm around her waist and pulled her down on his chest. "'E really need ta keep up with yer passport, sweetheart." Kerry renewed her efforts to snatch her passport from him, knowing he was enjoying this too much by the mirth shining in his eyes. "'E owe me now, don't 'e think? Enough to continue that mind-blowin' kiss you started?"

Kerry stopped scrambling for the passport and searched his face. "I didn't really start that, did I?" She scrambled off his lap and sat opposite him once again. "That's so not like me. I was dreaming," she remembered. "It was storming but you were holding me and I felt so safe. And it just seemed natural to…I mean I felt comfortable with…what is wrong with me? We just met and I'm scandalously taking liberties with a man I hardly know."

Merrek tried to tease her out of her panic. "Well, I've been told I'm some irresistible…so…" he smiled when his words got the reaction he intended. She now looked more exasperated than humiliated, rolling her eyes at his arrogant attitude. With a quick chuckle, he held out her passport, which she quickly grabbed and returned to the money belt on her thigh. While he watched the inadvertent enticing display, he remembered her words and was inordinately pleased that her unconscious mind had trusted him, had known he would protect her. But tease her he would. "As to yer taking liberties, luv," he smiled as he leaned back in his seat, his arms stretched across the back, "I'm at your disposal."

Kerry's lips quirked as the blush that was ever so quick to appear stained her cheeks. "You're dangerous," she stated quietly.

On cue, Merrek's eyes turned dark and penetrating. "'E're captivatin'," he drawled, and watched her eyes grow wide and thought he could probably warm his hands to the fire on her face.

After a long moment, Kerry spoke quietly, "Don't you find it weird— what we found at your sister's party?"

Merrek looked out of the train window and saw the St. Austell station approaching. He turned back to Kerry, all his teasing set aside. "It was intriguin', curious—some fascinatin' even." His move to sit next to her was quick and fluid and his arms as they went around her were warm and reassuring. "But what's not weird is the fact that I've enjoyed gettin' to know 'e, Kerry. I've had fun for the first time in a long while." He turned her so that they faced each other. "And I want ta see 'e again. Cultural experiences and genealogy be damned. I want to see you again."

⚓

Min was still up when they arrived at the B&B. She met them in the hallway to the kitchen, all aflutter. "So, 'ow was your day? What did ya think about Golowan? So much ta see and do, especially in just one day! 'Ow was the family?"

When she took a breath Merrek cut in with a tired voice. "The festival was great. The family? Trev was his usual insolent self, wasted no time in makin' passes at Kerry. Me sisters have Kerry suspectin' she may be a ghost from the dark past, or believin' I'm some reincarnated starvin' artist, and Lowenna actually accused Kerry of havin' dishonorable intentions for me. The usual bloody mess. The food was quite good, though."

Min shook her head back and forth during his account. She looked at Kerry, her round face scrunched in apology. "What about an oggie and a cup of tea? A little whiskey maybe?"

"Oh, it was a fine evening, Merrek," argued Kerry. "I thought it was fascinating—all those people, old and young all together. Min, you belong to a wonderful family. I wish you could have come tonight. The crowd was so…alive with conversation and laughter, the food was excellent and plentiful. All the little cousins running around playing together, there was…dancing…" Her eyes met his and she felt her face go hot. "It was actually all quite wonderful, it really was. But I am exhausted, and I have a trip to make tomorrow, so…thank you for a very nice time, Merrek. I do enjoy spending time with you."

Merrek had been stuffing an oggie into his mouth. He choked, coughed, and then interrogated. "A trip? Tomorrow? Where are you going?"

"I told you—I'm going to Porth."

Min's face crumpled and a small sound of distress escaped her. Merrek wasn't nearly so quiet. His voice sounded thunderous in the small room. "Porth? Again this with Porth? Kerry, 'tis not the safest place in Cornwall." Min was nodding her head in agreement.

"Your sister Elowen said it was a quaint little village built…"

"…Elowen is a sheltered mother of four who likes to look at travel magazines. Porth is picturesque no doubt, but 'tis also a drunken fishin' village fulla rough men who see nothin' new for years. You'd be a curious interest, if ye follow me meanin'. I've worked in these places, Kerry. I know what I'm talkin' about. If yer the trouble magnet 'e say 'e are, you'll be sure to attract some in a place like Porth."

Kerry flashed him a look of determination. "But I have to go. I may find something about my family in Porth." She heaved a heavy sigh at his unrelenting glare, "If it makes you feel better, in preparation for this trip I took a course in self-defense. My instructor said I was lethal."

"Lethal?" Merrek almost laughed.

"That's what he said," and to punctuate that statement she punched Merrek in the arm, "lethal." She began to bounce back and forth like a boxer with her fists at the ready.

But it didn't get the chuckle out of Merrek she was going for. His scowl returned even hotter than before as he watched her. "What was this instructor's name? Jean Claude Mauviette or some such?"

Kerry bounced into a basket of onions sitting on the floor nearby, sending several rolling in all directions. Casting Min an apologetic glance she turned on Merrek. "You just crack yourself up, don't you? I took French in college. I know mauviette means wimp, and he was not a wimp. He was very fit and a good instructor. He taught me how to defend myself."

"That so?" Merrek's eyes glinted. "Alright then, let's see what ye've got."

Before Kerry realized what he was about, Merrek took two long strides toward her, grabbed her arms and shoved her against Min's pantry door. He placed both her hands over her head and held them there with one of his. She struggled with all her might to free herself, tried to put into play the moves she had learned in class.

Moving swiftly to the side, Merrek caught her knee on its way up, pushed it back against the door and twisted so that he pinned her with his hip. Much to Min's horror, he reached up under Kerry's skirt with his free hand, and deftly unbuckled the money belt that held her passport, credit cards, and a hundred British pounds, and threw it onto the table behind him. Min was beside herself, not knowing what to do other than move her oggies out of the way.

"How long did that take me?" Merrek asked, his velvety voice gone hard, his face so close to hers that it seemed his dark, ominous eyes filled her entire world. "Ten seconds? Maybe less? And all I took were your things." Without backing out of her face, he took her hands in both of his and held them against the wall on either side of her head, her body still trapped by his. "If I was that man, Kerry, in less than five minutes I could take..." his eyes dipped to the neckline of her shirt and then came back to hers, hot and intense, "...whatever I wanted...even your life." As realization dawned on her face, he loosened his hold slightly. "Now, I've no claim on 'e that would allow me ta make demands, but I am pleadin' with 'e as someone who cares. Understand when a thing's not about freedom or self-reliance or bravery, but is just plain stupid." He watched her eyes as offense fought with determination and found himself promising her, "I'll take 'e t' Porth, luv. 'Ye'll have to wait a few days, a week at the outside, but I'll take 'e. Ye'll be safe with me. Will 'e do that?"

Kerry tore her eyes away from his and peeked around him to Min who was nodding in hopeful agreement. She nodded her head slightly, "Okay,

I'll wait," she said softly.

"Aye?"

She stole a glance at his face. He had that look in his eyes again that brooked no argument or compromise. Kerry's temper rose, but she knew he was right. "Yes, I'll wait for you," she answered tightly.

Satisfied, his hands released her, but his eyes still held hers until he was sure of the promise in them. Then, still tense, he turned to Min. "Sorry, Min, but I'm glad you were here ta back me. Thanks for waitin' up. Great oggies tonight." He wrapped one in a napkin, stuffed it in his pocket for the walk to Gorron's, and looked back at Kerry. He felt contrite when he took in her confused and defeated expression. His chest tightened as he recognized the hint of fear in her eyes when they reluctantly met his. Knowing that he was responsible for that wary stare, he could not bring himself to leave her just yet. "Walk me to the door, then?" He took her hand and pulled her along with him. "Good night, Min."

At the door, Merrek turned off the porch light, drew Kerry outside and shut the door. "Ah, Kerry…did I hurt you at all? I was just tryin' to make 'e understand, luv, not scare the wits outta 'e."

"No…no. You didn't hurt me. But you made one thing very clear. I should ask for my money back from ol' Jean Claude."

Lord, how easily she could make him smile. "I jus' caught 'e off yer guard, darlin', which is realistic, not like in class where 'e're expectin' it. Surprise is the deadliest weapon." He studied her for a moment. She was of a smaller build than all his sisters, and no one had prepped her as he had them. He had made sure his sisters knew how to be alert. He had taught them a street kind of self-defense. Lowenna and Rosen might be unwise in their wench-like ways, but heaven help the man whose attentions were not acceptable. Except for some gymnastics she had learned from Jean Claude, Kerry was defenseless. What kind of brother was this Owen?

"I…I had no idea…your strength…I was helpless."

"Aye, so. And I was trying not to hurt ya. Truthfully, Kerry, some men little older than Trev are made more o' strength than heart. And fists?" He placed a hand on each side of her head, held her gently in place while his eyes traveled over her. "Oh, my God, Kerry, I don't even want to think about what a man's fist could do to your bonny face." He kissed her forehead, and then lost his intention to leave it at that when she tilted her head back and he fell into her trusting eyes. He could not resist brushing his lips lightly over hers, and then along her jaw to the soft and fragrant skin of her neck. He lifted his head with a slowly indrawn breath, her scent causing havoc in his brain and elsewhere.

Kerry shivered as she felt the fingers of his large hand curl around her neck and his other splay at her back, pulling her close against his chest. "Ol' Jean Claude was right about one thing, darlin'," he breathed close to her ear. "'E are some lethal." He settled his mouth lightly on hers, nibbling and nipping, trying to tease her into a response. When the fragments of scattered thoughts finally began to come back together in Kerry's mind, she pushed back from Merrek's kiss and searched his eyes for clues of his intent while he gazed at her expectantly. "Somethin' wrong, luv?"

Surprising herself with her bluntness, Kerry asked, "Are you pursuing me?"

At first his eyes widened in surprise, and then he smiled, slow and lazy. "Me sisters 'ave been speculatin', aye? And if I am?"

Kerry kept her hands braced against his chest. "You know, back home in North Carolina, foxes pursue turkeys—mountain lions pursue wild boar. It doesn't usually end well for the pursued."

Merrek let out a long sigh, brushed a wisp of hair out of her face, his dark eyes shining affectionately. "And 'e know, darlin', treasures are also pursued...and then cherished and protected. I'm not your mountain lion out to hurt 'ee, Kerry. I'm just...so...damn...smitten." His mouth took possession of hers again, this time demanding a response.

And, God help her, she gave it to him. Her hands moved up his chest and found their way up around his neck and into the hair that curled at his nape. She stood on tiptoes to press her body more solidly against him and, letting instinct guide her, opened her mouth in invitation. The force of Kerry's formerly untapped passion suddenly surfaced, and its potency caught Merrek by surprise. Kerry felt the tremor that traveled through his body and felt her first thrill of sensual power.

With a sharp intake of breath, Merrek gently but firmly pushed her away from him and held her at arm's length while his dark eyes, smoldering with desire, searched the bemused green depths of hers. "Jesus, luv, wantin' trouble ta find you right here on Min's front porch?" Had he realized the affect his words would have on her he would never have uttered them, but it was too late. Kerry's earlier triumph hit a brick wall and crumbled into mortification.

"I'm sorry—I'm so sorry," she stammered, her eyes pained with shame. "God, I can't even do this right..."

Merrek's breath whooshed out in a short bark of a laugh. "Oh, I would disagree wi' 'e there, luv. I would say 'e did it some perfect," Merrek pulled in a calming breath. "I just need a minute 'ere," he chuckled wryly, "Maybe a douse o' cold water."

Kerry wiggled out of his hold and stepped back, "You must think I'm some kind of..."

"Hush," Merrek cut her off. Concern for her iced his fervor and he pulled her back into his arms, rested his chin on the top of her head, "We both know better than that. I've known from the first that 'e're... not like that." *Thank God. However, she was a natural seductress and did not even know it.* "And don't be sorry. God knows I'm not sorry," he chuckled again. "My clients in Dublin may be, as I'll be thinkin' of little else over the next few days." He sighed over the top of her head. "'E know...you and I...we're headed inta uncharted seas here. But I think I've known it from the start, and I'm not wantin' ta turn back now." *Hell, I don't think I could*, he thought with a certainty. "There's somethin' powerful between us, Kerry girl. Somethin' special I'm thinkin'. So wait for me, will 'e? Here at Min's where I know 'e'll be safe? I'll be back in a couple o' days. I want us ta spend some time getting' ta know each other. I'll show 'e around Cornwall, includin' Porth."

Kerry had been fervently praying that Min's porch would open up and swallow her. *Where was a good accident when she needed one?*

Merrek moved his head and leaned back, his hands tightening slightly on her upper arms. "Look at me, Kerry."

Shoot, he is so arrogantly demanding, she thought irritably even as she raised her eyes, darkened with humiliation.

Merrek literally felt his heart tumble in response to the unguarded candor in her eyes. *Lord help me, is she as innocent as she seems?* A powerful feeling of protectiveness seized him and with it an undeniable surge of possessiveness as well. He would have to mull that over later. Right now, all he wanted to do was reassure Kerry and maybe coax a smile from her before he left. "All is good, luv. Trust me—'e've done nothing ta be embarrassed about. I should be the one embarrassed." He grinned at her. "'E seem ta bring out the devil in me."

She couldn't help but smile at that, "Something tells me it's not very far below the surface."

He chuckled. "I could say the same about you, luv. So..." he began as he backed away and took both her hands in his, "...do we 'ave a date when I return to Cornwall?"

131

"Alright," her answer was hesitant but affirmative.

"Good. Anythin' you'd like to see or do—I'll be your personal tour guide."

"I'd like that. I haven't seen the moors yet." Smiling, she reached a hand down into the deep pocket of her skirt and drew out a card she had prepared for him earlier that day. "You can call me." She smiled timidly.

"Well, then. Three dates before ya finally surrender yer phone number. Makes me wonder…"

"Wonder what?" Her eyes were wide and deeply green.

He chuckled. "Jus' makes me wonder." He kissed her forehead lightly and stuck the card in his shirt pocket. "Good night, Kerenza. Make sure 'e retrieve yer passport from Min's table, aye?" Wanting to put some spirit back in her demeanor, he added, "Think 'e can keep up with it until I get back?"

She did not disappoint him. Her green eyes flashed, "Oh, you can be a real smart *arse*."

He was chuckling as he walked away. But she drew him up short with, "Won't you be needing these?" She held up his keys and jingled them. "Or were you thinking of pushing your bike home from the train station tomorrow?" He quickly checked his pockets and then turned and looked at her in disbelief.

"Brute force isn't the only way to pick a pocket," she crooned.

He shook his head in amazement, and then slowly climbed the steps to take the keys she held out to him. "Ah, Kerry, me darlin'. I knew 'e were goin' ta be a handful from the minute…well, aye, from the minute me hands were full of ya. 'E'll be here, aye?"

"I'll be here," she smiled.

His hand closed over the keys and her hand, holding both for several seconds as he searched her face. "Aye, a hell of a 'andful you'll be," his tone suggesting he was not unhappy about it. He took his keys and, after waiting to hear the door lock click safely behind her, started up the road toward the Gilliflower, a broad and toothy smile on his face.

⚓

Pumping the pedals in time to the music drumming in her ears, Kerry raced along the road back to Min's on the borrowed bicycle. An unexpected rain had caught her halfway between the market where she had gone to pick up things for Min and the B&B. Thankfully, it was just a light shower, but she was soaked to the skin, having wrapped

132

the produce and other items in her rain slicker and placed them in the handlebar basket. These sudden rain showers started out at sea and were oftentimes unpredictable, which drove her to distraction, but this one did not seem to have much strength. Still, it would be nice to be indoors, dry and warm.

When Kerry padded barefoot into Min's kitchen with the small bag of groceries, she heard Min on the phone. "Ah, she's just walked in, dearie. I'll get 'er for ya."

Kerry raised her eyebrows in question as she took the phone. "E's Lowenna," Min whispered. "I'll get you a towel."

"Hello, Lowenna," Kerry said into the phone, making sure she stood in one place so as not to drip all over the floor.

"Ay, Kerry. Listen, I want to apologize for my behavior last night. That was really not considerate."

Kerry smiled to herself. "Did Merrek ask you to call?"

"Yes, 'e did. But 'e's right. I used 'e, a guest in me sister's house, ta make a point with me brother. 'E wasn't nice o' me."

"Well, thank you, Lowenna. I appreciate you calling me. And might I just say…you are lucky to have a brother who cares so much for you. He worries about your safety and happiness…" Min took the groceries and threw a large towel around her. Kerry smiled her appreciation.

"Aye, I know it. 'E's jus' that 'e don't know the lengths he will sometimes go ta jus'ta make 'is point." *Don't be so sure about that,* Kerry's face burned as she recalled his formidable strength holding her captive against Min's pantry door. "'E's personally scared off half the boys in the county, an' the other half jus' by reputation. I'm going ta be an ol' maid, and Rosen as well. I know Da didn't have this in mind when he asked Merrek to watch out for us."

"He just wants to protect you, make sure you don't end up hurt by the wrong kind of man." *He means to protect me too, it seems.* That thought brought a secret smile to her lips.

"Aye, well, right now it doesn't seem as though a right man exists. But enough with that. The second reason I'm callin' is I talked wi' Da and me granfer and they said that paintin' has been in the family forever and has some value but they know nothing else about it—what do fishermen know of art, aye? But since it's presumed valuable, grandfer wanted it restored. It's been in the attic for years. So before Elowen took it to the conservator, Genna and I examined it with a magnifyin' glass and found a signature—well, a mark really." She paused for effect. "The initials…

M…W. Is that insane? Since yer so good at research, maybe 'e could find out who 'e is? Who she is. If 'e have time, ya know."

MW. Another fantastic coincidence? "Lowenna, I'll make time. To use your words, this just gets spookier at every turn. Does Merrek know about this discovery?"

"No, he left early this mornin' before I got up. But MW? And the woman in the paintin'—she looks just like you. And you and Merrek…"

Merrek and I…? Kerry felt a rush of emotions, unable to pin one of them down for consideration.

"…all this gives me the headlighters," Lowenna continued.

Kerry could not suppress her laugh. "Yes it does. Thanks, Lowenna. I'll dig in and see what I can find out. And don't worry about the other—all is well. It was so nice to meet all of you."

"I think we'll be seein' 'e again soon, Kerry. I'm lookin' forward to gettin' ta know 'e. Ta then."

Min pretended not to have been eavesdropping when Kerry returned to the kitchen. "Wot did Lowenna 'ave ta say?" she casually asked.

Kerry did not want to tell Min all that had transpired yesterday. Min was just too…Cornish. She would read meaning into every piece of coincidental trivia and right now Kerry needed stability. "She just called to apologize for ripping into Merrek in front of me. Those girls are so pretty."

"Aye. Too much for their own good. An' wild as panthers, both. But 'ave ye looked in a mirror lately yourself? Ye came 'ere lookin' like a cheel an' now you're blossumin' before me very eyes." Her own eyes were absolutely pixie-like, shining with mischief. "Merrek 'ave anythin' to do wi' that I'm wonderin'? 'E's smitten wi' ya. Makes me wonder…"

You don't know the half of it, thought Kerry. She paused on her way to the stairs and turned back to Min. "Didn't you tell me there was a painter in your family amongst the fishermen and miners? *Your only claim to fame* I believe you said?"

"Aye, I did. Backalong a couple o'centuries ago. Why?"

Kerry could not wait to start her research. "Just curious. I've a newly found interest in art."

- 11 -

Love is but the discovery of ourselves in others,
And the delight is in the recognition.
—Alexander Smith

Merrek stirred a teaspoon of sugar into his morning cup of tea while he worked with his computer. He loved early Sunday mornings at his parents' home. It was quiet before the others were up. He had enjoyed this time since he was a young boy—a little solitude in an otherwise very full and lively household. It was a good time to think.

He had been thinking of Kerry since long before dawn. His experience with past relationships had left him with no interest of having another, but this was different. Kerry was different. It went beyond the fact that she was the sweetest, most unguarded and sincere woman he had ever met. The difference was that somehow, for reasons he could not fathom, he recognized her as his.

Possessiveness had never been a part of his nature, but now that Kerry was in his life he wanted to keep her there, and he would do whatever necessary to ensure her safety.

Given her tendencies to misfortune, it could come to that. He stood and looked out the window where he could see the sun rising over the water, casting gold glitter on the gentle waves. Why, he thought, would a woman with Kerry's quiet beauty and obvious intelligence be so lacking in confidence and self worth? She was not a spineless pushover, but like an unmoored boat, tossed by the will of the water and pushed around by the winds. *She had no anchor.*

He glanced toward the docks over in Newbury and from this vantage point could just see the tops of the masts of two antiquated fishing boats his great grandfather and granddad had owned and operated before his father had added one with more modern conveniences and capabilities. There was his anchor, he realized. Family. Tradition. Work. The same components of living that had run through the veins of generations of

Walles men. As sure as the physical trait of red hair either popped out unexpectedly on the head of a new Walles infant or glinted in a certain light off his sisters' dark crowns, so did the personality traits that made him who he was. His traits were a throwback to earlier generations and he understood that. That knowledge grounded him.

If Kerry's ancestors were indeed from Porth, she came from a creative breed of people who had dared to not only survive, but to prosper in spite of their circumstances. Even though she was a gentle soul, Kerry had the wit and intelligence of a survivor, and in her kisses, he could taste the determined passion that she had obviously been secretly carrying, *smuggling*, all her life.

She had, however, been orphaned before she was quite an adult, and with no extended family, save one apathetic brother, was sadly much like a stranger to herself. Merrek could imagine the ambiguity caused by such a disconnection. She had no moor to keep her safe, no keel to steady her in times of uncertainty. No wonder she was predisposed to accidents. She was a lone craft tossed by a fickle sea.

He wanted to be her keel. *Her anchor.*

Merrek looked up as his dad entered the room. Walles, Sr. also enjoyed this time at home, but not only on Sundays anymore. A few years ago, he was on the sea before the sun made its appearance over the water, his older son working beside him. However, since his heart attack, every morning was Sunday. He missed the purpose that drove him as it was now driving his son.

"Always workin'," his father greeted him as he shuffled to the table. "I thought when I encouraged ye ta go ta university that I was savin' 'e from a life o' nothin' but hard work."

"Ah, Da, 'e's in me blood, no matter what. But I'm actually not workin' right now. I'm jus' searchin' around. Here, sit. I'll get 'e some tea."

His father sat and glanced at the computer screen. "What's this? Lookin' ta buy real estate, are ye?"

Merrek set a cup of tea in front of his father. "Aye. Thinkin' about it. Yer doin' much better, lookin' to retire the business. Trev will be goin' off to school soon; the girls are almost grown. I'm thirty-two. It's time, Da."

His father looked at him keenly. "How long have 'e been thinkin' this way?"

"I've been mullin' it around for awhile. Me business 'as done well, and Phillip 'as reached a position ta buy me out as planned. I've been pickin' up more assignments for the photography business—it just seems like everythin' is suddenly fallin' inta place."

His father leaned forward and narrowed his eyes. "That little American with 'e las' night. Where's she fallin'?"

Merrek grinned at his dad. "Inta place would be me hope. By me side—*me partner in life*."

The senior Walles had a grim, worried face. "Ah, bloody hell, son. Where do 'e really expect she'll fall? Here, in Cornwall? More likely back in America. She won't leave…"

"She doesna have anyone there, Da. One brother who cares so little for 'er 'e 'asn't even called ta see if she's doin' well 'ere."

The older man leaned back in his chair. "How long 'ave 'e known this girl?"

Merrek looked straight into his father's eyes and stated undauntedly, "The better part of a week."

The scowl on his father's face morphed into an incredulous stare, "*A week?*" he almost shouted. Calming himself, he cautioned, "You don't really even know this little…"

"Watch what 'e say, Da. She's easy ta know—'e's all right there in 'er eyes. I feel like I've known 'er…forever."

Bushy gray eyebrows shot up. Before he could speak, Merrek's mother walked quietly into view. "The paintin'," she said, "Lowenna told me. I'm surprised to 'ear yer caught up in… legends. Not that I'm inclined to shrug it off—it's facinatin' that the paintin' 'as been in the Walles family for years with hardly a thought and then your Kerry shows up—the spittin' image of the one painted. Yer just the last person I'd think would even consider…"

"'E's na the paintin'," Merrek interrupted. "That's a curiosity, no doubt, but Kerry…she's an old soul like me, aye? There's na many of us around. It's only been a week, aye, but I know 'er because we connect. I've ne'er felt that way with anyone else."

Walles, Sr. sent his wife a look of concern. Turning back to Merrek, he warned, "Yer not a green twig anymore, m'boy. 'E might not bend so easily this time."

Merrek froze briefly, and then stood, began clearing the table of his papers and laptop. His mother laid a calming hand on his arm, made him look at her. "We know not to ever mention it, Merrek, and we won't. Your father is just worried. Ye take things so seriously and he doesn't want to see 'e hurt again."

"I wasna hurt…" Merrek snapped, then softened his voice respectfully,

"…before. I was callow, and now I'm…educated. This time it's an educated decision, if 'e will."

Walles, Sr. let out a sigh, and his wife smiled. "Bring yer girl ta dinner soon. Let us get ta know her, too."

Merrek nodded, "I'd like that. When I get back from Dublin. I'll let 'e know." He glanced at his father and saw his worried but supportive smile. He slapped the older man affectionately on the back as he left the room.

Merrek spent the rest of his Sunday working on a photography assignment. He wished Kerry were staying in Penzance so he could see her for at least a little while, but then he thought his distance might be good for them. It would give them some breathing room and some time to cool before they saw each other again.

⚓

Merrek called Kerry from Dublin on Monday night to see if she would like to spend Wednesday afternoon with him on the Bodmin Moors and then accompany him on the first of several photo shoots later in the day. One of England's most prestigious environmental periodicals had contacted him for the job.

Kerry was very enthusiastic. First, she was excited about the moors, reciting all the reasons that one should never consider visiting Cornwall without touring the moors. He chuckled at the thought that she sounded as colorful as a tourist flyer.

Secondly, she was genuinely pleased and excited that Merrek's photography talent had caught the attention of a premier periodical. *Deservingly so*, she had said. He was looking forward to having her with him on the shoot. Her admiration of his work gave him a sharper and more appreciative edge.

He also had to admit he was looking forward to discussing his relative's mysterious connection to Kerry's look-alike. Knowing Kerry, she had been burning the midnight oil in research. Wednesday was agonizingly slow in its arrival.

When Wednesday finally dawned, however, the day did not go at all as Merrek had planned. When Min answered his knock early that afternoon, he knew immediately by the look on her face something was wrong. He felt his chest tighten. "What?" he was curt and demanding. "Did she go on 'er own after all?"

"No…no, m'dear. She's here. We tried to call 'e but things got hectic. Kerry's 'ad… an incident. She can't see 'e today."

Merrek was of another opinion. He eased past Min and headed toward the stairs. Pausing on the bottom step, he turned back to Min who followed close behind. "What's amiss? I talked to 'er yesterday mornin' and she was fine. An *incident* 'e say?" Possible scenarios flashed through his mind. "Is she 'urt?" Then he froze, trying to tamp down the anger that was already starting to build. "Did someone 'urt 'er?"

Min could not get the beginning of an answer out of her mouth before Merrek was at the top of the stairs. He glanced into the big room through the open door. It was unoccupied, so he turned to the smaller room and knocked on the closed door. "Kerry? Kerry, luv, what's happened?"

He could barely hear her weak and muffled voice. "I'm sorry, Merrek. I can't see you today."

He turned to Min who had continued to follow him up the steps. His eyes stabbed hers with a look of uncompromising intent. "Kerry," he called in warning, "I'm comin' in."

He could not believe the depth of emotion that surged through him over the welfare of this young woman he had met less than a fortnight ago. As he pushed open the door to her room, he steeled himself against what he would see, and what he would feel compelled to do as a result.

Kerry was lying on the bed on her stomach under a light sheet, her face buried in the pillows. Her head jerked up when Merrek entered the room and his heart sank when he saw unshed tears swimming in her eyes. What he could see of her seemed unmarked, but he noted before she collapsed into the pillows that she did not attempt to move the lower part of her body. He started toward the bed, but Min rushed around him and blocked his way. "Her pride's been wounded, too, m'boy. Best be gentle about this."

Merrek looked over Min's head to Kerry who still had not made a move to turn over, and his eyes followed the line and curves of her beneath the thin sheet. His body would have reacted to the fact that she was obviously nude under that sheet, but his mind was too fearful for her wellbeing. His voice was gruffer than he intended. "God, Min, tell me what's happened."

"Stingin' nettles," Min answered with a sympathetic grimace.

Merrek's eyes jerked to Min's, his expression incredulous. It took him a moment to grasp what she had said. "Did 'e say stingin' nettles?"

"Aye," said the older woman with a sorrowful shake of her head.

Merrek looked back at Kerry, his emotions in a tumble. He sank down in the room's wing-backed chair and ran his hands over his face and back through his hair. After a couple of calming breaths, he braced his hands on his knees and looked back up at Min with a mixture of relief and irritation in his expression. "Stingin' nettles," he repeated flatly.

Min nodded her head in silence, her eyes reminding him to tread carefully. He looked back to the unmoving form on the bed. It had to be more than that, especially since his heart was still racing. He had thought she was made of stronger stuff, and he made the mistake of not heeding Min's warning about censoring his words. "I'm sorry, luv, I just can't quite…I never took 'e for…"

Kerry's head came up and when she turned to face him her eyes flashed with indignation. "Took me for what? A cry baby? A wuss? An…idiot?" Down went her head again, her humiliation apparent.

Merrek glanced back at Min's accusing look and winced. Still assuming Kerry was more mortified than hurt, he experienced some relief. Mortification he could fix. However, her position suggested there was more to this and bid him to ask, "Where exactly…?"

A smothered groan came from the bed. Min laid a hand on Merrek's arm and whispered, "Her backside and upper thighs mostly…and…parts thereof," Min winced, her eyes full of pity. "She might be over the worst of it by noon tomorrow, but I'm thinkin' recovery might take the full forty-eight hours in this case."

Understanding flooded, and the relief that it was only an everyday topical allergy fled. Her backside? Jesus…*and parts thereof?*

Again, his recalcitrant mouth ran out ahead of his tact, "Kerry…how did you manage ta come inta contact wi' stingin' nettles…wi' yer bare arse?"

Kerry groaned more audibly into the pillow and Min found her first smile of the day, albeit a sad one. "Kerry took the bike down ta Pensky's field this mornin' ta gather some wildflowers for me vases. I've got me some visitors from Austria comin'. They check in around teatime tomorrow. Nice soundin' folk on the phone. They…"

"Min, please," Merrek's patience gone.

"Oh, sorry. Well, what happened at Pensky's…the uh…call o' nature was the instigator."

When Merrek remained in confused silence, Kerry lifted her head and turned a beet red face toward him. "There was no one around—I could see for miles. I was hidden…nobody could see me." Then she buried her face again.

Merrek pictured the field in his mind. Once used by Min's aging neighbor to graze goats, weeds and wildflowers now covered the field. The side nearest the road was steep, hiding that part of the field from the notice of passersby, but the view from there encompassed parts of the city and the sea beyond. "That's some steep hill over ta Pensky's field. Lots o' nettles growin' there I'd imagine."

"Aye," Min agreed. "And 'e's some steep, 'tis true."

"And I slipped," added the mortified voice in the pillow. "Just as I...well...I slipped and slid."

Merrek felt his chest cave. She was *hurt*, not just embarrassed, and here he was giving her a hard time. "Ah, bloody hell, Kerry. That's...sad. I've never heard o' anyone..." *and there goes my blathering mouth again*, "I mean...I guess 'e are in a lot o' pain, darlin'?" He finished gently.

He heard an errant whimper escape the victim, the first he'd heard from her. He was not sure if it was from pain or disgust. "I told you trouble finds me." She sounded weak. "Sorry about our date today, Merrek," her words sounded slurred. "I was so looking forward to it."

"I gave 'er a good dose of antihistamine," Min explained. "She'll be asleep soon."

Merrek ignored Min's warning and walked over to the bed. He let his fingers wind through Kerry's springy hair. "I'm sorry, too, luv. Jus' get well. We'll do the moors another time. Rest easy, now. I'll call 'e later?"

His answer was a slight shake of her head. She was asleep before he reached the door.

Back down in the kitchen, Min made herself and Merrek a cup of tea. Merrek savored it along with the knowledge that Kerry was not seriously hurt. His hands were still shaking slightly as he lowered his cup to the saucer.

Min was chattering. "The cheel wanted to get out and breathe some fresh air. She'd locked herself away with her research all morning and needed ta get away from it for a while. So since she was goin' that way, I asked her to see if there were any decent bouquets growing near Pensky's. She was gone so long I started to worry, and I knew as soon as she walked in with that basket o' flowers she was in pain. I thought maybe she sprained an ankle or got bit by some wee pest. I stayed after 'er until she fessed up. I thought I'd ne're again see skin as red as 'er pretty face when she told me, but then I saw 'er poor arse. Almost purple with welts upon welts. I don't know 'ow she walked back from Pensky's in those jeans pushin' that ol' bike, poor cheel."

"She musta felt on fire," Merrek shook his head with much sympathy and not a little respect. "Nettles are bad enough anywhere, but in such a tender area…bloody hell. I can't believe she walked back. She should have called out for help."

"She's a hardy one, I'd say. She also don't like a lot of fuss. And then there was embarrassment as well."

"I don't think I've ever known anyone so prone to accidents, Min. It's scary."

"Could be she's cursed. Livin' in the States don't keep an old Cornish curse from runnin' through the veins."

"Well, then I've got t' find a way t' break such a curse. I canna 'ave 'er in danger o' being seriously hurt, and I'll be losin' me bloody mind worrin' after 'er." He grimaced slightly. "Sorry, Min. I've lost control of me mouth it seems."

Min smiled knowingly at her young cousin. "Ah, then. A curse o' another kind 'as gotten ahold o' ye, is it?

"Aye, well right now it seems me curse is in findin' a way t' keep 'er in one piece."

⚓

By Thursday afternoon, Kerry could put on soft pajamas and sit, but she still stayed in her room. Min was busy with her new "big room" guests and that gave Kerry the time and solitude to continue her research of MW. Through the websites and search engines she had found most helpful, she painstakingly began to pull MW out of obscurity and back into existence. Kerry basked once again in the power she felt when able to give a forgotten person remembrance. It was like restoring the individual's…worth.

As from the beginning of her genealogical research, she envied those that had memories of the past generations that forged the reality of where they were today. She reflected that whatever traits our ancestors leave in the gene pools, those we carry with us, mostly hidden in the fibers that make us who we are and who future generations become.

Reading over her notes, Kerry's resourcefulness began to fill in the blanks on the subject of MW. There was only one local artist from eighteenth century Cornwall with those initials. He was Myghal Walles and Merrek's ancestral uncle. Apparently he had been very talented— enough to support himself with his paintings. Portraits were his forte, although he did paint landscapes and a few still life attempts. Min was correct—that ancient relative she had mentioned did have a few paintings showcased in a local museum, and some hung in family estates scattered over Britain. She found him living in Dorset at the turn of the century. He had died eleven years later, but she could not find a gravesite for him in Dorset.

Turning her attention back to Cornwall, she searched death records for the year 1811 and found him and his burial site at St. Sennen's Church in Sennen, down the coast from Penzance. He must have gone home to his final resting place, since the Walles were all from that general area, and according to Merrek, had been for centuries. Looking at the pictures of Sennen online, it just seemed the perfect place to have produced an artist.

According to the census records, Myghal had lived alone in Dorset and died alone in Sennen. So who was Kerry's double? The painting was not mentioned anywhere, was not listed among his works, but had been passed down to Merrek's branch of the Walles family. Had the woman in the painting come from his imagination, or had she also resided in the area? If only she had a name. Kerry had to find out who she was.

Merrek roared in on his motorbike just in time for tea Friday morning. As from the beginning, his presence heightened all Kerry's senses. Her mind was skeptical that she could have such a strong connection to a man she'd only known a short time, but her heart accepted it without reservation.

Min set out the fresh batch of scones she had made for her new guests arriving later in the day while Kerry poured the tea. Merrek settled himself on a kitchen chair and watched the sway of Kerry's hips as she walked back to the stove to return the teakettle. "It appears most o' the swellin' 'as gone away." he tried to keep a straight face and braced himself.

Kerry jerked around, her eyes round and wide and *green*. "What do you mean? It's *all* gone."

"Really?" He sounded unconvinced as his gaze tried to slip behind her. He laughed outright at the expression on her face.

Min had been chortling throughout the couple's exchange. "Listen ta the two o' 'e. It's like ye've gone on for years."

Their eyes met over Min's head and something sparked between them. After a long moment of silence, Merrek nodded his head slowly. "Aye," he stated, "there is that."

While the two of them simultaneously considered the implications of

Kerry's research, Min fell into motion. "I packed a picnic fer the two o' 'e. Nothin' much, jus' some fruit and cheese, some o' the fresh bread I made this mornin'. Merrek, maybe 'e can pick up a bottle o' wine on the way?"

"I can do that. Are 'e ready for an afternoon on the moors, Kerry Carter?" He picked up the basket Min had sat on the table, a mischievous grin curling his mouth. "Might be a good idea to be sure and make use o' the facilities afore we leave."

A low growl escaped Kerry as her face went red once again. "Oh, you are a…a buster, that's what you are, and not a very nice one at the moment."

Merrek laughed. "Ah, listen to 'er now, Min. Usin' our Cornish words she is, and it's a buster I am."

In spite of her best efforts, Kerry returned his grin. "You're in rare form this morning. What's got you all frisky?"

He leveled those glinting dark eyes on her. "You," was his simple and direct answer. Kerry was sure steam was now coming off her face and she glanced awkwardly at Min who was suddenly engrossed in the newspaper. When she looked back at Merrek, he winked at her. She stuck her tongue out at him.

He plopped the picnic basket back onto the table as he lunged toward her. Kerry was out the kitchen door and halfway across Min's herb garden when Merrek caught her and pulled her into his arms, both of them laughing like children. "Ah, Kerry darlin'," he buried his hands in her hair and tilted her head up to his. "'Tis some good to see 'e recovered. It near toppled me t'see 'e…incapacitated as 'e were."

Kerry lowered her forehead to his chest. "I didn't want you to know. It was bad enough that Min knew, although I wouldn't have been able to bear it without her help."

"Aye, well, and *baring it*'s what got 'e inta trouble in the first place, 'e know." He could not resist teasing her.

She gasped and pushed hard against his chest. She might as well have pushed against a brick wall. "Brute! Let me assure you I don't go around dropping my drawers just anywhere. I really had to go and this Penski's field is a not just a hop, skip and a jump from here you know. Oh, God I was so embarrassed."

"Ah, luv, and how would 'e have known? Do 'e 'ave nettles in the States?"

"I've heard of them. Where I'm from we mostly have to look out for poison ivy and poison oak. I know what those look like."

"Well, I've bodged as tour guide, I 'ave, not warnin' 'e about such 'ere in Cornwall. 'Tis sorry I am that 'e 'ad to learn the 'ard way, but now 'e know." He cupped her chin in his hand and raised her face to his. "And now 'e also know I won't be put off when it comes ta yer welfare, Kerry. We've this thing between us, aye? This thing we need ta discuss. So whatever yer worries or troubles trust me with 'em. I can't...I won't have 'e defenseless or uncared for here in me own country. And I won't 'ave 'e dismal if I can do anythin' ta make 'e happy." Before she could respond, he kissed her to emphasize his point. He had meant it to be a quick and mandating kind of kiss, but the second his lips touched hers the kiss transformed into anything but quick and became more of a plea than a command. Her quivers brought him around and he ended the kiss, smiled at her dazed expression. "I know what 'e mean, luv. We'd better go finish our tea and then ride over t' the moors, what say 'e?"

⚓

Kerry found the moors a study of desolate, haunting beauty. The granite added an uncompromising component to the starkness, while here and there rivers and waterfalls softened the landscape, as did green valleys and charming hamlets. She did not see how anyone could ever become bored with the area—eighty square miles of variations and surprises. In a brochure she had picked up to read along the way, she found Daphne du Maurier's description of these moors, 'They have a fascination unlike any other; they are a survival of another age.' Kerry smiled to herself as she recalled the meaning of Merrek's name. How appropriate. He was certainly fascinating unlike anyone she had ever met, and he sometimes seemed of another age with his old-fashioned ideals and almost warrior-like resolve.

She glanced up at him, caught his tender regard of her and blushed. As with the moors, it did seem that something tinged with magic sparked and sizzled between them.

Merrek found Kerry's reaction to the moors beautiful and intriguing. She had gone quiet, almost reverent. While he studied her, a contented smile spread over her pretty face and serenity settled in eyes that were as green and vibrant as the moorland valleys. The ever-present wind of the moors lifted her hair, and his hands itched to bury themselves in its silkiness.

She attracted him to be sure. She made him laugh, she had a kind heart, she could make his pulse race with a smile or a touch, and most importantly, he trusted her.

"So," Merrek began once they'd settled in for their picnic, "that paintin' that's been stored away in me granfer's attic of a woman bearin' your resemblance is the work o' me own relative some two centuries and seven generations agone?"

Kerry smeared honey that Min had packed onto a scone and took a bite. She resisted, barely, her eyes from rolling back in her head. "Well, there is a Myghal Walles in your family tree, an uncle actually, who was a painter in the late 1700's. He did portraits mostly, and, according to my research, the painting your grandfather owns is in Myghal's style, and it was marked with the initials MW. There was no other successful artist in that century from this part of Britain with those initials, so…what?"

Merrek was not sure he could have restated what she had just said, but he was confident he could describe in sensuous detail the way her tongue licked that honey from her fingers. He made himself look away and say something conversational. "'E know, too much honey can give you collywobbles."

She gasped slightly. "Is that bad? Please tell me English bees don't make honey from flowering nettles."

He laughed. It was a relief to laugh. "No, that crock is most likely from heather, but sometimes too much sweet can cause stomach upset—collywobbles."

"Collywobbles," she tested the word. "Yeah, when you say the word it feels like a stomach that's upset."

"Aye…and sometimes sounds."

Her smile grew wide. "I love your Cornish words. They…encompass the senses."

Merrek considered that. "Aye, I never thought o' it before, but yer right."

Kerry laughed and said it again, slowly, this time in a low gurgling voice, "Col–ly–wob–bles."

Merrek could not find his laughter this time, and attributed it to the sight of the word flowing slowly over her lips. That definitely encompassed his senses. He shifted his position and then attempted to bring them back on subject. "Now, tell me more about Myghal Walles. All I know of him is his excellent taste in women. Ye think she was real or imaginary?"

"That's the next part of the puzzle," Kerry turned serious. "He wasn't married—ever. No children, apparently. But he traveled all over the

British Isles. She could be from anywhere, could be anyone. Or, like you said, he could have just made her up."

"I think that would be even weirder. A likeness due to genetic makeup is feasible. Dreamin' up someone who appears in the flesh two centuries later is…uncomfortable. Aye, well now it looks as though ye've got yerself an additional genealogy project. Maybe this relative o'mine could be another path t'findin' yer own ancestors. Could be she was a relative. That would make us…what? Cousins maybe? I don't know why my family's never traced back as yer doin' now with yours."

Kerry chuckled softly. "Y'all have enough to do to keep up with all the relatives you have at present."

Merrek gave her a crooked grin. "*Y'all* do, me Southern belle." He pulled the cork from the wine bottle. "More wine? I'm drivin' so the rest is yers."

"My dear, Mr. Walles," Kerry cast aside her southern traces in imitation of a proper and saucy eighteenth-century English lady. "Are you bent on rendering a lady intoxicated?"

Merrek cocked an eyebrow at her and pushed the cork firmly back into the wine. "I think we're a bit past the tryin', luv," he said as he put the bottle back in the basket. "Think 'e can walk back to the bike or should I carry 'e?"

Green eyes flashed at him. "I think you should be a bit less insulting is what I think. I'm not the least…how do you Brits say it? *Trolleyed?*"

"Pissed," he countered. "Up 'e go now." He took her hands and pulled her to her feet.

"No, I'm not angry yet, but keep treating me like I can't hold my…*oh!*" she finished as she lost her footing.

Merrek had let go of her hands to pick up the basket at the same time she stepped back. Her ankle turned under her and she stumbled sideways. Merrek moved lightening fast, wrapped his arms around her and twisted beneath her in one motion. He took the brunt of the fall on his back with Kerry sprawled on top of him. Her eyes flew to his to assess his damage but he just as quickly flipped her over onto her back, bracing himself above her. "'E alright, luv?"

"My ankle turned. I must have stepped on something."

He did a backward crawl down her body to her feet. "Which one?"

"The right one." she flexed it and winced.

He took off her shoe and her sock and examined her ankle, messaged it, gently maneuvered her foot. She watched his ministrations with an increasing awareness that he was touching her, and she closed her eyes to concentrate on the heavenly sensation. She could not help but wonder how those big calloused hands would feel…

Merrek replaced her sock and shoe. "Let's try puttin' some weight on it," he was all business. He pulled her to her feet and let her try a few steps while he held her to his side. "Easy now. Think 'e can make it?"

"It will be fine, thank you. It's getting dark. Min says there are cats that roam these moors. *Cats what rip things up* is the way she put it."

"Aye, well, between the pixies, the cats, and the blindin' mists, we'd best be off. Take it slow. I've got ye."

Thankfully, it was only a few minutes to where Merrek had parked the bike. The darkness was closing in on them but Kerry felt completely safe until a flash of light in the distance caught her attention. The familiar knots began to form in her middle.

"Do 'e have denner plans?" Merrek strapped on the picnic basket and handed Kerry her helmet.

"What? I'm sorry?"

Merrek followed her eyes and saw the dark clouds gathering in the west. "Denner," he tried again. "Do 'e 'ave plans?"

Kerry was definitely distracted but she managed to answer. "I…need to pack my things and get ready to check out of the B&B tomorrow. Min has both rooms booked and I'm glad for her. I found a hostel just inside Penzance. There are several sites I want to see there." Her eyes darted back to the horizon. "Do you think it's going to storm tonight?"

"'E's hard ta tell about storms 'round 'ere. Maybe. Look, Kerry, why don't we pick up your things and we'll go ta me parents' home for denner—Mum's been askin' me ta bring 'e, and then I'll take 'e to your hostel after. Check it out for 'e."

He got her attention with that. "You don't need to check anything out for me, Merrek. I researched this hostel—I'm sure everything is fine."

Merrek held up his hands in defense. "No insult intended, Yankee. I'm jus' concerned." He pulled out his phone.

While he was busy in conversation, Kerry studied the sky again. She had checked the weather forecast that morning and there was no mention of a storm, but it sure looked as if one was brewing. She felt the knots in her stomach move toward nausea at the thought of enduring a storm in an unfamiliar hostel.

Merrek did not miss the worry on Kerry's face. He thought maybe that it was due to the idea of meeting his family again. "Mum is delighted, and Lowenna is ecstatic. Ye've opened 'er eyes to the fascination of genealogical research—she'll most likely want yer help on the Walles family tree."

Kerry smiled but looked back at the gathering clouds. She just wanted to get somewhere before the weather turned sour, "Can we carry my pack on your bike?"

He smiled in assurance, "We'll manage."

Kerry's new predicament was almost as terrifying as an approaching storm. After a long goodbye at Min's with promises to see her again before leaving Cornwall, Merrek slipped his arms into the straps of Kerry's backpack and straddled the bike behind her. He moved his arms around her and his hands covered hers on the handlebars. "May as well learn 'ow ta drive one, aye?"

"You've got to be kidding me. I'll kill us both."

"Nah," he chuckled. "I'm right behind 'e. Ye've driven a car with standard transmission, aye?"

"No."

He blew out a breath. "Aye, well then we should be in for an interestin' ride." He felt Kerry stiffen against him and smiled as he brought his mouth close to her ear, his breath warm as it stirred the wisps of hair that had escaped her ponytail. "Jus' messin' with 'e, sweetheart. We'll be fine." She softened against him again like warm honey. Her trust made him feel invincible. He chuckled again with irony as he felt himself stiffen. *Interesting ride, indeed.*

Merrek's parents lived in a modest two-story house on a quiet residential street half the distance to Newlyn where they moored their boats. It was crowded inside, as expected of a home that had once housed a family of eight. The parlor doubled as Merrek's bedroom in the front that opened to a dining room with a table that barely fit in the space. There was just enough room left for the buffet under a double window. There was also an ample kitchen, and three bedrooms and a bath upstairs. The realization that four girls had shared that one bathroom with not only their parents but with two brothers as well garnered her respect. They must have considered it a mixed blessing when the two older sisters married and moved out.

⚓

Merrek's mother and father, Nessa and Mick, greeted Kerry warmly. When she had first met Merrek's dad at Elowen's vacation rental, he was sitting down. Now she saw that he towered over her just like his son, and his eyes were shrewd but kind. His mother was welcoming enough, but seemed a little nervous. Kerry thought she might be apprehensive about what her husband might say based on their last meeting.

Merrek and Kerry greeted his sisters in the dining room where they were setting the table. After a quick glance, Merrek raised an eyebrow at Rosen. "There's one too many places set. Didde miscount?"

Rosen shot a peeved glance at their mother, and then confided, somewhat apologetically, "No. We've another guest comin'."

At just that moment there was a knock on the front door and Trev, coming downstairs, was just in time to admit that other guest through the front door. Merrek took one look at the priest and gave his mother an exasperated look.

"Kerry, dear, I'd like you to meet our priest, Father Larkin." Taking Kerry's hand, Nessa pulled her to stand directly in front of the priest, "This is Kerry Carter, Merrek's guest tonight. She's from America, and has been staying in St. Austell."

Kerry felt panic race through her, afraid of what raucous she was destined to cause tonight. That must have been in Merrek's thoughts also, hence the disgruntled look. She would try her best not to do anything that might embarrass him. But what were the odds? Kerry smiled in spite of her misgivings and held out her hand, "I'm very pleased to meet you, Reverend Larkin."

Was the priest's smile the tiniest bit askew as he took her hand?

"Likewise, Miss Carter from America. What brings you to Cornwall?"

Merrek had been pouring whiskey from a decanter on the buffet into three glasses and now passed one to the priest, one to his father, and kept the last one. "Kerry is actually here for two reasons, *Father* Larkin." He indicated with a wave of his glass in the priest's direction that she should continue.

Kerry felt the heat rising to her face when she realized her mistake in titles, but took her cue from Merrek and charged on. "Yes, two reasons. The first is to gather material for my Social Studies class. I teach British history and culture to thirteen and fourteen year olds, so I'm creating a portfolio that will not fail to hold their attention. Hopefully not fail, that is."

Father Larkin smiled. "Ah, yes, a difficult age that. I admire you for your obvious dedication."

Kerry began to relax a bit. "Thank you, Father. And the other reason is to find out about my ancestors who lived here in Cornwall. Merrek is very kindly helping me with both." *There. That should ease the tension she sensed from Mrs. Walles.* Or it might have if the woman happened to miss the warm smile and affectionate wink Merrek gave Kerry. She felt her face burning again.

Father Larkin studied her for a moment. "Carter. Carters from Cornwall you say?"

"Yes Father, I've traced them to Porth, but I haven't made it there yet to continue my research. I've been touring, gathering materials for my classroom."

"Hmm. Genealogy sometimes flushes secrets out of the closet. Are you prepared for that?"

Now that was an original question. Who so far had not asked her that? So even though she tried, she could not quite keep all the sarcasm out of her response. "Well of course I don't expect all the Carters to be saints." She heard Trev's smothered laugh aloud and looked at Merrek, who was smiling into his drink, and realized what she had just said. "I mean... well...I'm sure *none* of the Carters were *saints*...like your St. Peter or St..." she waved her hand in a circular motion, like it would draw the names from her mouth, "whatever...I mean... you know. But, yes, I'm prepared. I expect it, actually," she lifted her chin as if to prove a point.

There was a hint of a grin on Merrek's face as he walked to her side and took her hand. "Kerry can handle a smuggler here or a pirate there, or at least she should be able to after spendin' an evenin' with *this* family—aye, Father?"

The priest laughed and agreed in wry amusement. Merrek's mom wrung her hands and quietly suggested they sit down to dinner. Mick and Father Larkin sat at the ends of the table, with Kerry and Mrs. Walles to the right and left of the priest. Kerry felt as trapped as a fish in one of their nets, but Merrek smiled at her and she tried to relax. During the dinner service, the conversation remained light with topics covering the weather, the storm it seemed they had avoided, and recent news events. Then Father Larkin questioned Kerry again. "So, Kerry, you are not Catholic, I presume?"

So this was the reason for including the priest, thought Kerry and noticed the quick glance of interest Nessa flashed her way. She also felt the comforting pat Merrek gave her thigh under the table.

"No, I'm not. My brother is, though. He converted to Catholicism to marry my sister-in-law."

The priest's bushy eyebrows rose in interest. "Sometimes that's how God calls us, child—through others who have been called before us."

Kerry sighed heavily. "Father, I doubt very seriously that God called Owen. My sister-in-law is beautiful. I'm sure it was more of an *earthy* calling my brother answered."

Merrek coughed into his napkin, Lowenna jumped up to refresh the tea, and Trev leaned back in his chair, obviously enjoying a study of Kerry's face. Rosen and Mick kept eating as if they hadn't heard a word. Mrs. Walles looked from the priest to Kerry and back.

Father Larken, eyes twinkling, tried again. "But you do have a religious preference?"

Mrs. Walles gave her full attention then, and Kerry understood what was going on. Merrek's mom was afraid her son was becoming too interested in this American/Carter descendant and she wanted to know if his soul was in jeopardy. Kerry did not know where the impishness came from, but she gave into it and let it drive her.

"Yes, I do. I prefer religious freedom, as promised by my constitution."

Merrek raised his glass of whiskey in salute and then finished it in one gulp. He glanced at his dad and saw the smirk teasing the older man's mouth. He leaned back and willed Kerry to look at him, and when she did, he relished that touch of Yankee defiance in her eyes.

Mrs. Walles finally got down to the grit of what she needed to know. "Do 'e believe in God, Kerry?"

"'E didn't realize 'e would have to satisfy the church jus' to eat denner in me home, did 'e, luv?" Merrek addressed Kerry but his eyes snapped to his mother.

The woman was unfazed. "Father Larkin is here, and in his presence I think we should speak of more than the latest Cricket scores, aye?"

"It's alright," Kerry laid her hand on Merrek's thigh under the table. He was just barely able to conceal the affect her light touch had on him. "Yes, I do believe in God. I've just never actually joined a specific church. To quote Abraham Lincoln..."

"Ah, and 'ere we go," Merrek leaned back in his chair with a smile. "She's actually better than I am at this."

His dad smiled and his siblings joined in a chorus of teasing groans. "Not another one."

"Seriously?"

"Birds of a feather…"

"No I think it's misery loves company."

Nessa hushed them all. "Such rudeness. Go ahead Kerry, Lincoln once said…?"

"President Lincoln said, 'When I do good, I feel good. When I do bad, I feel bad. That is my religion.' I like that quote. I guess that's pretty much how I feel about it."

There were nods around the table as everyone considered the simplicity of that belief. Mrs. Walles still looked a bit stressed.

"What of your parents? Are they believers?" Father Larkin asked.

"They were. They're both deceased."

Mrs. Walles clucked her tongue in genuine sympathy. "It must be such a comfort to know your parents are looking out for you from heaven."

"Ummm…" Kerry did not want to be dishonest but could not think of a diplomatic response.

"You do believe that don't you dear?" Mrs. Walles eyes were wide with expectation.

"Honestly?" Kerry sighed.

Merrek smiled broadly at her, "Are 'e even capable o' any other answer?"

Mrs. Walles looked to her priest, who smiled at Kerry. "I respect honesty," he said reassuringly. "Do you believe your parents are watching over you from heaven?"

"Oh, God…er, goodness, I sincerely hope that's not true. I can't believe that and have any comfort at all. I think it would be torture for them to observe me day in and day out."

Father Larkin covered her hand with his. "Child, we all fall from time to time. That's what forgiveness is all about. Wouldn't it be comforting to know your parents are there to help guide you, to help you recover?"

Merrek put his arm around Kerry's shoulder and gave her a slight squeeze. "She dussna mean to fall from grace, Father. She means literally *to fall*."

Father Larkin raised his eyebrows again. Kerry sighed. "I'm a klutz. I'm always falling and injuring myself or getting into some sort of trouble. It drove my parents crazy with worry when they were alive. I'd hate to think they are spending the peace they've finally attained watching me stumble from one incident to the next. I'd rather think they are finally able to enjoy a deep, worry-free sleep, at least for a while."

Mrs. Walles looked to her priest, her breath caught in her throat.

153

Father Larkin looked at Kerry for a long moment, and then nodded. "Well, the young lady has apparently given this some thought and if her belief is a comfort to her, then…isn't that what our beliefs are supposed to be? Now Kerry, cheel, please pass me those scones and Trev—I've been wantin' to know how long 'e been workin' on that technique that earned 'e the goal in the third quarter o' last week's game? That was some impressive."

Moments later, Merrek looked around the table as conversation became normal and lively and realized Kerry had merged into his family with her open and straightforward demeanor. His sisters and his mother were laughing at something Kerry had just said. His Da looked at ease and as if he was enjoying his conversation with the priest while frequently casting looks of approval in Kerry's direction. Trev could not keep his eyes off Kerry. Merrek decided as long as he kept his eyes on just her face, the little buster might make it through the evening without injury.

Kerry turned suddenly and Merrek's eyes locked with hers. Unable to help himself in spite of being in full view of his family and the priest, he planted a quick kiss on her mouth, then sat back to enjoy the fireworks display on her face. He really should not embarrass her on purpose, but he loved to watch her reactions. Aye, he was more than smitten with this one. He was done in.

After dinner, Kerry insisted on helping clean up and Merrek's mom allowed her into the kitchen. Merrek knew how telling that was. Moreover, hearing Kerry's lilting laughter mixed with his sisters' was comforting and peaceful and…right.

Father Larkin left shortly after dinner. Mrs. Walles sat down with some knitting, and Merrek accompanied Mick on the older man's prescribed ritual of walking the mile trek to the carriageway and back. Trev went upstairs to study, and Rosen left to visit a girlfriend who lived two houses down. Kerry pulled out her iPad from her pack and invited Lowenna to explore with her what she'd found about MW. Lowenna shared the family tree she and her grandfather had drawn up. Within twenty minutes, Lowenna was hooked on ancestry, and she could not wait to find out more about Myghal Walles' paintings—especially about the subject of the painting he'd left in the family.

"It's some fascinatin'," Merrek heard his mother say when he and his father entered the house. "Merrek, 'e need ta take Kerry to Porth soon. I'm anxious ta find out what she can learn there. Mick, didde know that painter, who 'appens t'be your ancient grandfather's brother, lived and died in Sennen? Ah, son, 'e should take Kerry to Sennen as well. Beautiful place, that."

"I've already told 'er I'd take 'er wherever she wishes ta go," he said with a smile at Kerry.

Kerry absently noticed the raindrops that clung to his hair and jacket, but was mesmerized by his smile. "Yes," she stated. "There are some fascinating things in this area I want to see, starting with the Jubilee Pool."

A few moments of pleasant conversation later, when Kerry was relaxed and unguarded, a flash of lightning hit very close to the house and the crack of thunder that followed sounded as if cannon had fired. They were all startled. Mrs. Walles crossed herself, Lowenna gasped, a whoop from Trev traveled down the stairs. Even the men raised eyebrows at the magnitude. Kerry's reaction was much more dramatic.

Merrek glanced at her just in time to see the color drain from her face and her eyes glass over. He was across the room in two strides. As he was gathering her into his arms, he realized her breaths were shallow and coming much too fast. Sure she was going to faint, he gently but firmly eased her into a chair and pushed her head down between her knees. "Lo—whiskey. Deep breaths, sweetheart. Breathe."

Lowenna made quick work of the task, worry etched on her young features. When Kerry began to pull in deep breaths, Merrek righted her and looped his arm around her shoulders. When her eyes cleared, he coaxed her to take a sip of the whiskey. She did, then gasped and coughed and sputtered, but obeyed his command to drink some more. Finally, the color came back into her face, and then kept coming with embarrassment.

"Are you alright, my dear?" Mr. Walles concern was evident in both his voice and his face. Kerry gave a slight nod, but Merrek felt her tremble with the next loud roll of thunder. He tightened his hold on her. "Nah, not again, luv. Stay w'me." He held the glass of whiskey to her lips again. "Swallow," his voice was low and authoritative, and Kerry could do nothing but follow his commands. The whiskey warmed her, strengthened her, but did nothing to alleviate her embarrassment. Five sets of eyes stared at her now since Trev had come downstairs to join the group.

"Merrek, we can't send that child to a hostel tonight in this storm," said Mrs. Walles determinedly. "Lowenna, go change the sheets on Rosen's bed and then call the Billingsly's and ask if Rosen can stay the night. Kerry, dear, let's get you upstairs and settled in a warm bed."

Kerry met Merrek's look of concern with a silent plea. He answered that plea with a slight nod and then turned to Mrs. Walles. "Kerry and I will stay down 'ere for a while, Mum. We'll watch the storm and let 'e know if it takes a bad turn."

Mr. Walles gently pushed his wife toward the stairs. "They'll be fine down 'ere, m'luv. Sleep well, Kerry. Believe me when I say that most o' Cornwall's storms 'ave more bluster than bite. Don't sit up too late, son. 'E have an early trip to London, aye? Trev, Lowenna, up stairs with 'e. I'm sure 'e both 'ave studies."

⚓

It was approaching midnight when silence settled over the Walles' home. Thunder still rolled in the distance, but the worst of the storm had passed. Merrek still held Kerry cradled on his lap on the couch in the parlor.

"I'm not a child, you know. You don't have to hold me like this." But she kept her head tucked under his chin, savoring the warm safety of his embrace.

"You don't like it 'ere?"

She was quiet for a moment, then, "I didn't say that."

He tightened his arms around her. "Then we're in agreement there. An' by the way—I 'ave noticed yer not a child, and the fact that we are sittin' 'ere on me bed makes me e'en more aware o' that fact."

Kerry chuckled in spite of herself. "I almost made it, didn't I? If it hadn't been for that storm, I might have made it through the night without making a fool of myself or upsetting your parents. At least I didn't break anything…yet."

"Come on, luv. Ma and Da don't upset easily. Trust me, raisin' the six o'us 'ere in this cramped house prepared 'em for most anythin', includin' civil war." Merrek tipped her chin up with his long fingers so he could see her eyes. *Damn, but she was pretty.* "Kerry…what 'appened 'ere tonight? It looked some like a seizure, darlin'."

Kerry made a move to get off his lap but he held her secure. Surrendering to his greater strength, she settled in and began her confession, starting with childhood terrors leading up to the shameful adult panic attacks.

"When did all this start?" he asked.

"That's a good question but one I don't have an answer to. Maybe

156

when I was a baby, but my parents could never pinpoint it. It's just been this way as long as I can remember. I always watch the weather to make sure I'm not caught out where I'll make a fool of myself. I've cancelled appointments, dates, even parent conferences due to weather forecasts. But here, the storms gather and turn so fast. You really never know, do you?"

"'Tis true. We 'ave to watch the sky constantly when out in the boats. We've been caught out more than once tryin' ta get in just one more catch before seekin' shore. 'E learn quickly ta try and stay one step ahead o' that fickle sea, but she's a sly one. 'Tis na always possible."

The hand that held her head tucked against his throat moved to her nape, where he began to stroke her tenderly. It comforted, gave her confidence. "It always starts in my stomach. It hurts and threatens to make me sick. Then I can't breathe. I feel trapped and so…alone. I want to scream for help, but I can't because I can't breathe and…I have no one to call. And it all feels like it's my fault somehow. That I wasn't careful enough, smart enough, strong enough…I know it doesn't seem so, but I try to be careful. In spite of my efforts, though, my phobias rule me. I have friends but…I just feel there's no one I…" she waved her hand, trying to grasp the word the she was looking for. "No one I…"

"Trust," Merrek supplied the word succinctly.

Knowingly.

Correctly.

In his arms Kerry went very still. He could almost hear her thinking, and knew there was a lot riding on the next few minutes.

Somewhere in the house, a clock chimed the end of the day, the beginning of another. Kerry moved as if on cue. "I should let you go to bed," she said even as she snuggled deeper in his arms. His lips curved against her hair. He had been holding his breath for that signal from her—that he had somehow, thank God and every saint he knew, won her trust.

Kerry glanced around the room, the only thing that made it his own was the computer desk and bookshelf filled with files in the corner. Other than that, it looked like a regular living room—couch, chairs, lamps, coffee table, and a small television. "Have you always been in this room?" she asked.

"When we were kids, Trev and I shared it. It looked like a fitty bedroom back then. The girls shared the two rooms upstairs, but when Elowyn and Genna married and I moved to London, Trev moved upstairs and Mum got her parlor. Since I've moved back, I just sleep here on the couch. I can come and go as needed without disturbin' anyone. 'Tis temporary. I've started lookin' at homes around Cornwall. As soon as Da's doctor gives 'im the good word, I plan to move inta me own place."

"How nice," Kerry yawned. "I dream of having a place of my own someday. A place to decorate, a little yard where I can plant flowers...a safe place to ride out the storms...like right here. This feels so good."

A few quiet moments later, Merrek felt Kerry's body go lax with sleep. He wanted to just lie down and pull her beside him, go to sleep feeling the warmth of her body against his, listen to her breathe, surrounded by her sweet scent. But there is always a right and wrong time for everything. So he gently shook Kerry awake and then walked her up the stairs to Rosen's bedroom, pointed out the water closet and handed her a fresh towel.

He returned to the lonely parlor/bedroom, flopped down on the sofa/bed, and stared at the ceiling. God help him—accidents *and* a phobia. Complicated was Gorran's word, but Merrek preferred intricate. Kerry was layers of guileless complexities. He wanted to know them all.

On impulse, he reached under the nearby desk and retrieved his camera. He flipped through the numerous candid shots he had taken of an unsuspecting Kerry at the Golowan party and studied her face. He had caught faint glimpses before of what was plain to see in the time-captured photos—that abandoned look behind a cheery smile, uncertainty, longing.

He replaced the camera and returned to the sofa. He closed his eyes so he could see his mind's computer screen, a mental trick he employed frequently. He watched all his carefully outlined but random goals move across that imaginary monitor to connect to one central purpose. That purpose, it seemed, was now sleeping peacefully one floor above his head.

⚓

Kerry spread her sleeping bag across the hostel bed and looked around the room. So far, she had it to herself. She missed Min and the comfort of her room at the B&B. She was already missing the warmth and safety of Merrek's home and family. She had apologized to everyone for making such a scene the night before, and she was amazed and relieved at how easily they all accepted her fear with only empathy and concern.

"Merrek really likes you," Lowenna had told her as she repacked her backpack in the girls' bedroom "It's written all over his face. I hope you like him back." It had been more of a demand than a question, and made Kerry smile.

Merrek had taken her on his bike to the new hostel and left her with a sightseeing plan accompanied by maps with highlighted routes and his admonition to be back in the hostel well before dark. He had business in London and would see her the following day.

"When did you make up these plans?" Kerry had asked him, partly touched that he would be so considerate and partly irked at his archaic domineering tendencies.

"This mornin' while 'e were still snoozin' the sunrise away," he smiled. *How could she be irritated with him after a smile like that?* "Sorry, luv. I know 'e don't care ta be cosseted, but I can't 'elp meself." Merrek gave her a scorching kiss that turned her objections to ash. Then he had cinched the deal—*they would go to Porth on Saturday.*

Kerry pulled out her iPad and sat in the middle of her sleeping bag. The first thing she did was to check the weather forecasts for Porth—not that two days out meant any form of surety, but it was habit. So far, there were no scary possibilities.

The next thing on her list was a long email to Mrs. Tesmer. She wrote of her genealogy findings, the moors, the Golowan festival, the interesting people she had met at Min's B&B, and her plans for the day that Merrek had meticulously laid out for her, only she didn't mention Merrek Walles. Not yet. At present, she was reticent to share Merrek with anyone other than Tania.

After sending that email, she locked her belongings in her locker and picked up the highlighted maps. They were so precise she could not get lost unless she misplaced the maps. There was a measure of comfort in that, but the point of this trip was to build self-reliance, and that would be hard to cultivate if Merrek kept taking care of her. After last night, she knew it would be hard not to fall into that trap. His arms offered warmth and safety, his smile promised comfort and care, all the things she had craved since the loss of her parents.

She would have to be careful not to depend on him. It did not help that she liked him—*a lot.* She liked his smile and his laugh. His dark brown eyes that glinted with golden highlights when he teased captivated her, and she knew that those same eyes could deepen to almost black with steely glints when he became irritated. She liked the way he smelled—a masculine mixture of sea breezes and cedar. The attraction she felt for him was something new to her. She felt...sparks. A wide smile lit up her face. *I can spark, Tania. I just needed a fitty match.*

The tone on her iPad signaled the timely arrival of an email from Tania. It was a long missive, so Kerry took her iPad, locked the door, and went to the commons area to sip a cup of tea while she read. She almost shrieked her delight at the news of Tania's marriage proposal from Robert. He had even managed to do it in a romantic way. Then there was the news of the expansion of their favorite coffee shop to include a bakery, and hello's and good wishes from all her friends. There was no mention of Owen, however. Tania would not forget to pass along his inquiries or greetings, so there apparently had been none. Most of the email consisted of wedding plans, honeymoon options, and dreams for the future. Kerry took a few minutes to look out on the streets of Penzance, sip her tea and lose herself in dreams of her own.

The storms of the night before had receded, but left this new day drenched and gray. Merrek had drawn her touring plans carefully to keep her as dry as possible and entertained with many "cultural experiences" as he would say. He had planned well.

Merrek met her at her hostel early the next morning and took her to see the fascinating Jubilee Pool. As they walked the perimeter of the triangular pool they laughed together at the faces of those entering the pool for the first time, the shock from the cold apparent in their expressions and their squeals. Kerry got the shivers just watching them, and Merrek quickly chased them away when he wrapped his arms around her and pressed her back close against his warm chest. Unable to resist, he nuzzled her neck, nibbled on her earlobe, and then kissed her mouth when she turned her head and tilted her face up to his in invitation.

"Mayhap I should take a dip in that cold water," he chuckled softly, putting her away from him and taking her hand. "Ready to go for a ride?"

They took Merrek's bike to the docks at Newlyn where Merrek showed Kerry the Walles' fishing fleet. As he showed her the workings of the boats and explained the strengths of each design, she imagined him as he would have appeared centuries before, both as a fisherman and a pirate. With his dark features and his muscular body, his incredible balance and his dancing eyes, he would have fit either role well. How did he see her? A klutzy maid always in distress? Why couldn't she be like those fearless women smugglers about whom she had read? One was even captain of her own ship. *I'm a disgrace to the women's movement*, she thought, *no matter the century.*

For dinner, Merrek took her to a quiet and impressive little restaurant she had seen advertised as one of the places one should not miss while visiting Cornwall. It did not disappoint…except for one detail.

Kerry had just returned to their table from the restroom and they had begun to peruse the dessert menu when a shadow accompanied by the staccato of spiked heels darkened their table. Kerry looked up when she heard Merrek audibly groan. Turning her head, Kerry almost gawked at the approach of a woman oozing sophistication and elegance.

The woman was stunning, somewhere in her mid-thirties—not a real beauty, but very attractive mostly because of her poise, confidence, and immaculate, expensive clothes. She had her dark hair cut in a chic and sassy style, and it swished around her jaw line when she tossed her head. Kerry was glad she had worn her Golowan outfit instead of her customary jeans and t-shirt, but she still felt dowdy beside this sophisticated Venus. The woman's smile was nice enough, but Kerry noticed her artfully made-up brown eyes remained hard and calculating.

"Merrek, I thought that was you." Her voice reminded Kerry of honey—sticky honey, the aggravating kind that somehow transfers from your fingers to your clothes to your hair like a crafty and annoying spider web. "It's been a long time. I never see you in London anymore." She did not even acknowledge Kerry.

"Sophia. What are you doing in Cornwall?" Merrek's words were clipped, polite but not quite friendly. Kerry glanced at Merrek's face. His expression was hard, and his features flushed.

Still ignoring Kerry, Sophia answered, "I'm hosting a charity function here in Penzance at the Jubilee Pool. I recently moved to a young but fast growing banking firm headquartered in the Square Mile. I am personal assistant to the president, who sought me outrageously with an *irresistible* sign-on bonus and a handsome salary. I joined his group in January. It's been a good move for me."

"So your disloyalty even reaches to the corporate levels, aye?" was Merrek's stony reply.

"It's business, darling, and I'm good at it. Why don't you come with me to the function this evening?"

Merrek reached across the table and took Kerry's hand. "Kerry, please forgive us. Sophia, this is Kerry Carter, a teacher from North Carolina, America. Kerry, Sophia Weston."

Kerry gave her usual sweet smile. "It's nice to meet you, Sophia. That's such a pretty name."

The woman blinked at her, then turned back to Merrek. "It's going to be a fabulous party. You really should come. You would be delicious eye candy, and I could introduce you to some lucrative contacts. Are you still trying to get that little photography business off the ground? I know people, you know."

Merrek smiled at Kerry. "Kerry and I have already been to the Jubilee Pool this afternoon. It was very…stimulating, wouldn't you agree, luv?"

Kerry could not keep the blush from her face, but she was pleased that her voice was smooth and level. "Very, although I preferred the moors. I love the primitive and sacred feel of that place. It's sort of mystifying, secretive, you know what I mean?" She looked up to include Sophia in the conversation.

Sophia gave Kerry a quick scan and then dismissed her again. Turning back to Merrek, she laid a hand glittering with rings and bracelets on his shoulder, "Taking one of Rosen's little friends sightseeing, dear? How sweet of you, although I'd be careful if I were you. Some might find it a bit sick."

Merrek's eyes darkened dangerously. "Mayhap in yer advancin' years 'e need ta invest in 'earing aides, Sophia. Didna 'e just 'ere me say Kerry's an educator from America? She's also here ta do research pertainin' to 'er family's genealogy. A worthy endeavor, that."

A pinched look passed quickly over Sophia's face, but she recovered quickly with a toss of her head, which sent her shimmering hair swinging and then bouncing back into place. She must spend a fortune on hair products to achieve such an effect, thought Kerry, and she wondered if this was the woman Genna and her sister had spoken of at Elowen's bonfire. If so, Merrek and this Sophia woman had been intimate, and Kerry was surprised at the degree of resentment that stabbed her.

She could imagine Merrek and Sophia walking gracefully side by side, a bold and beautiful pair, his hand proudly at her back—not like the picture she and Merrek presented, his hand always at her elbow to catch her when she stumbled. She quickly looked down at the dessert menu and tried to pretend she was not even there.

But Sophia broke through her pretense when she crooned, "Merrek, did you ever come across those David Yurman earrings I used to wear back when we lived in the London apartment…*together*?" she added with that last with emphasis, obviously for Kerry's benefit.

Merrek caught Kerry's quick glance, and in that brief meeting he saw a kaleidoscope of emotions flash in her wonderfully readable eyes before she lowered them back to the menu. He had seen disgust, anger, sympathy even, but it was the insecurity and hurt that made his blood boil. *Damn Sophia for that.*

Fixing the woman with hard eyes, he drawled, "I promise 'e I removed every tiny remnant of yer person from that apartment, and then scrubbed it clean, and after four years no earrings 'ave been found anywhere."

Sophia bristled at his harsh words, but even though she had lost that battle, she was not yet through with the war. Running her fingers across his back, she almost purred, "Maybe I should come over and help you look again. They are subtle, but very valuable. I hate to give up on them completely."

"Then 'e'll 'ave ta speak with the landlord. I moved out...and on. So that settled, 'e'll excuse us while Kerry and I order dessert."

Sophia could not hide the fact that she was incensed he would so casually dismiss her. Her voice turned low, harsh and more than a bit tetchy. "You probably pawned them, you dockside trash."

Kerry's head snapped up at that. This was between the two of them, but she would not stay and listen to this ill-mannered twit degrade Merrek or his family, no matter how well put together and *subtle* she tried to be. Gathering up her things, she rose and glared up into Sophia's haughty face but spoke to Merrek. "I think I'll forego dessert," she said softly, and after making a show of raking her eyes over Sophia's voluptuous curves, added, "I'm suddenly reminded of the results of such indulgence." And with that, she turned and walked straight to the doorway without a backward glance, her head high and her backside trailing a tail of toilet paper that clung to the back of her skirt.

Merrek felt a strong tug on his heart and knew he would do whatever was necessary to keep Sophia from witnessing Kerry's otherwise stately exit. Luckily, Sophia had yet to recover from the shock of that set down by a woman she no doubt considered beneath her, and was still blinking at the table. Merrek took out his wallet, waited until Kerry was out the door, and then waved the British currency in Sophia's face to gain her attention. "Be a dear and drop this in your charity bucket for me, will 'e, old girl? Me dessert's awaitin' outside," and with a wiggle of eyebrows and a delighted grin, he laid the money on the table, stopped by the desk to pay the tab, and rushed out to find Kerry.

He found her pacing the sidewalk half a block away. As soon as he reached her, he jerked the toilet paper out of its static cling and wadded it up in his hand, grabbed her elbow with the other and pulled her to his side. "Touché, luv," he chuckled in her ear, "Very well done of 'e."

But Kerry jerked away. The anger still hot in her eyes, she hissed, "What a nasty piece of fluff she is. How in the world were you ever... with her?"

As if he had not asked himself the same question thousands of times, and *how did Kerry even know about Sophia? Oh, yeah, his interfering sisters.* "I don't know, luv. I was a young dobleck...she was older...she played on me stupid naivety...me ego..."

"Did you love her?" Kerry's eyes communicated her dread of that answer.

"No," his answer came quickly, emphatically. "Oh, I thought I did at the time and bein' a believer in the marriage institution I was entertainin' thoughts o' proposin'. But all I ever felt after I found out...after I broke it off...was humiliation and anger...and then relief. I never felt loss. Betrayal, yes, but not loss. So, no, I assure 'e, I never loved her. I was just a typical young bloke who had to learn the difference between love and... well..."

Kerry advanced on him, stabbed her finger at his chest to emphasize her words, "Well, I hope it didn't take you too long to learn how to toss her out on her Alexander-McQueen-clad ass." He backed up a step, but she continued her rant. "The nerve of her suggesting you would steal from her, and that slur she threw at your family...what a *nasty* woman."

A huge grin spread across Merrek's features. He thought this was one of her most splendid moments, looking like an indignant Viking princess with her flaming hair blowing about her head in the breeze, her green eyes snapping like firecrackers. "Aye," he assured her, "I did just that, me wee warrior. Except it might o' been on 'er Michael-Khors-clad ass, but who cares? I've found meself partial to Levi's these days." He pulled her back into his arms and kissed the rigidness from her right there on the street.

And that did not take long. Kerry could not help but respond. The man certainly knew how to kiss. But the thought of him kissing Sophia made her push away from him again. He raised his eyebrows and she huffed. "I'll bet Sophia never falls into stinging nettles or slops raspberry sauce on her clothes," she said dolefully.

Merrek stepped close and brushed her cheek with the backs of his fingers. Hell, he could not keep his hands off her. "I doubt the word 'hike' is in Sophia's vocabulary and I know for sure she'd never offer ta pick flowers for Min, not ta mention the fact that stinging nettles 'ave standards, too. As for the other—her wardrobe may be rich, but 'tis bloody borin'—no scrapbook o' memories there."

"I should wear a bib," Kerry lamented as she brushed at some crumbs still clinging to her blouse.

He chuckled at that. "Ah, Kerry, then people would think I was robbin' the cradle for sure." She huffed again at that. "'E may disparage of those youthful looks now, but I'd bet me bike you'll still be a knock-out at sixty."

Her color high, Kerry looked shyly at Merrek. "You think I'm a knock-out?"

"Ah, darlin', me an most the male population. 'E don't see the heads that turn?"

"Now you're teasing me. Compared to Sophia, I…"

Merrek cut her off. "Don't ever attempt to compare yerself to the likes o' her. 'Twould be like comparing an angelfish to a shark. Kerry, I love your honesty and your wholesomeness. What can I do to convince 'e…"

Kerry's smile came slowly across her face, the imp showing itself again through her eyes. "You might try kissing me again," she shyly interrupted.

Merrek's eyes softened and the golden glints that always accompanied his smile returned. "Aye," his voice seductive in her ear as he pulled her close. "'Ow does the sayin' go? *'E never know til 'e try*? Who said that?" His lips brushed hers lightly.

"Who cares?" Kerry whispered just before Merrek's lips covered hers.

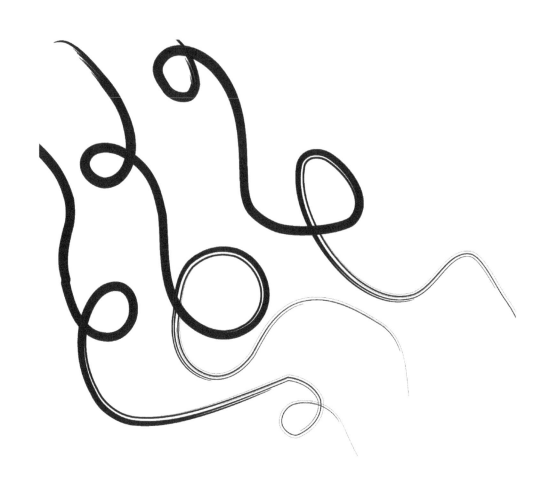

- 12 -

When we illuminate the road back to our ancestors,
They have a way of reaching out, of manifesting themselves...
Sometimes even physically.
—Raquel Cepeda

Even though Saturday morning's clouds hung low in the sky and the blustery wind had a bite to it, Merrek was in an unusually sunny mood on his way to meet Kerry at her hostel. He was actually glad now that the surprise confrontation with Sophia had occurred. He had known they would have to discuss his prior relationship with Sophia eventually, and now that it was over, he felt a huge burden fall from his shoulders—and not just where Kerry was concerned. Seeing Sophia again was like a baptism in ice-cold water. *What had he ever seen in the woman?* He felt young again—new, clean and ready to take on a world full of promises.

Kerry was waiting for him when pulled his bike into the parking lot. She was dressed in her usual jeans and t-shirt, stains hidden beneath her windbreaker, and she had braided her hair in preparation for the bike ride. She looked all of sixteen; her bright smile a beacon in the cloudy day. How dull his life had been until that cyclist had pushed her into his arms. *Fate? Luck?* Now even he was beginning to listen to pixies.

"Takin' yer backpack, are 'e?" He smiled in greeting.

"I thought I would, just in case...I don't know what. It just seemed to be the thing. I'll wear it though, so you can do the driving without worrying with it. I carried it all over London, right?" She smiled, "Before you came along."

He handed her a helmet and smiled as she put it on and snapped it in place, adjusted the chinstraps like a pro. "That would be best I'm guessin'. With this wind, you'll need me as a shield. We're just going to the train station anyway. If the weather turns bad, we don't want ta be on the bike."

Kerry froze, "I checked this morning—it's supposed to be a light rain if any. Have you heard differently?"

167

"I'm just cautious when it looks like this," he studied her worried face. "I packed a small bag also, just in case. But don't fret, luv. I'll be with 'e should it storm." She answered with a trusting smile and nod, and then they were off.

⚓

Porth proved to be a beautiful gem of a village tucked between towering cliffs on three sides, the fourth opening up to a lovely beach and harbor. Fishing boats, neatly tethered on one side of the harbor, left the rest of the beach open. The cottages built into and among the cliffs gave the village an ancient look and feel. Kerry felt as though they had stepped back in time. Her anticipation ran high, anxious to find whatever Porth had to offer her in terms of family.

After acquiring directions to the cemetery, she and Merrek climbed the steep hills up to the graveyard. The view from the top was breathtaking. The cliffs that guarded the little hamlet boasted sheer drops to the ocean below where the water crashed into outcroppings of rocks. The village stirred with activity, most of the boats safely tied at the harbor by now although they could see a few still scattered about on the green water. The wind that whipped around them tasted of salt and excitement. Kerry wondered what it would be like to live here, and what it had been like centuries ago.

Merrek suggested they split up to search the ancient cemetery. There were quite a few Carter markers. Kerry frantically wrote down names and dates to match up later. Finally, she found them—Rowse and Mary Carter, and to Kerry's gush of delight, Rowse's parents, all buried together near an overgrowth of native shrubbery that was threatening to take over that portion of the cemetery.

"Talan and Annik Carter," Kerry read from the stone markers. "Look, Annik lived from 1743 to 1770, making her only twenty-seven when she died. Talan lived almost nine more years. 1721 to 1779. He would have been fifty-eight."

"That was a might good age, I'd think, for backalong those days."

Kerry's delight was effusive. "These are my people, Merrek! My family!"

She checked her notes and did some quick calculations. "Rowse, the son, born in 1761, would only have been nine years old when he lost his mother and eighteen when his father died."

"Hardly a man. Little older than Trev. Too young ta be buryin' one's parents." He glanced at Kerry's downcast eyes and winced. "But then, you would know all about that. Sorry, luv."

"Yeah," sighed Kerry. "It's okay." She looked up at the clouds. "It looks like that rain is holding. Do you think we have time to clear back this greenery? No one has seen to these graves in a long time. I feel like it's my responsibility now. I'd also like to take some pictures."

Merrek followed her skyward glance. "Aye, just enough."

The next few minutes they worked in quiet as they hurried to pull back the encroaching vines and shrubs. Kerry pulled at an especially stubborn vine, and when it finally gave way she stumbled backward, falling over something hard and unmoving hidden in the shrubs behind the two older Carter graves. Merrek was there almost immediately, his face taut with concern as he gently pulled her free of green tentacles. "You okay, Kerry?"

She rubbed her side where it was already starting to swell. "Yeah, I fell over a rock or something in there. I think my money belt actually saved my skin." She started to get up, but Merrek pushed her back down.

"Catch yer breath, luv. I'll finish 'ere."

Kerry did not argue, but watched with interest as Merrek worked on the vines and shrubs. "Do you see anything in that clump there? Whatever it is made me painfully aware of its existence."

"I'll see to it. Might 'ave to give it a solid thrashin' for hurtin' 'e."

When Kerry heard a throaty gasp from Merrek, she jumped up, in spite of the stitch in her side. "Are you all right?" she asked, but his face showed more fascination than pain. "Merrek? What is it?"

He lifted his head to meet her curious eyes. He said in a disbelieving tone, "'E've got to see this." She stepped around the shrubbery to stand beside him. He pulled back the shrubs and vines and announced, "Kerenza Carter...meet *Kerenza Carter.*"

Kerry was sure the world tilted slightly when her eyes fell on the stone. Merrek's dependable arms were already there to steady her. "Oh, Merrek, this is truly creepy. I feel like I just stepped on my own grave. What are the odds of something like this? It's not as if I'm named after her. Dad didn't even know these people existed."

She stared at the old marker in amazement as Merrek stooped down to read the worn inscription underneath the name, "*Born 1767. Lost at sea 1792.* So this is just a memorial stone, not an actual grave."

"She was twenty-five—my age. Wait...she must have been Rowse's little sister. She would have been only three when her mother died, poor little thing."

"She was around twelve when her da died. If Rowse was eighteen, he must have raised her to an adult. I guess he's the one responsible for the marker."

Thunder rolled in the distance but Kerry did not react, so caught up she was in their extraordinary discovery. "Look, there's more wording, just below the dirt," observed Kerry. "See the tops of the letters there?"

"Aye." Merrek began digging. "Over the years, the stone has sunk or dirt has washed up around here." He straightened and looked around. "Hand me over that stone there behind yer foot."

Kerry picked up the stone and laid it in his outstretched hand. His fingers closed around it and her hand. He held both briefly for a moment, their locked eyes glittering in mutual wonderment and excitement. Then he took the rock from her and continued digging. When Merrek had uncovered the last of the inscription, they both sat back on their heels as the magnitude of what they had discovered washed over them both. The rest of the inscription read, *I will wait for you forever, my darling. ~ MW.*

- 13 -

There are cultures in which it is believed that a name
contains all a person's mystical power...
This it seemed was such a name.
—Diane Setterfield

"It's her," Kerry finally released the breath she had been holding. "The woman in the painting? *I know it's her.* MW—the same signature as on the canvas. She's my...what? Ancestral aunt? And it's got to be him—Myghal Walles—your uncle several generations removed." Kerry stood and began to pace. "Oh...my...Merrek, this is truly stranger than fiction. They knew each other, my ancestor and yours."

"T'would seem to be so," he answered in a quiet, reverent voice. "An' 'ere we are, some two hundred years later."

Before they could begin to contemplate the intricacies of this discovery, they became acutely aware of an impending storm. Out over the water, dark clouds were beginning to swirl and move toward the shore. Merrek swore in both English and Cornish as lightning flashed in the distance and the clap of thunder that followed it caused the color to leave Kerry's face. He threw on her backpack, scooped her and his bag up in his arms and began the descent toward the little town. The sky suddenly opened up and rain poured as he cautiously made his way down the slippery slopes.

"Put me down. I can run with you." Kerry surprised him with her sharp demand. He stopped and searched her face for assurance. "You'll hurt yourself carrying all this weight." Kerry explained.

"'E weigh nothing, luv, but if I slip 'e'll go down w' me." He put her on her feet, but he took her hand in his. "Sorry, sweetheart. The storm slipped up on me. I would not have exposed 'e to this. Yer good? Yer side?"

"My side won't matter if we're struck by lightning. Let's just go."

As lightning flashed all around them, Kerry felt as if they were running through a battlefield, but the firm grip of Merrek's strong hand abated her terror. Finally, they reached the edge of the village and ducked under the eaves of a grocer for shelter. For a moment, they stood there, gasping for breath, mesmerized by the lightning display. Kerry trembled, but did not seem faint. Merrek leaned down to her ear. "Happy July Fourth, Darlin'. Looks like you're gettin' your fireworks after all."

The last traces of Kerry's uneasiness vanished as she smiled at him in sudden realization, delighted with the distraction. "Thank you. I didn't expect anyone here to think of it. I actually forgot about it myself."

"Well, first off, I can be a fitty diplomat I can. And second—if it has anythin' to do with you, darlin', I've thought of it." He looked up and down the street while those words settled in her mind. "Let's see what we've got 'ere."

There was a pub across the street, and the thought of food and the warm and settling effect of whiskey brought them to a quick agreement. Merrek took a minute to let his eyes travel over Kerry. "Where's yer slicker?"

"I took it off at the cemetery. It's in my pack."

"'E might want ta put it back on."

Kerry looked at him in amused puzzlement. "Little good it will do me now. I'm already soaked to the skin."

"Aye, that you are. And not much about you is left to the imagination in your current state there, luv." He chuckled when Kerry gasp in sudden understanding and unzipped her pack. "Not that I mind," he continued. "Not in the least. But I'm not willin' ta share that scenery with the other blokes in the pub. Ready?"

Zipped up in her rain jacket, Kerry put her hand in Merrek's and they raced across the street and into the cheery but puddle-laden pub.

"Common zon," laughed a middle-aged woman carrying a tray of beer. "'Ee look like a cupla half-drowned wharf rats. Sit over there by some fire afore 'e git all rumped up. I'll be short'wit'e."

"*Rumped up*? Now there's a new one." Kerry said through chattering teeth.

"Aye, rumped up…cold…'e know, like a baby's position when tryin' to stay warm."

"Ah!" Kerry beamed. "That makes total sense. Just more…graphic."

Merrek laughed. "Like 'e said before, Cornish is nothin' if not colorful."

They took turns in the restroom changing into dry clothes, and then fortunately found a table near the fire. Merrek ordered shots of whiskey and an assortment of meat pasties and potatoes. Over their meal, they discussed their discovery.

"I still can't get over 'ow boldly those family genes have resurfaced after all these years," he mused. "If the woman in my uncle Myghal's painting is the Kerenza Carter that went missin' all those years ago, there is no doubt she's related to 'e. 'E could be sisters."

"How well do you think they knew each other, my relative and yours?" Kerry's green eyes sparkled.

"Well enough for her to pose as his model for that paintin'. Unless, of course, he painted her from memory—in which case, he'd dwelt on her extensively I'd think."

"You think they were lovers then?"

He looked up, and for a moment, his eyes focused on her whiskey-moistened mouth. "If she was anythin' like you…and he was at all like me…" his eyes finally broke free from her lips and seized hers. "…I think there's a brilliant chance."

Kerry's breath caught and she felt her heart slam against her chest. She was feeling warmer by the minute, could feel her flushed face, and knew that it had nothing to do with the whiskey or her proximity to the fire. Somehow, she found the fortitude to continue, "And she had my name. *Unbelievable.* It would be just too much if the painter's name was Merrek Walles."

Merrek coughed slightly and set his drink down slowly. "Well, now, and 'ere's where I'm to blow yer mind, luv—Myghal's the old Cornish derivation of Michael, and as fantastic as it seems, me full name is Merrek Michael Walles."

Kerry felt a familiar chill run down her spine, familiar because she had experienced it several times since uncovering Kerenza's memorial stone. How was it that an American girl answering a *call* and a Cornishman idly walking down the street collided, and not only had fireworks ignited, but a strong sense of belonging as well? If the Kerenza and Myghal of the 1700's were lovers, had they brought together their namesakes to continue an interrupted love affair? *I'll wait for you forever, my darling.*

"It's almost as if they've brought us together somehow," she mused, embarrassed when she realized she had spoken that thought aloud.

Merrek slung back his whiskey, and then a ghost of speculation crossed over his handsome features. "So then whose call was it 'e heard, luv? Kerenza's? Or maybe it was Myghal's. And I can't believe I'm even thinkin' this way." He shook his head and glanced dubiously at his empty whiskey glass.

Kerry sucked in a breath. "Or maybe there is something as simple as life after death, and since I ended up with her name, she feels she's been given a second chance and she's guiding me, trying to keep me safe by...I don't know...infusing me with these phobias," she could not stop her imagination from flowing, "I wonder how she became lost at sea. Maybe she was prone to accidents, like me, and fell off a boat? Rowse was probably a fisherman; do you think he would take his sister to help out? Or maybe she was swept out to sea somehow. I suppose you do have hurricanes here?"

"Oh, aye. Fierce 'uns they can be, too. We should look up storms of that era—see if there was one in 1792. And then, there's also the fact that in the late 1700's, this part o' England would've been ripe w' smugglers 'n pirates, and she was a Carter. Mayhap she caught the fancy of some pirate cap'n and he asked her to join 'im aboard 'is vessel."

"If that's so, then he must have caught her fancy, too. Not good for Myghal. After all, she could have said 'no'."

Merrek poured a little more whiskey in her glass, his eyes taking on a devilish gleam. "Ah, but 'ere's the thing, luv. Didde know there is na an old Cornish word that specifically means 'no'? Best keep that in mind, darlin'," he warned with a wicked smile and a wink.

"Really? But surely there's a word that means...uh-uh?" Merrek shook his head and smiled. "Nix?...veto?..." Merrek continued to shake his head, his smile spreading wider as Kerry continued, "...ain't happenin'? No way, Jose? Don't? St..." she caught herself.

But Merrek had been waiting for it. "*Don't stop?*" Those devilish eyes sparkled. "Aye, we Cornish men hear that often."

Kerry's breath threatened to freeze, but her quick wit came to her rescue. "How about 'By Tre, Pol, and Pen you'll know true Cornish men?'" She teased. "You don't have any of those prefixes in your name, so...are you a true Cornish man, in that sense?"

Merrek smiled broadly, reached across the table and captured her hand. He so enjoyed bantering with her. "We genuine, authentic, bona fide Cornish men don't need prefixes ta prove our Cornish manliness—in *that* sense."

Kerry laughed. "Cornish? Maybe you mean corny-ish?"

An explosion of light suddenly filled the room and then all went very dark. Two seconds later a deep and ground shaking roll of thunder announced another terrific downpour accompanied by substantial winds.

Kerry gasped and squeezed Merrek's hand that held hers. He could feel her tremors and brought her hand to his lips. "Twill be alright, luv," Merrek's voice came to her softly in the darkness. "Put yer fear aside. I'm right 'ere."

Shortly, several areas of soft light broke through the blackness. "Good," Merrek sighed, "they're lighting lanterns. Aye, we're going nowhere tonight—good thing we brought our bags. I'm goin' ta walk over and ask that bar maid if there's a place we can stay the night." He peeled her fingers away from his hand. "I'll be right back. Stay here."

Kerry watched him walk across the room. In spite of her nervousness over the storm outside, she could not help but admire the self-assuredness that showed in the way he moved. How did one acquire such confidence?

When he turned the corner in search of information, Kerry looked for another distraction from the building storm. She bent to take her notebook out of her pack, thinking to look over the information they had just obtained from the cemetery. When she pulled on the notebook, the pen flew out and rolled across the floor. Not thinking, she got up and chased it…right into the arms and lap of a rough looking, foul smelling character whose fast and sure hands belied the amount of ale he had most likely consumed.

"Come ta give ole Delwain a kiss?" He pulled her closer to his toothless smile. His hands seemed to be everywhere at once while his inebriated drinking buddies cheered him on.

"No!" Kerry shrieked. Delwain did not seem to understand the word and did not let up on his attack. Kerry groaned, "Oh, you blasted Cornish!" She wildly snatched a full tankard from the table and swung it hard at the man's face, catching him broadside in the ear and sloshing dark ale over both of them. "Did that translate?" she shouted. Another time the man might have laughed at her defense, but not this time. His ear was still ringing as he raised his meaty hand for the hard slap he intended to inflict when he felt his arm captured in a vise-like grip he could not break. A dark shadow fell across the table and the man looked up into granite-hard black eyes.

Without raising his voice, Merrek warned him, "'E'll not be wantin' ta do that, mate. Trust me. Let 'er go."

Sober enough to know he did not want to test the naked threat in those eyes nor challenge the strength in the man's grip, the brute took his other arm from around Kerry's waist, even used it to push her gently from his lap.

Merrek took Kerry's arm with his free hand and guided her behind him. Without taking his eyes off the drunken man, and alert to the movements of his buddies, Merrek let go of the man's arm and backed away to their table, keeping Kerry pressed close.

The jovial barmaid, who had witnessed the tense scene yelled out, "Next drink is on the house!" rendering the incident forgotten in the enthusiasm for free beer. Merrek nodded his appreciation to the woman, although he knew one round of free beer was a fraction of the cost and bother of a brawl-damaged room.

Turning toward Kerry, Merrek anticipated the alarm he expected to find in her eyes and how he was going to deal with it. Instead, she surprised him by the fiery anger and livid disgust that blazed in those beautiful green eyes, her delicate jaws firmly set in anticipation of a fight. That surprised him more than her display of passion earlier in the week. He could not keep the smile from spreading over his face. *Dear Lord, she was a catch.* "'E look like yer ready for trouble there, luv."

Kerry sighed in resignation. "I told you trouble finds me."

Merrek slipped his arms around her. "Aye, 'e 'ave." Before Kerry knew what he was about, Merrek drew her up to him, embraced her possessively and planted a lengthy and assertive kiss on her mouth amid whoops, wolf calls, and lewd remarks from the men that filled the pub.

When he raised his head, he smiled at her confused expression, and then whispered in her ear, "Just markin' me territory, darlin'. That should preclude any more misunderstandin's amongst the clientele."

Kerry glanced briefly over his shoulder at the numerous men sitting around the room in various levels of drunkenness, stuck here by the storm with nothing else to do but drink more. This would not be the place for a woman alone, Merrek had been right about that. She lifted her eyes back to Merrek's and was extremely glad he had insisted on coming with her, "Thank you for coming to my rescue."

"You were puttin' up a fair fight on yer own there. I'm beginnin' ta think I underestimated Ole' Jean Claude and those self-defense classes."

"Am I your territory then?"

Direct and to the point she was. He hedged at it, uncertain of her feelings. "As far as everyone 'ere tonight is concerned, aye, 'e are. I don't want 'e ta worry, luv. 'E'll come t' no 'arm."

She looked up into dark eyes that gleamed with the truth of that arrogant statement. The question was out of her mouth almost as soon as she thought it. "How can you be so sure?"

He did not miss a beat. "I'll not allow it."

She wondered briefly if Myghal had been this resolute would the sea have taken Kerenza away? The conviction that burned in Merrek's eyes looked to be capable of defying even a stormy sea. He made her feel so safe, and…worthy. She had never felt like that in her life, and another foreign realization came to her as she lost herself in those eyes.

I think I love him.

Merrek studied her from across the table. He had grown up with in-your-face-beautiful women, but Kerry had an exquisite, soft beauty. Even now as her rain and ale dampened hair dried into an array of soft curls in no particular style but their own and her lustrous eyes gleamed with affection. Every time he looked at her she became dearer, and he was becoming obsessed with looking at her.

I think I love her.

"Luck is with us by the way," he told her. "I found us a place to stay the night if 'e don't mind sleepin' in a brothel."

"You're kidding me," but her expression was unsure.

Merrek laughed. "Upstairs there's rooms what was once a brothel backalong…years ago. Like the saloons in your western movies, aye? They've been renovated inta a small hotel. The lady at the bar says they're some nice."

"Well, that's handy. We won't have to get back out in the storm."

"There's only one thing," he eyed her warily. "We'll be stayin' in the same room. All these people here are lookin' for places ta stay. We shouldn't take up two rooms, and besides, I don't want 'e down the hall from me. I hope you'll agree."

Kerry did a quick survey of the characters in the room. "I don't want to be more than two feet away from you," she said decisively.

Merrek kept a straight face but his eyes glinted. "We can make that 'appen."

The ex-brothel room was indeed quite nice. Not as nice as Min's, but clean and comfortable and much homier than the hostels Kerry had become accustomed to. Decorated in keeping with the old brothel days, it even included an ornate wooden dressing screen in one corner shielding a small area for an old-fashioned toilette. They had to share the bathroom down the hall with two other rooms, but since showers were out of the question anyway with all the lightning activity outside and the power outage, they had to be content with an old timey bowl and pitcher behind

177

the screen. Merrek brought water from the hallway bathroom for Kerry to use, then removed it and brought in some fresh for himself, having her lock the door each time he left the room.

"This is like going back in time—taking a sponge bath by candlelight," Kerry said as she walked aimlessly around the room in clean jeans and tank top while trying to work the tangles from her hair. "You know, you can get a decent bath from a bowl of soapy water. But I'd really love to wash my hair. It smells like stale beer."

Merrek chuckled from behind the screen. "I imagine it does—you doused the both o' 'e in that scuffle downstairs. I can help 'e with that. It'll only take a minute to go get some fresh water." He stepped into the room from behind the screen, shirtless, and smiled at her.

Kerry was not expecting to see him without a shirt. She froze for a moment, unable to keep her eyes from sweeping across the definition in his arms and trunk. His body was magnificent, and although she had been impressed with his intimidating strength that night at Min's, she now understood that she'd only experienced a fraction of his capability. She willed her eyes off his muscular and tanned torso and focused on the pajama pants that set loosely on his narrow hips. They were black with little white skulls and cross bones scattered over them.

"What?" his eyes followed hers.

"I was just wondering if you'd like me to help you track down the joker that packed those pants for you so you can…get revenge?"

Merrek looked down at his pants and then back up to stare at her in playful defense. "What's wrong wi' me knickers? Rosen gave 'em to me for Christmas las' year. I wore 'em tonight 'specially for you, luv. They coordinate wi'the whole pirate/smugglin' theme goin' on 'ere."

She smiled at his response. "Did they come with a matching shirt?"

"I don't sleep in shirts." His left eyebrow arched slightly and he motioned to her jeans. "Do you usually sleep in those?"

Kerry glanced down at her jeans and felt the blush spreading up from her neck. "I don't usually share a room with a man."

His mouth twitched with the hint of a smile. "Unlike the former occupants of this room then, aye?"

Kerry looked around the room and remembered its former use as a brothel. "Oh, that's right," she breathed. "Oh, man…If these walls could talk…"

"…You'd be blushin' so hard you'd catch fire. Back in a jiffy—lock the door."

When Merrek returned, Kerry lathered her hair using a small amount of the fresh water and then leaned over the basin while Merrek poured the rest slowly over her head. After squeezing out as much water as she could, she leaned over and captured the tresses in a towel which she twisted turban style. When she righted herself, a smile of contentment on her face, she found Merrek watching her with a glint in those compelling black eyes. "What?" she asked, a little embarrassed.

His eyes softened, and he looked a little embarrassed himself. "I'll clean this up and get us some fresh water for the mornin'. Go ahead and finish with your hair."

While Merrek was gone, Kerry scrunched and fluffed her hair with her fingers. When he came back with fresh water, he double locked their door. "Things are getting a little loud down in the bar," he explained.

Just then they heard a threatening roll of thunder. "It's getting loud again out there," observed Kerry, worry etched in her features. "It sounds like a new storm wave is coming in."

"Aye. Not good odds for much sleep tonight, either way. Are 'e feelin' okay? No panic?"

"No," Kerry answered quickly, surprised. "A little apprehension, but no...no panic. I feel...safe."

Merrek glanced her way a couple of times while he straightened things up around the room. "Well," he said finally. "Can't watch the telly." He motioned to her backpack. "No signal for yer iPad, so no recreation there. I didn't see any cards anywhere, so I suppose we could jus'...listen to the storm and...talk?"

Kerry sat on the edge of the bed—the *only* place to sit. "Sure. How long do you think the storm will last? Have you heard how bad it's predicted to get?"

Merrek sat down beside her. "'E's supposed to last all night, and storms like this are hard to predict. Could turn nasty, could jus' wear itself out."

Kerry glanced at him and then away. "We have storms like that back home, too. I'm usually huddled in my bed under the covers scared to death." Merrek breathed a shaky sigh. "Are we goin' to spend the night talkin' about the weather, then?"

Kerry stood, aimlessly walked to the window and opened the curtain. "Well," she was unsure of what to do or say. "Well..."

A blinding flash of white light suddenly flooded the room accompanied by a cracking sound from outside the window where Kerry stood. In one fluid motion, Merrek left the bed and pushed Kerry away from the window. He pressed her against the wall, sheltered her by bracing his arms on either side of her. "Woman, don't 'e know not ta stand in a window during a lightnin' storm?"

"I do. Of course, I do," she declared, staring eye-level at the small medallion he wore around his neck that was nestled in the hair that covered his chest. It was St. Andrew. He had told her that, days ago when she'd noticed the chain around his neck. St. Andrew was the patron saint of fishermen and was a gift from his mother. Lifting her eyes to his, she swallowed. "I don't know what I was thinking."

Those deep green eyes were dazed and a bit confused. Merrek held her gaze a long moment. He read wariness there, timidity, but no fear or mistrust, which greatly pleased him. Without moving his hands from the wall, he slowly leaned his head down and buried his face in the soft, slightly damp curls that fell over the curve of her neck and inhaled deeply. "'E know what I'm thinkin'?" he murmured as he exhaled slowly. "I'm thinkin' yer hair smells some nice." He nosed the locks out of his way to taste the smooth and fragrant skin just below her ear. "And I'm thinkin' yer skin is some tasty."

He heard her soft gasp, felt the pulse beneath his lips jump and quicken, her body tremble. She flinched as another flash of light and clamorous rumble filled the room. "Shhh…shh, easy now," he soothed, and slowly moved his lips over her delicate jaw to capture her mouth with his.

Her response was immediate and uninhibited. He felt her hands slide up his bare chest and curl around his neck. His hands came away from the wall of their own accord to slide around her torso, and when he heard soft little groans come from the back of her throat his arms tightened on impulse. He realized he was crushing her lips and made himself raise his head. The lashes of her closed eyes stood out against her pale skin. Swollen and rosy lips parted as she sighed. Her lids fluttered open and revealed clouded and bewildered eyes near the color of jade. He thought her the most precious thing he had ever held in his arms.

"Kerry, sweetheart," he almost did not recognize the gruff sound of his own voice. "I've been wonderin'—you'd never been on a motorbike, you've never been in the ocean, and 'e haven't danced much. And since 'e don't usually spend time in rooms with half-naked men, does that mean 'e've never…?"

She hesitated a moment until his meaning sank in, then lowered her eyes and slowly nodded her head. Merrek pushed her head beneath his chin with a sigh. "I just knew you were goin' ta say that," he whispered with a wry chuckle.

Kerry pushed back and searched his eyes. "Does that matter to you? Because it doesn't to me."

He stared back in surprise. "Of course it matters to me. You matter to me. I've had me own reasons for stayin' uninvolved the last few years...'e must have yours, too. Whatever those reasons are, I won't..."

"More like not interested...until now."

He held his breath while he studied her, then exhaled and gave her a weak smile. "Are 'e sure that's not just passion talkin'? 'E have more than a fair share, 'e do. Maybe it's momentarily clouded yer brain. You'd regret it later."

"You think I'm *passionate*?" She asked with surprise.

"Darlin', 'e literally vibrate with it," he grinned at her blushing face, a devilish gleam in his eyes. "I'm thinkin' 'e could be damn squally."

"*Squally?*"

"Aye, 'tis a seaman's term," his eyes held fast to hers. "Means some wild storm." For the space of a few seconds, Kerry could not find her breath.

She stared at Merrek, wondered what that would be like. "I've never felt...I'd started to fear that I couldn't..."

"Aye, well, 'e couldn't dance either, could 'e now?" He cupped her face in his hands, rubbed his thumbs over her pink cheeks. "It's all about chemistry, luv. And e've got to admit...we do seem to have some powerful chemistry between us."

She peered tentatively up into his face, and then a smile curved her pretty mouth—a somewhat naughty smile that stopped his breath. He watched in fascination as the pixie in her emerged and lit an impish sparkle in her eyes. "So then why do you think I'd regret it? Aren't you any good?"

Merrek's eyes widened with astonishment. She was forever unpredictable. Just when he had once again settled into thinking she was a timid innocent, she shocked him with that sassy boldness. He yanked her close to his chest and bent his head to hers, nose to nose. "Are 'e baitin' me, lass?"

"I'm trying to," she was breathless, and, as usual, honest to a fault.

He loosened his grip and his eyes dropped to her mouth, which he immediately recognized as a mistake and so took up a study of the wallpaper pattern above her head. "Kerry, I have some rather old-fashioned ideas about beddin' virgins. 'E seem...

"Untouchable?"

"Vulnerable," his eyes captured hers again. "I'm doin' me best ta protect 'e here, luv."

"From…?"

"Me."

Kerry's breath caught again for a moment, then her brows furrowed. "You would never hurt me, I know it."

"Kerry, I'm an old soul in a vastly changed world. I'm no casual lover. I'll want more. 'E have a life in America that e'll go back to eventually. You'd be leavin' an irretrievable part of yerself behind. Trust me, you'd regret it. 'Tis unwise and…" he blew out a long breath, "bloody unfortunate."

A defeated sigh escaped her. "Damn, Merrek. The first time I've ever felt turned on has to be with a guy who's got scruples, a real gentleman." She turned away from him just before another thought crossed her mind. She whirled back around with green fire in her eyes and said with an adorable pout in an accusing tone, "You're afraid I might break your… whatever…somehow."

How she could make him laugh and make him melt at the same time was beyond him. He tried to reinforce his splintering resolve and then admitted with defeat, "Aye, I'll admit to being some afraid of 'e, but not for that reason." With a throaty sound that was part laugh and part groan, part triumph and part defeat, Merrek stepped forward, scooped her up in his arms and carried her to the bed. He laid her down and covered her with his body, plied her with gentle kisses. She was small beneath him, delicate. *Absolute heaven.* He could indulge up to a point and retain his control, right? *But did she seriously have to smell and feel so good?*

Kerry felt herself shiver as Merrek's mouth traveled across her cheek and down her neck. The scrape of his day-old stubble excited her as his mouth traveled to her tank top, lingered there. She felt a force within her gaining strength like the lightning and thunder outside the window, and when Merrek slowly pulled the loose straps of her top aside and lowered the shirt to give his mouth better access, she felt herself coming apart.

Merrek felt it, too. Her startled gasp and tremors brought him back to his senses. He had never experienced want and need such as this, but he made himself raise his head. "Kerry? Look at me, luv," when she did, he was amazed at the passion simmering in her eyes. "'Tis the truth—I've been wantin' 'ee since I first held 'e in me arms and dove inta those sea green eyes o'yers, but 'e give me the word and I promise I'll stop. I'll sleep on the floor or outside the door…anythin' you want…"

"What I want is for you to shut up and kiss me again," she almost pleaded through shallow breaths.

A slow smile curled his lips. "Ah, God help us, darlin'. You really don't know, do 'e, how damned seductive 'e are? So bloody enchantin'," he kissed the side of her mouth. "So perishin' allurin'," he kissed the opposite side. "Enticin' as…hell." He covered her mouth with his and plundered, devoured, pleasured. He groaned quietly when he lifted away from her minutes later. "God forgive me, Kerry, but I can't help m'self. There is one thing I need ta know before we…go forward—are 'e sure this has nothing to do with you thinkin' we are supposed ta…because of Kerenza and Myghal?"

Kerry's eyes grew wide, and pleased him with the honesty that once again glimmered there. It was her answer, however, that threw fuel on the spark already ignited between them. "Oh, gosh, Merrek. I haven't thought of those two since you came into the room without your shirt."

Desire exploded through him. He buried his hands in her hair and held her head captive. "Are 'e sure, luv? I'll protect 'e, but this canna be undone."

In answer, she moved her arms around him and pulled herself more tightly against him, seeking his assurance and acceptance.

Merrek knew he had lost the battle but *oh, what he had won*. His raspy whisper was shaky in her ear, "Only thing is I've no experience being a woman's first. I'll most likely need to employ some restraint." He raised himself and looked at her–soft, lovely and willing. "And I've got ta tell 'e, m'darlin', that's a tall order in light of our ancestors' probable interrupted love affair. It seems I've over two hundred years of pent up passion ta deal with 'ere."

Kerry laughed softly and took his face between her hands. She softly assured him, "Merrek, you do realize that Kerenza and Myghal never had offspring. We are not their descendents, there is no direct line. This is just between you and me. So…" Merrek's eyes followed her hands as they pushed her jeans down over her hips, revealing a tantalizing scrap of lilac lace, "…*don't stop*."

Merrek smiled broadly at her reference to their earlier conversation. She was absolutely exhilarating.

"Aye, and there it is, luv. Music to every Cornishman's ears."

Kerry could have sworn there was actual fire just behind those dark eyes as he kneeled over her to pull the jeans down her legs and over her feet. She let out a shaky sigh.

Merrek gave her a warm smile. "And Kerry, m'sweet luv, I do appreciate your encouragin' genealogy lesson, but this still feels like over two hundred years o' pent up passion t' me."

⚓

Merrek watched her sleep and imagined what it would be like to wake up with her every morning warmed with memories of the night before and anticipating another just like it come sunset. Those thoughts blanketed him in contentment, and peace and longing.

The sounds outside their window drew him out of bed to check on the storm. The rain was coming down in sheets, and the strong wind made the window shutters vibrate. He began formulating a plan to get to safety should they need…

A movement from the bed caught his attention, and before he could climb back in beside her, Kerry was in the throes of a nightmare. She fought with the bed covers and her whimpers were working up to a full scream as he reached for her. "Kerry. Kerry, luv, wake up. Yer dreamin'," he soothed.

"Merrek?"

The terror in her tearful plea tore at his heart. He wrapped her in his arms and cradled her against his hard chest. "I'm right 'ere, luv. I've got 'e."

She clung to him like a lifeline. He tasted her tears when he kissed her face. He stroked her hair and whispered an old Cornish rhyme he'd learned as a child, relieved when he felt her body relax as she settled. When she opened her eyes, they were drenched with relief and lingering tears. "I was drowning. Again."

While he still held her close with one arm, he used his free hand to arrange the bedcovers over them and then grabbed a tissue for her from the nightstand. "Tell me," he prodded. "The telling often lessens the reality."

Kerry had never felt this utter security in the aftermath of a nightmare. As she lay there surrounded by his heat and tenderness, she unloaded the fearsome details of the repetitive dream. Merrek listened patiently and with empathy.

When she was finished, the gale still raged outside their window, so Merrek coaxed her down on the bed and with his hands, mouth and body took her away from the terrors of storms and nightmares.

Sometime later, she fell into a deep and nightmare-free sleep.

- 14 -

There are things we don't want to happen but have to accept,
things we don't want to know but have to learn,
and people we can't live without but have to let go.
—Unknown

Kerry woke slowly, turned in Merrek's arms and languidly stretched. Sun was streaming in through the window, and she could hear the cries of sea birds. Her movement brought Merrek out of his sleep. "Again, Kerry?" he groaned through his yawn. "'E know, 'e can take the *don't stop* thing some too far…"

Kerry came up on her elbow to face him, bringing the bedcovers with her. Merrek popped open one eye, laughed at her incredulous expression, and then folded his arms around her. "Did 'e get any sleep a'tall, luv? I tried to will the thunder and wind to stop so you could rest with no more nightmares."

She snuggled against him. "You must have succeeded then. I don't even remember hearing the storm after…well, what we did. I just remember feeling warm and safe…and nicely tired."

Without warning, he pushed her onto her back and loomed over her, his eyes dark and serious. "I have ta tell 'e, Kerry, this has been some incredible. Outrageously incredible. I was a virgin meself to that kind o' pleasure."

"Really? I mean, I thought it was…beyond words, but you…?"

"Trust me…aye, beyond words. The storm outside paled in comparison to the tempest in 'ere."

Kerry blushed and turned her head toward the window with a sad smile. "Well, it seems the storm is over."

Merrek chuckled hoarsely. "Ah, Darlin'," he yanked the covers from her. "Methinks it's just begun." She shrieked when he bent over her to spread tickling kisses over her abdomen.

He jerked up suddenly. "Jesus, Kerry. That's quite a bruise 'e've got

187

there."

Kerry looked down at her side where in the light of the morning a hand-sized discoloration showed angrily against her creamy skin. "Oh, that's where I fell over Kerenza's memorial stone yesterday. I knew it was going to leave a mark, but it's just a bruise, nothing more."

Merrek ran his fingers gently over the dark blue and purple wound. "'E sure there's nothin' hurt internally?" He stiffened as a thought occurred. "I hope I did nothing to cause 'e more pain there …" his eyes flew to her face. "Did I, luv?"

"No, not at all," she peered into skeptical eyes, "Merrek, seriously, it looks worse than it is."

He relaxed slightly and his eyes followed his fingers down to her thigh where an old scar showed clearly in the morning light. "This?"

"I fell down a ravine while hiking with some friends. That was where a broken pine branch caught me for eighteen stitches." He kissed the scarred skin and moved to her knee where the skin puckered slightly. "That is a combination of injuries from childhood and recently when I fell down some stairs at my school." She impatiently batted his hand away and pulled the covers back up to her neck. "I told you I was clumsy, more so when I was younger. I've tried to become more cautious—I've had people depending on me. But like my friend, Tania, says, I'm kind of a trouble magnet. Accidents seem to find me."

"A fitty Calamity Jane 'e are, aye?" he asked softly, not smiling but with tenderness in his eyes.

Kerry grinned. "You sure know a lot about American culture for a Cornishman."

He shrugged. "I know a little about a lot of things. I like ta read."

Kerry reached up to feather his hair off his forehead. "I had guessed that. Your everyday vocabulary speaks to it, as well as your impressive anthology of quotes. I'll bet you were every teacher's dream student."

"Well, I don't know about that." She felt his hand under the covers slowly creeping up her leg. "All I care about is makin' sure I'm the only one in this teacher's dreams."

Kerry's breaths became quick and shallow, and her body responded to his touch as he watched her eyes lose focus.

⚓

Later that morning, after a real shower and a breakfast of sausage and eggs, Kerry and Merrek walked down the main street of the tiny village and onto the wharf in the harbor. There they watched men and women clean up debris from the storm and check out the damage to their tethered fishing boats. It was more than a bit eerie for them both, knowing that they were walking where two others had probably walked over two hundred years before. Perhaps lovers, like themselves.

The water was still choppy, but the tide was out, and from their vantage point on the pier they could see a crop of jagged rocks rising out of the water just a few kilometers from shore. "I feel like I know this place," she whispered. "I'd be willing to bet Kerenza drowned *right out there*. I'm convinced she's the reason I'm afraid of the ocean. She's been warning me my whole life. And if there happened to be a storm when she…do you think it's possible I have those fears because of what she went through?"

Merrek could not suppress the shiver that ran through him as well. *Had Myghal somehow forwarded his anger and frustration with the sea to his future nephew?*

They stood there in silence until Merrek suddenly reached up and freed Kerry's unruly hair from its clasp. The ocean breeze picked up the silky curls and had them dancing around her head. Her eyes, soft and spring green, looked questioningly into his.

"Ye look like 'e belong 'ere, like 'e fit."

"And yet you were worried about me coming to Porth."

"Aye. Let me rephrase that. Ye look like 'e belong 'ere…with me."

Kerry's heart jumped in her chest. But she didn't have time to ask him what he meant before her phone rang. When she saw Owen's name on the screen she let out a delighted sound. He was thinking of her after all.

"Owen! How nice to…" her voice faded away.

Merrek watched as the delight on her face darkened to despair and he knew, just knew, and steadied himself against the anguish that was to come. Kerry lifted tear-rimmed eyes to his. "Of course, Millicent," she said into the phone. "I'm on my way."

Merrek fought to keep his composure, but he felt as if he had just taken a sword to the gut. "Bad news I take it."

"Owen's been in a horrible accident. He's hurt so badly the hospital has him in an induced coma for now. The doctors aren't sure if he'll…they need me, Merrek. As soon as possible."

He simply nodded and took her hand. Bringing it to his lips, he stared for a moment at the jagged rocks and the sea beyond. Fate brought this lovely girl into his life only to snatch her away, just like the one before her. He felt a sudden stab of kinship with his ancient uncle—felt the same violent ripping in his own chest.

But, he reminded himself, his Kerenza was still alive and well, and that mattered more than anything else. "I'm so sorry," he said as he guided her back to the pub to gather their things. They mutually understood how much ground that sentiment covered.

Kerry did not know how she would have made her flight arrangements without Merrek's calm steadiness. She herself was a wreck when she called Mrs. Tesmer to say goodbye. The young man at the desk said Mrs. Tesmer was busy with a guest, and that he would give her a message. "Please tell her thanks for everything, but due to a family emergency, I'm leaving today on the 3:30 flight to the States."

"Is this Miss Carter?"

"It is."

"I was here the night you came in. I'll make sure Mrs. Tesmer gets your message as soon as possible. And…I'm so sorry to hear of your troubles."

"I don't think I can make it through a conversation with Min," Kerry told Merrek as she stared at her phone. "We got so close, and she's not as stoic as Mrs. Tesmer."

"I'll explain everythin' to 'er. She'll understand. We need ta get 'e through this as easy as possible."

Merrek continued to be very supportive during the train ride back to London, but she still felt the need to justify, maybe as much to herself as to him. "Not only do I need to see him in case he doesn't…you know, but while he's in the hospital I'm sure Millicent will need me to take care of the baby. Her family is in Colorado, and I'm on leave, after all, and…"

Placing his hands on her shoulders, Merrek turned her so she faced him. "Kerry, luv, 'e don't need ta explain family duties ta me of all people. Sure 'e 'ave ta go. He's all the family 'e 'ave. 'E need to go for yourself as much as for 'im." He pulled her close. "But I will miss you, my Kerenza." He kissed her softly. A worried expression on his face, he spoke intimately, "About last night…I was very careful. But you will let me know immediately if…"

Kerry's eyes grew wide and then filled with tears. She could only nod her agreement. As their train pulled into the London station, Merrek squeezed her tight. "You know how to get in touch with me. I know you'll be busy, but I'd like ta hear from 'e—as often as 'e can manage."

Kerry hugged him tighter. "Beaufort is so far away," she murmured.

"Aye, luv." He sighed in resignation. "I've always hated that bloody ocean. Now I know why."

Merrek handed Kerry out of the cab and slung her backpack over his shoulder one last time. When they entered the airport lobby, Mrs. Tesmer was waiting there. She glanced at Merrek in surprise. "Kerry, dear," taking Kerry's hand in both of hers. "I am so sorry you have to leave us so soon and for such heartbreaking reasons." She turned to Merrek, held out her hand. "Olivia Tesmer."

"Merrek Walles, Mrs. Tesmer," he responded, his large hand swallowing her tiny one. "I've heard a lot about 'e."

"All good, I hope?" Mrs. Tesmer's sharp little eyes flitted back and forth between the two young people. In her shrewd, Mrs. Tesmer way, she was quick to discern the depth of their relationship. Feeling a squeeze to her heart, she focused on Kerry's stricken face. "I don't know where to begin, dear. It's been such a pleasure. I've enjoyed our teas more than you can know. I'm going to miss you."

"Oh, Mrs. Tesmer, I don't know what I would have done without you. You've been such a good friend." She hugged Mrs. Tesmer, feeling the tears already pooling in her eyes. When she turned to Merrek, she saw his restrained devastation and wished with all her heart there was something she could do to alleviate the hurt—for both of them. Grimacing inwardly, she had to admit he had been right about last night. There was no way to break the bond they now shared, and leaving him seemed an impossible feat.

Olivia Tesmer missed none of it. She needed to say something encouraging but was at a loss. "Take care, Kerry. Drop me a line occasionally. I'll give you two some alone time now."

Kerry smiled her sincere thanks and gave her friend one last hug. She turned to Merrek when Mrs. Tesmer faded into the crowd. What could she say in the few seconds they had left? His sad smile and slight shake of his head put away her need to say anything. He bent down and kissed her softly on her cheek. He helped her don her backpack, and asked her if she had her passport handy. That brought a bit of a smile to her face. "Tania will be so surprised. Almost two months here and I never had to get a replacement." The smile faded when she looked directly at him. "Merrek, I…"

He stopped her with a finger to her lips, and starting with her eyes that were swimming in unshed tears, he began a slow perusal of her face, memorizing every detail, as an artist would.

Kerry watched him, not breathing, and when his eyes dove once again into hers, she felt him extract her heart and soul. And she let him take them, gave them freely. Then he kissed her slowly, gently, imparting his own in return. "Take great care, Kerenza, m'love. When the storms come, remember the feel of me arms around 'e and please don't be afraid." Kerry was battling the tears threatening to break through, and the forlorn look in her eyes was painful to see. He hugged her to him. "The distance between us isn't nearly as great as that between Myghal and his Kerenza. Mayhap we'll bridge that gap in the near future. Until then, take care, m'sweet."

In response to the announcement that came too soon concerning her flight, Kerry's voice trembled as she spoke softly. "I have to go now." She smiled goodbye, took a step toward the security area, then turned and threw herself in Merrek's ready arms. He held her tightly, one arm around her waist, the other hand buried in her hair. "I'll never forget you," she whispered in his ear just before she pushed herself away and hurried into the crowd.

- 15 -

Ignorantly is how we all fall in love; for it is a kind of fall.
Closing our eyes, we leap from that cliff in hope of a soft landing.
Nor is it always soft; but still, without that leap nobody comes to life.
—Salman Rushdie, The Moor's Last Sigh

Merrek had no idea how long he had stood there in the midst of people pushing past him. He seemed frozen to the spot even though he knew she would not...could not change her mind and come back.

With great effort, he made himself look away from the last place he had seen her before watching her disappear into the throngs of people rushing toward the gates.

She was *gone*.

He felt...*empty*.

When he turned, his eyes locked with Mrs. Tesmer's. He tried to offer her an empathetic smile, but his mouth just would not work.

"Oh, my boy," she sighed as he approached. "I think we could both use a stiff drink. Would you escort an old lady into one of these bars? My treat."

Merrek started to shake his head, but the tiny woman looked as though she shared his loss. "I'll tell 'e what—'e buy the first round, I'll buy the next."

Merrek downed his first shot of whiskey in one swallow in hopes that its burn would cauterize the gaping hole left by Kerry's swift departure. Mrs. Tesmer sipped hers between sentences. "Kerry's such a sweet, special kind of person. I loved her from the moment I met her. It would make my day to see those sparkling, optimistic eyes; that bright smile. I've had a void in my life since my daughter died. For two months Kerry did much to fill it." After emptying her glass, she added, "Unfortunately, it seems she may have left a void in yours."

Merrek ordered another round and took more time with this one. He was not one to talk much about his private life, especially with a stranger,

193

but the little woman's eyes shone with sincere concern. He owed her a response. "Aye, you're right there, and I didna see it comin'. None of it." His brows drew together in a frown. "I 'ope her brother does well. She's 'ad too much loss in 'er life already."

Mrs. Tesmer studied the strikingly handsome man across from her. She doubted Kerry would find a better match back in the states, but she hoped her young friend would find one as fitting for her as this one might have been.

When the lady had drained her glass, Merrek asked if he could get her a cab back to the hotel.

Mrs. Tesmer smiled. "No, but thank you. I think I'll sit here and watch the crowds for a while, let the liquor wear off, and then catch a ride with the hotel van."

He stood slowly, laid some coins on the table, along with his business card. "Nice meetin' you, Mrs. Tesmer. I've got ta catch the train back to Cornwall. Let me know, will 'e? If 'e hear from 'er? I'll do the same?"

Mrs. Tesmer searched his face. "My late husband was an American. We had a few unsettled years, but it made those we had later even more worthwhile. I am sorry for this turn of events, Merrek. You seem to have Kerry's welfare in mind more than your own, and that speaks well of you. I wish you the best, whatever happens. And yes, we'll be in touch, I'm sure."

⚓

The trip back to Cornwall was a blur. Merrek saw none of the scenery that sped by outside the train window even though it seemed his eyes focused there. Memories of meeting Kerry that first time in St. Austell kept replaying in his mind. He remembered that freshness about her, an unpretentious innocence he had mistaken at first for youth until he'd felt the womanly shape of her as he'd held her close out of harm's way.

He understood his parent's concern that he had only known her for a very short time, and that their relationship had since bloomed like his mother's foxglove in the time-lapsed video he had made when he was a boy. However he had not needed time to get to know Kerry—it was more as if, as Gorron had said days ago, he had *recognized* her—had been waiting for her.

He knew as soon as he had gazed upon that expressive, honest face that held no secrets and played no wily female games. He knew as soon as he had delved into those green eyes in whose depths past and future somehow intertwined. He found delight in her intelligence and easy humor, admired her ability to laugh at herself, and his effortless ability to make her blush endeared her even more.

Then, of course, there was Kerry in bed. That freshness and honesty extended to her lovemaking, and the trust she had given him fueled his passions beyond anything he had ever experienced.

Sweet Jesus... he did love her.

A scowl transformed his face as another new realization slammed into him. He had taken all that freshness and honesty, innocence and trust—and made of her a one-night-stand. Unknowingly, unintentionally...but he hated himself for it nevertheless, even though he would cherish the memory with all his heart...the heart that was at that moment flying toward the other side of the Atlantic.

⚓

Kerry felt shell-shocked as she watched the clouds outside the plane's window. So much had happened to her in the last twenty-four hours—life-changing events. She had gone from the triumph of finding her family home to the shock and excitement of discovering her eighteenth-century Aunt Kerenza to experiencing extraordinary passion and utter contentment in the arms of her first lover to the agitating worry for her injured and maybe dying brother. If that was not enough, she was also fraught with an agonizing, sorrowful loss of what might have been. She was on shutdown, unable to read, eat, sleep or react in any way. The woman next to her had long since given up trying to converse and the flight attendant was perceptive enough to leave her alone.

Alone.

So she was back to being alone. Except...*When the storms come, think of me arms around 'e and please don't be afraid.* Knowing Merrek Walles was on the same planet with her was comfort enough that she was able to shake herself out of the clouds and ask the attendant for a cup of tea. Somewhat fortified, she opened her book of quotes and her eyes immediately fell on Emerson's words she had recited to Tania weeks ago, 'Every man is a quotation of all his ancestors.'

Those words, in light of recent discoveries, triggered a riot of thoughts in Kerry's mind. She had not had the chance to research Kerenza, but apparently, phobias had not kept her ancestor out of the sea, and neither did it seem she had been opposed to taking risks. Kerry had seen firsthand how quickly Cornish storms materialized and how intense they could be. It seemed probable that a storm could have been instrumental in Kerenza's disappearance. Maybe Kerenza's brother, Rowse, because of his sister's calamity, had admonished his children to stay away from the sea, to be cautious, that tragedies can happen during storms. Thus his son, Rowen, had moved further inland to St. Austell to work in the mines instead of the sea, and Rowen's son, Stephan, had moved even further away to London.

Kerry relinquished her teacup to the attendant, and slumped back into her seat with her thoughts. Owen had not emerged from the gene pool with those traits. He had been on Duke University's water polo team and was a certified sailor. He seemed to enjoy his job, and stockbrokers could not be risk averse. But perhaps Rowse had also contributed the notion that younger sisters can be a time-consuming burden. Maybe that explained Owen's distance. It was not a conscious decision to ignore his sister, he was what he was.

By contrast, Merrek's ancestors may have talked about the lonely uncle who had lost the love of his life. *So sad. He should have been more attentive, not become so isolated.* That would explain the inherent devotion that encapsulated Merrek and that triggered both affection and vexation in those he cared for.

Quotations are we? With a few strokes of her iPad keyboard, Kerry found what she considered scientific collaboration for that theory in the words of John Maynard Smith, Geneticist, 'Genetics is about how information is stored and transmitted between generations.'

⚓

Merrek got off the train in St. Austell and hailed a cab to the Gilliflower. He needed another drink. Gorron was standing at the bar and saw him come in. His welcoming smile faded when he perceived Merrek's mood. He spoke to one of the servers, and then motioned Merrek to follow him to the privacy at end of the bar.

"Why am I thinkin' this stormy face o' yers 'as something to do with little green-eyes 'e were with before?" He thanked the server and set a glass of scotch in front of Merrek. "She get scared off by the infamous Walles?"

Merrek took a long sip of the scotch. Gorron had given him the good stuff. Too bad he couldn't fully appreciate it. Tonight he would have been easily satisfied with the rotgut he deserved. "There was a family emergency in the States. 'Er brother was almost killed – may not make it still. She's on 'er way back. I jus' came from takin' 'er to the airport."

"Aw, now that's a bloody shame. The lass is pretty shaken up I'd guess. 'E don't look so good yerself. Anythin' I can do?"

Merrek put the glass to his forehead, and rolled it back and forth a few times and then set it down. "'E know, Gor... for the last few years, I've tried ta encourage...no, more than that...I've *preached* at me siblins ta stay controlled, not ta make the kind of impetuous decisions that can make a mess o' their lives or do damage t' someone else's. Not t' jump inta things too fast or without thinkin' things through—and then what do I do? And God, Gor, she was a virgin, and I'm sendin' her back across the Atlantic...not one. I won't even be there t' give 'er the reassurance she'll most likely need. And what if she's conceived my child? I'm a damned hypocrite and a bloody bastard t' boot."

Gorron's eyebrows drew together sharply. "Is it possible...?"

Merrek took another long sip, and then just drained the glass while Gorron looked on. "Anythin's possible, but 'e's not probable—I was at least careful o' that. But 'e know what her last words t' me were? The bastard what took from 'er what can't be restored and then sent 'er on along 'er way? She promised not to forget me. Oh, well I bloody well made damn sure o' that, aye? 'Tis not what I'd 'ave 'er remember me for—a spoiler o' innocence." He set his empty glass on the bar and vowed, "Though I'll remember 'er til the day I die, I can promise 'e that."

Gorron studied his cousin, then turned and waved to the young server. "Well, let's refill yer glass and think this through. Firstly, don't forget it takes two, me boy. I don't mean ta maze ya up 'ere, but do ya really think yer that irresistibly seductive? That ye swept 'er inta somethin' she really didn't want t' do? Maybe it was 'e what got swept away. I saw 'er. If 'e'll remember, I told 'e to watch out for that one."

Merrek turned to stare at Gorron with eyes that were beginning to glaze over. "Did 'e really take 'er for a wily wench lookin' ta bed a Cornishman afore goin' back ta the states, man?"

Gorron quickly backtracked, afraid of offending his cousin with common talk about his new friend. He shook his head. "Nah. She seemed...I don't know...fresh-faced...kind of an old soul. Perfect for 'e if ye ask me. But wi' a mind of 'er own, remember that."

Merrek let Gorron's words settle in. "I did try to talk her out of it," Gorron raised his brows. "I did. I even offered t' sleep on the floor."

"Well, then, there 'e go," Gorron slapped him on the back. "It was 'er decision. Quit beatin' yerself up. Virginity's a passin' stage in life anyway.

197

If not you, then some other…" Gorron swallowed his next words when met with the sinister look Merrek flung his way. "Oh, I see 'ow 'tis, then."

"Jesus, thanks, Gor. I didna think I could feel any worse. The thought of another man…" he threw back the drink that had been set before him.

Gorron put his hand on Merrek's shoulder. "But, come on, me lad. Relationships come and go in today's world. Some things just aren't meant t' be." When he saw the jaw muscles in his friend's face clench, he removed his hand and continued, "and then some things are worth fightin' for. I've never known 'e t' back down from a fight, boyyo."

Merrek pushed his glass away. He was beginning to feel the effects of the scotch and he had to get the rest of the way home. "'E think it's even possible t' cultivate a relationship across a thousand miles o' sea and five time zones?"

"Difficult aye, but if she's worth it to 'ee ye'll find a way. With all the bloody technology 'e 'ave at yer fingertips these days, 'e've got a better chance than 'e would 'ave ten…even five years ago. I'd 'ave done anythin' for my Hedra, and would again even after all these years. Hell…" he mused, "especially after all these years. But then, we 'ave a history. Ye and this wee Yankee, there's no history to build on."

Merrek chuckled dryly. "Trust me, Gor, this all started with history."

⚓

Back on the train to Penzance, Merrek mulled over his conversation with Gorron. The scotch had begun to settle some of his turmoil and allowed a cheerier glow to cast hopeful light on his predicament. He still was not sure of the logistics, but this he knew for sure—if this Walles and Carter union was meant to be he would do everything on his end to ensure it was done.

⚓

It was almost midnight in Penzance when Kerry called Merrek's cell phone. He hadn't realized how taut his nerves had been until he felt them relax upon hearing her voice.

The reprieve did not last long. The heartbreak in her voice still rang in his ears, "It's just like Mama all over again." He had wanted to board the next westbound plane immediately. She should not have to deal with this alone.

It was not because Kerry was weak. She had already proven her strength. In spite of her fears and feelings of inadequacy, she had accepted her duty as befitted a stoic queen. But he would spare her the sense of being alone.

Four nights after Kerry's departure, Merrek sat at his desk in his mother's parlor, listening to the silence of the sleeping household. Lowenna had left a note on the desk—a copy of a quote she had found.

'Don't let the fear of the time it will take to accomplish something stand in the way of your doing it. The time will pass anyway; we might just as well put that passing time to the best possible use.' Earl Nightingale.

Merrek read Mr. Nightingale's quote several times, letting its relevance fuel his resolve. The only way he could deal with the day to day without losing his mind was to use the time he had without her to build toward their potential future together. He would not think of having to settle for *without* her. He needed to work. And put the damn passing time to use.

- 16 -

Our chief want is someone who will inspire us
to be what we know we could be.
—Ralph Waldo Emerson

Merrek exhaled slowly with a soft groan as he glanced at the computer screen. The image had switched to screensaver while he had brooded over the sales lingo. He had programmed the screensaver to display the photo of Kerry on the seawall taken at Elowen's Galowon party. Those challenging green eyes never failed to spur him toward his goals. Switching back to his document, he completed and sent the sale proposal.

Then he checked the weather again for Beaufort, North Carolina.

"What are 'e about today, Merk, me brother?" Lowena flopped down on her stomach on the couch that doubled as Merrek's temporary bed.

Merrek suppressed a smile at her use of the name she had called him when she was a toddler. Instead, he presented a serious face with raised eyebrow. "What are 'e doin' home from school so early?"

"Well, 'e are lookin' at the bloody genius who performed first rate on her economics examination and has won exoneration from Professor Erdict's damned class for the rest o' the week." Her eyes lit up more over the last part of her statement than the part where she aced the exam.

Merrek kept his face expressionless, daunting. "And so that gives 'e the right ta swear in yer mum's parlor, does it?"

She had the good grace to seem a little set back. "Aren't 'e proud o' me? I'm number one in the class."

Merrek started with a grin, "Aye, 'tis proud I am, ta be sure…" and then he reached over to tug her long raven curls "…*m'lady* Lowenna," he concluded with a ferocious scowl.

"I'll see to me language, brother, if 'e'll relax that horrible frown."

"'Tis unladylike, Lo. 'E don't want t' give anyone reason to call 'e dockside trash, 'cos then I'd 'ave t' remedy their perceptions." He let go of her hair and sat back to consider her. Lowenna Walles was going to lead some poor soul a merry dance soon, but she could stand to be a bit more demure. He thought of Kerry. Lowenna could learn from her. "So...'e 'ave some free time this afternoon then? Would 'e like ta go wi' me on an investigation?"

Lowenna jumped off the couch in one movement. "Genealogy investigation, mayhap? For Kerry?"

"Aye, I thought I'd continue 'er research. Find out some about our old uncle as well. Interested?"

His sister threw her arms around his neck and gave his cheek a resounding smack. "I'll see if Mum needs anything, and if not—'e've got yerself an assistant sleuth."

⚓

In Beaufort, Kerry was letting her morning cup of tea steep while listening for little Alexandra to wake up. She glanced at the coffee pot and smiled weakly at how easily English tea had replaced the American coffee ritual in the two months she had spent immersed in her ancestral culture. A wave of homesickness swept through her, more intense than anything she had felt for North Carolina during her first weeks in London.

The last four days had taken Kerry back to a time she thought she'd buried with her mother—the cold hospital vigils and the apprehension of being around equipment used to keep a mindless body functioning. Back was the frustration of limited information from hospital staff, and long hours that ticked by with no change, drowning hope tick by tick.

When she was not at the hospital, Kerry cared for Alexandra, which would have been a wonderful diversion if not for the constant fear of a mishap to the only blood relative she may have left. At night, when she should refuel her reserves for the next day, the nightmares would only allow her light, fitful snatches of sleep.

The dreams themselves were less intense than before, for in every one Merrek materialized to wrap her in his strong arms and hold her until the horror dissipated as she woke. Then, however, the longing would take over and deep sleep eluded her.

While she lay awake, she often thought of Kerenza. She would mentally write and rewrite scenarios of what might have happened to her. Had her ancestor drowned or had she managed to find a scrap of something to hold onto until she reached some distant shore? Had she longed for Myghal as Kerry found herself longing for Merrek?

She closed her eyes for a moment, the tea cup warm in her hands, and allowed herself to picture dark, playful eyes and charming sideways grins, and oh but what she would give for just five minutes in the shelter of his arms, clutched to that warm solid chest where she was guaranteed absolute support and security. She doubted Merrek could ever comprehend how much those memories were helping her ride through this current storm. *Had Kerenza worn memories of Myghal as her armor as well?*

Alexandra called from her crib in the nursery, breaking Kerry's mental meanderings. She hurriedly slurped a sip of tea and braced herself for another day.

⚓

"He never gave up on her, did 'e?" Lowenna stood by Merrek, staring at the tombstone in the Sennen cemetery. The caretaker had shown them a map of the plots, revealing two purchased by Myghal Walles in 1792. The plot next to his was empty.

"Seems not, if that's indeed who the other plot was meant for. Of course, he could 'ave purchased two together in hopes 'e would marry eventually, but just never did. And we still 'ave no absolute proof that Kerenza and Myghal were even...together."

"Oh, come on Merk. *I will wait for you...forever?* Please...could 'e need more proof?"

"Aye, I could...I do. And it's there—I can feel it. We jus' need ta ferret it out." A westerly wind blew warm against them.

"What's the news from Kerry?" Lowenna asked, surprising Merrek that she would think of Kerry at the feel of the soft, warm wind as he had himself.

"'Er brother's still in the coma, 'is brain's still swollen. Kerry sounds tired."

"You look tired, too, Merk. This 'as taken a toll on 'e."

"Well, aye, 'e's taken a bit out o'everyone involved, I'd say. 'E's life, Lo. Life's na' easy. But, if 'e make good with what 'e have, it can be fulfillin'. At least that's me hope."

Later that week, *The Ecologist Magazine*, one of the ten top environmentally inspired periodicals in the UK, called to hire Merrek. They wanted photographs to go along with an article on the preservation of England's peat bogs. The thrust of the article was to explain the ban on the use of peat for gardening and landscaping.

His guide was a dedicated environmentalist about his own age, very energetic and enthusiastic. He showed Merrek around the areas currently protected by the ISSI, and while Merrek explored various angles and perspectives with his camera, his guide lectured him on the greenhouse effects of the peat bogs. "They absorb carbon, and when peat is extracted, the carbon is released into the atmosphere," the guide explained. "As far as a habitat, there are species there that can't live in any other biome. Another thing about the bogs is their ability to preserve. Miners have found the ancient remains of all kinds of life in the bogs very well preserved. It's kinda like a mummifying burial ground."

"They ever find human bodies?"

"There have been bodies found as recently lost as World War II. Rare, but it has happened."

"Interestin'. I've seen stacks o'peat in Scotland and parts o' Ireland. Still used as a fuel for heatin', is it?"

"Some still burn it, but mostly, here in England, it's used for gardening. It takes hundreds of years to build back, and we've been mining it at a dizzying rate. It won't ever catch up, especially if we don't discontinue the practice."

"Is there any minin' currently takin' place in England, then?"

"Extracted for landscapin', no. All the contracts expired in 2014. The only reason for extraction now is for new construction, but by law, it has to be preserved and then put back when the building is complete. Tomorrow we begin a documentary style article showing this process. Your photos are to demonstrate the timeline of such an endeavor."

It was fascinating work, and as Merrek edited his photos on his computer later that night he craved Kerry's presence. She had an eye for the heavy hitters. Later while he tossed and turned in his own bed reliving his most recent phone conversation with Kerry, he realized that her confidence and pride in his work meant more to him than any praise he received from clients or any amount written on a paycheck. *He missed her terribly.*

⚓

Kerry rolled over with a groan. It was 1:30 in the morning. Alexandra was cutting teeth and it had been a miserable night of fever and fretting, but she was finally sleeping soundly. Kerry on the other hand was having difficulty getting relaxed. It was breakfast time in England. Min would be pulling her oggies out of the oven, and Merrek would be…

The ping from the computer signaled an incoming email. Kerry's breath caught in her throat and in spite of her fatigue, she jumped out of bed in anticipation. Her heartbeat began to race when she saw it was from Merrek.

⚓

Good morning, bonny Yankee. I know you are still asleep as it is the middle of the night there, but hopefully you'll have time to read this when you wake up. I have some research results for you.

Lowenna and I went to Sennen to find Myghal's gravesite. According to cemetery records, Myghal purchased the space beside him in the early 1790's at the same time he purchased his own—probably for his spouse, but it is empty.

We were desperate to prove he'd purchased the other gravesite for Kerenza, so we put our heads together and came up with the idea to search for old archived newspaper articles. We were very excited to discover the Cornish Studies Centre in Redruth. Fascinating place. There we found copies of an old newspaper called the The Sherborne Mercury, established in Dorset in 1737. It had been a very influential newspaper in its time and kept five counties of the United Kingdom informed, Cornwall being one of them.

After three hours of searching through weeks of articles of the year 1792, we found an article dated November 12 about the disappearance of Kerenza Carter of Porth during an unexpectedly intense storm. Her only surviving relative, brother Rowse Carter, was a remnant of the Carter smuggling ring in the Mount Bay area. Since his boat was also missing, it was suspected that the young woman was caught by the storm in the act of bringing in contraband from a French ship that was seized by authorities after it was run aground near Falmouth by the same storm. As of the date of the article, she was still missing—no body. The article stated that Kerenza also left behind her fiancé, Myghal Walles, a prominent portraitist from the area near Sennen. They were to have been married shortly after the New Year.

So we were right, my sweet. Your auntie and my uncle were lovers. I wanted to call you with this news so I could hear the excitement in your voice, but I was unsure of your schedule.

I hesitate to ask if there's been any change in your brother's condition—I know how painful this is for you. I hope it is a comfort to know that I try every night to will some of that pain away, as I try to will the storms away from the North Carolina coast. You are stronger than you think, my Kerenza. And I am here.

Merrek

Kerry hit the reply button, hoping to catch him before he left the computer. *Merrek, it's so good to hear from you. Are you still there?* (Send)

Kerry waited a few minutes, stifling yawns and tapping her fingers while she waited for Merrek's reply. She did not have too wait long.

What are you doing awake, lass? You should be sleeping in the wee hours.

She could picture him in the parlor at his parents' house, in front of his computer, sipping morning tea while dawn streaked across the Cornish sky. He was with her, now, in real time. If she could just reach through the computer screen and touch him.

Outstanding research you and Lowenna have done! How exciting this is—to find proof of what we suspected. But how tragic and sad, too. It seems as though Kerenza was a bit too brave and daring for her own good. Do you believe it eerily possible that the lessons of her mistakes influence me today? Overdone, true, but those lessons have kept me cautious, which is fortunate given my proclivity to accidents, and it would explain the reason for my fears.

Anyway, you are my hero for finding this information. I wish I had been there to share the work—and the thrill of discovery. I miss Cornwall. I miss you.

I'm still up because a wee little girl was cutting wee little teeth until these wee hours of the morning. There's been no change in Owen yet, but doctors are optimistic. Millicent is a mess. She's never been through anything like this before. How are you doing? (Send)

A pause while she waited…then,

Optimism is good, Kerry. I know you've been through this too many times but please remember to take care of yourself. I'm still feeling a bit like a rug was pulled out from under me, but I'm coping. It seems that Myghal bequeathed to me a weakness for redheaded sirens with green eyes named Kerenza. I miss you too, my sweet.

I'm leaving soon for a photo shoot on Sicily Island. An article about the history of tsunami activity captured in the shoreline deposits. Anything before I have to leave?

Kerry's mind searched frantically for something to say, and then her fingers flew hurriedly over the keyboard. *Take care of yourself for me.* (Send)

Kerry's eyes grew heavier and heavier but she was determined to stay awake for his reply. He didn't disappoint her:

I will do anything for you. The weather promises to behave all week there in Beaufort. Good luck with the teething. Try and get some sleep, will you? Take care, my love.

Kerry read the last line of his email several times. She knew very well that *my love* was a more common endearment in Cornwall than in the States, used casually in greeting anybody and everybody. It still made her feel warm inside to hope he may have meant it a little *less* Cornishly.

- 17 -

When all is said and done, the weather and love
are the two elements about which one can never be sure.
—Unknown

Six months later, the week before Christmas, Kerry convinced Millicent she needed a brief break in order to help Tania with her upcoming wedding. When she had arrived at the apartment, Tania was shocked that the drab creature Kerry had become was the same lively girl that had been her roommate. Tania worried over her friend's tired eyes and downtrodden spirit.

"Kerry," Tania tried a second time to interrupt her friend's deep thoughts. Sad green eyes finally turned her way. "Look, Kerry, let's put all this wedding stuff aside for a few minutes, make some hot cocoa, sit at the window and watch the snowflakes blow around. Who knows when we might get another opportunity to do that?"

Kerry turned to look out the window. The snow was a surprise, and it had increased in the last hour, clinging to tree limbs and dusting the ground. This time last year, she would have been delighted to see snow this close to Christmas, but today all she could think about was the drive back to her brother's house. She had not even thought to check the tread on his tires. She would have to cross her fingers that the roads would not be too slick.

"Yeah, okay," she smiled weakly at Tania. "You'll be seeing lots of snow shortly. You'll have to send me videos." Kerry still had not gotten over the shock that Tania and Robert were moving to New York after their Valentine's Day wedding. "If you have time, of course. That new job you've taken sounds pretty demanding. And then there's Robert," she added with a little chuckle.

"Yes," Tania smiled dreamily, "and then there's Robert." Putting aside the bows she and Kerry had been working on for the last two hours, Tania stole a quick assessing glance at her sad friend. "When was the last time you heard from Merrek?"

Kerry got up to run water into Tania's kettle and then placed it on the stovetop. She reached into the cabinet where Tania still kept the instant hot chocolate and measured an amount into two coffee mugs. "Merrek has been so busy," she said finally. "Did I tell you he bought a house? He's doing the renovations himself, so between that, his photography and his family obligations he doesn't have much time, I guess. You know how it goes. I stay busy too since I somehow became Owen's primary caregiver. Communication is a frustrating endeavor, and…we're losing touch, Tania. Nobody's fault, just…circumstances are working against us. I don't know…it just stinks."

"Go sit down and take a load off. I'll bring the cocoa."

Kerry took a chair that Tania had positioned in front of the window and let the shameful hurt wash over her again. She despised herself for wallowing in self-pity but she could not seem to stop.

When Tania joined her with the two steaming mugs, Kerry was self-consciously wiping away tears. She reached up to take the mug from Tania and saw the concern in the girl's eyes. "I'm sorry, Tania. I really am ashamed of myself."

"For what? Your life had just started when Owen's accident jerked you back from Cornwall to help with his and now here you are, bullied into a payless full time job taking care of him and his family. Finding out your best friend is taking off to New York. Missing that hunk o' male flesh you left over there in the mother country. What have *you* got to feel ashamed of?"

"It's no harder on me than anyone else—except maybe you, you lucky thing. But Owen has to learn to walk again, Millicent has to watch him struggle and endure his moods, and Merrek—you should have seen his face when I left, hear the loneliness in his voice every time we've talked. So I shouldn't be smothering in this self pity."

"Well, you know you can bare your soul to me, girlfriend. Maybe it would help to talk about it."

Kerry sipped her cocoa, felt herself going back in time when it was just she and Tania sharing the small apartment as well as all their worries and dreams, such as they were. "It's just that…everyone else seems to be making progress of some kind. Owen is rehabilitating, slowly but surely. Millicent's business is growing as is Merrek's and he's bought a house, Tania, a home. You're getting married and moving on and I'm…going nowhere. I feel like I'm being buried alive. And I shouldn't. It's selfish and self-centered. I should be more…"

"…of a *saint*?" Tania offered. "You're twenty-six now, Kerry, and you had your first taste of happiness last summer. Who could fault you for grieving that loss? It's just like you to add guilt to your pain."

"Everyone has had to make adjustments. He's my brother. What else can I do?"

"Have you talked to Millicent or Owen about how you feel? I mean it's been six months and this is the only break you've had in all that time. And let me tell you, girl, as long as you will give they will take until you're drained. And then what? Which one of them would take care of you?"

"I've thought of that, Tania, and I feel so alone."

"Look, you were a terrific daughter, and you are an uncommonly generous sister. This stuff has pulled you down. You need to save yourself. It's time Owen and Millicent found a way to work this out like other people do without putting it all on your shoulders. This is not your on-going responsibility. Talk to them. Surely, they understand your leave of absence is ending and you have some decisions to make about going back to Cornwall and pick up what you started there or pick up your career here, get an apartment, buy a car. You need to get on with your life, Kerry. *Your* life."

Poking along on the icy interstate back to Beaufort, Kerry thought about the conversation she needed to have with Owen and Millicent. Tania made sense, and Merrek had hinted at the same thing the last time they had communicated. His frustration with her brother and sister-in-law had come through during that last phone conversation and she had been a little too defensive in her response. But Merrek had not pushed her. *Was he giving up on her? Was she to give up on Owen, her only flesh and blood?* Oh, but she longed for Merrek. Her bond with him had gone so deep so fast. If he did break it, and she would understand it if he did, she knew he would also break her heart.

Merrek walked back into his parlor after seeing his guests on their way and admired the new addition to the room. He had asked his family over to see his newly finished home and they had brought him a housewarming gift—the renovated painting his ancestor had made of Kerry's beautiful reckless aunt.

It was perfect. He had intended to enlarge and frame the photo he had taken of Kerry. This, however, was much more stunning, and what a poignant piece of art to possess.

Myghal's painting of Kerenza drew the eye as soon as one entered the room. Hanging over the mantel, the windows opposite the fireplace shed a playful light on Kerenza during the daylight hours, and at night, the soft light cast by the recessed spotlights in the ceiling exposed her soul.

The conservator had done a fantastic job with the restoration. The lines were sharper, finer, and the rich, dramatic colors Myghal had used were once again vibrant. The man had truly been a talented artist. Kerenza's green eyes gleamed with that challenging sassiness he loved to see in Kerry's, and there was the allusion that he could reach into the painting and bury his hands in the thick, magnificent tresses. Even the peridot necklace she wore seemed to sparkle.

The strong ache overcame him and moved him to the bar in the adjoining room. After pouring a good measure of whiskey in a glass, he could not help but return to stare at the painting. *What do I do now, Kerenza-luv?*

He did not know how long he would have to wait in the house he had restored for her. The planters on and around the patio were filled with soil and waiting for her flowers and herbs, and the grill had just been delivered for her American style deck. In the bedroom, the bed was in place opposite the French doors that opened to a private patio, but he had yet to sleep there. Every night, on a cot that he had slept on during the renovation, he battled his impatience with Kerry, his frustration at their situation, and the anger that was building toward Kerry's family.

He thought of how Myghal must have suffered, waiting years while praying his Kerenza would return. Perhaps he had held onto the hope that she had been carried to another shore, clinging onto a piece of wreckage, or possibly picked up by another vessel. He had to admire the man's faithfulness and tenacity. It had only been six months since Kerry left, and though Merrek kept busy, his patience stretched tight and his optimism was shrinking. He no longer felt sure she would come back to him, but he was positive he did not want to live in this house without her.

Merrek stopped by his computer on his way to retire and checked the weather for Beaufort, a routine he had developed since Kerry's departure. It was snowing there. Snow was okay—no thunder or lightning. But in his gut he felt another kind of storm building.

He jerked around to stare at Kerry's likeness on Myghal's canvas. Those eyes seemed to bore into his soul, laced with warning, challenging him to act. He emptied the glass slowly, lost in thought. Finally, he made up his mind. He would give it until after the New Year, and then he would take matters into his own hands.

- 18 -

There is no difference between being
Rescued and being captured.
— Jane Mendelsohn

Kerry was growing restless even though she stayed busy with household duties, childcare and rehabilitating Owen. At first, she had done so with thanksgiving that she could help. Then the home healthcare nurse impressed the importance of training someone to take over Owen's daily physical therapy, and before Kerry knew what was happening, that burden became hers. Now, as she sometimes pled and other times fought with him to follow through with his exercises, all that willingness to help was, despite her best efforts, spiraling into resentfulness. Millicent still depended solely on Kerry's willingness. She had not yet mentioned that it might be time for Kerry to resume her own life. She probably assumed Kerry had no life.

When Owen first came home from rehab and Kerry began his care, she thought this would be the catalyst for a closer relationship with her brother. However, his wild ranting and not always just verbal abuse had forced another wedge between them. Kerry tried to remind herself that Owen couldn't control his actions due to his head injury, but as the weeks crept by she began to suspect that Owen considered the effort to do so a waste of energy. After all, it was too easy to take out his frustration and anger on someone who was more than willing to take the brunt of it and who was not worth the effort of better behavior anyway. The notion that she might actually be an obstacle in his recovery began to worry her.

Then there was Alexandra. The little girl and Kerry had become very close. Kerry sometimes thought Millicent a little jealous of the tight bond that had formed between the two of them while Millicent had been preoccupied in the first weeks following Owen's accident. Alexandra made up for, in one giggle or sloppy kiss, any ill-treatment Owen could inflict.

215

Near the window of the south-facing room where she was staying in her brother's house sat a beautiful, healthy Kalachoe that Kerry lovingly pampered toward blooming in the spring. Merrek had sent it to her for Christmas—along with the peridot pendant she wore around her neck that he had designed as a replica of the one Kerenza wore in Myghal's painting.

Whenever she had some time to herself, which was usually in the early hours just after midnight, Kerry would sit on the bed with her journal and iPad, finger the necklace, and write stories about a relentless and reckless eighteenth century female pirate of the Cornwall coast. She called her little collection of stories *Fearless*. Although she never entertained thoughts of anyone else reading them, they provided her an escape into another character. One that was not a plain and bumbling oaf, but beautiful and brave, free and a bit wild, accomplished and respected.

The stories, however, did not provide her escape from Merrek. He became every hero in the Kerenza stories—strong, attentive, and protective, but never crushing the heroine's spirit or self-confidence. Merrek was never far from her thoughts, and after seven months of separation and strained communication, he became even more embedded in her dreams.

A week before Tania's wedding, Kerry found out rather abruptly that her life was once again to take a turn. Millicent informed her that she had sold their house and she, Owen and Alexandra would be relocating to Colorado where Millicent's family lived and couldprovide the support they needed. Kerry was shocked at the suddenness of the decision. Millicent was surprised at Kerry's reaction.

So...you're *leaving* me here?"

"Well, you can come visit for sure, but isn't your life in Wilmington? Your teaching job...your friends? Honestly, Kerry, we're doing you a favor."

⚓

"I can't believe she said that to you," Tania fumed two weeks later as she and Kerry sewed more pew bows at Tania's apartment in Wilmington. "No 'thanks for all you've *done*'? Just...'by the way, now that we don't need you anymore you're on your *own*'?"

"I don't know, Tania," Kerry's brows pulled together in worry. "Something else is going on but I can't pin it down. Since Owen came home from rehab, he has been tense and moody. I thought it was the head injury as would be expected. But Millicent has recently started acting...scared. Not because of Owen's physical condition, but she freaks out at phone rings and doorbells. She won't let me take Alexandra to the park anymore. Owen about came unglued when I almost answered his cell phone one morning, and they've not been generous at all with my use of Owen's car. That's why I took the bus this time. The car just sets in the garage. It would do it good to get it out every now and then. I know I'm clumsy but I've never had a car accident. Now this hushed selling of the house but there were never for sale signs out front, no one coming to see the house. This sudden move to Colorado? It just doesn't sound—*normal.*"

"Well, what's normal?" Tania sighed. "I mean I would think anyone would act strangely after a loved one's near brush with death. Maybe Millicent does need to be close to her family right now. What upsets me is...you need family, too. Did Millicent even bring up your moving with them? I can't believe they would just leave you here on the other side of the country."

"But I don't want to move to Colorado anymore than I want to take up residence in Beaufort. I don't even want to resume my life in Wilmington without *you* here."

"Oh gosh, Kerry, I feel like I'm abandoning you, too."

"No, my friend, don't you feel guilty about realizing your dreams. You give me hope...that it can happen. Anyway, I told Millicent I'd have to have Monday off so I can go by the Administration Building and fill out the paperwork to return from my leave of absence. She's taking off work to stay with Owen and Alexandra. Oh, and by the way, have there been any takers on this apartment?"

"There have been a few lookers. Nothing for sure."

Kerry looked up from her stitchery and caught Tania's stricken face. "Oh, Tania, I'll be fine. That trip to England, short as it was, gave me a taste of self-confidence and...worthiness."

Merrek had given her that.

"Maybe you'll start dating again?" Tania ventured, but Kerry bristled. "Oh, come on, girl. You need to stop pining after your first mating and discover there is a whole sea of men out there who can do the same thing. Eventually you'll meet another someone. You'll settle down, maybe start a family. By the way, I've arranged an escort for you for the rehearsal dinner tonight. I think you'll like him," and with a wicked wiggle of her eyebrows added, "who knows where it might go..."

Kerry groaned. "Not this again, Tania. I can go by myself."

"I won't hear of it. Have you not heard the weather reports? It's supposed to get horrible tonight. I don't want you to be alone."

Kerry suppressed a shudder and pricked her finger in the process. She had been following the news of the tropical storm that was moving up the Atlantic—an early one this year. She was just reaching for a tissue to wrap around her *bleeding* finger when her phone rang. Her heart jumped in her chest when she saw the call was from Merrek. She had not heard from him except in short, business-like texts, in three weeks. "Hi, stranger," Kerry answered with a tentative voice. She could here traffic noise in the background. "Where are you?"

"Uh…look, luv—I'll get right to the point. Truth is…I can't do this long distance relationship thing. It's killin' me. Affectin' me work, me sleep…"

Kerry knew Tania was watching her, but she could not keep her face from falling at his words. "I understand…"

Before she knew what Tania was about, her friend grabbed the phone. "So you're going to break her heart after all, are you—you limey bastard? I should come over there and scratch your eyes out for stringing her along all this ti…"

"*Tania!*" Kerry was furious, grabbing for the phone. "He called *me.*"

Tania was drawing breath, already reloading for another round, but she suddenly shoved the phone back in Kerry's hand, a stunned look on her face. "He said he'd make it easy for me, whatever that means, and to give the phone back to you—in no uncertain British terms, I might add."

"Well?" Kerry glared at her friend. Then she spoke into the phone, "Sorry for that Merrek. Tania is…overly dramatic. You were saying?"

Merrek's voice was tight. "I was sayin' I'm not doin' this anymore. So please tell this cabby the address of your current location…and please be there."

"Hello?" said a voice with a Jamaican accent. Kerry could not think. "*Hello?*" repeated the strange voice through the phone. Kerry finally rattled off Tania's address and put down the phone, her mind slowly wrapping around what was going on, a brilliant smile spreading across her face. "He's here! Tania, he's here! I can't believe this! Oh!" Her hand went to her hair, wrapped up under an oversized bandana, loose strands curling wildly about her face. "Oh, Tania, I'm a mess."

Tania jumped up and pulled her friend into the bathroom, handed her a fresh towel and a hair dryer. "You're a mess? I've made a mess. The least I can do is help you fix your mess."

Half an hour later, freshly showered and groomed, Kerry waited while Tania answered the impatient knock on her door. She waited still as Tania quietly stood back to allow entrance to the darkly handsome, travel-rumpled, unshaven giant of a man whose intense eyes were avidly focused on Kerry's face. He looked…hopeful but unsure. Kerry smiled all over her face.

It was all the reassurance he needed. Merrek crossed the threshold, dropped his bags on the floor and walked directly into her outstretched arms. He scooped her up, fisted one hand into her freshly washed hair and buried his face in the curve of her neck. He breathed deeply, as if he had been starving for air. "God how I've missed you," he mumbled in her ear.

It thrilled Kerry as she clung to him that it seemed he would pull her inside him so they would never be apart again. "What are you doing here?" she asked, still shocked at his sudden appearance. "I mean, how…?"

"I have ta be in Washington, DC ta meet wi' *National Geographic* on Monday. I added on this side trip ta make sure I didn't just dream 'ee up—over and over, night after bloody night."

Kerry was giddy with emotion, but suddenly remembered her friend standing by the door. She gently pushed at Merrek. "Merrek, I'd like to introduce you to my best friend, Tania."

But Merrek kept her close and shook his head. "We've met," he whispered hoarsely. "If I turn around, there's a chance she'll scratch me eyes out and I'm not nearly through lookin' at ye."

Kerry giggled and pushed again. Merrek set her back down and slowly turned to face Kerry's bold friend. "So, Tania…do we 'ave a problem, you and I?"

The man's size, his dark eyes, and his astonishingly handsome face intimidated Tania, but she did manage to square her stance and look him directly in the eyes. "I'm not sure. I am sorry for reaming you out on the phone before I had all the facts, but still, if I thought for a minute you meant trouble for my friend there, I'd make good on that promise, you feel me? So you'd best convince me otherwise."

Merrek studied her a moment. "Truth is I wouldn't have worried so much about Kerry all this time 'ad I known she 'ad such a fierce watchdog at 'er side."

Tania's eyes narrowed. "Uh…excuse me? Is that some limey way of calling me a bitch?"

Humor glinted in Merrek's tired dark eyes. He turned to Kerry and smiled. "I see why ya like 'er. She's quick." Kerry chuckled at the look on Tania's face.

But Tania gave in. "Well, forgive me, then?"

Merrek held up a hand. "One condition. *Limey bastard?* 'E's highly offensive...on multiple levels."

"Deal. No name calling...on either side..." Tania emphasized as she held out her hand. "Friends?"

Merrek took Tania's hand. "Nice ta meet ya, Tania. And congratulations are in order, aye? When's the big day?"

"Tomorrow," both girls spoke at once.

"*Tomorrow?* Damn, I didn't mean ta get in the way..."

"Not at all," Tania assured him as Kerry shook her head, "you are herewith invited to the wedding, and you can escort Kerry to the rehearsal dinner, too. I'll cancel your other date, Kerry, or at least find him something else to do."

Merrek's eyebrows drew together sharply. "*What other date?*"

"Oh, don't worry," Tania assured him. "He's a date...er, an escort rather, that I arranged for her. All this wedding stuff, you know, requires escorts."

"Well," replied Merrek, pulling Kerry to him. "I'll gladly take it from here if there are no objections from 'e, luv?"

"Oh, God, Merrek. I still can't believe you're here. And I'm so glad you're safe. Did you know there's a storm coming? Was it a horrible flight across?"

"A bit, but no worries, luv. I could not have timed it better had I tried," he said as his eyes darted around the room, taking in for the first time the wedding paraphernalia, "but I see you're busy here, and I need ta get cleaned up, rest a bit. I've been on a plane from London ta Atlanta, then ta Beaufort, a cab ta yer brother's 'ouse, a cab back to Beaufort, a bus here ta Wilmington, and a cab here. I'm some tired."

"Oh, Merrek—all that trouble!" exclaimed Kerry.

"Aye, well, I predicted 'e'd be a 'andful, didn't I now?"

"Did you see my brother?"

"Aye, we 'ad a nice conversation once I convinced Millicent I wasn't a serial killer and talked me way in. She's a timid one, aye? I didn't expect that. But your brother—'e looks good, Kerry. 'E's lucky."

"You had a conversation with Owen? What did he say?"

"He wanted ta know what my intentions were with his little sister."

"Owen said that to you? After all this time he's now trying to be my guardian or something?"

"No, luv, 'e's tryin' ta be yer older brother. Let 'im."

Kerry didn't argue. "What did you tell him?"

"I told him my intentions were honorably dishonorable."

Kerry gasped and Tania laughed. "What did he say?" they asked in unison.

"He laughed, shook me 'and and gave me his blessin'. He actually looked relieved I think."

Tania held her hand up to Merrek for a high five. "I like you already, Merrek Walles."

Merrek slapped Tania's hand and continued, "Anyway, 'e told me you'd taken the bus to Wilmington yesterday, so I followed. Is there a hotel nearby? I'll get out the way…"

Kerry laughed. "Oh, things couldn't have worked out better if you had let me in on this surprise plan of yours. Come with me. Tania—I'll be back to help you a little later on?"

"Don't worry about it. We are almost done here anyway, and my sister will be here shortly. She'll want something to do. See you tonight."

⚓

Kerry took Merrek to the hotel nearby where she was staying for the weekend. Merrek would not touch Kerry again until he had showered and shaved. She turned down the bed and closed the curtains, straightened the room, laid out her clothes for dinner. She could not curb her jitters at being alone with Merrek again.

He came out of the bathroom, looking somewhat refreshed and certainly fit, a towel wrapped around his hips. "That's some nice shower in there. Are all American water closets that big?"

"No," Kerry chuckled. "Not all. That one's a hotel perk." She watched in shy fascination as his eyes traveled over her, darkening with intent.

"Are all American women this exciting?" He moved purposely toward her but stopped when he noticed her wary smile and almost imperceptible retreat. He looked at her questioningly, then with understanding. "Is this a bad time, luv? I'd be more than content ta jus' 'old 'e."

"I…no, I just…" and the blush he loved so much began to creep into her face as her eyes swept over his body.

"Aw, Kerry, sweetheart—'e've seen me before, luv. I promise nothin' 'bout me 'as changed in the last eight months." Nevertheless, he left the towel on as he approached her, reached out and pulled her close. "I'm exactly as 'e left me, darlin'." She pushed away slightly so she could look up into his face. Recognizing truth there, she relaxed against him. He continued with a sigh, "'Ceptin' a might randier, knowin' that all I'll ever want was way beyond me reach…until now." Finished with verbal assurances he kissed her with eight months of need and unspent desire. Her uncertainties melted in the heat.

When he finally lifted his head, he said, "I've been waitin' for this moment to return since we stood on that wharf in Porth, been wantin' ta finish what I started there. To tell 'e even though I realize it's been a whirlwind relationship that's now been kept an ocean apart for almost nine months, I know I love 'e, my Kerenza. I've known from the start that 'e were the one for me. I want 'e ta be mine—always."

Kerry gazed into the dark eyes she'd missed so much. In them, it seemed she saw centuries of dedication. "I've been yours since…all along. I've never, ever considered anyone else."

His eyes lit up. "You asked me once what I believed about life after death. I'm still not sure, but this much I'll go ta me own grave believin'. That call to Cornwall was for me. I know it. Whether it was Kerenza or Myghal, the pixies, St. Andrew, or God Almighty, I'll thank whatever entity sent 'e ta me as long as I live."

⚓

Kerry shifted slightly to look at the clock and Merrek's arm tightened to pin her against him. He never even broke his breathing pattern, causing Kerry to smile. He was exhausted—if not just from the trip then surely from the addition of their lovemaking, but he held onto her fast even in his sleep.

She finally craned her neck back far enough to see by the clock that it was not quite as late as she thought, but she needed to start getting ready for the rehearsal dinner. Merrek stirred slightly, but his eyes remained closed, his thick, long lashes lying against his sun-bronzed skin. "Somewhere 'e need ta be, luv?" he asked thickly.

"Yeah, I'm afraid so. The rehearsal dinner is in two hours. Want to go with me or would you rather sleep?"

"And let some other bloke escort ya? I don't think so. I'm goin'."

"Good. I'm going to take a shower, so you have a few more minutes. I'll wake you when you need to start getting ready. Oh, did you bring a suit?"

"Yeah, I did. Probably needs ta be steamed. I'll check in a minute."

Kerry was in the middle of lathering her hair when she heard Merrek come into the bathroom and hang his suit on a hook near the steam rising out of the shower. Then the shower door opened and he stepped in.

"'E could 'ave a fitty party in 'ere," he commented in amazement as his eyes scanned the large shower enclosure. Kerry turned her back to him, still uncomfortable with his total disregard of modesty, especially hers. "'E look cute wi' short, sudsy hair," he smiled, and as his eyes raked over her he chuckled, "and 'e blush all over yer body, didde know that?"

"It's probably the hot water, don't you think?"

"Aw, now, Kerry, m'luv, don't go ruinin' it for me. Makin' 'e blush is one of me best pleasures in life."

Kerry made a face at him over her shoulder and then stepped under the water. As the suds slid from her hair, Merrek chased them with his fingers down the small of her back and over her hips. "Seems all me best pleasures have somethin' ta do with 'e."

Kerry shivered and found that breathing evenly was becoming difficult. "Want the soap?" she asked for diversion.

"Nah, not jus' yet."

"What are you doing in here then?" Kerry asked, looking over her shoulder with a timid smile.

And there it was—that smile that never ceased to destroy her equilibrium. "Ever heard o' shower sex, darlin'? I've no experience in the activity m'self, but at the moment I can't seem ta think of anythin' else."

When she could catch her breath again, Kerry eyed him dubiously. "Is it me or this shower that's turned you on so?"

That brought a chuckle from him. "'E's some powerful combination, that I can tell 'e." He moved with her under the flowing water, wrapped her up in his embrace. "And 'e said 'e had a couple o' hours still, aye?"

"You're incorrigible," Kerry sighed as her head fell back against his chest.

"Oh, sweetheart," he whispered gruffly in her ear. "'E 'ave no idea…"

⚓

Kerry and Merrek had never seen each other dressed up. She was amazed that Merrek could look even broader in his navy suit, so commandingly handsome. Merrek found it hard to take his eyes off Kerry. The soft material of her dress flowed over her body, accentuating the delicate femininity he adored, and the spiked heels just about put him over the edge before he raised an eyebrow and caught her eyes.

She smiled at him with understanding. "A requirement by Tania. She says I have to have a practice run before tomorrow!"

He gave her a supportive smile. "You'll do just fine, m'luv. And yer breath-takin', 'e know that?"

Kerry felt her heart flutter. She held her hand out to him. "Are we ready?"

He took her hand, but when she turned and took a step toward the door, he stood firm, pulling her back. "A moment, please." He reached for her other hand and held them both, gently caressing them with his thumbs. "I realize I'm askin' a lot o' 'e—more than I should expect, but I'm goin' ta ask 'e all the same. I want 'e ta come home wi' me, Kerry. Ta my home. *Your home.* 'E's ready for 'e, and Owen seems ta be on the mend—enough ta let 'e go." Freeing her hands, he reached into his suit pocket and brought out a small box. "I meant what I said. I love 'e and I want 'e wi' me always." He opened the box toward her. "*Marry me, Kerenza.*"

She had a fleeting glance at a peridot solitaire surrounded by sparkling little diamonds as her eyes flew to his face. *Was he serious?* Her mind exploded with all the reasons she should take some time to consider this—not the least of which was the short time they'd known each other, but each and every thought sputtered and fizzled and fell until there was nothing left but the dark quiet of his eyes. All her dreams were in those eyes. "Yes!" Kerry threw her arms around his neck and buried her face there, heady from his scent, and reveled in the protective feel of his hard, strong body.

He held her close, reverently. "'E've made me a happy man, luv, the happiest. I'll do everythin' I can ta do the same for 'ee, so there will never be regrets. Wanna try on the ring?"

Kerry pushed back away from him and held out her left hand. Merrek carefully removed the ring from the box and slipped it on her ring finger, a perfect fit. "Do 'e like it? It matches yer eyes."

"It's beautiful, Merrek." She turned the ring in the light, mesmerized by the sparkle. "But I would have said yes to a cigar band. I love *you.*"

His brows furrowed slightly. "I wish I'd known that—me Da keeps a box in 'is study…"

"No, no…" Kerry laughed with delight. "I love it. My birthstone…it matches my necklace…it's awesome! And I love the setting. How did you guess the size?"

"That was Elowen's doin'. She used ta work in a jewelry store. She's developed a good eye. Wanna get married next week?"

"What?" Her expression was incredulous. "I don't know if we can, Merrek. I'll have to see what the state laws are regarding a marriage license. There may be special forms to file since you are a UK citizen and…"

"Marry me, luv. Next week. I'll fly back 'ere after me meeting in Washington and we'll do it all—legal and non-retractable. I'll get a lawyer if need be. I want ta take 'e back ta Cornwall as me wife, not as me roommate."

Kerry's mind was whirling again. "Where?"

"At yer brother's house in Beaufort, maybe? So your brother can be present?"

Kerry felt her eyes tearing up. "That is so thoughtful, Merrek, but won't your family be upset?"

"Not if they don't miss out on a celebration. I thought we could get married here, with your family, and then 'ave a reception in London later wi' mine."

"In London?"

"Aye, in the ballroom of the Traveler's Haven Hotel—at the insistence of Ralph Wilesky and Olivia Tesmer." He smiled when Kerry's eyebrows arched. "I've run inta Olivia several times. We've been exchangin' news and updates. She invited me ta dinner with Mr. Wilesky six weeks ago. They started makin' plans the second I mentioned my intentions. Does that set well with 'ee, luv? I hope so, seein' as how me mum and sisters are also in on those plans, and the mood in Da's household will be sour if they're disappointed."

"So they know, too? I mean, that you were going to ask me?"

"Aye, and that's some risk I've taken wi' me ego there—that you'd say yes."

Kerry moved into his arms, enjoying the extra height her heels gave her. "Did you ever seriously doubt it?" she asked, nibbling at his neck.

"Nope." He quickly and confidently uttered the single word and then smiled in a way that reminded her of Trev.

"So, cockiness runs in the family, then?"

He smiled, took her hand and pulled her to the door, "Yer perception is one of yer most amazin' attributes, luv." He held open the door and let her precede him. He followed, shut the door behind them and watched her walk toward the elevator ahead of him. "Apart from the obvious ones, that is."

"So…you're the English dude?" Robert's face registered surprise as he shook hands with Merrek.

"Cornish…dude… ta be exact, aye."

"I was expecting a pretty Little Lord Fauntleroy, I guess. You're not little by any means, and that's quite a grip you have there."

"Ah. Twenty years o' pullin' in loaded fishnets.""He is pretty, though," noted Blake. He tried to ignore the hand Merrek held out and moved forward for a hug, but Merrek grabbed his elbow to stay him and enveloped Blake's hand in his own. Blake undauntedly accepted the handshake and introduced himself with an indulgent smile. "Blake Sheldon here. Brandon Fuller there. We've known Kerry for going on three years. Sweet girl. You're a lucky guy."

Merrek shook hands with Brandon. "Aye, she is, and aye, I am. Kerry's talked fondly of 'ee both. Nice ta make yer acquaintance."

Blake batted his eyes and smiled in delight as he laid a hand on Merrek's chest. "Oh, I could listen to you talk for hours. That accent kills."

Merrek looked more than slightly uncomfortable. "Aye, well, I don't talk all that much."

"Really?" Blake drawled out while his smile and eyes grew wider.

Kerry took Merrek's arm. "I think we are getting ready to sit down. Blake, Brandon, see you later?"

Merrek patted Kerry's hand where it lay on his arm. "Thanks, luv. He wasn't hittin' on me, was he?"

Kerry laughed. "Blake hits on everyone—he can't help himself. But he's harmless. He and Brandon have been together for eight years. Brandon plays the cello and Blake the violin. They're providing the music during the wedding. Beautiful music—you'll see."

Merrek held Kerry's chair out for her, then leaned down and whispered in her ear, "I think we make beautiful music together, don't you agree, luv?"

Kerry smiled at him, the sparkle in her green eyes matching that of the peridot in her new ring. "Aye, that I do."

Tania arrived with her parents and sister. After greeting Robert's mother, she began making the rounds to speak quickly with all the guests before the meal service began. When she came to Kerry, it took her less than five seconds to link Kerry's glowing face to the gleaming ring on her finger. She gave both Kerry and Merrek congratulatory hugs. Then she punched Merrek playfully in the arm.

2. "So you're going to take her away from us, are you?"

"Well, I'm not leavin' 'er 'ere, trust me."

Tania caught Kerry in a fierce hug. "Rescued and captured all in the same day!"

⚓

The anticipated storm finally blew in shortly after midnight, lighting up the dark sky and producing thunder rolls that shook all of Wilmington. High winds and slashing rain caused many to worry about toppled trees and power outages, flash floods and washed out bridges. But not Kerry. She never even stirred, but slept peacefully in Merrek's arms.

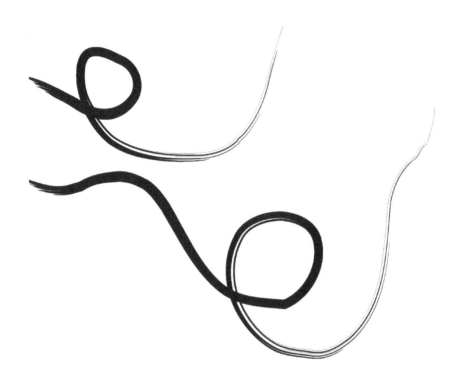

- 19 -

I have had dreams, and I have had nightmares.
I overcame the nightmares because of my dreams.
—Jonas Salk

Kerry waved goodbye to Tania and Robert as they left for their Charleston honeymoon. In her hands, she held both her bouquet and the bride's bouquet that Tania had delivered into her hands like a gifted quarterback to his most bumbling receiver. The crowd had held a collective breath as a determined Kerry dove for the bouquet in the direction of a potted hydrangea and caught it just as Merrek circumvented a collision by wrapping his arm around Kerry's waist and hauling her to safety against his side. The crowd had erupted in cheers when Kerry stretched both bouquets over her head, her face beaming with victory.

Merrek stood beside her, one hand at the small of Kerry's back, the other twirling the easily won bride's garter on his finger. "She looks radiant."

Kerry smiled and blew a kiss to the happy couple. Merrek peered down into her wistful face and tried to picture Kerry in a white bridal gown with a long trailing train. For the life of him, he could not get the image to superimpose over the picture she presented now in the red slinky bridesmaid's dress that was driving him crazy. "Why do 'e think Tania chose for 'e to wear that dress? Me sisters made sure their bridesmaids couldn't come near to takin' attention away from themselves."

"You're the only one that noticed me, Merrek. And besides, Tania doesn't think that way. She's a costume designer—give her a theme, a budget, a model and she's off. It's *Valentine's Day*. You think she'd have had me wear a puffy-pastel-blue?"

"Could've used a puffy-pink, aye? It's been bloody hell today trying to function normally through these fantasies I keep havin' about 'e and this red dress. 'E's gettin' some uncomfortable."

229

"Really," Kerry crooned. "But candy-heart-pink clashes awfully with my hair color. Tania knew just the shade of red I could pull off."

He noticed when she shivered, and removed his suit jacket to wrap around her shoulders. "I've been thinkin' about our weddin' and I'm feelin' a little bad, luv, that 'e won't have all this—the long train, the bubbles, havin' yer moment in the spotlight. We could 'ave a big weddin' in London if you'd rather."

Kerry turned her full attention to him, her eyes sparkling. "What, and embarrass you by tripping on a long train in front of all those people? Not a chance. Trust me, a small wedding is more my style, more in my comfort zone. And while we're on the subject I've been thinking, we should probably change your wedding vows a bit. Like instead of *for better or worse*, we should add something like for *slip or fall*, for *trip or tumble*…you know what I mean?"

With his arm around her, he led her back toward the reception hall. "Aye, I get it. Somethin' along the lines o' *for mayhem or mishap*—that sort of thing?"

Kerry pushed him away with a playful scowl. "Now, that's going a little far, don't you think?" She chuckled at his skeptical glance. "But vows are serious, right? You want to have a crystal clear idea of what you're getting into."

At that, Merrek gave her a lustful smirk. "Darlin', as long as I'm gettin' inta y…"

"Shhh!" She cut him off and looked around to see if anyone was in hearing range, her face beet red. "You are bad!"

He chuckled, leaned forward and planted a quick kiss on her mouth. "Just keepin' it crystal clear, Kerenza, luv."

She stopped abruptly to look at him. He raised an eyebrow in question. "What?" He smiled when she continued to stare at him.

"I was just wondering if Myghal was anything like you."

"You mean besides bein' a Walles? Tall probably, dark features most likely, certainly good in bed…"

Kerry interrupted with an incredulous snort and interjected, "You think he was as assertive and protective?"

"'E know, I've thought a lot about how Kerenza disappeared. Where was Myghal? How did he let that 'appen?"

"Well, what could he have done if he was…say…out of town? Couples can't be together 24/7 you know."

"But she was evidently headstrong and foolish. He should've taken charge o' that."

"Oh, boy—listen to you. All that macho chivalry. I'm clumsy and prone to accidents. What are you going to do with me? Lock me up in a padded cell when you're not around?"

The plethora of emotions that flash in his dark eyes—determination, fear, anger, worry—was fascinating to watch. Finally, his jaw set with resolve he stated, "For one thing, yer not foolish, although a might headstrong. I feel for Myghal's loss, but Kerenza should never have been out in that boat by 'erself with a storm brewin' if that's what did 'appen. Me uncle should have known her mind, and prevented it. Aye, he was shortsighted, and he lost her." Merrek turned Kerry around to face him. *"I'll not lose you."*

Kerry could not help but believe him, and that was a comforting feeling regardless of the arrogance in the statement. "But Merrek, you've got to be realistic. We don't have to look past our own families to know that health issues arise, accidents happen. We're not always in total control of our lives."

"All that is true, but some things can be avoided with awareness and action." He tightened his big hands around her upper arms and pulled her against his chest. "You want to have a crystal clear idea of how it's goin' ta be with me? 'E might as well know that I'm a possessive and controllin' devil. Just ask me sisters. I protect what's mine."

Kerry pulled in a quick breath and pushed away from him. She turned in a complete circle, letting her eyes roam quickly over the modern surroundings before facing him again. She shook her head slightly, as if to clear it. "I thought for a moment there I'd gone back in time. You sound like you just walked out of an eighteenth-century romance novel."

His eyes flashed. "You'd rather I was more like yer twenty-first century brother?"

Kerry gave him a soothing smile. "It wasn't a criticism, Merrek, just an observation." She moved close, stood on tiptoe and kissed his cheek. "I've always loved those eighteenth century heroes. Like you, they're honorable and strong, reliable and protective, and…"

"Good in bed?" He arched and wiggled his eyebrows.

Kerry stepped back and flashed him an exasperated grin. "Like stallions. Their egos were big, too."

"Too?"

Kerry rolled her eyes. The devil controlled this man for sure.

"What else do these heroes have in common with me?" Merrek asked.

A new blush superimposed the previous blush, and Kerry glanced around them quickly for spectators. Finding none, she put her hands on her hips and lifted her chin in irritation. "Their capacity to…"

He cut her off with a kiss that stole her breath. "Overwhelm?" he smiled into dazed green eyes. With a smug grin, he watched Kerry's face as she obviously worked to collect her scattered wits. He loved the fact that he could do that to her. He took her hand and started up the steps of the church, pulling her along. "What were eighteenthcentury heroines like?" He watched in amusement as Kerry tilted her head and began to list attributes.

"Beautiful, intelligent, spirited…oh, and they always…always…no matter if they've been dragged through a swamp, ridden on a horse for days, or spent hours working in the fields in scorching temperatures… they always smelled good."

Merrek let out a burst of laughter. "In a time without sanitation laws and limited hygiene products, I doubt they could 'ave smelled noticeably bad to anyone."

Kerry's giggle was music to his ears. "I never thought about that."

"Did the heroines of said novels evoke unprecedented desire in their heroes?"

"Oh, sure, that's a predominate theme. He would desire her above all others and then fall helplessly in love, even though he fought it every step of the way."

"So…after getting' 'im some worked up, was she pleasin' in 'is bed?"

Kerry glanced at him with a disgruntled face. "Is that all you ever think about?"

"Aye," he answered without skipping a beat. He loved watching her face turn rosy, "Well?"

"She couldn't help herself from being anything but wildly responsive to her hero, but to him only."

"And was she also a bit o' a handful, would 'e say?"

"Well, yeah, she wasn't perfect. She had a few little…quirks."

"Well then, Kerenza m'luv, considerin' all that, 'e are some blast from the past yerself." Pausing just before entering the reception hall, Merrek leaned down and captured Kerry's mouth with his. "'E smell good, too," he whispered in her ear as they went inside to join the rest of the reception clean-up crew.

⚓

Another wave of the tropical storm started to blow through not long after the wedding. Kerry and Merrek made it back to the hotel just before the clouds spilled over. Merrek did not waste any time acting out the fantasy he had imagined throughout the day. As soon as he had closed and locked their door, he turned Kerry away from him, ever so slowly unzipped the lengthy enclosure down the back of that Valentine red dress, and then gently moved it off her shoulders. It sluiced down her body to pool at her feet, and then he started a slow removal of her dainty red under things, except for the hose and lacy garters—those he left alone.

The storm outside their window did nothing to squelch Kerry's enthusiasm for fulfilling the rest of the fantasy, and when they were sated, she slept once again undisturbed, sheltered in Merrek's protective embrace.

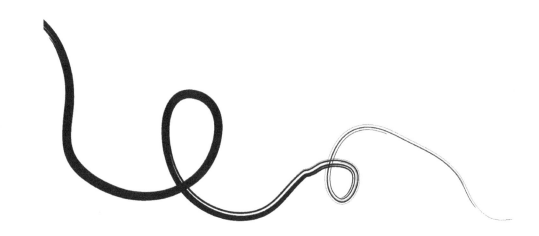

- 20 -

Beyond mind, there is an awareness that is intrinsic...
—Osho

Merrek's meeting with the supervisors at *National Geographic* went very well in spite of the sinking feeling in his gut that trouble was brewing. He had called home first, fearing his father was having another go at heart failure, but all was well there. His next call was Kerry's cell phone. His call went immediately to voicemail. He waited a few minutes and called again with the same result.

Frustration caused his temperament to become edgy, and he tried again a few minutes later while walking through security at Dulles International, and again as he hurried to his gate. No answer. No answer.

As soon as he found a seat at the gate, he pulled out his laptop and searched for other contact numbers, berating himself for never obtaining emergency information for Kerry. There was no listing for Owen Carter in Beaufort. That did not surprise him as not many people have both a cell and land number, but it did irritate him. Next he Googled Millicent Carter and found the number for her dance studio. The lady who answered the phone told Merrek that Millicent went home early, unexpectedly, and no, she absolutely could not give out Millicent's private cell phone number.

Once seated on the plane, Merrek fought the panic that threatened to overtake him. Nothing from Kerry, and Millicent had gone home early. Even if something had happened to Owen, Kerry would surely have called him by now.

A flight attendant asked if he wanted a drink. *No he didn't want a drink. He just wanted the bloody plane to move.* He silently cursed every passenger that took extra precious seconds arranging luggage and settling in seats. He envisioned the fiery annihilation of the five planes in front of his that were delaying takeoff, and then checked his watch every two minutes or so during the forty-minute flight to Atlanta where he had thirty minutes to catch the plane to Beaufort. Although he tried repeatedly on his way from one terminal to the next, Kerry's voicemail was all he could reach. He left a message, "I've called several times, luv, and you're not answerin'. Please call me—leave a message. I'm a bit worried."

As soon as the plane's wheels touched the Beaufort runway, he turned his phone on and checked for calls. Nothing from Kerry. When he called her phone, again her voicemail answered immediately. He left another message, then texted, *You're killing me, love. Call me.*

Once in a taxi headed to the Carter home, he began to chide himself for his possible overreaction. Maybe she had lost her phone somewhere like she had her passport in Cornwall, or just simply forgot to charge it. Nevertheless, no amount of chiding would rid him of the innate feeling that something was dreadfully wrong.

⚓

It had started out as a somewhat typical morning for Kerry. Millicent left for the studio at eight to get ready for her nine o'clock Interpretive Movement class and Kerry made breakfast for Owen, Alexandra and herself. After breakfast, Alexandra watched a princess movie while Kerry led Owen through his morning physical therapy routine. It was then that the day started downhill.

"Damn! Are you fucking trying to kill me?" Owen roared at her when she coaxed him to push a little harder.

"Owen, what is wrong with you? Alexandra is right in the next room."

He had the decency to look somewhat repentant. "Look, let's just forego this...S-H-I-T today. I can't take it right now."

"This isn't my idea, Owen. These are your doctor's orders. No pain, no gain. You know that. You're getting more range in your movement every day. You don't want to stop now."

"Kerry, I...can't concentrate on this today, and when I can't concentrate the pain takes over. *I'm done for the day!* Get me a pain pill."

Kerry sighed, lowered the wheelchair's footrest and guided Owen's right leg back into place. "Owen, you're tapering off, remember? You can't have another one this soon. What's truly wrong, Owen? What can I do?"

Owen let out a harsh bark of sarcastic laughter. "Well, Dorothy, can you click your ruby red slippers together three times and zip us to Colorado?" His expression was surly, but looking past that she recognized the worry and the...*fear?* Owen had insisted they cancel his doctor's appointment today. Had he developed a new physical problem he was afraid to face?

"What's going on, Owen? What's got you so upset?"

Owen looked up at her, the expression on his face indecisive. "Look," she told him as she handed him a glass of ice water, "I'm going to walk Alexandra up the street for her play date with Emily and when I get back, let's talk."

Owen shook his head furiously. "No! No, Alex needs to stay here—at home. At home. Here—at home."

Kerry knew her brother was extra agitated because since the accident he tended to repeat himself when stressed.

"It's only two houses down, Owen. I'll stay just long enough to find out what time Grace needs me to pick Alex up and then I will hurry back. Ten minutes at the most. Then you'll talk to me?"

"DO NOT TAKE ALEX OUT OF THE HOUSE, KERRY," he roared at her. When he saw her stricken and confused face he tried to explain. "It's dangerous out there."

Owen was obviously in the grips of some fear. Kerry had read that those with head injuries could develop paranoia, but..."Owen, seriously, what is going on?"

"Everything was going to be fine. I had it under control, and then this f...freaking accident. How can they blame me for what I had no control over, right? No control."

Kerry felt a throbbing begin in her temples. "Who is blaming you, Owen, and what did you lose control of?" She knew instinctively this was something she really did not want to know, something that would have broken their parents' hearts. He finally told her, whining and yelling, crying and raging all the way through the discourse while the princess movie played on in the other room.

When he was finally spent, so was Kerry, as well as so disappointed to understand that Owen considered himself a victim only, and was actually looking to her to somehow make it all go away. To take care of the Carter family as she always had. She suddenly felt very tired.

⚓

When Merrek arrived at the Carter's home a little before three o'clock that afternoon, Kerry had been missing between five and six hours. Millicent explained, "Kerry called me at work just as my first class was underway and told me Owen was having an extra bad morning. I came home and tried to calm things down, but Kerry left while I was preoccupied with both Owen and Alex. She left I guess around 9:30 in Owen's car. She hasn't been back and we haven't heard from her. She's not answering her phone."

"I know," nodded Merrek. "I've been callin' since before I left Washington. E's na like her. E'ave any clue to where she might've gone?"

"I told her not to take the car anywhere. It's a valuable car. Very valuable," said Owen flatly.

Was it bad form to tear into someone confined to a wheelchair?

Holding onto his temper, just barely, Merrek inquired in a deceptively calm voice, "Yer sister is missin' and yer worried about yer car?"

Millicent went to stand beside Owen. "He's worried about Kerry because she is in his car. She might be in danger, Merrek—she *might* be." She turned her head to look at Owen, who was holding his head in his hands. "Owen is in trouble with some bad people. We had hoped to be in Colorado before it came to a head, but…they know Owen's car, Merrek."

Merrek felt all the air leave his lungs. The need to sit down beckoned but he wanted freedom of movement, the room to pace if need be. "Owen?" When Kerry's brother looked up, Merrek stared intently into eyes the same color as Kerry's, but so different in luminosity. Whereas he could almost drown in the shimmering depths of hers, he could barely get his feet wet in the shallows of Owen's. They were worlds apart, these siblings. "Owen, I need 'e to tell me everythin'. Don't leave anythin' out." He raised his voice when Owen's head dropped to his chest, "And I don't care how taxin' it is for 'e, and I don't give a rat's ass if yer head is splittin' or yer back's in spasms. Yer goin' to tell me everythin'—now. The clock's tickin', and you know every minute counts for her if she is truly in trouble." He grimaced as Kerry's words suddenly slammed into him— *Trouble finds me.*

Millicent's eyes widened and she dropped down beside her husband so she could look up into his face. "Owen? Did you ask Kerry for the money? Do you think she went to the bank?"

"What bank?" Merrek already had his phone out.

"First Bank of Beaufort," Millicent answered, her eyes never leaving Owen's face.

Merrek walked out onto the porch to make the call. He needed air. He was suffocating in dread of hearing Owen's explanation and its implications regarding Kerry. But the heavy, humid air that greeted him sent him further into despair. It told him a storm was probable. Kerry

238

was terrified of storms, and he did not know where she was.

When he found the number for the bank, he came back inside and gave the phone to Owen. "You're their client, you know who to talk to. Find out."

Owen sounded a bit shaky, but still arrogantly authoritative and was able to ascertain that Kerry had been in around 10:00 that morning to have $75,000 wired from her branch in Wilmington into Owen's account. That was five hours ago. With Merrek's guidance, Owen asked if she had been alone during the process. The answer was yes and no. She was alone when she came in, but a man joined her as she was exiting. Merrek's hands itched to encircle Owen's throat, but he needed the man to be able to talk. And in the face of Merrek's wrath, talk he did.

"I have a friend," Owen began, "who works for Landen and Lowry, a law firm in DC. He has been giving me tips on certain acquisitions and so forth that enabled me to help my clients increase their bank accounts—substantially—and for a while my own as well."

Merrek thought for a moment. Then his eyes narrowed. "Insider tradin'? But that's illegal in this country, aye?"

"Yes."

Merrek stared at the man for a second and then turned is eyes on the picture of Owen, Millicent and Alex that stood on the baby grand piano in the expensively furnished living room. Turning back to Owen, he asked, "Why, man? Why would you risk...everythin'?"

"To cover the many risks I'd already taken. I...gamble. Sometimes I win—*big*," the sweep of his hands indicated the room's furnishings. "Sometimes I lose, and I had a terrible losing streak the months before the accident. I lost so much I had to borrow money to pay my debts. I eventually exhausted my limits from the reputable institutions, so I was forced to turn to a...seedier supplier." He hurried on when he saw Merrek's shocked expression, "I had it all under control with the money coming in from the inside trade deals...but then this idiot driver comes out of nowhere and my life is over. I can't work, and disability insurance won't pay all the medical bills *plus* the high interest gambling debt. I have mouths to feed...I'm broke. We've sold the house and Millicent's studio and business, and I thought it was enough to buy us some time to get out of town. However, this morning I got the message that...it wasn't. They've demanded more."

Merrek knew he could not give in to the panic that was threatening to take away his ability to think...to breathe. He would be no good to Kerry if he did. He forced logical thoughts. "Kerry had $75,000?"

"Yes, from the sale of our parents' estate. That was her half. Mine was wiped out months ago."

"So if she had the money transferred electronically into your account, you would have to wait at least a couple of days to withdraw it, right?"

"Yes, that's the way it is." Owen made a whimpering sound. "Look, I never asked her for the money. She did this on her own. It was her decision."

The man's whimper was lost on Merrek. "'E had to know she'd do it for 'e. 'E were counting on it. So bloody well have the guts ta place the blame where it belongs." He pointed to the phone lying in Owen's lap. "Call the police."

Owen shook his head in protest and Millicent made a small sound of shock. "Merrek, if we involve the police…"

"I don't give a flyin' f…" Merrek paused to reign in his control. "I don't care if 'e go ta jail, Owen. I want Kerry back safe."

"Listen, Merrek," Owen pleaded. "Likely, *if* someone has taken Kerry…and we don't know that yet…but if someone has, he is likely just planning to hold her as collateral until I can withdraw the money. We'll probably hear from them soon. But if we involve the police, and whoever is with Kerry has someone watching the house, they may not…treat the collateral nicely."

Merrek felt panic and helplessness weigh hard on his chest. He had told Kerry, with the arrogance of a fool that had never felt Myghal's pain that he would never lose her, as Kerenza had been lost. That he would take charge and prevent catastrophe from happening in their lives. But here they were. He was off guard—just like Myghal. *And what could he do?*

"At least call and report yer car stolen. If she's in it they'll arrest her and we can work it all out later, but at least she'd be out of harm's way." Owen looked shocked at this suggestion, and Merrek continued in exasperation. "Look, I'm just throwin' things out here. Tryin' not ta lose me mind. 'E think anyone at the bank got a look at the guy that left with Kerry?"

At that moment, Owen's phone rang. They all three looked at it as if it was a creature of horror. Then Merrek said, "Answer it—on speaker."

As Owen was saying hello, Merrek pulled out his own phone and openeded his voice memo app.

"Owen?" Kerry's tight voice came through the speaker. Merrek's breath froze.

"Kerry, are you alright? Where are you?" Owen stammered.

"They took your car, Owen. You'll be able to access your account on Friday for withdrawal. I won't see you again until you've paid them so please do it as soon as possible. Tell Merrek I..." There were sounds of a shuffle and the connection went dead. Millicent put a hand over her mouth and left the room.

"Call back," demanded Merrek. But when Owen tried, a computerized voice said the number was no longer in service.

At that moment, Owen was more afraid of the man glaring at him than he was of the loan sharks that were circling or the law that might become involved. Merrek could read that fear in Owen's eyes, and he did nothing to alleviate it. For one thing, he truly hated this man for Kerry's current circumstance; for another, it was handy when you could use a person's fear as a control mechanism. However, what could he control Owen to do? Trade places with Kerry? He could not even trade himself because they had no way to contact these people. He would not be effective collateral, anyway. He was not convinced even Kerry was a sure thing to hold over Owen.

Think. He had done some tracking before. When Trev got himself mixed up with that bunch of druggies and went missing for two days. When Lowenna missed curfew by three hours and he traced her to a party where he found her drugged and on her way to a bedroom accompanied by a sleezy toad ten years her senior. *Think.*

At that moment, he became aware of the phone in his hand. Dobeck! He replayed the recording of Kerry's voice, listening carefully for clues of any kind. He listened repeatedly, forcing his concentration away from the tears and terrors he heard in her voice and honing in on the background noises. Finally, he heard it, understood it. "She's on a boat. Listen and tell me if those sounds right after Kerry says *your car* tells 'e anythin'."

Owen listened and frowned. "It sounds like wind."

"No," insisted Merrek. "There's a pattern to it, like waves slapping against a solid structure. And there's a whistle, right after she says 'withdraw'...right...there. That's a maritime whistle." He played it three times before recognition slid across Owen's face. "One long blast— *moving forward with low visibility.* I've signaled the same many times m'self. The storm's movin' in. Your Coast Guard will want all boats docked."

"But there's many boats, Merrek. To find the one she may be on will be like looking for the proverbial needle in the haystack."

"Then I'll go to the police. I know they won't want to do anything until she's been missing for, what, seventy-two hours? But I'll try an' convince 'em of…somethin'. I don't know what, but I'm startin' now. I can't just do naught. Just lettin' 'e know what I'm about." He handed Owen his business card. "Call me if 'e hear anythin'."

Owen and Millicent both pleaded with Merrek not to leave them, as if he offered protection. He had a heart, he did, but he could do nothing for them until Kerry was taken care of, and that's just the way it was.

He slipped out through the kitchen door, called and met a cab at a drug store not far from the house, all the while looking for men in parked cars. He took the cab to the waterway first as his impatience to find Kerry was overwhelming.

Standing on the docks a few minutes later, he strained to see through the low-lying fog that blanketed the area. He could make out a few boats still working their way inland, and he could see the flashes of light from the Coast Guard boat. He closed his eyes and concentrated on the familiar sounds he knew from fishing with his dad all those years. He was at home around water and boats. What he was listening for he was not sure, but he would know it. Instinct would tell him.

He heard again the warning blast from the Coast Guard out on the water. That warning directed all vessels back to the docks. That was one in his favor, *but how was he going to find the one that held Kerry?*

⚓

The water was so choppy Kerry was afraid she was going to be sick. Huddled against the wall of the storeroom they had shoved and locked her into, Kerry struggled to assemble her wits and think her way out of this situation. She also took a wild stab at mental telepathy in order to send a message to Merrek. If he knew where she was, she had no doubt he could rescue her, *but how was he to know?* With a shaky sigh, she accepted that the possibility of escape was largely up to her.

To keep her fear and anxiety controlled, Kerry tried to mentally write her brave heroine out of this room and off the boat while eluding her captors. Kerenza, the fictional counterpart Kerry had created, would succeed at this she thought. Of course, that likely might involve some swimming—*in the ocean. How did this happen?*

She had thought only of getting Owen out of trouble and his family out of danger. She had almost enough money in her account—a good faith payment. She had not noticed the car following her. She had not paid much attention to the deceptively kind looking man that held the door for her and followed her into the bank, and if she had not been so distracted with Owen's predicament, she might have noticed that the man seemed to follow her every move. By the time she became suspicious, he was following her to the car. At that point, Kerry began to suspect that he knew she had just surrendered everything she had to vindicate her only family member.

He came up behind her with unpredicted speed, apparently not as senior as she had guessed, and as soon as she had unlocked and opened the car door he shoved her to the passenger seat and took over. Enraged, she had put up a fight, but a properly placed male fist had put a quick end to her struggles.

She was semi-conscious by the time they had reached the docks and she tried her best to focus. Two men half-carried and half-dragged Kerry down the docks towards a boat. "A little too much to drink," her bank escort had chortled to a curious passerby, "a good thing Dad was in town."

"Kids," was the response, with an empathizing shake of the head as he strolled on by. Kerry opened her mouth to speak, but the grip that threatened to break her arm made her too nauseous to utter a sound, and over the man's shoulder, she saw Owen's car leaving the docks.

A bucket of cold water thrown in her face had awakened her fully. She was on a boat, in the hull, and after the man from the bank coached her through the phone call to Owen, he left her alone in the locked storeroom.

The boat rose and then fell on a particularly rough wave, and Kerry's stomach lurched. She heard the repeated blasts from a horn, possibly from the Coast Guard. With the weather turning bad, the boat she was on would have to turn back inland or find itself subject to suspicion. It was the first time she ever remembered being grateful for a storm.

⚓

From the docks, Merrek heard several warning blasts from what visually he could barely make out as a US Coast Guard vessel. Off to its right, he saw the running lights of a smaller craft making its way slowly but steadily toward the slips. He started to jog in that direction but the sound of impact and splintering wood brought him up short. A distress signal cut through the fog shortly after that ripping sound. His gut told him that was his sign.

He ran again out onto the slips at the southern-most end of the docks. A man was there holding binoculars to his eyes. Merrek asked as he approached, "Can you make anythin' out in this muck?"

"Some. The boat hit had no lights on—*can you believe that?* Who would do that unless they were trying to hide? Bad mistake. That other boat couldn't see her and plowed right in. By the way she's taking in water, the captain's gonna lose her. She screamed like a woman on impact."

⚓

Water was pouring in the hole caused by the collision. Kerry could hear the activity above her as the crew scrambled about. She tried the door to her prison, but it would not budge. Looking down, she watched in horror as the water swirled around her feet, rising quickly over her ankles.

She looked around frantically for something to stuff into the gaping hole, but was not sure she could reach it even if she found something. She was in a death trap. She had to let someone know where she was.

The other boat had signaled distress. Maybe they could hear her. Maybe the Coast Guard she had heard out there would hear her. She began to scream, yell and pound on the walls. Then she remembered she was below the water line now, no one would likely hear her. She would save her energy for a worthier activity—like swimming—if she could only find a way out.

⚓

"'E heard a woman scream?" Merrek felt his heart skip. "How far out is it, 'e think?"

"About a quarter of a mile. I'd say those folks have about ten minutes before that storm moves in. See the line of it over there?"

Merrek looked in the direction the man indicated. Dark, threatening clouds were moving in fast, and he could already see the rain they were bringing with them. If Kerry was in that boat, she needed to get off soon. "'E 'ave a boat 'ere, mate? A radio?"

"Yeah, behind us there—the *Sabre Cruiser*. Why?"

⚓

The water was now over Kerry's knees and rising fast. The boat was rolling slightly to the side, back end down, increasing the speed at which it took in water in the hull where Kerry remained trapped. Trouble had really outdone itself this time and Kerry had walked into it as naively as a lamb to its slaughter.

She rubbed her hands over her face and massaged her temples. When she felt the water lapping at her thighs, she threw her head back and sobbed in desperation. That was when she spotted the axe.

The water had moved a chest away from the wall and exposed the peg from which the axe hung. Kerry pushed through the water and slipped it out of its sling. Then she moved to the locked door and swung the heavy axe as hard as she could at the door. She felt a rush of adrenaline when she felt the wood give way. It took her a few seconds to work the axe free of the door, and then she swung again. When she had hacked a hole large enough to slip her arm through, she felt around for the latch outside the door. She felt a thrill of accomplishment when she located the latch, but her spirits plumeted when she felt the padlock holding the latch in place.

Finding her resolve, she slipped under the water to find the ax she had thrown aside. When her hand closed around the handle, she emerged from the water with renewed energy and purpose. She attacked the door again at a spot above the water level, which was almost to her chin now. Her arms began to ache from swinging the ax so high, but there was no help for it. She tried not to think past opening the door. She would focus on one problem at a time.

When she finally had the hole big enough to crawl through, she grabbed the top of the doorframe, heaved herself up and kicked hard. That widened the opening but the water began to rush through it into the stairwell, taking Kerry with it. She twisted into the stairwell and tried to catch herself but ended up slamming her head on the rail. She also had several cuts and scrapes from the splintered door, but she barely noticed the pain.

"*Somebody help me!*," she yelled as she climbed the stairs leading to the galley. There was no one on the boat. It seemed the crew had jumped and left her to go down with the ship instead of incriminating themselves. *What kind of people had Owen done business with?*

It was already growing dark from the approaching storm. She could see lightning behind clouds that were beginning to swirl with the wind. She ran to the helm and found the radio. She also found the button for the horn and while she struggled to operate the transmitter, she pushed one long blast and a short one followed by another long blast: *S. O. S.* Almost immediately, she heard a muffled voice come through the speaker, "Kerry Carter?" Kerry went limp with relief.

245

⚓

Merrek released the breath he had been unconsciously holding since he had stepped from the *Saber Cruiser* onto the Coast Guard boat. No thanks needed for the captain of the *Sabre Cruiser*, he was happy to help.

"Damn, Englishman," said the captain with awe. "You were right! I see her!" Then louder, directly into the mouthpiece, "Hang on, Miss Carter. We're on our way."

Kerry had almost collapsed with the assurance that the Coast Guard was coming and Merrek was with them, but a huge gust of wind and a high rolling wave snatched her relief and filled her with a new fear. She listened to the creaks and moans of the boat, and the sucking sound of water as it pulled the small yacht down and over. She clung to the rail and realized that the approaching Coast Guard boat she could just barely make out would not reach her in time. If she did not get clear of the boat quickly, it would suck her under on its way to the ocean floor, and she might not survive the trip.

Steady in the face of this reality, Kerry reached for the life preserver hanging near the radio and pulled it on. She remembered Merrek's words back at Min's the day he talked her out of going to Porth alone— *Know when a thing isn't brave, but just plain stupid.* Kerenza had been impetuous, not brave. She had been reckless, not particularly sensible. Sensible meant one knew what was wise, and bravery was doing that wise thing even though it terrified you. It seemed that now, in spite of all her past and present fears Kerry was going for a swim in the ocean after all. Hopefully, she truly was *braver than she thought.*

⚓

"Can she swim?" asked the captain, worry etched on his face as he watched the injured boat list severely.

"Not well, and she has a fear of deep water," Merrek's voice was strained but strong. "I'll go get 'er. I'll keep 'er calm till 'e get close enough to pull 'er aboard."

"Absolutely not," stated the captain. "I'll send in one or two of the crew members."

Merrek turned on the captain, his eyes blazing, and his body rigid. "Don't try to stop me," he growled.

"I can't let you do it," the captain reasoned with him. "What if you don't reach her in time and it goes under. We could lose both of you. We won't risk civilians."

"She'll fight 'em, cap'n. 'Er fear will insist she fight. Your men would be at risk. She won't fight me. I'll bring 'er to 'e."

The captain searched Merrek's face and recognized the stubborn tenacity. He quickly came to a decision he was not happy about. He motioned for someone to give Merrek a life jacket while he tried to keep Kerry in his sight through his binoculars. The sharp rise and fall of both boats made that difficult.

Merrek fastened the life jacket around him as one sailor gave him instructions on how to release the rope that tethered him to the boat and another handed him the cord to an inflatable raft, which he wrapped around his wrist. He gave both men a quick nod of thanks, and they both returned one of encouragement.

A heartbeat later, the captain took in a sharp breath, let the binoculars drop to his chest and turned the wheel sharply. "She jumped. It looked like she jumped clear and just in time, too. We'll be right behind you."

Merrek stepped out into wind and rain that blinded him. He felt his way and cautiously but quickly climbed over the rail, hugged the inflatable boat to his chest and hurled himself away from the boat and into the agitated waters.

It was more difficult to get one's bearings than it had appeared from the boat and *Oh, God* was it cold. Merrek was amazed that Kerry had jumped, and he was so grateful that she did. Her act of bravery may have saved them both as finding her in a sunken vessel before they both ran out of breath might have proved impossible.

At first, he could not see her, but wasting no time, he began to swim in what instinctively seemed to be the right direction. Through the fog, he thought he saw a mast reaching toward the sky, as if in hope that some hand might reach down and save it from its inevitable decent. Then on the crest of a wave, he got a glimpse of her yellow life preserver, and began calling to her repeatedly as he fought against the water. If she could just control her panic until he could reach her.

Kerry had known in the depths of her being that she would have to abandon the boat or go down with it. She figured her best option would be to take control rather than be at the mercy of a sinking ship, so she had forced herself to leap into the churning water.

Never had she felt so disoriented. She could hear the boat she had just escaped creak and shudder and splinter as it went down. The wind and water seemed to join forces against her, causing confusion and terror. She found herself in the middle of all those years of nightmares, only this was real. She could not wake up from this.

Then she heard Merrek's voice calling. Moreover, just as clearly, she heard another voice from somewhere deep within her very being. *Not again, Kerenza. We're not going to repeat this. Swim. Even though you think you cannot—swim toward his voice.*

Kerry began to kick and paddle for all she was worth in the direction of Merrek's calls. The rain blinded her while the late February temperatures rendered her movements slow and lethargic, but she struggled on. Her one fear now was that she would fail to meet Merrek half way and that would put him in greater peril.

Just when she thought she could not stay conscious any longer, she felt Merrek's strong hand grab her forearm, and then his arms were around her. She vaguely heard his encouraging words—*so proud... very brave... there now, I've got 'e.*

Merrek clung to Kerry with one arm while he pulled the string that engaged the inflation mechanism on the lifeboat. Getting Kerry in it was not easy, having to synchronize lifting her up in cadence with the undulating water. Nevertheless, she seemed to come to life at his touch, and was able to help pull her body up and over the side, and then she actually helped Merrek drag in as well.

He immediately laid her down in the bottom of the boat and covered her with his body in hopes of sharing what heat he had. She was trembling violently and her teeth were chattering. She felt so small beneath him, so cold. When she opened her eyes, however, he saw that wonderful blaze of determination—that fight that made her his Kerenza, and that did much to lessen his worry that she was too fragile to survive.

As the Coast Guard pulled them by the tether towards the boat, Merrek rained kisses over Kerry's face. An hour ago, he was afraid he had lost her. Thank God, the waves had actually pushed her closer to him instead of carrying her out to sea. Maybe the combined efforts of God, Myghal and Kerenza delivered Kerry into his arms. Maybe the sea was making up for the past. Maybe it was pixies or just the ying and yang of life, but by the time the Coast Guard rescued them from the water, Merrek honestly did not care. He thanked them all.

⚓

It had been a harrowing experience, and Merrek had to admire the captain and crew for getting them safely docked in the midst of such a storm. He had never seen a crew work so well together—almost like parts of a well-designed machine, putting apart their human side as they pressed toward their goal.

Once out of danger, every one of them came to shake Merrek's hand, actually thanked him for being the key to a successful rescue. Merrek expressed his gratitude to them as well, glancing frequently at the blanket wrapped woman he held. Her skin was still pale and cold, but she was breathing.

He kissed the top of her head and she stirred, snuggled closer. He smiled against her damp forehead. She had proven to be the fighter he had known she would be—against her fears, against the odds…for him and their life together.

- 21 -

Truth is stranger than fiction,
but it is because fiction is obliged to stick to possibilities.
Truth isn't.
—Mark Twain

Merrek and Kerry were up all night answering questions. On the way to the hospital, the Coast Guard captain questioned Kerry about her imprisonment inside the sinking boat. At the hospital, doctors examined them both for hypothermia and Kerry's injuries were treated. During this time, they learned detectives were waiting at Owen's house.

Once the hospital released them, an officer took the dry and revived couple to police headquarters where they answered questions regarding the kidnapping, the car theft, and what they knew of the criminal lending group and their collection methods. Kerry also looked through forty or so mug shots and was able to identify her abductor. Then they went to Owen's house.

A detective in a suit, accompanied by a squad of uniformed officers, met them on Owen's front lawn. "Miss Kerry Carter?" the suit asked with a grim smile. "There is no one here. Do you know where your brother and his family might be?"

Kerry shook her head, dumbstruck. "I can't believe they would leave the house. They were both very scared. You don't think…"

"No," the detective assured her. "There's absolutely no evidence of forced entry or struggles. Their neighbors have seen nothing unusual. It looks more like a planned evacuation. Go on inside and take a look around—see what you make of it," he instructed.

Merrek followed Kerry into the house. It was indeed quiet. A quick look into the garage revealed Millicent's car was gone. They looked into closets and drawers, in Alexandra's room, noticed the missing pictures and keepsakes that had adorned the house. It became apparent that the Carters had not hung around to find out the outcome of Kerry's abduction. They had fled the scene before the police got involved.

"They didn't even leave me a note…in case I made it back alive," Kerry was stunned, but too tired to react. "I don't even know Millicent's family in Colorado. I suppose I should try to find out how to contact them."

Merrek pulled her into his arms and delivered another undisputable fact, "And he has your $75,000 at his disposal tomorrow, sweetheart. You may as well kiss that inheritance goodbye."

"Oh, I already knew the money would be gone as soon as I learned he was addicted to gambling. And then there were the loan sharks. Either way, I knew I'd never see my inheritance again. *What was I to do?* He's my brother." She sighed heavily. "I thought this kind of thing only happened in the movies."

Merrek tightened his hold, still reveling in the fact that she was in his arms, warm and alive after their rescue a few hours ago, "How easy is it to be married here?"

Kerry jerked in surprise, but laughed. "In North Carolina? Turns out, we could get married if we were first cousins, no blood tests, no waiting period."

"Interesting place," he smiled. "Do 'e think 'e can leave it to live in Cornwall?"

"Will you be there?"

His eyes glowed with warmth and affection. "When I'm not on assignment for *National Geographic*, aye, I'll be there."

"Oh, my goodness!" She pummeled his chest lightly with both fists. "With everything going on, I forgot about the interview. You got the job?"

"I did. I forgot about it, too, until now. God, Kerry. I was so afraid I'd lost 'e and I'd promised 'e that I wouldn't."

"The second I knew you were on that Coast Guard boat I knew I was going to be okay. I jumped, Merrek, did you know that? *Into the ocean.* I voluntarily jumped." She cocked her head, and her eyes filled with wonder. "It wasn't so bad."

Merrek laughed, took his arms from around her and framed her face with his hands. He grimaced at the dark bruise that covered her left cheek. "I didn't know whether to be angry with 'e for putting yourself in danger for your brother or proud of 'e for what 'e tried to do. How did 'e get this bruise, luv?"

Kerry told him about hitting her head on the stairwell of the boat, having decided to cause him less fury by keeping secret the fact that she now knew what a man's fist could do.

The officers came back from their own search of the house. One of them looked at her kindly. "Do you have any personal items here that you would like to retrieve before we lock this place down?"

"I do," said Kerry. "A few clothes, an autographed photo from an extremely talented photographer, and a plant. It will only take me a minute."

"I'll help you," Merrek offered. "What are you going ta do with that plant?"

"I can't leave it here. It's meant so much to me. It would feel wrong to abandon it. Can't we ship it?"

Merrek's eyebrows drew together. "I can get 'e another."

Kerry let her fingers dance over the leaves. "Maybe we can find a good home for it. Let's take it with us for now."

"I'll agree to that. Then we'll find a hotel, preferably with one o'those huge water closets, and then we'll crash. When we wake up, we'll go get 'hitched' as they say. I want ta get 'e away from 'ere, Kerry. 'E's got bad vibes."

Kerry was as anxious to leave as he was. She had only sad memories here, except for her time with her little niece. She passed by the piano where Owen's family picture used to sit. It was gone now, of course. "I sure hope they take care of Alex. She's a sweetheart."

Merrek smiled encouragingly. "With those good genes she shares with 'er Aunt Kerry and 'er aunt Kerenza, I 'ave a feelin' she'll do fine for 'erself. I've got yer bag. You carry the plant."

After some much needed sleep, Kerry and Merrek drove back to Wilmington where Kerry tied up loose ends. She gave away her teaching materials she had in summer storage and turned in her resignation at the county office. She and Merrek met with Kerry's friends, minus Tania and Robert, to say goodbye…again. Kerry packed only the things she needed to get by until she could shop in London. Merrek took care of procuring a marriage license and getting Kerry an airline ticket on his return flight.

Early the next afternoon, the Coast Guard captain who had rescued Merrek and Kerry married them in the clothes they had worn to Tania's rehearsal dinner. It seemed fitting that he should perform the ceremony on his boat, with his crew as witnesses. The new bride and groom gifted him a good bottle of whiskey and a healthy Kalachoe plant that he assured them his wife would enjoy. The whiskey he would share with his crew.

It was a fine wedding—the only thing that was a bit out of place was the bride's bright red dress and her bruised face. But nothing about their wedding was traditional anyway and Merrek did love that dress. Tania and Robert listened in over a speakerphone, and when the Captain pronounced them husband and wife, Merrek lifted his new bride over his head and spun her around before lowering her to his smiling mouth.

Back at their hotel, the couple consummated their vows several times, slowly and tenderly as well as heated and in wild abandon. They were ravenous by the dinner hour. Their flight to Heathrow was later that night, and they had just finished a sumptuous meal in the hotel's restaurant when Merrek's phone rang. The call was from England.

Merrek thought it was another congratulatory call from home, and put the phone on speaker to share with Kerry. Lowenna's voice was frantic. "Merrek, you and Kerry have to come home *now*."

Merrek's face contorted. "Is it Da?"

"Oh, no…no. Merk, I'm sorry. I shouldn't have blurted it out like that. I should have known 'e would be an instant bag o'worries. No…Everyone here is top o' the mark. 'Tis this, Merrek. You know that site where you took pictures for that environmental magazine? The place where they're doin' the green buildin' on the peat bog? Diggin' out and replacin' the peat?"

Merrek took a deep breath and rolled his eyes, making Kerry giggle. "Aye, Lo, get on with it, then?"

"Well, yesterday during their excavation, a body washed out. It's been all over the news. They've determined it to be an eighteenth-century female body, fairly preserved in the peat, and…get this…*still wearin' a peridot pendant*…" after a few seconds of silence, Lowenna spoke again. "Merrek? Kerry? Are you there?"

The couple stared at each other in eerie disbelief.

Who else could it be?

- 22 -

I believe there's a calling for all of us...
that every human being has value and purpose.
The real work of our lives is to become aware.
And awakened. To answer the call.
—Oprah Winfrey

Merrek's remodeling continued on the house he had bought almost a
year ago, making it into a home where Kerry would thrive. And thrive
she did, in beauty, in poise and in grace.

She now had her riot of flowers and herbs that grew in the boxes
Merrek built for her. The third bedroom was a writing haven where Kerry
wove her stories and corresponded with her agent. Merrek was in the
process of building on to the garage behind the house where he would
move his photography studio from Penzance. That left the bedroom
across the hall from theirs available as a nursery.

On the mantel under Kerenza's portrait was a collection of photos.
One of them, a picture of Kerry in a cream-colored lace cocktail dress
adorned only with the peridot necklace Merrek had given her. As a
wedding gift, he had given her peridot earrings to match. She looked
exquisite beside her tall, broad-shouldered husband who was dressed
entirely in black except for his cream colored necktie embellished with
the little bicycle stud Kerry had designed for him.

Another photo was of the newlyweds with Merrek's immediate family
along with Ralph Wilesky and Olivia Tesmer. In the photo, Kerry held
an old framed photo of her own parents on their wedding day.

The rest of the pictures were candid shots taken by Merrek himself.
During the dinner and the dance that followed, he somehow managed
to include every member of his enormous family—the family to which
Kerry now belonged. With his lens, he captured the love and support that
shimmered through the frolic and raucous laughter as they celebrated
with each other and with close friends. Her father would have been so

pleased.

Kerry was content with her new family, but she refused to give up on Owen. He would heal, recuperate, pay his debts, and come around. It was his calling.

This day Merrek and Kerry stood together on the Sennen cliffside, the autumn sea breezes ruffling their hair and bringing with it the smells Kerry had adopted as the scents of home. She stood in the circle of Merrek's arms, her back braced against his hard form, his big hands caressing the slight mound that had replaced Kerry's flat belly. She closed her eyes in contentment and leaned back into her husband's embrace.

In front of them were two gravesites, both now occupied, finally, after almost two hundred years. Kerenza was finally home.

It took five months after Kerenza's body had broken away from the peat protector that had held her for two centuries to pass into Kerry's custody as the only living relative of the deceased. Since DNA testing could not offer solid proof, all the information that Kerry and Merrek had gathered since they had met finally satisfied the authorities, especially the portrait that Myghal had miraculously had the foresight to leave with the family.

Kerry had heeded Kerenza's call. She and Merrek had rescued the eighteenth-century woman from whatever eternal storeroom of forensic science the white coats would have eventually found for her. Thanks to her niece and another Walles champion, she was now where she belonged—resting beside her beloved Myghal for the rest of eternity. The time between the times was over, and Kerenza had found her atonement.

⚓

One year later, Merrek and Kerry brought the baby Michael to visit Min. They left the two rocking and cooing to walk off the oggies Min had 'forced' them to eat. They found themselves on Fore Street hand in hand, where they met two years before.

"Got a good quote for us now, m'luv?" Merrek squeezed her hand, remembering that meeting and knowing she would not disappoint.

"As it happens, I do. I found it just this morning when we were on the train. You and Michael were busy showing off, so I took the opportunity to catch up on my reading."

Merrek's dark eyebrows drew together. "We weren't showin' off. We were playin' peep-eye."

Kerry chuckled. "Well you had the attention of everyone in our car.

The ooh's and aah's were thick as smoke. I could barely see what I was reading."

"Well, we make a fine pair, me and me son. Both handsome devils, intelligent, witty…"

"*Cocky?*"

"Cornish Walles through and through, m'luv. It's in the blood. What quote did e' find?"

"This is from novelist Toba Beta, 'You are the fairy tale told by your ancestors'." Kerry stood on tiptoes to kiss Merrek's cheek. "I am the fairy tale, and you made it come true."

The End

Acknowledgements

The hobby of spinning stories for my own amusement took a serious turn about two years ago.

At the request of my daughter-in-law I pulled a ten-year-old manuscript from my files, that had provided me with hours of writing fun, and I let her read it. As a result of over a year's worth of hard work together editing, designing the cover, fundraising, printing, marketing and everything else involved, my dream has been realized.

The second person to read the manuscript was my husband, Doug McCoy. He has been my wealth of enthusiastic support and my number one fan.

I would also like to acknowledge those early supporters who believed in me enough to make a sight-unseen contribution to fund the project. Richard and Virginia Edgar, long-time and treasured friends; Dave and Carol Armitage, newer but dear friends as well; sister Cindy Suda Martinez, who shares a love of writing; family member Debbie Riggs Shufelt; and my cherished friends of the Reading Roadies Book Club.

Extras

Discussion Questions

1. Discuss today's interest in genealogy. What are your personal experiences? How do you relate to Kerry's need to know about her ancestors and her roots?

2. Have you traveled outside of your home country? What effect can experiencing other cultures have on a person?

3. Do you believe in fate, that things happen for a reason? Do you believe that our lives are predestined, that our choices are up to us, or both? Discuss why you feel that way.

4. Discuss the meaning of the quote that opens chapter five and how it applied to Kerry and her meeting with Ralph Wilesky. *Our actions are like ships we may watch put out to sea, and not know when or with what cargo they will return to port. (Iris Murdock,* The Bell*)* How often do you feel this applies to you? How does this play into fate?

5. Chapter six opens with the quote *When the traveler goes alone he gets aquainted with himself. (Liberty Hyde Bailey)* What does that mean? How frequently do you travel alone? Discuss experiences you have had.

6. Compare and contrast the qualities you observed in Kerry and Kerenza; Merrek and Myghal. Which qualities do you admire? Which ones annoy you? Why do you think the characters are the way they are and were the way they were?

7. Kerry says people are the same everywhere. What did she mean? What examples in the book support that statement? How does this belief sync with your views of global society?

8. Compare and contrast Kerry's new friends Olivia Tesmer and Merrek's cousin Min. Kerry bonded with both women even though they are very different. What qualities were responsible for this bond?

9. Have you ever known someone with an addiction? Was Owen a typical case? Why or why not?

10. What does *atonement* mean and how did eighteenth-century Kerenza achieve it?

11. What did Merrek mean when he compared Kerry to an unmoored ship? How can family anchor us?

12. What do you think of collecting and referencing quotes? Why is Kerry's collection important to her? Do you have a collection of your own?

Notes

Quote Index

p_. It has always seemed to me I had to answer questions which fate had posed to my forefathers which had not yet been answered, or as if I had to complete, or perhaps continue, things which previous ages had left unfinished. —Carl Jung

p i. It is easy to be wise after the event. —English 17th Century

p1. It is in your moments of decision that your destiny is shaped. —Tony Robbins

p11. An important key to self-confidence is preparation. —Arthur Ashe

p17. Every man is a quotation from all his ancestors. —Ralph Waldo Emerson

p17. With every goodbye, you learn. —Veronica A. Shoffstall

p19. The more unsustained I am, the more I will respect myself. —Charlotte Bronte

p21. Always remember— you're braver than you believe. —A.A. Milne

p22. How lucky I am to have something that makes saying goodbye so hard. —A.A. Milne

p23. We are all formed of frailty and error; Let us pardon reciprocally each other's folly—that is the first law of nature. —Voltaire

p31. Our actions are like ships we may watch put out to sea, and not know when or with what cargo they will return to port. —Iris Murdock, The Bell

p37. When the traveler goes alone he gets acquainted with himself. —Liberty Hyde Bailey

Intuition is nothing but the outcome of earlier intellectual experience. —A. Einstein

p.38. That which we manifest is before us, we are the creators of our own destiny. —Garth Stein

p39. Never, never, never give up. —Winston Churchill

p41. London is an old lady who mutters and has the second sight. She is slightly deaf, and doesn't suffer fools gladly. —A.A. Gill

p46. Last night I dreamt I went to Manderly again… —Daphne du Murier

p51. No one can make you feel inferior without your consent. —Eleanor Roosevelt.

p53. Those who desire to understand the Cornish, and their country, must use their imagination and travel back in time. —Daphne du Murier, Vanishing Cornwall

p55. All things are subject to interpretation. —Nietzsche

Facts do not cease to exist because they are ignored. —Aldous Huxley

p59. Beauty —be not caused—it just is. —Emily Dickinson

p60. I see myself as an intelligent sensitive human with the soul of a clown, which forces me to blow it at the most important moments. —Jim Morrison

p62. History remembers only the celebrated, genealogy remembers them all. —Laurence Overmire

p75. Fertility of imagination and an abundance of guesses at the truth are among the first requisites of discovery. —William Jevons

p94. This has been the most wonderful evening I've had in some long time. —?

p95. If ever in doubt as to whether to kiss a pretty girl, always give 'er the benefit of the doubt. —Scotsman Thomas Carlyle

p101. We all become great explorers during our first few days in a new city, or a new love affair. —Mignon McLaughlin

p103. The best way to know if a man is trustworthy is to trust him. —Ernest Hemingway

p104. Trust dies but mistrust blossoms. —Sophocles

p110. A ship is safe in harbor, but that's not what ships are for. —John A. Shedd

p113. Man maintains his balance, poise and sense of security only as he is moving forward. —Maltz

p135. Love is but the discovery of ourselves in others, and the delight is in the recognition. —Alexander Smith

p145. They have a fascination unlike any other; they are a survival of another age. —Daphne du Maurier's description of the Moors

p152. When I do good, I feel good. When I do bad, I feel bad. That is my religion. —Abraham Lincoln

p167. When we illuminate the road back to our ancestors, They have a way of reaching out, of manifesting themselves... Sometimes even physically. —Raquel Cepeda

p171. There are cultures in which it is believed that a name contains all a person's mystical power... This it seemed was such a name. —Diane Setterfield

p187. There are things we don't want to happen but have to accept, things we don't want to know but have to learn, and people we can't live without but have to let go. —Unknown

p193. Ignorantly is how we all fall in love; for it is a kind of fall. Closing our eyes, we leap from that cliff in hope of a soft landing. Nor is it always soft; but still, without that leap nobody comes to life. —Salman Rushdie, The Moor's Last Sigh

p195. Every man is a quotation of all his ancestors. —Ralph Waldo Emerson

p196. Genetics is about how information is stored and transmitted between generations. —John Maynard Smith

p199. Don't let the fear of the time it will take to accomplish something stand in the way of your doing it. The time will pass anyway; we might just as well put that passing time to the best possible use. —Earl Nightingale

p201. Our chief want is someone who will inspire us to be what we know we could be. —Ralph Waldo Emerson

p209. When all is said and done, the weather and love are the two elements about which one can never be sure. —Unknown

p215. There is no difference between being rescued and being captured. —Jane Mendelsohn

p229. I have had dreams, and I have had nightmares. I overcame the nightmares because of my dreams. —Jonas Salk

p235. Beyond mind, there is an awareness that is intrinsic... —Osho

p249. Truth is stranger than fiction, but it is because fiction is obliged to stick to possibilities. Truth isn't. —Mark Twain

p255. I believe there's a calling for all of us...that every human being has value and purpose. The real work of our lives is to become aware. And awakened. To answer the call. —Oprah Winfrey

p255. You are the fairy tale told by your ancestors. —Toba Beta

Author Bio

Teresa McCoy is a retired primary school teacher who lives in North Georgia with her husband, Doug, of forty-seven years. They have four children and eight grandchildren—a noisy and lively group on Thanksgiving. Teresa and Doug have spent years researching family history, starting in the 70's and 80's with microfilmed records in the University of Georgia Library. In recent years they visited the archives in Utah, used various genealogy websites, DNA testing, and have learned how to effectively search state courthouses and cemeteries. The discovery that they both had Scottish roots resulted in three trips to the United Kingdom. Both have become active members of the American Scottish Foundation as well as the Clan MacKay and Clan Gregor Societies of America and Scotland.

Teresa's hobbies include writing, reading, gardening and travel, and she loves being with her grandchildren. She also enjoys spending time at their cabin in the woods of the North Georgia Mountains. Teresa is a member of The Reading Roadies, a traveling book club; and P.E.O., an organization that provides scholarships for women worldwide. Both Teresa and Doug are avid University of Georgia football fans.